THE BOOK OF DEATH

THE AZIMAR ARCHIVES BOOK ONE

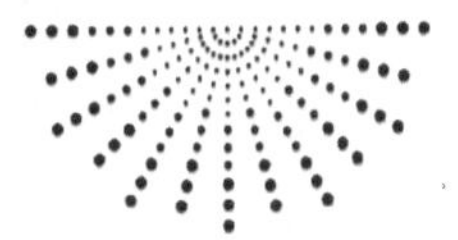

JACKLYN HENNION

For my husband- my greatest ally and my best friend.

1

DARS

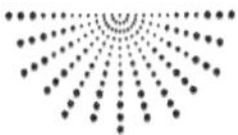

Dars, First Knight of the King's Guard, took the lead position of the party as they walked down first one hallway then another, longer one. His heavy boots clicked against the stone and his sword bounced lightly against his hip with each step. The four other knights with him brought up the rear guard, their footsteps echoing his. Between them three more men walked, unarmed and unhurried.

"Is this all still really necessary?" a quiet voice asked behind him.

"It is a tradition. And we must follow tradition."

The heavy double doors at the end of the hall loomed closer with each step until the whole group had come to a halt before it. Dars turned, surveying the group and the empty hall behind them.

All was as it should be.

"After you, First Knight," the eldest of the men among them said.

Dars held the door to the small council room open as three of the most powerful men in Etritia stepped into the brightly lit chamber.

King Areanath entered first, as was his right, and stood at

1

the head of the table, waiting as the others joined in their customary places around him. His long, wiry hair was a tad unkempt, as it usually was, and his long beard had been half braided and tied off with a spare length of leather, much in the way a dwarf might have fastened his own beard. But he stood tall and solidly, both hands wrapped over the top of his council seat.

Dars watched as Areanath's brother followed in behind him, casting dark glares around the room at the knights of the King's Guard posted at each corner of the room, stopping to stand behind the chair across from Areanath. Mothlenor folded his arms together, the wide sleeves of his heavy robes draping down to his waist.

And lastly, Hasani, the young left hand to the King, his dark hair neatly trimmed and plain, slim-fitted clothing giving him the appearance of a respected and wealthy Etritian merchant, rather than one of the most influential denizens of all of Azimar. As Hasani passed him, he gave Dars a small smile and a nod, which Dars happily returned.

"Ajax has told me that congratulations are in order. You're making him an uncle," Dars said to the young man before he could walk out of earshot. Hasani turned, a faint red rising to his cheeks. "And what does that make me, exactly?"

Hasani's faint smile grew deeper and he took Dars into a hug. "You can be a grandfather, if you'd like. Or a great uncle. Whatever you want to be called." He released Dars, giving his shoulders a squeeze. "At any rate, you're family, Dars."

"You're fucking right I am," he said, returning Hasani's affections with a thump on the young man's back. "I wish you'd told me sooner, Hasani."

Hasani sighed, his nose scrunching into a grimace. "I wanted to—I really did. But Silvana asked to wait. To make sure the baby would stay well with her."

Dars had suspected as much, and Ajax had confirmed it when he'd brought the news, so Dars could only nod, grateful the news about his chosen daughter's pregnancy had been good.

"Hasani," a cool voice called from the council table. "We should get started."

Hasani and Dars both looked to the center of the room to see Mothlenor glaring at them. "I'd rather it not take all day. I have other things to attend to."

"Of course, Mothlenor." Hasani gave Dars another nod and a smile, then stood to wait behind the seat to Areanath's left. The seat to Areanath's right remained unclaimed, as it had for more years than Dars could recall.

"I believe we're ready to begin, Dars." Areanath's voice was remarkably similar to his brother's, though warmer and not quite so deep. He motioned towards Dars. "If you would, please."

Dars bowed to his king then turned and shut the heavy door to the council room, turning the large key in the lock until a loud click echoed throughout the room. He tucked the key into his breast pocket and settled to stand with his back to the door, hand on his sword.

Areanath and the others took their seats simultaneously as if on cue. There was a moment of noise as chairs scraped against stone, but the three council members settled themselves quickly enough.

"Now, the first order of business. Hasani, if you don't mind beginning. Much like my brother, I don't relish the thought of this lasting for the whole day."

Hasani nodded, flipping open a large ledger that he had brought in under one arm. "Fall harvest is nearly on us, as we all know. I've been gathering information about the potential gross production values for some time, and I should have a final report within the week."

"Good news?" Areanath asked.

"Very good. The last signs of the drought we experienced a few years ago seem to be …"

Dars let his mind drift. It was always the same. Taxes will be good this year. Crops are doing well. The Free Cities have requested this or that nonsense. Does the king see fit to make this or that change to the conduct codes for Etritia? Yes, Hasani, your assessments seem adequate, as always …

Dars was grateful to be considered faithful enough to the crown to be head of the King's Guard during council meetings, but the meetings grew tedious and boring after listening to more than a few of them.

And I shouldn't be here. It should be Ajax standing here, bored enough to rip his fucking ears off.

But the annual King's Guard recruitment was nearly over, and it was Ajax's duty as commander to oversee the last few weeks of training for the young men eager to take on the mantle of knighthood. And so the task of protecting the small council from threat had fallen to Dars, though it had long been a mostly ceremonial position.

Voices were being raised and Dars gathered his attention back to the small council table just in time to see Mothlenor stand up and lean over the table towards his older brother, eyes dark and staring daggers. "You can't seriously be considering the proposal. It's insanity!"

"It's my decision to make, brother. And Hasani agrees that it would be wise," Areanath said, his voice only slightly quieter than Mothlenor's, but calmer.

"If we had someone in that fourth chair," Mothlenor stabbed a finger at the vacant military council seat to Areanath's right, "they would argue against it. It is unwise. It is a foolish decision and it will only bring more harm than good!"

Areanath stood quickly, his chair nearly toppling over as he did. "First Knight Dars!"

Dars straightened, squaring his shoulders. "Yes, my lord."

"Please take a seat at the small council table." Areanath's voice had dropped to a more reasonable level, and he indicated the empty seat beside him, his eyes never leaving his brother's.

Hasani's eyes widened and his lips were pressed into a thin line. Mothlenor only glared deeper at his brother. Dars's old heart nearly failed right there; he tightened his grip on his sword, hoping it might steady him. "I'm sorry?"

"My brother wants the fourth seat to be filled for this argument. I will concede to his wishes and put the most qualified man available into the position as the head of the Etritian military arm." Areanath turned to Dars, giving him a sly smile. "Just for a few minutes, at any rate."

Dars could feel his mouth opening and closing, and finally managed to stammer out, "B-but it shouldn't be me, it should be Ajax …"

"Commander Ajax has his hands full with the newest would-be recruits. He chose you to take his place guarding the small council hall. I'm sure he would be happy with you taking his place in this exercise as well."

Dars reluctantly stepped to the remaining chair at the small council table. He almost expected it to be covered in dust and old cobwebs, but whichever servants were in charge of cleaning the hall never seemed to neglect the vacant seat. The smooth wood of the chair gleamed dully in the light cast by the chandelier overhead and the fireplace set in the opposite wall. Dars sat slowly and, as he did, both Areanath and Mothlenor took their seats once more.

"Welcome to the small council table, Dars, First Knight of the King's Guard. Though your tenure will be short, I'm confident that you will do your best to serve the people of Etritia." Areanath leaned back into his chair, steepling his fingers together and resting them against his chin. "Now, what do you think of this proposal?"

Dars hesitated, his breath caught for a moment. He caught Hasani's eye and the young man gave him a small smirk. Dars almost laughed. *The little shit knows I wasn't paying attention.* Dars let out his held breath in one long exhale. "If I'm to be honest, my lord—"

"You have no idea what we were talking about, do you?" Areanath chuckled.

"That would be correct, my lord. I apologize, but I was …" Dars heard his voice trail, unsure of what Areanath might find acceptable.

"Bored?" Areanath supplied helpfully.

"Yes."

"You weren't the only one, First Knight." Areanath straightened, ignoring the scoff from the far end of the table, though it made Dars turn his head. "Try to pay attention for the next few moments, and all will be forgiven."

"Of course, my lord."

"Hasani has just brought us news that our elven neighbors to the east, in Thessala to be precise, have requested our aid. They are concerned for their young, because they believe the coming winter will be a particularly harsh one and they find themselves unable to be wholly prepared."

Dars shifted uncomfortably in the seat, folding his hands awkwardly into his lap rather than resting them on the table. "What can we do to help?"

At his words, Mothlenor scoffed again, and Areanath gave his younger brother a small smile, his head tilted slightly. Mothlenor folded his arms across his chest, scowling around the table at them all. "He doesn't understand the whole situation."

"He understands enough, Mothlenor. You wanted a military arm at the table. You wanted another opinion." Areanath's smile deepened, and Dars wasn't sure if it was sincere or a condescending smirk. "I've done more than enough to please you. But you shouldn't be surprised to find that no one else shares your concerns."

"Why the fuss over aiding Thessala?" Dars asked. "The elves have been our allies for over a century. They've helped

Etritia when we've needed it. Why not do the same for them?"

Areanath dipped his head to Dars. "A very good question, First Knight." Areanath turned his attention to Mothlenor, giving him a look somewhere between a glare and an impatient stare. "Well, brother?"

Mothlenor's fingers were drumming against the table, his hawkish eyes narrowed. "Thessala only seeks to weaken us," he said softly. "We should not provide aid to another when doing so would be a detriment to ourselves."

Areanath's nostrils flared and a muscle near his jaw flexed slightly. "Are you suggesting that I consider some sort of trade, then?"

Mothlenor slammed his hand against the tabletop. "I am suggesting that you do nothing!" There was a stunned moment of silence, during which Mothlenor seemed to struggle to get his temper under control once more. Finally, Mothlenor spoke again, his voice calmer and softer. "We cannot afford to assist them without bringing danger to our people. Therefore, we should offer no aid at all. We must remain strong, and may the Great Elir damn Thessala for her foolishness."

"You would ask me to doom elven children to their deaths so that no Etritian citizen may suffer any discomfort?"

"I would ask you, brother, to reconsider any proposal that might weaken Etritia," Mothlenor pleaded. The anger in Mothlenor's voice was all but gone, and Dars was surprised to find himself nearly pitying the king's younger brother.

Areanath was silent for a long moment, staring at his brother. Mothlenor returned the gaze, still as a statue.

"I'll reconsider it."

Mothlenor exhaled loudly. "Thank you—"

"First Knight Dars," Areanath said, cutting the rest of his brother's words off. "Unless there is an objection, I will go ahead and revoke your seat on the small council."

Dars snorted. "You'll hear no complaint from me."

"Good. I believe we're finished." Areanath stood, and Dars and the others rose with him. "Get me out of this room, Dars. I need a glass of wine and some rest."

"Of course, my lord." Dars fumbled to fish the key from his pocket, hurrying to unlock the double doors to the small council hall.

Never before had Dars been so grateful to leave that room behind him.

MOTHLENOR

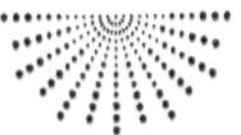

Mothlenor was the first to break from the small council, turning to walk down a vacant hall without a word to his brother. No one had made so much as a sigh since the First Knight had unlocked the council room doors and led the party out. Dars was his usual quiet self, as were the other King's Guards with him, but Mothlenor sensed relief in the way the old man walked back in the direction of Areanath's chambers. Hasani was also quiet, though Mothlenor suspected that he would break his silence as soon as they had walked out of hearing distance. Hasani knew how to be prudent and could read people almost as well as Mothlenor himself could, and he knew when to keep his mouth shut.

As for Areanath, Mothlenor knew his brother's feelings better than most. When Mothlenor had chanced a glance at his older brother, Areanath's face was blank, his eyes staring straight ahead impassively. It was those flat, staring eyes that made it easy for Mothlenor to tell that his brother was deeply angered by what had occurred in the small council hall.

And that, Mothlenor thought as he tugged open the small

wooden door that led to his tower, *is likely the only thing we have in common. That, and our faces.*

Mothlenor climbed the curved stairs to his tower study slowly, relishing the sudden chill that crept into his bones from the surrounding stone. The old tower smelled of arcane energy, of power.

My power.

Mothlenor let the fingers of one hand trail against the large square stones that comprised the walls, and the residual energy of years of arcane work coursed over him, making the skin of his arm stand out like gooseflesh. It settled back over his body, mingling with the energy already filling him. He could have taken that old energy back into himself if he had wanted. But he didn't, instead letting it sink back into the stones of the tower as he continued his climb.

Besides, there was something more pressing waiting for him up ahead.

The door to his study was open just a crack and flickering candlelight fell onto the topmost steps. The door had been shut and locked when Mothlenor had left for the small council meeting.

Mothlenor didn't even slow his steps. He knew what waited for him, and he knew better than most how to defend himself if there was danger in the rooms beyond.

The first thing Mothlenor spotted upon widening the door enough for him to enter was a rather large chest, plain and unremarkable, sitting squarely on his worktable.

There had been papers cluttering his desk, there nearly always were, but they had been nicely organized and set aside to make room for the wooden box. The latches had been unfastened and were facing him as he walked closer, inviting him to open the box and peruse its contents. Mothlenor already knew what lay inside and his palms itched with anticipation.

But a small movement at the far end of the room caught

his eye; he looked up to find a thin broad-shouldered man with dark hair and eyes watching him from across his study.

"You must be Ferrand," Mothlenor said. He looked the man over, searching for any hint of hostility, and found nothing.

"That's right." Ferrand didn't move from where he stood, arms folded over his chest. His skin was oddly pale, almost sickly so, and the thick and dark clothes he wore made his appearance all the more disturbing.

"You're a northerner," Mothlenor said. "A true northerner. From beyond the mountains."

Ferrand's teeth flashed in a smile. "That's right," he repeated.

Mothlenor arched an eyebrow, giving Ferrand a more scrutinizing look. "What's it like beyond the mountains?"

"Cold," Ferrand answered. "And dark." He moved, dropping his arms to his side and taking a half step closer to the desk. "You're welcome to take a look. To make sure it's to your satisfaction."

Mothlenor nodded, returning his attention to the chest. He lifted the lid slowly, peering at the contents. He couldn't help the smile that crept across his face at the large golden rock within. He lifted it from the lined interior, cradling it carefully in his hands. "It's smaller than I imagined it would be. But it will do nicely."

"Good." Ferrand flashed another smile.

"You've received your payment already, yes?"

"I have," Ferrand said with a small nod. "However ..."

Mothlenor gave him a hard look, setting the oblong golden stone back in its place. "We made a deal, Ferrand." *If he tries to cross me ...*

Ferrand lifted a hand. "We made a deal. It's yours, and I won't ask for a copper more." With his other hand, he pulled a smaller box from an inner pocket of his vest. "However, I have another item that might interest you as well."

Mothlenor took the offered box, his eyes trained on Ferrand. The man was braver than he'd thought. Or more foolish. The box was surprisingly heavy for its small size, but fit neatly in his palm. He weighed it experimentally in his hand, considering it. "What is it?"

"See for yourself. If you're interested, I'll name my price."

Mothlenor snorted. He already had what he wanted. There was little more Ferrand could offer him that would interest him nearly as much as what lay in the chest before him. But he opened the box, prying the lid off with a quick jerk.

The sight of the small orb inside nearly stopped his heart.

He stared at it for a moment before quickly jamming the lid back into place. He took a long breath, hoping his face hadn't betrayed the sudden excitement he'd felt. "Is this what I think it is?"

Ferrand's teeth flashed again. "A dragon's eye, yes."

At Ferrand's confirmation, Mothlenor couldn't help the rush that came to his words. "As a collector's item alone, it would be worth—"

"Quite a lot, I'm sure." Ferrand took another half step towards Mothlenor, crossing his arms over his chest again.

"Was it Farnean's?" Mothlenor asked idly.

Ferrand snorted. "Farnean's eyes were destroyed over a century ago. They were too large to fit in this room." Ferrand jerked his chin towards the box in Mothlenor's hands. "That belonged to a young one. Barely more than an infant."

Mothlenor's hand caressed the lid of the box absentmindedly. "How much?"

"I'm not asking for money."

"Oh?" *He wants the chest back. He'll offer a trade. And I'll have to kill him and keep both for myself ...*

"No," Ferrand said, his chin lifting in an arrogant jut. "I want a seat beside you when the time comes."

Mothlenor frowned; his words had a hard bite to them when he answered. "I'm not sure I know what you mean."

Ferrand smiled again, more slowly this time, and Mothlenor realized with disgust that Ferrand had played him for a fool. "I think you do." Ferrand's head tilted slightly to one side as he stared at Mothlenor, that odd smile making him look like a madman. "I can smell the winds of change coming, Mothlenor. And when they reach Etritia, I want to be here to take advantage of them."

They stared at each other for a moment as Mothlenor weighed his options. He could reject Ferrand, and lose the dragon's eye. He would still have the chest, in that case. Or he could chance working with Ferrand and have both items. Surely he could make very good use of the dragon's eye …

"The eye for a seat on my council? That's all you ask?"

Ferrand nodded. "That's all I ask. I'm sure you'll find yourself in need of someone with my talents eventually. Why not just take me, and get the eye as well?"

Mothlenor placed the smaller box next to the chest and offered his hand out to Ferrand. "You have a deal."

3

AREANATH

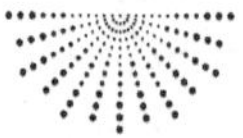

Areanath awoke with a start. He listened for a moment, but the world seemed quiet. He slipped from his bed, his knee protesting as he straightened and slipped on a heavy robe. There were guards posted at his bedroom door, of course, and they would refuse to let him leave unaccompanied this late at night. It was their job to protect him, but this was something he needed to do on his own. Fortunately, there was more than one way to leave his rooms.

Areanath limped to a far wall of his study, stepping around one of the plush chairs that adorned the mostly empty room. The scent of rose oil drifted to his nose as he circumvented it, and his steps slowed for a long moment.

Nevina ...

Areanath shook himself lightly, reminding himself that haste was essential; he stopped to stand as close to the empty stretch of wall as he could, almost hugging the cold stone.

There was a hall on the other side of this wall, far enough from the guards that he would not be spotted. The only trouble was traversing the half a meter or so of solid stone.

Areanath closed his eyes, stilling his mind and momentarily forgetting the task that lay ahead of him. After a quiet moment he was ready, hands trembling slightly against the wall. A half-murmured word and a few seconds of nauseating motion, and his hands were no longer brushing against the cool stone wall of his study.

Slowly, carefully, Areanath opened his eyes.

He stood out in the dimly lit hall, his back against the far side of the wall that divided his study from the rest of the castle. Areanath released a quiet sigh, unsurprised to realize he had been holding his breath. A quick check around the corner showed him the two men standing to either side of his chamber door, silently guarding a now empty set of rooms.

Another quiet sigh and Areanath was off, limping into the soft darkness of the long hallway.

His quest took him to the far corner of the castle, and he hurried along as quickly as his knee allowed him. The soft leather shoes he wore were silent against the stone floor, and only the occasional torch hanging on the wall lit his path. It didn't take long for him to reach his destination. The castle was quiet and still, and he passed no one.

There was a stretch of softly lit hall ahead of him, lined on either side with wooden doors at regular intervals. Areanath counted doors as he walked, stopping at the eighth door on the left near the end of the hall. He hesitated, raising a hand to knock.

But what if he doesn't answer? Or worse, what if Silvana answers?

Areanath turned to face one shoulder against the door, letting the long fingers of his left hand trail lightly against the smooth wood. He took a small step further down the hall, and another, concentrating on the spots where his fingertips touched.

Wooden door turned to stone wall, and Areanath continued walking, taking one small step after another. He had nearly reached the ninth door, and the next set of rooms, when his searching hand found what he was looking for.

Here ... He tapped the spot once, thinking.

There was nothing on the other side of this section of wall. Nothing closer than the meter or so of space he needed. Areanath once more shut his eyes, concentrating on that empty spot just beyond the wall in front of him. After a dizzying moment, he stood in the dark interior of his adviser's rooms.

He could see nothing, but he heard the faint sound of light, even breathing, punctuated by a delicate snore. Areanath waited in the dark for his eyes to adjust, standing motionless, surveying his surroundings as they came into view. There was a bed on the adjacent wall and a sleeping figure lying in it. He could make out long red curls against the covers. *Silvana.* He looked away, uneasy at seeing his adviser's wife in such a vulnerable position. In the darkness of the bedroom, Areanath rapped three fingers against his collarbone. *Great Ones forgive me for this trespass.* There was no one else in the bedroom, but Areanath could see the man he was looking for in the next room, hunched over a desk with his back to Areanath.

He slipped around the edge of the bed, put a light hand on his adviser's shoulder and a finger to his lips as the startled man turned to look at him.

Once his mission was complete, and his adviser had shown him back out into the hall, Areanath began the slow walk back to his quarters. He'd hardly gone a dozen steps before deciding that he wasn't fully prepared to return to his bed. The quiet of the night was too relaxing to pass up when given the opportunity to enjoy it. There were a number of places Areanath knew he could eventually be found if someone came looking for him. The library, for one. He could go there, light some candles, and read for an hour or so until he was too tired to hold his eyes open. Or the kitchens.

Who didn't get the craving for some of Cookie's apple tart in the middle of the night? Or his most recent night haunt, the southern balcony, which overlooked a good portion of Etritia. If only he had brought his pipe with him … He checked his robe pockets and there it was, along with a small leather tobacco pouch. He smiled in the darkness and adjusted course.

———

Areanath leaned against the stone parapet, unlit pipe in hand, relishing the way the cool wind nipped at him. Summer was coming to an end; he could feel it in the air. But there was still some time. He chewed on the end of his pipe, staring up at the night. The stars peered down on him from every corner of the clear sky. Nearly every summer night this year had been clear and beautifully lit with scattered stars, and he had taken to admiring them at every chance.

The guards would be looking for him soon if they weren't already. He didn't care if they found him now; his work was done. For tonight, at any rate. He was content to stand on the balcony until someone discovered him. Or until his old knee started to give out again. He rubbed at it out of habit, but the pressure just made it twitch uncomfortably. It would be the knee, surely.

He stood for a few more minutes, chewing on his pipe, staring at the stars. A falling star rolled across the night sky. He watched it go by, forgetting himself for a moment.

The sound of nearby footsteps pulled him away from his dreaming. He looked back at the door behind him. He had left it slightly ajar; surely someone would notice it. He quietly turned his back to the door again, intent on finding just one more moment of serenity.

But it was not long before the door creaked open. He

sighed, his eyes still on the stars. "Can't a king be allowed some privacy to contemplate?"

"Certainly, my lord. Your guards only ask that you tell them where you are going."

Areanath winced at the voice, turning. The man standing before him was unimpressive in appearance, with long and slightly greying hair falling limp against his thin face and shoulders. He stood stiff and straight, his dark green eyes watching Areanath intently. He might have looked unassuming at first glance, but he gave off an aura that demanded respect, perhaps even fear. For Areanath, it was like looking in a mirror, his slightly warped reflection staring back. "Mothlenor. I didn't intend for you to be stirred from your tower on my behalf."

Mothlenor waved his hand, dismissing Areanath's concerns. "I was already up and about, dear brother. I came across one of your guardsmen in the hallway." He paused. "He mistook me for you, of course." There was more than a hint of distaste in his voice.

"I'm sure it's harder to tell the difference by candlelight, Mothlenor. I hope you can forgive him."

"Never mind him. I'm more intrigued by how you always manage to leave your room without the guards posted at your door ever noticing." Mothlenor stepped to the edge of the balcony, turning to face his brother. "I must know how you do it." There was a sly smile playing his lips.

Areanath smiled in return, but his mind raced. "If I told you, brother, I feel that my midnight meditations would come to a halt." Mothlenor's eyes darkened, and his mouth turned down into a small frown. Areanath had anticipated as much. In an effort to quell further questions, he offered out his pipe. "Do you mind, brother? I seem to have forgotten my tinderbox."

Mothlenor glared slightly before taking the pipe in hand. He cupped a palm over the bowl of the pipe, and Areanath immediately saw the faint glow of embers between his brother's fingers. Mothlenor passed the pipe back, not even glancing to see if the spell had worked. "I would hope that my arcane abilities would extend to uses beyond lighting your pipes, but I live to serve."

"You are very skilled, brother. I wish I could perform the same magics that you can, but I think we both know how poorly my natural talent is in that particular art." He slipped the pipe back into his mouth, inhaling deeply and releasing small plumes of smoke. He was glad to have changed the topic. The hatred he would deal with, for a time.

"It would be far wiser to invest more energy into learning magic and less into midnight excursions just for the enjoyment of a little fresh air and smoking. I am well aware of your deficiencies, brother." Mothlenor smirked. "And I hope you can forgive me for saying that you only have yourself to blame."

Again, Areanath noticed the thinly veiled disgust, but he was not surprised. He had grown accustomed to it over the years; his younger brother had developed a habit of pointing out Areanath's failings. He sucked deeply on his pipe once more, releasing more plumes of smoke. A moment passed, and Areanath once again stared out across the parapet. Rather than looking up to the stars, he instead looked out across the land. Visible just below them was the market square, quiet now in the middle of the night. Areanath's eyes followed the paths of the streets south, away from the castle, first to the residential areas, then to the great castle wall. Beyond the wall were farms dotted with homes and stables and the glistening waters of the Knife close by. He wondered briefly if the farmers were awake yet. The harvest season would be on them soon; surely that meant longer days for the men in the fields.

"What do you see when you look out across the land?"

Areanath was surprised by his own question. But he didn't retract it, curious what his brother might say.

Mothlenor sighed, casually casting a side glance out over the balcony's edge. "I see your people."

"My people? Are they not also your people?"

"I am not king."

Yet. He hadn't said it, but Areanath could hear it in his voice. Areanath nodded. He chewed on the end of his pipe, thinking. "Do you know what I see?"

"What do you see?" Mothlenor's words were a disinterested monotone, and Areanath was sure that his younger brother was only humoring him.

What do I see, exactly? The words were already out of his mouth before he could gauge their weight. "I see people. Not really *my* people, but just people." He sighed, smoke unfurling from his nostrils as he did. "I see people living their lives. People it is my sworn duty to protect from danger, from evil, until my death." He turned to his brother, watching for his reaction.

Mothlenor only smiled, his eyes glinting. "I suppose that is one thing we can agree on."

Areanath chewed on his pipe, looking his brother up and down. He huffed slightly. "I suppose." His knee twitched again and he rubbed it, but it only made the pain worse. "I think this old body of mine has decided that it's finally time for some rest. Would you like to walk with me back to my room, Mothlenor?"

Mothlenor scowled angrily, but quickly motioned Areanath through the open door. "Of course, my liege. As I said, I live to serve." They walked through the doorway, which Mothlenor closed behind them, and continued down a series of long hallways. The light of the few torches lining the walls cast eerie shadows on the stone floor and Mothlenor's heavy footsteps echoed loudly all around them. Ahead, more footsteps could be heard, perhaps from a few guards still canvassing the hallways in search of King Areanath. "Actually, brother, I'm glad that I was the one who found you out and about tonight. I have something I'd like to discuss with you, but we haven't had many chances to talk lately," Mothlenor said, his words bouncing loudly around them.

"Oh? And what would that be?"

"The Last Hunt," Mothlenor answered, voice flat.

"Ah." Areanath frowned. "Right." The Last Hunt, the royal signal of the end of summer and the beginning of the fall harvest season. He had been trying to avoid this conversation with his brother for several weeks.

"It should have been last week, at the latest." Mothlenor seemed to glower in the darkness beside him. "Some of the farmers have already begun bringing their crops in, even though the Hunt has not been completed."

"It's not their fault. Time will not wait for two old men to get their duties squared away." Areanath sighed. "The farmers know when their crops are ready. I cannot fault them for not wanting to wait for my permission."

"I've taken the liberty of making the necessary preparations. Everything can be ready the day after tomorrow." Mothlenor led Areanath back to his rooms. The guards were gone, presumably off searching for their king. Mothlenor pushed open the door and held it for his brother.

Areanath's heart sank. *So soon? I need more time ...* But to his brother, he said, "The day after tomorrow sounds excellent. Until then—"

"Until then, you should not be making any more midnight excursions and rousing half the castle on a mad search for you." He had surely meant his words to sound light and playful, but they instead sounded threatening. "I will go and inform the guards that you have been returned safely to your quarters, and I should hope that this won't happen again tonight."

Areanath thought back to his true intentions for slipping out of his room. *Everything is nearly in order. After tomorrow ...* "Don't worry, Mothlenor, it won't happen again." *Probably not ever again.* He smiled cheerily at his brother. "Now, I should be going to bed. This old leg, you know. It'll be bothering me all day if I don't get enough rest."

"Very well. Goodnight, then." Mothlenor huffed.

"Goodnight, brother." Areanath closed the door and paused behind it for a moment, waiting for Mothlenor's footsteps to fade away.

Once he was sure Mothlenor had retreated enough, he quickly hobbled across the room, one hand clutching his bad knee. Along the way, he motioned towards a small cluster of candles on a desk, which lit instantly. He continued across the room, guided by the soft light of the candles, until he reached a large dry basin in the corner of the room. He knelt beneath the basin and pulled out a large water pitcher, pouring the contents into the basin before setting it aside again. He waited a moment for the ripples to calm before taking both hands, fingers splayed, and stretching them over the surface of the water. He closed his eyes, concentrating, and waited for his magic to work. After a few seconds, the water darkened, and a vague figure appeared on the water's surface. Areanath opened his eyes, and the figure appeared to grow larger as if stepping closer to the surface of the water; the face grew clearer and more distinct with each second. Finally, a slender woman was visible, her light hair pinned away from her face and a white veil swept back over it. Her skin was almost porcelain and her eyes were a bright blue. She was young, much younger than Areanath, and her features were sharp, her voice kind. "Areanath."

"Nevina." Areanath smiled. "I should thank you for the waking potion you taught me to brew. It worked wonderfully."

The corners of her lips lifted slightly in a smile. "I'm glad I could be helpful. How did things go?"

"I was successful, though I did run into some … difficulty."

"Your brother? Does he suspect anything?"

Areanath sighed again, rubbing his hands over his face in exhaustion. "No, he still thinks I'm a dimwitted coward that can't even get dressed without assistance."

"That's good, I suppose."

"There's more."

Worry crossed Nevina's face. "Yes?"

Areanath drew a deep breath before slowly replying. "Mothlenor brought up the Last Hunt again. He wants to leave the day after tomorrow."

The worry on Nevina's face grew deeper. "He will kill you."

It wasn't a question. Areanath knew that, and he had known as much when he had agreed. He nodded. "I suspect he'll wait until we've been out for a few days before actually doing the deed, but it is inevitable. I am ready."

Nevina sighed. "Very well. Do you still have some final preparations to make?" Her voice was heavy.

"I do. Will you come to see me tomorrow? One last time? You have been a valuable friend in all of this. It would …" he stammered, "it would make me very happy, seeing you one last time before I go to my death."

Nevina smiled, eyes shining in the half light of the room. "Of course, Areanath. I'll come tomorrow."

He returned the smile. "Thank you. Goodnight, Nevina."

"Goodnight, Areanath." And with that, the image faded from the water.

4

MOTHLENOR

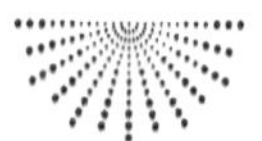

Mothlenor sat behind his disheveled desk, fingers steepled together and chin resting against the tips. "Areanath, you idiot," he muttered.

It wasn't the "midnight meditations" that his brother enjoyed so well that angered him, or even the fact that the castle guards had difficulty distinguishing him from his kingly twin at times – though that was annoying – it was his brother's refusal to see the error of his thinking, Areanath's inability to see reason that truly infuriated him.

"Your inaction will kill us all." Mothlenor shifted, drumming the fingers of one hand against the rough wood. The steady tapping usually helped to calm his anger and had become a habit when thinking about his older brother. "There is danger lurking in every corner, waiting for its chance to strike. And you do nothing." His fingers drummed again. "You claim it is your duty to protect the people, yet you continue to bend the knee to lesser creatures."

Drum.

"Idiot."

Mothlenor caught a whiff of burning wood and he pulled

his restless hand from the desk with a groan. Looking down, he counted four little burn marks where the tips of his fingers had drummed against the wood. There were other burn marks etched into the wood around him similar to the new ones he had just made. He sighed. *I continue to let my imbecile brother get the best of my emotions. But not for much longer. Just a few more days ...* "There is much work to be done." Mothlenor straightened to stand, but stopped when his eye caught a smooth grey orb pinning down a small stack of papers. "But first ..."

He plucked the orb from atop the pile. The stone fit neatly into the palm of his hand, cool to the touch. "What a pretty gift you were." He rotated the dragon's eye in his hand, peering at its dark surface. "Let's see what you're really capable of, shall we?" He clutched the stone tighter, pouring his energy into it. It instantly responded to the influx of power, the surface transmuting into a shimmering pool of shifting colors. Mothlenor grinned. *What is my foolish brother up to now?*

Mothlenor concentrated on his twin, imagining him as he last saw him, and the stone's surface began to change. The swirling colors muted, shifted into place, and were still. An image had formed on the surface of the dragon's eye. He lifted the stone closer, digesting the sight. His brother lying in bed, unmoving.

"Hmph." Mothlenor frowned at the sight of Areanath, and let the image melt from the stone. *Who else?* He thought for a moment, settling himself deeper into his chair. *There aren't that many people worth keeping an eye on, it would seem. Perhaps* ... He concentrated again, this time on his brother's adviser. The stone responded, again the bright colors dimmed and stood still. To Mothlenor's surprise, the young man was awake, bent over a small desk, a book in one hand, a quill in the other. His dark hair was tousled and he was still in his robes. Mothlenor huffed under his breath, again letting the image drift away. He watched as the colors within the stone writhed, transfixed.

There was one more ... *Nevina, that pretty little witch.* He had heard whispers that she had returned to Etritia. *No doubt to fill the king's head with her lies.* She could be a powerful ally if she could only be turned away from Areanath ...

Mothlenor peered into the dragon's eye again, concentrating on her image. In his mind's eye, he could see her thin frame, the white dress all Coven members wore, the long pale hair she rarely wore loose ... The curve of her hips, the sound of her voice, the way she almost glided when she walked ... But her eyes he had never seen. She had always kept her face hidden from him, from everyone. *Except Areanath*, he suspected. He continued to linger on her unfinished impression, but the stone would not respond. He tried again, and again the stone refused to reveal anything.

He gave up, stemming the tide of energy he had been feeding to the stone. It instantly went dark. He slowly rotated it in his palm, staring at it casually. It was noticeably warmer than it had been only moments ago. "Everything has its limitations, I suppose." He dropped the stone back onto the desk with a sigh. Standing, he turned his back on the orb. "There is still much to be done."

5

NEVINA

Nevina chewed on her lip as Areanath's image faded from the surface of the mirror in front of her. *Men can be so selfish,* she thought, pressing her eyes closed and willing her tears away. *Killing each other for the sake of power. Even their own family, Elir damn them.*

"So selfish," she muttered, sniffing delicately.

There was a soft knock at the door to her room, and Nevina jumped at the noise. "Just a moment!" she called, forcing her voice to remain steady. "I'm not decent."

She carefully draped a white veil down over her face, adjusting the ties that fastened it as she stood until it covered her eyes and rested gently against the bridge of her nose.

The door opened to reveal a tall girl with blonde tresses framing a face half covered by a similar white veil. The girl bowed slightly as Nevina pulled the door open wider. "Matriarch," she half whispered.

"Layle, what are you doing up?"

"One of the younger girls felt ill. I was caring for her," Layle answered.

"Was it Arella?" Nevina asked, moving to step around the girl. "Is she alright?"

Layle put an arm out to stop her. "She's alright, Matriarch." She quickly pulled her arm back as Nevina stepped away. "Just some homesickness, that's all," Layle added in another half whisper, wrapping her arms around her chest.

Nevina frowned slightly. "We'll only be away for a few days."

"I told her as much, Matriarch. She's asleep now."

Nevina sighed in relief. "Thank you for taking care of her." She reached out and caressed the side of Layle's head, feeling her soft hair under her fingers. "You're very good to the other girls, and I don't tell you often enough how grateful I am to have you under my care, and how much I—"

"I understand, Matriarch," Layle said, cutting her off.

"Alright, then," she said softly, pulling her hand away. "Did you need to see me for something? It's very late, you should get to bed."

"I thought I heard you talking to someone. Was it Grandmother?" Layle asked.

"No, though I should probably check in with her before sleeping, I suppose. It was the king. We were just discussing some minor details before tomorrow's meeting." Nevina shrugged. "Nothing terribly important."

"Oh," Layle said, her chin dropping slightly. "I was hoping it was Grandmother. I was going to ask if I could say goodnight to her, but …" Layle's words trailed.

Nevina chuckled. "I'll pass your message along, Layle. I'm sure she'll be grateful to know you were thinking of her." She gave the girl a quick nod. "Now, off to bed. It's late, and you need sleep. Goodnight, Layle."

"Goodnight, Matriarch." Layle bowed again slightly before walking away and slipping into a neighboring room in their rented cottage.

Nevina watched her departure for a moment before shutting the door and returning to her scrying mirror, which she had balanced atop the mantle to the fireplace in her room.

The fireplace was unlit, but there was a smattering of candles on the mantle and on the table a few feet away, and their combined glow was enough to see by.

Nevina thought of her mother, Layle's grandmother, and she hardened her will into a small knot of desire as she lightly touched the surface of the mirror. It instantly grew foggy, responding to Nevina's scrying magic and seeking out her mother.

She heard her mother's voice before she saw her image as anything more than a shadow on the glass. "Nevina? Is that you?" Her mother's voice was warbled, but strong and warm.

"It's me, Nevara." Nevina smiled as her mother came into view more clearly. Her long hair was down, more silver now than gold, and her robe clung to her thin frame. "You've forgotten your veil," she said, staring at her mother's milky eyes in disbelief. *How long had they been so dead?*

Her mother waved a hand in dismissal. "Forget the veil. It's no good to me anymore. I have nothing to fear from you seeing my face, darling."

"You're very beautiful." She meant it. She had only seen her mother's face a few times, but was always struck by how stunning she must have been in her prime. Even now, thin and nearly blind, her face was radiant.

"Nevina …" her mother chided lightly. She waved her hand again, and Nevina noticed a tremble in the thin fingers.

"Are you cold?" Nevina frowned, spotting a young woman in the background, waiting to attend to her mother. "Anna, can you get her a blanket? She looks half frozen."

The young woman snapped to attention, bowing and muttering a quick "Yes, Matriarch," before hurrying out of view. Nevina felt a momentary pang of jealousy that Anna, an Ungifted, could look on her mother's face every evening. It was safe for any Coven member to go unveiled around an Ungifted, and Anna was her mother's caretaker in her old age, but it still hurt. Anna was little more than a girl, and might one day be her own caretaker. Would Layle feel the same jealousy when that day came?

Nevara protested vainly as the young woman draped a heavy blanket over her shoulders. "Really, Nevina, it isn't necessary. I'm only up for a moment more, then Anna will help me to bed." She sighed as Anna rearranged the blanket to sit more comfortably on her. "I'm glad you Called on me, Nevina. I'm not sure I like you going to the castle right now."

"Did you See something?" Nevina asked. *Could she See anything, anymore?*

"No. Maybe. I'm not sure." Her mother sighed. "I just have this terrible feeling that you won't return home." She shook her head, smiling faintly. "I know it's silly, but will you Call on me again tomorrow night? Or the morning after? Whenever your ... duties are complete?"

There had been a slight pause, Nevina had heard it. And she knew why. Her mother was aware of her true intentions in coming to see Areanath. Although Nevina had let the rest of her Coven assume the visit was purely politically motivated, she couldn't keep the truth from the former Matriarch. *Is that why she was worried?*

"Of course, Mother. But don't wait up for me. If you haven't heard from me by nightfall tomorrow, I'll just wait until morning. You shouldn't stay up so late two nights in a row." Nevina tried to smile reassuringly before remembering her mother couldn't see it. "There is nothing to worry about. No harm will come to us while we can still call the king our friend."

Her mother sniffed delicately, one eyebrow arched in skepticism. "Very well, Matriarch."

Her words stung a bit. In only an instant, her mother had changed the tone of their conversation from one of a mother chatting with her daughter to one of a subordinate bending to the wishes of her master. It had not been that long ago since their roles had been reversed, and Nevina had been the one acquiescing to her mother's will.

Nevara must have sensed her unease in the silence. Her voice grew softer and her brows knitted together in concern. "Just come home quickly, and safely."

"Of course, Mother."

"Anything else, Little One?"

"Yes." Nevina's lips curled into a smile. "Layle wanted to wish her grandmother a good night."

"Oh, Nevina …" Her mother smiled, her eyes almost bright for a moment. "I wish you hadn't told her."

"It's hardly a secret, Mother. It was just as easy for her to figure out as it was for me, all those years ago."

Her mother sighed. "I suppose you're right. And it does an old heart good to feel loved by the youngest ones. Give her my love in return, and tell her not to tell a soul." Her lips thinned, one eyebrow rising critically. "If it'll even do much good anymore."

Nevina chuckled. "Goodnight, Mother."

"Goodnight, Nevina."

With that, her mother's image faded from the surface of the scrying mirror. Nevina untied the veil from her hair and laid it on the mantle beside the mirror; she slid into bed, already thinking of what tomorrow might bring.

6

SILVANA

S ilvana was awoken by the faintest hint of nausea; she rolled in her half sleep, reaching for Hasani's warmth. When she didn't find it, her eyes snapped open and she let out the smallest groan. *Already working. This can't continue when the baby comes.*

Silvana sat up in bed, blinking away the last traces of sleep and searching the half-lit room for her husband.

He was bent over his small writing desk, scribbling furiously. Silvana watched him for a moment until he dropped the quill on the desk and leaned back in his chair, rubbing his hands over his face.

"Hasani?" He turned, surprised. "Hasani, it's nearly morning. Have you been up all night?"

Hasani looked to the other side of the room, where grey light started to filter through the window covering. "So it is." He touched a slip of parchment on the desk, its edges curling slightly. "I'm sorry. I was working."

"Hasani …" Silvana pleaded, brushing a few errant strands of hair from her face.

"I know, I know. I'll stop working so late when the baby comes. I promise."

Silvana frowned at him, eyes narrowing, but she tugged back the covers and motioned for Hasani to join her. He stood, smiling sheepishly, and started for her.

"What are you working on?"

Hasani paused, glancing back at the curling parchment on his desk. "Rubbish, as it turns out." He snatched up the parchment, looking it over briefly. After a quiet hesitation, he walked out of her line of sight towards the hearth. She heard a faint crackling sound followed by Hasani's low mutter. "Complete nonsense."

"So you'll come to bed?"

Hasani stepped back into view, smiling at her. "I'll do whatever my lady desires." He walked across the room, pausing at the desk to pick up a small book, which he tucked into the inside pocket of his vest.

"What's that?"

"A book." Hasani shrugged a shoulder before planting a kiss on her forehead. "Areanath gave it to me."

"Is it any good?"

He shook his head firmly, a faint smile crossing his lips. "Not really." He crawled into bed and Silvana rolled over to her side, pressing her back against his chest. He wrapped an arm around her waist and buried his face in her hair. Silvana smiled in the dark as Hasani sighed contentedly and pulled her closer to him. He placed a hand on her swollen belly, rubbing it gently. The touch was soothing and Silvana could feel her body relax as Hasani held her. "Has our little boy started kicking yet?"

Silvana laced her fingers together with Hasani's, and together they held her stomach. "No, he's still too little." She turned, looking over her shoulder at him. "And how can you be sure it won't be a little girl?" She smiled, goading him.

She could see his dark eyes shining lightly in the dark. "I can just feel it. Our child will be a strong and healthy boy."

"And if she's not?"

"Then I will love her as much as I love her beautiful mother, and treat her just as kindly. And I would perhaps insist that we try again for a boy."

Silvana smirked. "And if we only ever have girls?"

Hasani sighed wistfully. "I would love them all." He pulled her closer, squeezing her gently. "But I would perhaps insist on trying again and again until we have a boy."

Silvana snorted, pulling away from him. "That's alright for you to say. I would be the one to carry and birth them all." But she rolled over to face him, planting a kiss on his cheek. "I hope, then, for both our sakes, that it is a boy." A faint pain in her abdomen brought her hand up to sit a bit higher on her belly. "There is already one unfortunate side effect of all this …"

Hasani leaned away from her, looking her over. "What's that?"

"I'm hungry. All the time." She groaned, unable to keep from smiling.

Hasani chuckled, kicking the covers back and sitting up. "I'll go see what Cookie can bring us."

"No, no, no." Silvana pushed him back down. "You stay in bed. *I'll* go see what Cookie can bring us." She pulled the blankets up to Hasani's chest and gave him another kiss on the cheek. "You were up working all night. You just rest for a bit."

Hasani grumbled incoherently, but she left the bed, taking a few minutes to change out of her bedclothes and into a loose-fitting dress. It hid her figure nicely, but wouldn't after another month or so. *I'll have to see about getting something larger made soon.* Silvana sighed, pulling her hair back and tying it with a length of green ribbon. She could feel Hasani's eyes on her as she crossed back and forth across the room, but she ignored him. He needed rest, and he would fall asleep within a few minutes if she let him be.

Leaving the bedroom, Silvana went to the hearth, grabbing her shoes and glancing at the cooling embers. There were traces of burned parchment in one far corner of the fireplace, covered in Hasani's neat script. It was not the first time Hasani had worked all night, and it surely wouldn't be the last. But Silvana had never heard Hasani refer to his work as rubbish, and never had a late night's work ended up tossed into the fire.

An ember popped suddenly, and the tiny clump of half-burned work curled and blackened away to ash. Silvana took her shoes and turned away from the little heap of black dust.

By the time she had put her shoes on and dabbed a drop of fresh perfumed oil behind each ear, Hasani was snoring lightly in the bedroom. Silvana watched him quietly for a moment until her stomach groaned and gently reminded her of the growing child in her womb. Silvana left their rooms as quietly as possible, letting the door shut behind her with the softest snap, and hurried down the quiet castle halls to the kitchens.

Cookie was already up and wearing her apron, of course, bustling about the kitchens with floured hands. Ishta, her oldest daughter, sat at the long prep table, peeling a basket of apples and dropping them to soak in a pail of water.

"Apple tart season already, Cookie?" Silvana asked as she entered.

"Has been for a week or so now, lovely. I keep making a few dozen or so, but *someone* likes to sneak in at night and gobble a few of them up." Cookie dusted her hands on her apron, rolling her eyes at the ceiling. She moved to a cabinet on the far wall, opened it and pulled down some platters. "Hungry, lovely?"

"Very," Silvana answered, seating herself next to Ishta. "Where are the other girls?"

"Illa has gone out to the market square to pick up some things. Irena is in bed with a cough, the poor thing," Ishta answered, dropping an apple into the pail and taking up another.

"The poor, lazy thing, you mean," Cookie corrected. There was a whisper of a southern accent in her voice, hinting that she had spent most of her youth along the southern coasts. But it had been so long ago, judging by the greying at her temples, that Silvana wondered how Cookie had managed to keep the rolling slur from ever leaving her speech. "That girl hasn't a thing wrong with her, except for a stubborn bout of utter indifference." Cookie held a long-handled wooden spoon aloft, giving Silvana a hard look. "Neither hand nor spoon can beat it out of her." Cookie turned her back to Silvana, dipping the spoon into a pot of white mush and scooping some into a nearby bowl. "She must have gotten it from her father's side, may Imis keep him." Cookie dropped the ladle back into the pot and quickly lifted her right hand; she tapped the first three fingers gently against the opposite collarbone, paying reverence to the Goddess Imis.

Silvana and Ishta exchanged a glance and Ishta rolled her eyes, dropping her freshly peeled apple into the pail of water.

Cookie set the bowl down in front of Silvana. "May you have better luck with yours than I have."

Silvana stared at the steaming bowl in front of her as Cookie drizzled a generous helping of dark honey over the top. "You know about it?"

Cookie snorted, turning away from Silvana again and bustling around the stone oven in the far corner. "Nearly everyone in the castle knows at this point, I think. Your brother was down here last night, just raving about it."

"Was he?" Silvana swallowed around the hard lump that had formed in her throat, pushing the porridge around with her spoon.

"He was very excited," Ishta said, glancing sideways at her.

"Everyone is very excited," Cookie said over her shoulder.

"As they should be." When she turned, she held a platter with warm bread spread liberally with soft butter in one hand and an old clay jar in the other. She slid the former to Silvana with the careless ease of someone who had done it a thousand times before. The clay jar she held out for Silvana to take. "I made this for you, lovely."

"What is it?" Silvana took the jar from her, lifting the lid to peer inside. A wave of something heavy and sour rolled up to her nose, and Silvana clamped the lid down again with a gag. "Great Ones take it, it smells horrible!"

Cookie laughed, taking the jar from her and setting it on the far end of the table. "Family secret. Two onions, picked under a half moon, soaking in goat's milk." Cookie turned, giving Silvana a coy shrug. "And a few extra things I'm not willing to share." She crossed her arms over her chest, nodding once at Silvana. "Eat it tonight before bed and you'll have yourself a little girl."

Silvana looked over at the jar, stomach rolling at the thought of eating the putrid contents. "And if I want a boy?"

Cookie snorted, shaking her head. "Is it you that wants a boy, or Hasani?"

Silvana said nothing, bringing the slice of bread to her mouth and inhaling deeply before taking a bite. The sweetness of the bread helped to remove the lingering scent of Cookie's onion and goat's milk mixture.

"Mother says that once a man gets a boy out of you, he'll never lie with you again," Ishta said calmly, dropping her last apple into the pail and wiping her hands clean on her apron.

"It's true," Cookie said, motioning towards the clay jar. "I used this to make sure I only ever had girls, so that my sweet husband would never leave my bed." Cookie smiled wickedly and Silvana nearly choked. "Not until his death, anyway, that is."

Silvana chanced another glance at the jar and turned away from it just as quickly. "I think we'll let the baby choose for itself what it wants to be." Silvana pulled the porridge closer to her, stirring the honey in and giving it a tentative taste. "Besides, I'm not sure I could ever bring myself to eat that, Cookie. It's certainly not your best dish."

Cookie let out a roaring laugh and returned to the oven. "Of course, lovely. Whatever you'd like." She bent to pull a baking stone of apple tarts from the oven and set them aside to cool. "It was just a thought, dear."

"I appreciate it, Cookie." Silvana savored another few mouthfuls of food, watching Cookie as she slipped another batch of apple tarts into the oven. "What did you mean when you said everyone should be excited about my baby?"

Cookie turned, wiping her hands on her apron thoughtfully. "Well …" She hesitated, crossing the room to sit across from Silvana. "I suppose it's just nice to have a baby in the castle, is all." Cookie shrugged. "Areanath hasn't had one of his own, Great Ones only know why. Any woman in Etritia would have gladly thrown themselves at him a decade ago, and many still would, I think. His brother doesn't seem keen to take a wife either." Cookie sighed, giving Silvana a frustrated look. "Yours is the closest thing we little folk will have to a royal baby, Silvana."

Silvana tried to protest, but the lump in her throat had returned, and no sound would come out.

"You shouldn't put so much stress on her, Cookie. It won't be good for the baby, royal or not," a gentle voice said from the doorway.

"Areanath." Silvana sighed, getting to her feet. The other two women also rose, Ishta bowing and hurrying from the kitchen and Cookie going to the cabinet again with a faintly derisive snort.

Areanath held his arms out for her, and Silvana hurried around the table to embrace him. He smelled lightly of tobacco, the scent of it clinging to his cloak and beard. He kissed her forehead and squeezed her gently. "Are you doing well, Silvana?"

"Excellent. And you?" Silvana waved him towards the table, but he shook his head.

"I was on my way to the gardens and I swore I could smell some freshly baked apple tarts," Areanath said pointedly, glancing at Cookie with a faint smile.

Cookie harrumphed, dropping a hot tart on a dish and bringing it over to him. "I bet you could smell them in your sleep. I've had to stop making them the night before they're needed because you keep scuttling in here like a little rat and nibbling away on all my goods."

Areanath smiled, taking the dish from Cookie. "You should take it as a compliment, Cookie. I like to think I'm much more discerning when it comes to food than a common rat." He took a small bite of the tart, his eyes closing as he chewed slowly. "Mm. Exquisite, as always."

Cookie scowled up at him, but her cheeks deepened to a faint red at his words. "I'll let you have one more on your way back through, but the rest will be served tonight, after dinner." She waved Areanath back towards the door. "Now, shoo. I've work to do, and I don't need a man getting underfoot in my kitchen."

Areanath smiled at Cookie, obediently stepping out of the kitchen and into the hallway beyond. "Would you care to join me, Silvana? The garden is quite peaceful so early in the morning."

"I'd love to," Silvana said. She turned to give Cookie a quick embrace. "Thank you for breakfast, and thank you for …" her eyes slid to the clay jar and its foul contents, "that."

Cookie chuckled. "Of course, lovely." She bustled over to Ishta's pail of apples, hoisting it up with both hands. "Should I send something up to Hasani?"

Silvana nodded, stepping to stand beside Areanath. "I'm sure he would be grateful, Cookie."

Cookie returned the nod. "I'll see it's done. May the Great Imis preserve you, Silvana. And the baby. And keep that old man out of trouble."

Silvana smiled, turning to see Areanath staring after Cookie, chewing slowly on a mouthful of tart.

They walked side by side in silence, leaving the castle proper and heading for the gardens. The exit closest to the kitchen opened close to the barracks, and Silvana could see young recruits milling about, preparing for their latest training. Her brother would be out there somewhere, though she couldn't see the bright splash of red hair among the handful of people outside the barracks.

Areanath finished his tart and, with a few low words, handed the empty plate to a servant girl who passed them. Silvana was sure the girl was Ishta's sister, Illa, though it might have been Ishta herself. They were close enough in age and had the same slightly olive-toned skin and dark hair. Silvana always had trouble telling the two apart.

"That Cookie," Areanath said with a low sigh. "She really knows her way to a man's stomach." He brushed a few fallen crumbs from the front of his cloak. "I'm grateful she's so hard on me, otherwise I would just eat myself into my grave."

Silvana smiled, looping her arm through his. "There's a bit of tart in your beard."

Areanath cursed, brushing at his beard with his free hand, and they continued in silence once more.

The morning was cool, with a gentle breeze blowing in around her feet, brushing away the first of the dying leaves of autumn. The sky was still mostly grey, and when Silvana glanced behind them, the streets of the market square were quiet. When they entered the shade of the garden, what little sounds she could hear dimmed away to nothing, and it suddenly seemed that she and Areanath were the only people in all of Azimar.

Areanath led her to a stone bench close to the entrance,

and they sat together. The bench was at the top of a low hill, facing east, and from where they sat, Silvana could see the streaks of orange-red sunrise as they stretched across the horizon. A fountain bubbled quietly not far from the bench, the Goddess Imis carved to stand in the center of the pool, water pouring from a pitcher in her hands to splash between her feet.

"This is my favorite spot in the garden," Areanath said, examining a climbing rose bush nearby. "If I get out here early enough, I can watch the sun rise. I can hear Etritia awaken and smell the flowers as they warm in the sunlight." He sighed, rubbing at his right knee gently. "And I can get back into the castle easily, if my old body wants it."

Silvana chuckled. "It's a good spot."

They resumed their silence, and Silvana took a moment to look around her at the flowering plants. The climbing rose bush closest to Areanath was the largest by far, with several heavy flowers. Silvana stood, walked over to it and brought a flower to her nose.

"It's during moments like this one that I wish I could stop time," Areanath said from the bench. His eyes were on the skyline, watching as the red-orange hues slowly crawled their way towards them. "Just stop it where it is, and savor every bit of life in it."

"That sounds wonderful," Silvana said. *It sounds lonely ...*

"But I think if I did, I'd never start it going again."

Silvana said nothing, bringing another rose towards her and inhaling its soft scent.

"Cookie was right, you know."

Areanath's eyes were on her when she turned to look at him. "Oh?" She dropped the rose, folding her hands in front of her. "About what?"

The king gave her a faint smile. "That your baby is the closest Etritia has had to a royal child in a long time." His head tilted slightly as he watched her, his warm eyes softening. "And that worries you, I think."

Silvana shook her head, trying to laugh his words away. "It's nothing, really." Her voice was strained.

Areanath motioned for her to sit beside him again, and Silvana reluctantly did so. "There's no one else here, if you want to voice your concerns." He waved an arm around them. "Tell Imis, if you can't tell me. I've found that she's a good listener."

This time Silvana did laugh, but it sounded hollow, even to her. She wrung her hands together in her lap, trying to make sense of the doubts and fears that had plagued her since the night before.

The sun continued to rise, the sky brightening with each passing moment. She stared at the silent statue of Imis, counting her heart beats as the fountain sprayed against the bare stone feet of the goddess of life and death.

"I worry that I'll mess everything up," she said finally. "That I'll do something wrong while carrying the baby, and it will be a dead birthing." She wrapped her hands together, winding her fingers so tightly around each other that her knuckles turned white. "Or that the birthing will go well, but he'll grow sick as an infant. Or that he'll grow strong and healthy, but will be a spoiled and unruly child. Or that he will be a good, kind man, and he will hate me for being his mother." She turned to face Areanath, not surprised to find him watching her. "I worry that if my son is the closest thing to a royal child, I will fail all of Etritia in raising him."

"That …" Areanath raised an eyebrow, frowning slightly, "is a lot to worry about."

SIlvana let out a frustrated chuckle.

"But normal, I think," Areanath added with a smile. He wrapped an arm around her, pulling her close. "I think you're doing well so far. I think you will continue to do well." He kissed the top of her head. "And you will not be going it alone, Silvana. All Etritia is cheering you on, and all Etritia will be there to help you. Even if your son will never actually be king."

Silvana sighed, letting her shoulders relax as Areanath hugged her. "Wise as always, Areanath." He laughed, the sound of it making her smile. "However, I think I would feel a lot more confident if there had been a queen for me to discuss these sorts of things with."

"Ah, and for that I am sorry, Silvana." He released her, taking her hand and wrapping it in his own. "But you can always come and talk to the goddess." He motioned towards the fountain, which seemed to glow in the brightening light. Imis's head was tilted, her face soft and caring. Her mouth was a gentle smile, and taking a long look at the goddess's likeness soothed Silvana. "She never really answers, but it might help."

The morning sun had risen, and Silvana could hear regular shouts and bursts of noise from the courtyard outside the barracks.

"Sounds like the commander has begun his training for the day," Areanath said, standing with a low groan. "I should be going myself. I have some work to see to." He knelt to give Silvana a light kiss on the forehead. "Take a few more moments for yourself here. And when you're ready, see if you can track down that husband of yours and head to the market square."

"The market square? Why?"

Areanath smiled, his eyes brightening in the sun. "Nevina should be arriving shortly."

Silvana's breath caught. "The Matriarch?" He nodded. "Areanath, why didn't you say anything sooner?"

He shrugged. "She gets upset if we make a fuss over her. Better just to surprise everyone, she thinks." He bent to kiss the top of her head once more. "I'll see you later, Silvana."

Silvana watched him leave, then began silently counting

down the seconds as they passed. *Areanath wants me to enjoy a few more minutes here, so I will.*

She watched the clouds as they moved across the sky, fidgeting where she sat. The minutes seemed to stretch into hours, first one, then two, until finally she stood with a huff.

"That's quite long enough to wait, Areanath. I hope you're ready for the Matriarch's company."

7

LAYLE

I t was technically Kall's turn to cook breakfast for
everyone, but Layle still seemed to be doing most of the
work. She was used to it by now. With the girls older than
her, she had to step in to keep the bread from burning in the
oven while they gossiped away about Great Ones only knew
what. With those younger than her, she was their guiding
hand, helping them when the Matriarch was otherwise
preoccupied. At least the younger ones listened to her. Millie
and Kall only snapped at her irritably when they realized she
had yet again done their chores for them, and insisted she
did it out of spite, or to gain the Matriarch's favor.

In truth, Layle only worked so hard because remaining
idle made her skin crawl uncomfortably, and caused her
mind to fixate on silly, small worries.

She never wanted the Matriarch's favor. But she got it
anyway. She and Arella both.

Layle had just finished dividing the food onto half a
dozen plates—a slice of toasted bread with freshly made
butter, two beautifully cooked eggs, and a generous slice of
ham each—when Arella, the youngest, came up to her, veil
and shoes in hand. "Layle, will you help me?"

Layle quickly turned her away from Millie and Kall, who were gossiping at the table, hoping the two hadn't seen her sister's face. Not that they hadn't seen it before. "Arella, you shouldn't have left your room without your veil on," Layle hissed. "You should have stayed put until I came for you."

"I called for you, I promise. But you didn't hear," Arella protested, her voice taking on an infantile whine.

Layle was already tying the white veil into place, smoothing her sister's golden hair as she did so. "It's alright. No harm done. Do you need help getting your shoes on?"

The little girl nodded, climbing into the closest chair. She took the slice of ham in both hands and bit into it, lifting her feet obediently as Layle laced the shoes. "Where are we going?"

Layle brushed a bit of dirt from Arella's dress and pointed at the utensils beside the plate of food. "Today we are going to the castle, so you have to be on your best behavior."

Arella took the utensils in hand and began stabbing ineffectually at her eggs. "Why?"

Layle tucked a large napkin into Arella's dress collar just in time for it to catch a dribble of yolk. "Because the king lives there, and he is a very good person. And it's nice to be good for good people."

Arella wiped a sticky hand onto the napkin and continued eating without the utensils. "Why is the king a good person?"

Layle had to think about that one. *Because he's our father,* she wanted to say. But that was only conjecture on her part. Her mother had many infatuates; any one of them could be her father, and another one Arella's. She wasn't even supposed to know that Arella was her sister. Or that the Matriarch was her mother. Arella certainly didn't know. But there were only three blonde-haired, blue-eyed women in the Coven—four if you counted Navara, who had gone grey in the last several years—and it was pretty easy to guess those sorts of things. And the Matriarch had told her that much, anyway.

"Well, he comes from a long line of very nice people." Layle thought for a moment, trying to find words someone so young might understand. "His great grandfather led mankind into the Great War, and was a good leader." Arella was staring up at her, chewing slowly at a mouthful of bread. There was a smear of butter on her cheek and Layle wiped it away. "His grandfather signed the peace treaties with the elves and dwarves after the Great War ended." Layle paused again, thinking. "His father gave the Coven and the Free Cities the right of sovereignty, and let us hide ourselves away from the rest of the world."

Arella made a sour face. "What's soventy?"

"Sovereignty," Layle corrected. "It's like … freedom."

Arella nodded. "So the Coven can take care of itself. Matriarch Nevara said so."

"Exactly," Layle said, smiling.

"What has King Areanath done to be good?" Arella asked.

Layle hesitated, unsure of the answer. *What* has *Areanath done?*

"King Areanath is a good man because he is fair and noble, and because he cares about those he rules over," came a voice from the doorway.

Layle turned startled. "M-matriarch. I didn't see you there." She had almost said "Mother."

The Matriarch smiled knowingly but continued. "Perhaps King Areanath hasn't done anything quite so grand as ending the Great War, but he's still a good man." She sat in the chair next to Arella, Layle standing between them. The last two girls followed in behind her and took their seats, thanking Kall for the food. "When the countryside was in drought some years ago, he commissioned the King's Guard to dig new wells for the farmers. Even though he knew he could pay any amount of money to keep himself and his household fed, he wanted to make sure that there was enough water to keep all the crops alive, so that the poorer people living in the city could still afford to feed themselves. When a great sea storm damaged the Free Cities of Emery and Hythe, and many people lost their homes and their way of life, he released them from taxes for the next five years and sent a large stipend and the finest craftsmen in the city south to help them rebuild." The Matriarch cut a piece of egg from the plate in front of her and ate it delicately. "History has many stories of kings who fought great battles, and of kings who did terrible things to the people they were supposed to protect. King Areanath is neither of those. But he is kind, and loving, and trustworthy. And I think it is those things that make him a good person."

Arella was smiling, her small hands balled around the last remaining bits of toast. "Can I meet him?"

The corner of the Matriarch's mouth curled up, dimpling one cheek. "Perhaps you can, someday."

It looks just like Arella's smile, Layle thought.

The Matriarch surveyed the table. The other Coven children were sitting, chatting idly amongst themselves as they ate. The Matriarch's smile faded. Layle knew what her mother had realized. There were six plates of food, including Arella's, which was now empty, but seven of them in total. "Are you not eating, Layle?"

"I've already eaten, Matriarch." It was a bit of a lie, and she was sure her mother knew. The loaf of bread Kall had baked had been too small, and she had gotten distracted while collecting eggs from the chickens kept cooped up behind the house, and had returned with far fewer than she should have. But Layle had eaten some of the ham, which she had cooked the night before in preparation for Kall's lack of planning.

"Would you like an egg?" the Matriarch asked quietly.

"No, thank you, Matriarch. I've already eaten," Layle repeated a bit forcefully. She took Arella by one sticky hand, pulling the napkin from her sister's dress and helping her to her feet. "I'll help Arella get cleaned up, and then the two of us will be ready to go."

The Matriarch only nodded, taking another delicate bite of her food.

The sun was bright, but not too warm. Fall would be coming soon, and there was a cooling breeze rolling in from the River Knife. Layle could hear the rushing waters off to their right, but she couldn't see any sign of the long river other than a far-off bridge. They walked in single file along the dirt road from their rented cottage to the castle, as they usually did when outside the Coven's walls. All except Arella, who walked beside Layle, one tiny hand in hers; Layle walked behind first Millie, then Kall. The countryside was pretty enough, in Layle's opinion. There were houses dotted along the long road to the castle, many of them with a stable and a horse or two. The smell of animals was somewhat refreshing. There were no horses in the Coven, and the heavy scent of them was relaxing.

Arella tried to count the farmhouses they walked past, but she repeatedly lost her place, usually around the count of two or three. So instead, at Layle's insistence, Arella took to naming the plants in the field they passed. Some were easy, just wheat and corn and what were probably potatoes. Others were more difficult, some of them strange even to Layle, and for those Arella made up names. A series of long rows of elongated purple plants were named "purple surprise," and the round fruit growing on a cluster of small potted trees in one field were named "ugly apples." Layle was tempted to pluck one of the green-yellow plants from the tree to try herself, but thought better of it. *Perhaps we'll see some when we reach the market square, and I can ask the Matri-arch to give us each a little spending money.*

The great curved wall surrounding Etritia loomed in front of them, seeming to grow taller with every step, as did the mountains the castle sat against. Layle had seen maps of Etritia and the surrounding lands, and while she knew that Etritia and the farmlands they passed on the road to the castle only made up a small part of Azimar, the size of it all as they drew nearer made her feel suddenly very tiny and insignificant. In the safety of the Coven she took up a bit of space, and she knew the surrounding land like few others. But here, looking up at the tower spires that poked up from behind Etritia's walls, she thought it impossible that any one person could come to intimately know every nook and cranny of such a large city.

They weren't the only ones on the road to the Etritia. Ahead of them walked an elderly couple, the man pulling a small cart behind him, his wife carrying a basket of what looked like baked goods and amber bottles of liquid. *A farmer taking his produce to sell in the city, and his wife with a nice lunch for them.* Layle smiled at their backs, but the Matriarch made no move to overtake them on the road.

They walked in relative silence, keeping pace with the elderly couple and maintaining a respectable distance. With each passing moment, the castle grew closer and closer, the walls of the city looming overhead as they drew nearer. The noise of a bustling market began to drift towards them, growing louder as they reached the main gate on the east side of the city. The guards standing watch on either side of the gate briefly inspected the farmer's cart, then his wife's lunch basket. They seemed to know the couple, exchanging words and laughter before waving them through. They hardly approached the Matriarch, recognizing instantly who she was from her veil and white dress. They quickly bowed and let them pass. The Matriarch returned the bow, then gave the elderly couple a polite nod as they filed past. The wife made a delighted sound of recognition, turning excitedly to her husband as the Matriarch and her followers filed past them. Layle smiled at the couple and Arella gave them an energetic wave, which they returned eagerly.

The gate they entered from opened onto a densely packed area that Layle could only assume was the market square. She could see the long steps leading to the front of the castle through the throng of people, but the Matriarch seemed to be in no hurry to reach them. And for that Layle was oddly grateful. There were too many things to see and experience, and Layle wanted a few moments to absorb as much as possible.

At a nearby vending stall, a thin woman in richly colored skirts bowed low to the Matriarch before holding out a long silver chain for her to examine. The Matriarch declined, and the merchant nodded politely before moving on to a woman in a high-necked dress with a young man at her elbow. Layle could smell the high scent of flowers and sweet breads, and she spotted two carts further down that seemed to be the source. She could hear chickens clucking, though she could not tell where the sound came from. And all around them, people shouted, bartered, laughed, and hurried about. Layle clutched Arella's hand tightly, and her little sister stepped closer to her, mouth agape in wonder. Layle followed the Matriarch, head turning at every new sight and sound, both thrilled and a little frightened.

They had reached Etritia.

8

NEVINA

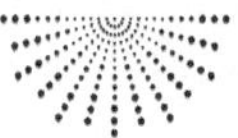

Nevina walked slowly through Etritia's market square, letting the girls trailing behind her take in the sights around them. She had been to Etritia on several occasions, but this was the first time her girls had come with her to the capital. The sights, the smells, the sheer number of people—it could be both fascinating and overwhelming. Their little faces and wide eyes showed as much each time she turned to check on them. Even Layle, usually so reserved, seemed to be enjoying herself.

Nevina slowed further, allowing her girls to follow a little more closely behind. She caught sight of a helmed guard tailing them, and she was both grateful and a little surprised by his presence. *Has the commander come to offer himself to me already?* She smiled to herself, thinking of the routine gesture she and Commander Ajax always found themselves making. But the guard kept his distance, watching the Matriarch and her girls from afar. Nevina found herself a little disappointed to realize that it wasn't Ajax. *But the day is still young.*

As they drew nearer to the castle, the city dwellers crept closer and closer to the little group of women, staring as they passed, trying to catch a glimpse of the faces beneath the white veils each woman wore. Merchants were the boldest, coming within touching distance to offer her their wares, and to try to sneak a look at what lay hidden behind each veil. Nevina waved each one away, purchasing nothing, not even truly looking at what was offered to her. After all, she wasn't here to shop for a new trinket or bauble. And Areanath was sure to keep the castle's kitchen well stocked with sweet breads and honeyed cakes, even when he wasn't expecting her.

Nevina continued to slow her pace as the crowd around them continued to swell. It would only take a few more moments before people began begging for answers, and she didn't want to lose one of her girls in the chaos. There was always chaos, wherever a Matriarch visited. Etritia was no exception.

"Please," a woman begged, pushing through the gathering crowd to kneel before Nevina, "my son, will he ever come home?"

Around them, a hush fell over the assembled onlookers as they waited to see if the Coven's newest Matriarch would share the insights her Gift gave her.

Nevina Saw the answer as soon as she looked into the woman's eyes. Her son, his hair and face much like his mother's, riding a weary horse through a twisting forest path. "He was traveling?" she asked the mother, almost unaware that the words had left her mouth.

"Yes," the woman sobbed. "He wanted to see the world. I thought he was so foolish, but I couldn't make him stay."

The vision Nevina watched in her mind's eye continued, and Nevina fought to coalesce the flood of images into one coherent thread that her mind could follow. Thieves ambushed the young man, knocking him from his horse and sending him sprawling to the ground. They took the animal and beat the son, robbing him of even the shirt and shoes he wore. When he knelt in the dirt, nose broken and bleeding, begging for his life, they cut his throat and left him on the side of the road. Nevina blinked, trying to hold back the tears stinging her eyes. "He is fine," she lied, taking the woman's hand and guiding her back to her feet. "He found something that he wasn't aware he had been searching for. In time, he will marry a beautiful woman, and they'll have a beautiful family," she said. "But you will never see or hear from him again."

The woman sobbed loudly, a sound full of anguish and joy, and Nevina's heart ached in sympathy.

The silence that followed was short-lived, and suddenly they were all speaking, all calling out to her.

"My crops. Why do they grow so poorly?"

"Will my wife and I ever have a baby?"

"Is my husband still sleeping with that harlot?"

The questions came in, one after another, and Nevina could hardly keep up. All the people. All the eyes, watching her. All the truths she Saw. It was too much. The former Matriarch had been so much better at quelling the crowds, at pleasing the people. At answering all the questions. Nevina had walked faithfully behind her for years, and still she had not mastered that ability. But they were close; the stone steps to the castle doors were only thirty or so yards away.

A small hand slid into hers, and she looked down to see Arella standing anxiously at her side. She was still so young, and she clung to Nevina in fear. She quietly cursed herself, looking through the crowd around them, hoping to catch the eye of the guard that had been following them. *I shouldn't have brought the girls ... but they need to see the world, and this is another part of it.*

She caught a flash of red hair on the stairs and her heart leapt. Ajax stood just outside the castle doors, scanning the crowd until he caught sight of them. Nevina smiled, glad that he had come to help her, though she would never admit it to him.

Hasani waited at the top of the stairs, his gaze seeming to track Ajax as the commander carved a path through to them. He eyed the commotion with some concern, one hand pressed against his chest, clutching at something within his vest. Nevina wanted to laugh. Areanath had said that his task the night before had been successful, but she should have guessed Hasani would be the one that Areanath would turn to.

Ajax was suddenly in front of her, his lips pursed, though his eyes were alight. "Always one to draw a crowd, aren't you?"

Nevina felt her cheeks warm, partly from embarrassment and partly from the sudden comfort she found in the commander's familiar voice. "I'm sorry, Commander. I haven't quite mastered the former Matriarch's command of the people yet." She waved at the girls waiting behind her, whose eyes were wide and frightened. Without a word, they filed past her and followed Ajax back to the castle steps. The crowd once more fell silent, the only sounds a few sighs of disappointment that their questions had not been answered.

The castle doors shut loudly behind them. All her girls were accounted for, if a little shaken, and Nevina released the breath she hadn't realized she had been holding. She laughed softly, steadying her nerves. "I miss the city so often. Yet when I return, I immediately begin to question my sanity."

Hasani smiled politely and Ajax laughed, the sound relaxing Nevina's anxieties. Arella tightened her grip on Nevina's hand, stepping to hide in Nevina's skirts. She ran her hand over the girl's head, soothing her.

"Nevina," a soft feminine voice called from behind her.

She turned. "Silvana." She reached for her friend and the two embraced, kissing each other's cheeks lightly. "I'm glad to see you again."

Silvana smiled, taking Nevina's free hand. "I was so happy

to hear that you would be coming today. It's been too long since your last visit."

Nevina returned the smile. "It has, and I will have to apologize to everyone for it." For a moment, Nevina was lost in Silvana's eyes. She Saw the woman pregnant and alone, wandering in the rain. And the moment was over, gone as quickly as it had come. Nevina shook off the sudden wave of uneasiness that had overcome her, focusing her attention once more on the present and ignoring the unsettling glimpse into a future that may or may not come to pass. "Do you mind, Silvana, if the girls go with you off somewhere, while I meet with Areanath?"

Silvana smiled at the five girls still standing behind Nevina, and then at Arella still holding Nevina's hand. "Of course not. I know just the quiet little nook where we can all enjoy some refreshments."

Nevina turned to the girls, gesturing for them to follow Silvana. And they did, without saying a word. Even Arella finally released Nevina's hand and took her place in line again. As they drifted out of earshot, Nevina turned towards the men. She bowed politely to Ajax. "It's nice to see you again, Commander."

"And you, Lady Matriarch." He returned the bow, a smirk playing on his lips.

Nevina could guess what he was thinking. *Play the reverent knight in your chosen brother's company, as you always do, Ajax. The second he turns away ...*

She turned to Hasani. "And you, Hasani. It's always nice to see Areanath's favorite adviser."

Hasani smiled. "It's easy to say that when the only other adviser is Mothlenor."

Nevina shrugged a shoulder in reply, taking the arm he offered her.

"The king will be pleased you have made a return visit. Although, if I remember correctly, you were not yet Matriarch when last you came, were you?" Hasani led the way to Areanath's chambers, leading Nevina gently while Ajax fell into step on her other side.

Nevina smiled. "When last I visited the king, Nevara was still Matriarch, yes. I had just taken on my fourth infatuate, and was here by her request, as a liaison."

"And how is Nevara doing?"

Nevina thought about the way her mother had looked the night before. The milky eyes, the tremble in her hands. Even her voice had seemed weaker than she remembered. "Nevara is fine. Her physical sight has begun to fail her, and it's become exceedingly difficult for her to use her Gift without it. She now spends her days instructing the women of the Coven, content to live out the rest of her days surrounded by her Coven daughters. Her wisdom is still available, should I ever need her." She briefly considered her mother's warning the night before but quickly brushed the thought away.

"I … understand that the Coven's numbers are shrinking. The king has been worried about it for some time. Is there anything we can do?" Hasani asked softly.

Nevina frowned slightly, considering the question. "Areanath and I have discussed that very topic at some length before, but we've yet to come to any helpful conclusions. The main issue is, of course, the gender disparity." Nevina looked between the two men. "As the Gift is found only in women, it can make maintaining our numbers difficult."

"But enjoyable, I would hope." Ajax smirked, his eyes bright. "Since each Coven sister takes on multiple infatuates to keep the Coven alive and healthy."

"It can be." Nevina returned his smirk before turning back to Hasani. "Most of the Coven's members are born as a result of another member bonding with one of her infatuates, but some are born outside our walls. We seek out those women gifted with the Sight while they are still young, and take them to care for and foster. We educate them, teach them the moralities that come with their Gift, and help them to better understand their role in the world." She shrugged slightly. "There is open communication between the king and the Matriarch regarding the possibility of Gifted girls here in Etritia. The Coven has similar connections in the Free Cities to the south, and with the human cities in the east, as well. That seems to be the most Areanath can do, at the moment."

"What about Vyris?" Ajax asked. "I've often wondered if there might be gifted children living among our western neighbors."

"I don't think there are any humans living in Vyris," Nevina said, shaking her head slightly. "If there are Gifted, they are elven, and are likely being cared for by their own people."

Hasani halted, turning to Nevina. "What happens to those children the Coven bear that are not gifted?"

Nevina bit her lip. It was not a question she was often asked. "If a daughter proves herself Ungifted, she is still accepted as a member herself. Her duties to the Coven differ, but she is still treated with the same love we give to our Gifted girls." She hesitated for a moment. "If a member of the Coven bears a son, he is cast out."

Hasani's eyes narrowed. "You just throw them out?"

Nevina quickly shook her head. "No, of course not." Hasani's shoulders relaxed, and Nevina continued. "They are taken to cities across the known world, where they are given to a family that will care for them. And we are told to forget them." She pursed her lips together, hoping the conversation would end there.

Hasani looked at her for a moment. "I think I understand, Matriarch."

Nevina drew a shaky breath, collecting herself. "Forgive me, but we should continue. Areanath is waiting for me."

"Yes, of course. We're nearly there."

They rounded one last corner before they found themselves before Areanath's chambers. Hasani reached for the
door. "I have some business with the king as well. Shall we go
in together?"

Nevina paused. "Will you be long?"

Hasani shrugged. "Just a moment. I had a few questions I
wanted to ask about … something." His voice trailed and his
hand instinctively went to the inner pocket of his vest.

Ah, Areanath's notes. Nevina smiled. "You go on, I'll wait
out here with the commander."

"Are you sure?" Hasani frowned slightly.

She nodded. "An adviser should have privacy when
meeting with his king. Even if the topic is a seemingly
innocuous one. Like literature," she added pointedly. She
smiled again as Hasani's eyes lit up, but he said nothing.

Hasani paused at the door, casting one last glance at
Nevina before letting himself into Areanath's room.

As the door closed behind Hasani, Nevina turned to see
Ajax staring at her, a strange expression on his face. "Is
something wrong, Commander?"

Ajax dropped his gaze. "No, of course not. I just …" He
paused, a sheepish grin playing on his lips. "I just found
myself wondering what the Matriarch of the Coven looks
like beneath her veil, to be honest." His eyes brightened. "You
are a strange woman, Nevina."

Nevina smirked. *Hasani is barely out of earshot, and he's
already falling into using first names.* "I've heard similar words
many times, Ajax, and it has yet to get me out of my veil,
never mind the rest of my clothing." She caught a glimpse of
his wide brown eyes, and there she Saw it. Simple curiosity,
and a desire to know her better.

And a little lust, of course.

Ajax smiled. "Well, there's my plan foiled. I suppose I'll
just have to try again some other time."

Nevina laughed. "You try every time I come to visit, Commander. The answer is always the same."

Ajax's smile deepened. "I still enjoy asking the question, Nevina."

She returned his smile. "I enjoy it too." She could feel her cheeks warm slightly at his smile.

Perhaps ... things could be different this time, Nevina thought. She was now Matriarch, and it was her duty to choose infatuates for Coven members, including herself. She could take Ajax, and there would be no one to tell her otherwise. But she also knew her visit would be a short one, and there was a good chance she wouldn't return to Etritia for a long while. The idea pained her.

Ajax stepped to Nevina's side, watching the door to Areanath's chambers with her. "Does it ever get to be too much?"

"What's that?"

"Your Gift." He shrugged slightly. "To know so many things about so many people. To know things about yourself, about your future," Ajax said. He turned to face her, his eyes scanning over her face. "Does it ever overwhelm you?" His eyes seemed to linger on her lips for an instant longer than necessary, but perhaps that was only her imagination.

She smiled thinly. "At times, yes. Fortunately, we are unable to See things about ourselves. And we've taken measures to ensure that we can't ask others in the Coven to See for us."

"The veils, you mean? You have to look into their eyes to See, right?" Ajax asked.

"Traditionally, yes," Nevina said, smirking slightly. "Though they haven't been used for that purpose in many, many years. The veils are mostly kept for tradition's sake, and to conceal ourselves from those outside the Coven. It's a sign of great respect if a Gifted unveils herself to an outsider." She turned to Ajax. "The more effective means of preventing any one of us from acting on such temptations are arcane based."

"The Coven does magic?" Ajax lifted a brow, surprised.

"Some of us are skilled in the arcane arts. But not all." Nevina tilted her head, looking Ajax over. "Does that bother you? The thought that I could be a witch?"

Ajax shrugged. "Not really, I suppose. The king's brother uses magic, and while Mothlenor might have his flaws, the people of Etritia still respect him."

And all the while, he plots to kill the King and take the throne, Nevina wanted to add. But she held her tongue. "Then I hope the same is true for the Coven."

Ajax smirked, one corner of his mouth curving in a way that Nevina found utterly charming. "Of course, Matriarch. If I can find it in myself to care for Mothlenor despite his oddities, I can certainly do the same for you."

She almost snorted. "You're too much, Ajax. But Great Ones take it, I would hope so."

At her words, Ajax let out a rolling laugh, surprising her. It was a good laugh, warm and comforting, and Nevina couldn't help the smile that came to her lips.

"Lady Nevina!"

They both turned at the voice and, at the sight of Mothlenor walking briskly down the hall to meet them, Nevina's smile faded. Beside her, Ajax's laughter stopped, and he took a careful step away from her, putting a more appropriate distance between them.

And with that small space between her and Ajax, Nevina felt suddenly alone as Mothlenor drew closer with every passing second.

9

HASANI

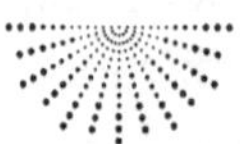

Hasani stepped into a brightly lit room, noting with a little surprise the numerous candles dotted around on every available surface. Areanath sat hunched over a writing desk scribbling on a bit of parchment. He wore simple clothing—Areanath was not one for fancy fabrics or heavy robes—and his long, slightly greying hair had been brushed and pinned back into a knot between his shoulder blades. His beard, usually scraggly and a tad unkempt, had been trimmed and oiled.

At the sound of Hasani's entrance, Areanath straightened. "Ah, good, you're here." He looked surprised to see his adviser there. "My apologies, Hasani, I'm expecting the Lady Matriarch."

"She's just outside, my lord." Hasani gestured to the door. "Ajax is with her."

"Then send her in, of course." Areanath turned back to his writing.

Hasani stepped closer to the king. "Actually, I was hoping I might have a moment of your time." Areanath looked up at Hasani again, an eyebrow raised. "I wondered if you might be able to better explain this for me." Hasani reached into his vest, pulling out the little book.

Areanath leapt up from his chair. "Oh, put that away, you fool." He hastily shoved it back into Hasani's vest. "I told you to keep it hidden away, didn't I?" He shook his head, frowning down at Hasani.

"So you did bring it to me—in the middle of the night?" Hasani grimaced. "I thought I was mad, you know."

Areanath's eyebrow raised again. "We're all a bit mad, I suppose."

Hasani shook his head. "But what does it even mean? The writing is nonsense."

"No offense taken," Areanath said, smirking. "So, you've read it then?"

"Well, it's a book, isn't it?"

Areanath snorted. "Don't worry about it yet. Just remember that it's there. Someday it'll make more sense." He turned away from Hasani, back to the desk. He shuffled a few loose papers almost idly. "Was there something else you wanted to discuss?"

"There was, actually ..." Hasani briefly thought about asking if Nevina knew about the book as well; she had seemed so coy ... *No, surely I'm just imagining it.* He instead addressed the other news Silvana had brought him. "This hunting trip with your brother ..." Areanath straightened at the mention of Mothlenor. "Do you have everything you need?" Hasani sighed. "Something for your knee, for example?"

Areanath turned back to Hasani. "I am well equipped, yes. Thank you for mothering me, Hasani." He smirked a little, his bright green eyes glinting.

"If you are prepared for the journey, then I suppose that's all I can do."

Areanath placed a hand on Hasani's shoulder. "You've done quite a bit." Areanath paused. "After all these years ..."

He gazed into Hasani's eyes, searching. "I've placed a heavy burden on your shoulders, and I apologize."

Hasani smirked. "On days like today, I must agree with you."

Areanath gave his shoulder a gentle pat before letting his hand drop away with a soft sigh. "Please bring the Matriarch in, Hasani."

"Of course, my lord."

MOTHLENOR

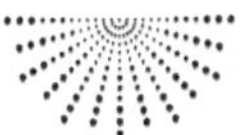

Mothlenor quickened his steps at the sight of the Matriarch. He'd heard a bit of the commotion of her entrance from his open tower window, but it wasn't until his guard had returned with news of Nevina's arrival that Mothlenor rose from his desk and descended his tower to the castle proper. *She's early today. Always subverting me, that Coven witch. She must have rented a room, to get here so soon. It's unlikely that the Coven keeps themselves so close to the castle. But still …* He made a mental note to have her followed as she left the castle. The former Matriarch had always been so careful to arrive at different times of the day, and from different locations. It had been impossible to figure out the location of the Coven. Perhaps the newest Matriarch wouldn't be so careful …

"Lady Nevina!" Mothlenor called, drawing her attention to him. He was almost glad to see the startled way she turned to look at him until her lips pressed together into a thin line. "I'm glad you were able to reach the castle so easily this morning." He came to a stop a few feet from her, bowing in greeting. The scent of her wafted to him, and he breathed it in, letting it roll over him. She always smelled of rose oil and unspent arcane energy, a combination that always reminded him of her. "I see our fine commander has escorted you here. Should I announce you to my brother?"

"That won't be necessary, Mothlenor." Nevina's voice was polite enough, but he could hear an anxious edge to it. "Hasani is in with him now, and will announce me momentarily."

He scowled, but continued. "Then perhaps I can have someone wait to escort you out of the castle? I'm sure you've found some fitting accommodations here in the inner city?"

Nevina smirked slightly, a trait which both infuriated and aroused him. "Actually, Ajax has agreed to escort me, but thank you for the offer."

Ajax moved slightly at her words, glancing quickly between them, saying nothing.

"Ajax?" *First name only?* "I see. Perhaps you can join us for dinner before you leave, then?" Mothlenor could feel his anger rising, but he held it in check.

Nevina frowned, clasping her hands neatly in front of her. "I'm sorry, but I'm not sure Areanath and I will make it to dinner tonight. We have much to discuss. I'm sure you can understand."

Now that was a surprise. An entire day with Areanath? What could they possibly need to discuss? *Unless ...*

Mothlenor dismissed the thought before it had even fully formed. The idea of such a young Matriarch taking on his brother as an infatuate was laughable. *Nevara, perhaps.* Areanath even deserved such an old crone as a lover. *But Nevina? Never.*

"Then do you mind terribly if I call in with my brother for a moment?" Just as he asked, the door to Areanath's chambers opened and Hasani stepped out into the hall. His brother's adviser held the door to Areanath's rooms open, looking from Mothlenor to the Matriarch and back again. Mothlenor only gave him a cursory look before addressing

Nevina again. "There's something I would like to discuss with my brother, and it's too urgent to wait until tomorrow."

"The king is expecting the Matriarch …" Hasani began, but his voice trailed as Mothlenor turned to stare at him.

"It will only take a moment," he growled. He looked once again to Nevina, breathing deeply before adding, "I insist, Matriarch."

"Let him in, Hasani," Areanath's cool voice called from the open doorway. He sounded almost annoyed at Mothlenor's insistence.

He has nothing to be annoyed with. Mothlenor bowed stiffly to Nevina again. "I thank you, Matriarch. I hope you can find your way to the castle again soon. Your company is enjoyed here, as I'm sure you know."

Nevina smiled, but it looked forced. "We shall see, Mothlenor. I hope the Coven can call ourselves friends of the king for many years to come."

Mothlenor raised an eyebrow, surveying her thin frame. "I can only hope for the same, Matriarch." He turned from the Matriarch and the silent commander. He stepped through the open door of his brother's rooms, glaring at Hasani as he passed him. Hasani only nodded politely back, which only angered Mothlenor more.

Mothlenor shut the door in Hasani's face. With a quick gesture of one hand, the door was locked, and the room soundproofed. The motion was half practiced act and half intentional insult against Nevina. She could try to listen in on his conversation but would find the spell. She could break it, but not without Mothlenor knowing. She would know she had been intentionally shut out, and the thought made him smirk slightly. It didn't matter that Areanath would likely tell her what they discussed, it was the arcane act of slamming the door against her that he wanted. *Perhaps that will teach you a bit of humility, Nevina.*

"That's not really necessary, Mothlenor."

Mothlenor turned in surprise to his brother. Had he guessed what Mothlenor had just done? "What isn't?"

"Your rudeness. It's not necessary. We are all friends here."

Mothlenor snorted lightly. "I suppose." He looked his brother over. A fresh shave, a new shirt, even some incense burning in the corner to cover the lingering scent of a weak old man. If the door to his brother's bedroom had been left open, Mothlenor might have been forced to reconsider the possibility that Nevina had chosen Areanath as an infatuate. As it was, the bedroom room was firmly shut, and Areanath instead looked the part of an impatient king.

"Why have you come, Mothlenor?" Areanath gestured towards a nearby chair, but Mothlenor chose to remain standing.

"Do discuss our other 'friends,' coincidentally."

"Meaning?"

"The elves in Thessala."

Areanath sighed heavily, leaning back in his chair. "Ah." He grabbed the half-full glass of wine from the nearby table. "The elves in Thessala." He took a sip, motioning for Mothlenor to continue.

"I thought you agreed to consider the matter longer before taking any action?"

"I did," Areanath said impatiently.

"Yet you helped them anyway?" Mothlenor's anger was returning, but he drew a steady breath and waited for his brother to sip at his wine again. "Why?"

Areanath set the glass aside and steepled his fingers together. "Because they are our friends, Mothlenor. And that is what friends do. You might not be terribly familiar with the concept, but—"

"Don't you dare mock me, Areanath."

Areanath waved a hand dismissively. "Forgive me." Areanath seemed to pause for a moment, considering his response. Mothlenor waited, his anger simmering away. Finally, Areanath continued, drumming his fingers together as he spoke. "Do you know why they asked for our helped?"

"Because they're greedy animals."

"Because their sheep had fallen ill, and many had died. Without the sheep, they could produce no wool. Without the wool—"

"Get to the point, Areanath." Mothlenor didn't have the time or patience for his brother's ramblings.

Areanath sighed. "They were worried about their children surviving the winter. The younger elves are not as resistant to weather extremes as the adults, and they are sure that this winter will be a particularly cold one." Areanath sipped at his wine again, apparently content to force Mothlenor to wait for him to continue. "Darith, only a day's journey south of Thessala, is still recovering from the droughts of a few years ago. They had already sent word to Hasani, requesting aid. So, when the elven elder in Thessala Called me after the council meeting yesterday—"

"You let the elves Call on you?" Mothlenor spat furiously. "How can you be such an imbecile?"

Areanath blinked slowly. "When he Called me yesterday, I suggested that he send someone down to Darith to propose a trade. Wool for crops." Areanath absently made small hand motions to indicate the trade. The motion only angered Mothlenor further.

"You'll let the elves arrange a trade with one of our cities?"

"Yes." Areanath's voice was unusually firm.

"And you will agree to the trade?"

"Of course I will!" Areanath growled. He closed his eyes, drawing a deep breath. When he spoke again, Mothlenor was sure his voice was still straining to conceal his frustration. "The elves are our friends, Mothlenor. And the trade helped our own people. Why would I refuse?"

"Because the elves are—"

"The elves are not animals, Mothlenor." He grabbed for his wine glass again. "And neither are the dwarves."

"You sound sure of yourself." He felt his anger burning its way through him. His brother was so blind when it came to the other races of Azimar. And rather than be suspicious of the strange elven land of Vyris, across the Knife, Areanath was fascinated by their elusiveness and mysterious mannerisms. *He is too foolish.*

"As do you, brother," Areanath replied, draining his glass and setting it aside once more.

"One of us is wrong, you must realize that."

Areanath sighed. "Yes, I realize that." He seemed to study Mothlenor for a moment. "Is there anything I can do to convince you that you are the one in the wrong?"

Mothlenor snorted. "Not likely."

Areanath nodded, apparently expecting that response. "Then please get out."

Mothlenor glared down at his brother. "Excuse me?"

"Get out, Mothlenor." Areanath met his gaze, looking tired. "You're dismissed. The Matriarch is waiting for me."

Mothlenor nodded stiffly. "I live to serve." He turned, opening the door out to the hall, simultaneously breaking the sound dampening spell he had put on it. He shut the door behind him, taking a deep breath of the fresh air and letting his anger melt away for a second. *This will all be over soon.*

Nevina was still waiting in the hall, the commander standing beside her. He could feel her eyes on him, and it made his skin crawl and flush.

"Matriarch." His voice came out in a raspy croak.

"Mothlenor," Nevina returned, inclining her head slightly.

He watched as Nevina looked at the commander then stepped closer to him. She paused only a step away from him. He could smell rose oil and arcane energy. His head was swimming.

She seemed to regard him for a moment before one hand raised slowly. "May I?"

Mothlenor looked down at her small frame, watching the lines of her neck as she looked up at him. *If I could only see her eyes ...* "What?"

"The door ..." Nevina said softly, pointing behind him. "Areanath is waiting for me."

Mothlenor started, realizing he was blocking the door to Areanath's chambers. "Of course, Matriarch. He's ready to see you." He stepped away from her, turning and hurrying down the hall, refusing to look back. He needed to get away from his brother, away from the Matriarch, away from the lingering scent of rose oil and magic ... *Just a little longer, and this will all be over ...*

NEVINA

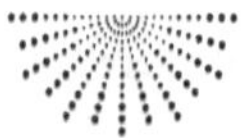

Hasani hardly winced as the door to Areanath's chambers slammed in his face. Nevina released a soft sigh, grateful Mothlenor was gone, even if only for a moment. To her surprise, Ajax did the same beside her. She looked over at him, and their eyes might have met if she were not wearing her veil. Ajax smiled wryly and it almost made her laugh. But her hands were shaking too hard where she held them clasped together, and there was an angry knot in her stomach. *Areanath's killer, though he has yet to strike.* The thought made the knot in her stomach tighten, and her fingernails dug painfully into the backs of her hands. *And the way he looks at me is too ... unsettling.* Mothlenor was always keen to look her over a few times when they met. Half of the men in the castle did the same, including Ajax. But his eyes always seemed too hungry, like an animal stalking prey.

Nevina's attention was pulled out of her thoughts by Hasani's voice.

"I'll go check on Silvana and the girls. Make sure they're all doing alright." Hasani sighed, running a hand through his dark hair. "I'm not sure I should be here when Mothlenor returns."

"Sure, sure. Go on, I'll wait with the Matriarch," Ajax said.

Nevina smiled at Hasani, "I'm sure Silvana would love her husband's company, especially given her pregnancy."

Hasani's mouth worked for a moment, before he finally choked out a small laugh. "Your Gift continues to astound me. I didn't even have the chance to tell you—"

"You didn't need to." Nevina smiled again. "She's a wonderful woman, Hasani. And she'll be a wonderful mother. Count yourself lucky."

"I do." His smile widened. "Every day." His brows pinched slightly. "Do you happen to know—"

"The gender? No, sorry." Nevina laughed delicately, her shoulders easing as her anger dissipated. "Even my powers have their limits, I'm afraid."

"Ah, well. It was too much to hope for." Hasani shrugged.

"Hoping for a boy, I take it?" she asked. Beside her, Ajax snorted.

"Hoping, yes. And praying, sometimes. To the Great Ones." Hasani's face reddened slightly at the admission.

"If the Great Ones are still able to hear you, perhaps they will answer your prayers." Nevina hoped it would be so, for Hasani's sake. But Azimar had been godless for centuries now, though faith in Elir and Imis still lingered. "It certainly doesn't hurt to try."

"Thank you, Matriarch." Hasani bowed low, straightening slowly. "I'll be off, then. I hope to see you again soon. Your presence makes the king very happy. I think he has some affection for you, and for the Coven." Hasani stepped to Ajax and thumped him on the back. "And I will see you for lunch."

Ajax returned the farewell, pounding Hasani between the shoulder blades as they embraced. "Give Silvana my love. I might be too busy in the next few days to see her much." Hasani nodded curtly before leaving Nevina and Ajax to stand alone in the hall.

Nevina smiled at Hasani's retreating back. "You care about him a great deal, don't you?"

"Of course." Ajax settled himself against the wall, facing the door to Areanath's chambers. "We grew up together. He's married to my little sister. He's a brother to me."

Nevina made a small sound of acknowledgment, settling herself beside Ajax.

"What about you, Matriarch? Do you have any family?"

She sighed, shrugging a shoulder. "We aren't actually supposed to know about our family. Everyone in the Coven is our sister, except for the Matriarch, who is our mother." The reminder of her new station always left goosebumps on her skin. I *am the mother to all of the Coven. What if I make a mistake?* But she continued to answer Ajax's question. "I know that I was born into the Coven, but I do not know precisely who my birth mother is." *Nevara, the former Matri-arch.* "I also know that I have birthed children into the Coven, but I do not know which children they are. I could guess, given their ages, but that still leaves a couple of possi-bilities." *But even that is a lie.*

"You've had children? How many?" Ajax's eyebrows rose in curiosity, and Nevina warmed under his interest.

"Two." *Three.* Nevina smiled, turning to face Ajax. "Both Gifted, I've been told."

"Fascinating. I had no idea." Ajax smiled, his brown eyes shining. "I have to say that I'm glad the king's brother is taking his time. It's given me the chance to—"

The door to Areanath's chambers was thrown open, and Mothlenor stepped out into the hall, snapping the door shut behind him.

Ajax gave Nevina a half smile, letting his words go unfinished.

Mothlenor seemed to quietly collect himself for a moment. His eyes were closed and his head leaned against the door. Nevina watched, her anger at him returning as he regulated his breathing. His eyes snapped open, finding her in an instant, and Nevina felt that overwhelming sense of hunger emanating from him once more.

"Matriarch." His voice was raspy as if he had been yelling.

"Mothlenor," Nevina returned, bowing slightly. She gave Ajax a final look before stepping towards Areanath's door.

Except that Mothlenor did not move. He continued to stare at her, his gaze forcing her to stop more than an arm's reach from him. She couldn't bear to stand too close to those eyes. She didn't want to See what they held.

Nevina raised a hand, pointing to the door at Mothlenor's back. "May I?"

Mothlenor's eyes darkened. "What?"

"The door …" Nevina said, trying not to look too closely at him. "Areanath is waiting for me."

Mothlenor stepped away from the door, blinking. "Of course, Matriarch. He's ready to see you." He turned, moving in an agitated hurry, and left without another word.

Nevina sighed, reaching for the door.

"Is it wrong of me …" Ajax began. Nevina turned to see him watching the departing Mothlenor. "Is it wrong of me to say that Mothlenor's behavior lately has me worried?"

Nevina gave him another half smile. "He worries me as well," she admitted. "More than I would normally care to say."

"Oh?" Ajax raised an eyebrow, his eyes still on Mothlenor.

"Yes," Nevina said softly. "When he looks at me, I don't think he sees the Matriarch of the Coven. I think he sees only a pretty prize that he can steal. And that frightens me a little."

Ajax's eyes snapped to her at her words. "Nevina …" He straightened, nodding politely to her. "I'll have someone wait here for you. They'll know where to find me when you are ready to leave the castle. And I'll be your guard on your way out." His shoulders relaxed a bit, the playful glint returning to his eyes. "You've already told him as much, anyway."

"Thank you, Ajax," Nevina said softly, her cheeks warming. She turned to open the door, but his voice stopped her again.

"Areanath doesn't know, does he? That his brother upsets you?"

"No," Nevina replied, still facing the door. "And I'd like to keep it that way."

Nevina opened the door to Areanath's room, shutting it carefully behind her. She locked it, sealing it with magic as she did. Nothing could get in or out now, not Mothlenor, not his magic, and nothing she and Areanath might share in their time together …

Areanath was emerging from his bedroom, a full wine glass in one hand, a small keg under the other arm. "Ah, Nevina, there you are. I'm glad you were able to come. I was just getting some more wine. Mothlenor has a way of making my wine glass empty itself when he's around." He carefully set both keg and glass down on the long writing desk against the wall beside them.

Nevina snorted, untying her veil and pulling it from her face. "Is there another glass or two in there for me?"

Areanath laughed, and the sound stabbed at her heart. *How many more times will I be able to hear that sound?*

"There's some in here for you, plus three more of these in the bedroom." He thumped the top of the keg softly, then set to filling a glass for her. "Vyrisian wine, from the elven king. He sends me some every year, for my birthday. I've been saving them, but …" He shrugged. "No sense in that anymore, now is there?"

"Areanath …" she began, but stopped as Areanath raised a dismissive hand.

"I am ready, Nevina." He held an arm out for her and she stepped into his embrace, wrapping her arms around his waist. He was warm. She would miss that warmth. "There are a few more preparations," he continued. "But I am ready."

Areanath didn't have to tell her that he was also terrified, and plagued by the idea that his work would fail him. That he dreaded the moment his brother would actually perform the deed. Nevina could See it all clearly in his eyes. She would miss those as well, so warm and green.

Nevina pulled her gaze away, her own eyes beginning to water. "You don't have to die like this, Areanath." She tightened her grip on his waist, not daring to let go for even a moment. "Leave with me. Let your brother keep your throne."

He ran a thin hand through her hair, a motion that always seemed to calm both of them. "It's not that simple. I wish it were." He leaned down, kissing the top of her head. The scent of woodsmoke and tobacco filled her nose as he did so, and it made her cling to him tighter. *So many things I'll never experience again.*

"Just stay with me today. Keep me company. It would make the going easier, tomorrow." He pulled her from him enough to look her in the eyes again. "Besides, I could still use your help."

Nevina nodded, releasing Areanath and wiping an errant tear from her face. She grabbed the glass of wine he had set aside for her. "Very well. If you have to go through with this, I can at least help you make sure everything will work." She finished the glass in one long pull. "And I'll stay with you today. This wine won't drink itself, after all." Nevina forced a smile, setting the empty glass next to the wine cask.

Areanath smiled, taking her free hand and giving it a light squeeze. "Thank you, Nevina."

He didn't have to tell her how much he cared for her, didn't have to explain that he would give anything to be able to run off with her. One look in those eyes, and she knew it all.

AJAX

Ajax waited until the door to Areanath's rooms closed behind the Matriarch before making his way back down the hall. Her words both troubled and surprised him. Mothlenor, overcome with lust for the Matriarch? To the point of causing her anxiety at the sight of him? Ajax could hardly believe it. Mothlenor had only ever seemed … upset by the presence of a Coven member. Nevina especially seemed to infuriate him, though he surely thought he was good at concealing it. No doubt it was his phobia of other races. Though the Coven were human, they lived outside the rule of the king, bound by their own secret laws and hidden from the rest of the world. To Mothlenor, they probably seemed no different from the elves or dwarves.

Ajax shook his head, quickening his pace. He could fulfill his promise to Nevina and keep a guard posted outside Areanath's rooms to wait for her. It was a small thing, and would ease her mind.

And he would do nearly anything for her.

His footsteps slowed again as he recalled her pleased smirk, and the hint of bright blue from under her veil as she once again rebuffed him. The rebuff didn't bother him—it never had. Theirs had been a long game, since her first visit to the castle, when she followed behind the Matriarch Nevara. With each visit, his advances became both bolder and sloppier, and he delighted in seeing her smile widen over the years as she came to expect them. After the last several years, he couldn't be sure which of the two of them enjoyed their banter more.

She had once confided in him that it was not her choice to make, but the Matriarch's. Even then, he never stopped secretly hoping that she might one day accept.

And now, Nevina was Matriarch.

Ajax blinked, suddenly finding himself outdoors. The sun was high and bright, and Ajax had found his way back to the training grounds without remembering the trip. The yard was empty, the youths he had been working with earlier apparently dismissed for the day.

Ajax shook his head free of thoughts of Nevina's affections and crossed the training grounds to the barracks on the other side. He needed someone he could trust to wait on the Matriarch, and he had just the man in mind.

Ajax found Dars inside, chastising a young recruit in the small room that served as the barracks kitchen. Thin and severe, Dars held a long wooden spoon dripping with juices in one hand, the other hand resting on the pommel of his sword. Ajax felt sorry for the poor bastard that had upset his second in command. Dars was on the older side, but he could still beat a full-grown man into submission when it was needed. And his sword skills were second only to Ajax's own.

"Now get yer bony little ass to the garden and find me a damned onion or two, so I can fix this fuckup ya call a meal," Dars grumbled. The boy nodded hastily and ran out the side door. Dars turned as though he sensed Ajax's presence behind him. "Little shits these days can't be damned to make a fucking stew." He jabbed the spoon into the simmering pot hanging in the fireplace. "Shit's all burned and tasteless," he grumbled again, shaking his head.

Ajax smiled, trying to hold back his laughter. He'd been on the receiving end of a few of Dars's angry rants about cooking before, and could empathize with the terrified soul that just fled the room. "He's just a boy, Dars. He'll learn in time. I did."

"Ya learned because I fucking taught ya, Ajax. A knight's gotta know how to feed himself out in the wild."

"Dars." Ajax chuckled, unable to help himself. "We're not in the wild. He will learn."

"Yer fucking right, he will, so help me." Dars slammed the heavy lid onto the top of the pot, setting the spoon aside. He fell onto a nearby bench, glaring angrily at the offending pot of stew. "By the time I was his age, my da had—"

"Taught you how to catch a fish, and taught you a dozen ways to clean and cook it." Ajax fell heavily onto the bench beside Dars. "I'm aware, Dars. And I'm sure you're passing those same skills on to your son."

Dars grunted. "Ain't no good fishing round here. But I do what I can." He straightened, turning to look at Ajax. "Speakin' of my son …" Dars's words trailed, and he looked Ajax over hesitantly.

"He's still thinking about recruiting?"

"Aye. Seems convinced to do it this next spring." Dars sighed, crossing his arms over his chest.

"You don't want him to try?"

Dars snorted. "Course I do. I just don't think he's ready yet is all." He huffed, glaring at the pot again. "But I can't make him wait any longer, neither. He'll be too old in another year."

"You've been training him?"

"Aye."

"Then I'm sure he'll be ready, Dars. No need to worry."

Dars sighed, brows pinching. "But if he ain't …" Dars's

voice trailed again. If he failed, there would be no second chance. The King's Guard only took the best youths of Etritia and the surrounding towns. They did not accept failures.

"He'll be fine," Ajax insisted, patting Dars on the shoulder.

Dars looked over at Ajax again, looking him up and down once more. "I s'pose you're right. Your da said the same things about you, and look at you now."

Ajax smiled. He'd never known that, but it certainly sounded like something his father might have said.

Dars shook his head. "I only ask that you don' go easy on him. He's got to earn his place, and I won' go asking favors from you, even if I don' think he's ready."

Ajax laughed, nodding. "If anything, I'd be harder on him. If you're training him, he's likely to show the other boys up without any effort."

Dars sniffed, spotting the young recruit returning with two medium onions in his grasp. "My little shit can cook, too," he mumbled under his breath. He stood, moving to intercept the boy before he dropped the vegetables whole into the pot.

"Wait, Dars. I have a favor to ask."

Dars barked at the boy to wait, then turned, eyebrow raised. "What's that?"

"After lunch, will you wait outside the king's chambers for the Matriarch? When she's ready to leave the castle, will you bring her to my rooms? I'd wait myself, but I have some work to see to."

Dars frowned. "Escorting the Matriarch out of the castle? That's uncommon."

"It'll be late. She'll be tired, and she has her followers with her this time. I'm sure she'd like to avoid any harassment, if possible," Ajax lied.

"Sure, sure." Dars glanced back to the boy, who was struggling to lift the heavy lid with a single hand. "Now, excuse me while I yell at this little fucker a bit." Dars stepped from the bench, then turned back as if he'd remembered something. "Ah, Ajax. Will you be joining us for lunch?"

Ajax laughed, shaking his head. "I don't think I will this time, Dars."

Dars grimaced. "Lucky bastard."

Ajax left the kitchen as Dars rounded on the boy once more for not listening to directions. He'd never been more grateful to have a lunch scheduled with his chosen brother.

AREANATH

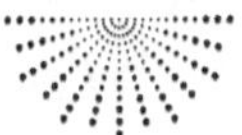

Areanath watched Nevina as she slept, the soft sheet pulled up over her chest, her face buried into the crook of one elbow. The toes of her bare feet peeked out from underneath the covers, despite the way she had tucked her knees in close to her body. In that moment, asleep in his bed, Nevina looked just as beautiful as she ever had before.

They had drunk a fair bit of wine, two of the casks now empty and stacked against the farthest wall. She had lent Areanath her Gift, then left him to work in the study. He didn't mind that she dozed in his bed while he completed his last task. It was better that way, anyway. She wouldn't know how to reverse his spell if she missed critical parts of its creation.

Her golden hair was loose, spilling across the sheets. Her clothing had been scattered around on the floor, but he had taken a moment to pick the pieces up and drape them over a nearby chair. There was nothing for him to do but watch her light breathing as she slept, and try to memorize the curves of her body and the angles of her face. He wanted to remember every detail for the last few days of his life.

Areanath padded over to his side of the bed and slipped

in beside her, draping an arm around her. She smelled of roses, his favorite flower. The thought of her dabbing on oils for his benefit made him smile. He kissed first her shoulder, then her neck, pulling her closer as he did.

She stirred, groaning softly and stretching her legs under the covers. "Areanath. I'm sorry I slept." She sat up, clutching the sheets to her chest and tousling her hair.

"It's alright. Our work makes you tired. You should sleep when you can." He sat beside her, running a hand through her hair and down her back. Had she worn her hair down for him because she knew he liked it that way?

"It makes me more tired than you?" Nevina snorted, giving him a playful smile. The sight of it pierced his heart. He would have to remember that smile when the time came.

"You do most of the work." He smiled, wrapping an arm around her waist.

"In here, yes." Nevina agreed. "But you're doing all the work out there." She nodded her chin in the direction of the door, indicating the study where Areanath built on his spell.

"The work is easier out there," he said, smiling. "But I'm not sure it's ready just yet. I have a few more questions that need answers." He turned, picking up a wine glass from the bedside table. "I brought you more wine, if you need it."

Nevina's eyes brightened as she took the glass from him. "I don't need more wine to be with you." She sipped it, making a small sound of satisfaction at the taste. "I do like the wine, though." She brought the glass to her lips again, blue eyes smiling at him over the rim.

"Should I find someone to take you home tonight? The day is only half over, and there is still more than a cask of the stuff left."

Nevina shook her head, draining the glass. "Ajax will be taking me home tonight. He said he would have someone waiting out in the hall for me."

"Ajax?" Areanath's eyebrow raised. "The commander?"

Nevina nodded, watching him. "Good. Better than letting you stumble off into the night."

"Areanath ..." Nevina chided, a small smirk playing her lips. The curve of her mouth brought out a small dimple, and Areanath's heart ached, knowing he might never see it again.

Nevina pulled him close, kissing him. The first one was gentle, the second passionate.

The third was fiery, burning its way through his body to his groin. He lost count after that, as Nevina's Sight overtook his own. Nevina gently pushed him to his back, settling her body against his. Her hands roved over his chest and down to his waist, and his skin pricked out in gooseflesh under her fingers. As her Gift overcame his senses, Nevina began to tug at the lacing of his robe, but he could only vaguely feel it.

Some small part of his mind could feel her warmth, could hear her breathing as she rode him. A small part of his mind could even feel the pleasure it gave him. But it was all pushed aside for the overwhelming power of Nevina's Gift. He could See, for a few brief moments, and he understood more than he would ever know again.

Images burned themselves into his mind. Mothlenor, sitting in the throne. A large, smooth egg, iridescent blue, settled in thick grass. Nevina, looking down at him, chest bare. A snowy mountaintop, hidden in the clouds. A crying baby, swaddled in white cloth. Nevina, straddling him, head tilted back in ecstasy. A dark-skinned child, stumbling barefoot after a muddy green-winged creature.

Just as Areanath's mind began to process each image, it would dissolve, only to be quickly replaced by another.

The endless stream of images continued, flashes of Nevina's face appearing more frequently as she neared her climax.

Finally, they slowed, until Areanath found himself face to face with his brother in a wooded area. Mothlenor's eyes flashed in anger, and then everything was black.

Areanath slowly opened his eyes, realizing the Sight was gone. His breath was heavy, and a light sweat had broken out across his skin. Nevina's weight was against him, and he could feel her breath on his neck. She had fallen on her side, one leg still draped over his, one arm settled across his chest.

"Was that enough?" she mumbled.

He took the hand resting on his chest and kissed the palm. "Yes, I think so." He rolled to his side, wrapping an arm around her waist. "Are you alright?"

Nevina nodded, breath still coming in soft pants. "Definitely," she said with a small laugh.

"Good." He ran his hand over her hair. "Sleep. I need to work before I forget everything. I'll be back." He kissed the top of her head, inhaling the scent of roses once more. Nevina only mumbled as he stood and draped the covers back over her naked body. He hurried from the bedroom, fastening his robe shut again as he went.

The images he had Seen ran through his head once more, but already they were fading. It would be enough, though. He was sure. He already knew most of what he had Seen, anyway.

But that last image …

Areanath's heart was beating fast as he lit more candles and settled into the chair at his desk.

He was sure that last Sight had been in the seconds before his death.

And that future, at least, was not too far away.

MOTHLENOR

Mothlenor

M othlenor bit back an angry snarl, tossing the dragon's eye back onto its plush cushion. "Damned thing. Utterly useless." The soft whirling colors of the stone winked out, leaving only the neutral tones of polished stone behind. He stared down at it, anger building. "What could they be up to?"

It had still been late morning when Nevina had stepped into his brother's chambers, but dark would be falling soon, and there was no sign of her leaving. *She said their meeting would run long, but I was sure she'd been trying to anger me.* What was left for the Coven to discuss with the king?

Their numbers were quickly dwindling, that was no secret. But Gifted girls could only be found, not plucked from thin air. There was nothing Areanath could do to help them. Except, perhaps …

Mothlenor pushed the thought away. It was impossible. His brother was feeble and too soft.

"In more than one way, surely," Mothlenor muttered to himself, amused by the idea. "It would be completely useless to her."

But they've had the whole day … Surely she could make it work eventually …

"Damn them both," Mothlenor growled. "It's not possible." He tugged open one drawer of his desk and swept the dragon's eye inside, slamming it shut. "And why would she choose him?"

And why not me?

He couldn't bring himself to ask the question, but it was there, simmering under the surface.

Asking it would only mean admitting that he wanted her, and she was a Coven witch.

The Coven was nearly as bad as the elves, always taking what they pleased, and asking for more. Only giving their squealing, unwanted young.

They were a disease, running rampant through all of Azimar.

And Azimar must be cleansed. Starting with Etritia and the castle.

A rough knock at his door pulled him from his thoughts. He realized that he had pulled another one of his possessions from its place on his desk; he sat with it resting in his lap, both hands tracing the whirls and ridges of the surface. He hardly remembered pulling the object from its place, yet there it was. He blinked several times before hurriedly tucking the object into the drawer next to the dragon's eye. "Enter," he growled before the knock could sound again.

Ferrand opened the heavy door and stepped over the threshold, wearing the black cloak of a King's Guard. It fit him nicely, accenting his pale skin and high cheekbones. "You called for me, sir?" His voice was smooth and deep, and the sound of it irked Mothlenor on some unspeakable level.

"Ferrand." Mothlenor stood, crossing his arms over his chest. "I have another job for you."

"Of course." Ferrand bowed slightly, eyes never straying from Mothlenor's own. They were dull and expressionless, like something not quite alive. "Following the Matriarch again?"

Mothlenor's lip twitched into a small snarl. "Yes, but this time I want her followed all the way back to whatever hole she's hiding in. Can you do that?"

Ferrand frowned thoughtfully. "I have someone in mind that could." The frown deepened slightly, as did his voice. "But I'll need a key to the prison."

Mothlenor blinked slowly. Of course Ferrand had a man in jail. "Why was he locked away?"

Ferrand shrugged. "He's a thief. He was caught."

Mothlenor huffed lightly. "Not a very good thief, then."

"No." Ferrand smirked, eyes darkening. "But he is small, and quiet, and will owe me a favor if I let him out."

"He'll tell you where she's staying?"

"And then?" Ferrand asked expectantly.

"And then you bring her to me."

15

NEVINA

Another few hours or so had passed since Nevina had last given Areanath her Gift. During that time, they had opened the last cask of Vyrisian wine, and now even it was nearly empty. Their time was nearly up, and they both knew it. Nevina fell back into a chair, wineglass in hand, tired. "You think this will work, when the time comes?" She draped her bare legs over the arm, feet dangling. She held a page of his notes in her other hand, studying it. She could understand some of it, but most of the writing looked like little more than nonsense to her.

Areanath sighed, refilling his glass once more and taking a small sip. "It has to work, or the world as it is now will be done for before long." He carefully tugged the page of notes from her hand and set it back on the nearby desk before taking the seat opposite hers. "I've checked and rechecked everything. It should work. It *has* to work."

"As soon as he lands the killing blow?"

Areanath nodded. "As soon as I die. Whether he does it himself or someone else does it. When I die ..." He paused, swallowing hard, and took a deep breath, giving her a sardonic smile. "When I die, the spell will be activated."

"And I'll be able to tell?" *Would I want to know?*

Areanath's brow furrowed. "Perhaps. You've been woven into everything. You might be able to feel when it ... activates." Areanath choked on the last word.

Nevina nodded her head. "I understand." She took a large sip of the wine, draining her glass. "Why are you doing this? What do you think your brother will try to do after taking the throne?"

Areanath frowned, swirling the remaining wine around in his glass. "You know about the Great War."

"Of course." She shrugged, standing to fill her glass. "Mankind's first chance to show the older races that we can be just as great and terrible as them?" She snorted. "The centuries since then have given us time to grow and prosper in peace."

"Yes, but the war itself left scars on all the races. Some of those scars are still fresh. A small wound could cause a tide of blood. A new war could be started, even."

Nevina turned to face Areanath, eyes widening. "Mothlenor wants to start the Great War all over again? Is that even possible?"

Areanath shook his head. "I don't think he wants to start it all over again. I think he plans to cause just enough trouble to set all the races on edge. Some of the older races can remember the Great War from their own lifetimes. They won't want to jump into another ordeal like that. But the men ..." Areanath sighed. "It's not war he wants, it's genocide."

Nevina shuddered, sinking back into her chair. "Imis preserve us," she whispered, bringing her hand to her collarbone without thinking. "Then there really is no other option for you?"

"There is no other option."

Nevina nodded slowly. *No wonder Areanath is going to such desperate lengths.* "Why do it now? Why not let someone else take your place in the Last Hunt and continue your life as you have … keep this spell inactive?"

Areanath smirked, staring into his wineglass. "You forget how old I am, Nevina. I will die eventually, as is the natural order of things. And my brother will take the throne then, and it will all be the same anyway."

"You aren't that old, Areanath,"

Areanath only shrugged. "Kings tend to have shorter lives than other men, I've noticed. Better to die protecting my people than from old age or disease. And Mothlenor might realize, given decades to watch me, that I have some arcane skill." His eyes met hers, tired and sad. "And what would he do then, I wonder?"

The resignation she found in his eyes frightened her. *He has already accepted it, and now he can only wait.* "What else can I do?"

Areanath's hand tightened around hers. "When it happens, get out. Go home. Don't leave the safety of the Coven. If he figures out what's happened he might come for you, to demand help in reversing it. It can't be reversed, not after being activated. Once he realizes he doesn't have the power to stop it himself, you're the next person he'll turn to."

Nevina squeezed his hand in return, smiling sadly. "Alright." She took another long sip from her wineglass and set the empty glass aside. "I don't want to leave you just yet."

"You can stay a bit longer—you don't have to leave."

She took Areanath's wineglass from his hand, setting it next to hers. His gaze followed her hands as she ran them up his chest to his shoulders. "This will be our last day together." Careful not to jar his knee, she pulled the skirt of her robe up to her thighs and straddled him.

"Nevina …" His eyes found hers, searching.

"Yes?" She untied the belt around her waist, letting the front of her robe fall open.

"Everything has been completed. You don't have to do this."

Nevina smiled sadly again. "I want to, Areanath." She pulled his arms around her waist.

"Why?"

She sighed. "Sometimes I wish you could See the way I do. That you could look into my eyes and know everything I am. Then you would know why." She kissed him, the taste of wine still on his lips. Leaning back, she looked into his eyes. "We are running out of time together. And I want to remember you. I want to remember this day. And I want to remember us together for a few moments. Without magic, without Sight. Like two normal people."

"Like we used to?" He ran a hand down her back and it sent goosebumps over her body.

She shook her head. "Not like we used to, not quite."

"How would it be different? There was no magic then."

She closed her eyes for a moment, relishing the touch of his hands on her hips. She opened them again to see him staring up at her expectantly. "Before, you were my infatuate. A man chosen by the Matriarch. I didn't know you, you didn't know me. We met to have children, nothing more."

"And it worked." He smiled thinly. "Twice, if I'm to understand correctly."

Nevina nodded. "Yes, it did." Her eyes were beginning to water, but she blinked the tears away. "I'd like to try for a third time. For a boy, perhaps. I could make sure he grows up somewhere safe, and then he can become King, and—"

"Nevina," Areanath interrupted. "You're the Matriarch now. You gave up your ability to have children. Didn't you?"

She bit her lip. "I haven't. Not yet. There was a ceremony, and I drank a potion, but Nevara and I agreed to make the potion useless. To give me one last chance with you." She laughed weakly. "Even Nevara's maiden, Anna, didn't know, and she did most of the potion work."

"Nevina …" Areanath chided. "You are lying to your people."

"I am. For you. For us." Nevina smiled. "If it doesn't work then I will happily take the potion and make myself barren. If it does work, then your death will allow my Coven to forgive my lie. They will accept any child born of our king and greatest friend, even one conceived in deceit. If it is a girl, she will be treasured, as her sisters are. If it is a boy, they will help me find the best place for him to be raised, and will help me bring him back to Etritia when the time is right."

"Sisters?" Areanath asked. His voice was soft and full of emotion. "I gave you daughters?"

"Yes, you did." Nevina's eyes blurred, but she smiled down at him, cupping his face in her hands. "They're both beautiful, and very talented." She considered his face for a moment, staring into his tired eyes. Normally, the idea she was entertaining would be out of the question. But considering the circumstances … *And I am Matriarch, now.* "I can bring them to you, if you would like to meet them. They're here, in the castle. It would only take a mom—"

"No, Nevina," Areanath said. "I'm not sure I could bear what is coming if I met them now. Just knowing that I gave you daughters and not sons is enough for me."

"I understand." She sighed, clutching one of his hands and bringing it to hold against her cheek. "I want to try for a third, Areanath. A boy, for you. But this time will be different, because we both know each other. And because I love you, Areanath."

He looked up at her for a moment, and she stared past her tears and into the soft green of his eyes. With one quick movement, he leaned up and kissed her, his grip tightening around her. She melted into him, content to never let go.

16

FERRAND

Ferrand's heels clicked loudly on the stone floor as he made his way through the castle. His thief was already free, that had been simple enough. But perhaps there was a simpler way to complete Mothlenor's task. And the thief would still owe him a favor …

Ferrand turned a sharp corner and faltered in his steps. *It seems the good Commander Ajax was a step ahead of me.*

A single King's Guard stood outside the door to Areanath's chambers, one hand on his sword. *Fortunate that this one is old. Those feeble of body are also feeble of mind, and this will be only too easy.*

Ferrand continued down the hall, stopping in front of the knight and bowing low, though it pained it him to do so. *This charade will not last much longer. Then I will have to bow to only one man.*

"Yes? What d'ya want?" the old knight drawled.

Ferrand forced his face to remain neutral. *Not just an old man, but a southerner. Where do they find such pathetic knights?*

"The commander has sent me to relieve you of your post, sir. He asked me to escort the Matriarch home tonight."

The knight sneered, looking him over. "I don' think so, boy."

"Excuse me?" Ferrand said, trying to keep the anger from his voice. "The commander asked me—"

"The commander asked me to wait here all damned day if need be. If he wanted me off to do something else, he would have come down here his own damned self with a new man to see the job through. Someone he trusts. And, what's more …" The old knight leaned closer to Ferrand, scrutinizing him. "I don' know ya."

Ferrand scoffed, angered by the old man's persistence. "That proves nothing. There's no way you could know all of the King's Guard, old man."

"Old man?" The knight stepped closer to Ferrand, beady eyes staring up at him. "Ya have no idea who you're even trying to fool, do ya? I'm Dars, First Knight of the King's Guard. I train every bullheaded fucker that sets foot in the barracks." His eyes narrowed as he continued to glare up at Ferrand. "And I'm saying I don' know ya."

"Step aside," Ferrand said coldly, dropping all pretense of respect for the old southerner. "I have business with the Matriarch."

"No," the knight growled. "Get the fuck out of here before I beat that face of yours into the floor, Elir guide my hand. I'll make you cry so damned loud, the elves in their old woods will hear you. And you'll be arrested."

Ferrand sneered down at the frail man. *He could never …* But it was pointless to continue. His thief was already free, after all. "Very well, First Knight." Ferrand turned and walked briskly away.

The old knight called after him, frail voice quavering. "I know ya now, you little shit head. Don' let me see your face again."

Ferrand hissed, hand flexing over the spot where a sword

should have been hanging from his hip. *Dars, First Knight. Ajax, Commander. The King's Guard needs some new blood, it seems.*

1 7

NEVINA

Nevina left Areanath's chambers, veil carefully tied into place, the soft fabric once more covering her eyes and brushing against the bridge of her nose. Her head ached from too much alcohol and she rubbed at her temples, knowing it would do little to ease the pain. They had finished all the wine, and she would surely regret it in the morning, but Nevina was happy to have those last few memories with Areanath.

An older knight stood guard across the hall, one hand on the hilt of his sword, the other combing through the scruff of beard on his chin. At her appearance, he straightened, giving her a low bow. "Lady Matriarch, I've been asked by the commander to offer myself as an escort, should you need it. I am Dars, First Knight of the King's Guard." The man's accent was southern, the consonants soft and rolling, and his lined and worn face seemed vaguely familiar.

"Have we met before?"

The knight smiled crookedly. "A time or two, yes. Nothing worth remembering, Matriarch."

"All the same," Nevina said with a tired sigh. "I'm glad you're here. The king and I had quite a lot of wine. I'm not sure I could find my way to the end of the hall at the moment."

Dars snorted lightly, his face lighting up. "I've escorted my fair share of tipsy ladies, Matriarch. Have no fear." He offered a supporting arm, and they started down the hall at a sedate pace.

They walked for several minutes, and after a few turns, Nevina was absolutely lost. She held Dars's arm as he led her through the castle, letting him talk and giving her mind the chance to slowly clear. Dars complained about the newest recruits they'd just received, using language that might have been unbecoming of a knight but that made Nevina smile.

In time, they came to a hall Nevina presumed could only be living quarters. A long row of heavy wooden doors lined each side, the walls between each set of doors decorated in thick tapestries. Dars seemed to consider for a second before choosing one a few feet down the hall and knocking on the door.

"Damned doors all look the same. I think this is the one."

There was a moment of shuffling before the door opened. Ajax stood in the doorway, a book in one hand. His clothing was different, Nevina noticed. His heavy armor and cloak of the King's Guard had been discarded, as had the sword he normally wore on his hip. Instead, he wore a plain tunic tucked into his pants. The effect was startling, making him seem both smaller and more human.

"Dars." Ajax's eyes shifted from his First Knight to Nevina, and he smiled as he looked at her. "Matriarch. I wasn't sure when to expect you. I hope everything went well with the king?"

Nevina nodded. "Very well, I think. The Coven knows it can always rely on Areanath's friendship and aid, and he on ours." It hurt Nevina to say the words, knowing that Areanath only had a little time left in the world.

"Ajax," Dars said, his voice suddenly stern. "A word, before I go."

Ajax glanced between his second and Nevina, one eyebrow rising. "Of course. Come in, both of you." He waved Nevina and Dars through the door and into the front room. "This should only take a moment, Matriarch, then we can be on our way."

Nevina nodded politely as Dars pulled Ajax a few steps away. She could hear anger in his rolling accent, despite the hushed whisper he spoke in. Nevina ignored the two men, taking a few moments to inspect Ajax's quarters.

The furnishings were sparse, but what little was present seemed to be well cared for. A plush chair sat close to the fireplace, empty at the moment, while a tidy desk was set against the far wall. There were papers and a few books arranged in neat stacks on the desk, and Nevina crossed the room in long, slow steps to investigate them.

Behind her, Ajax asked a question, his voice louder than Dars's had been.

The papers on the desk were covered in small, looping handwriting, each line meticulously penned out in even strokes. Nevina nudged the corner of one sheet with a finger, examining Ajax's notes on the performance of various members of the King's Guard.

She turned away from the notes, her eyes falling on the bed in the room beyond. Even that was carefully maintained, the covers smoothed and the single pillow fluffed and carefully placed at the head of the bed.

"Thank you, Dars," Ajax said, drawing her attention back to where the two men stood together. "I'll leave it to you. Keep me informed."

"Understood," Dars grunted, dipping his head in farewell to both Ajax and Nevina. "I'll be on my way, then. I'm sure ol' missus Dars is storming the barracks as we speak. Gotta go placate the lady before she scares away the other knights." He bowed again to Nevina. "Matriarch, it was nice to see you again. I hope you'll be returnin' soon."

She returned the bow. "Thank you, Sir Dars. Your company was a pleasure."

The old knight flashed her a quick crooked smile before seeing himself out, walking quickly down the hall and disappearing around the corner. Nevina watched him go for a moment before turning her attention back to Ajax.

His eyes were fixed on hers, despite the veil. It made her skin crawl, but not in an unsettling way.

"Has something happened?"

Ajax blinked, straightening. "Well, I'm not sure, to be honest." He made his way over to her, tapping the spine of the book he held against the open palm of his opposite hand. "Dars says that a man came to Areanath's door while he was standing guard. He was dressed as a King's Guard, but didn't seem to realize that it was the First Knight he was trying to trick into believing he was one of us." Ajax stopped less than a step from her, setting the book carefully in an open spot on the desk. The book fit perfectly, as if the spot had been made for it.

"What did he want?" Nevina could smell hay and horses on him, not an altogether unpleasant scent.

"To see you, apparently." Ajax tapped a finger on a stack of papers, surveying his desk. When he looked up at her, Nevina felt her cheeks warm. "Dars said he was tall, pale skinned, with dark hair and eyes. Sound like anyone you know?"

"Hasani?" Nevina blurted.

Ajax smirked. "Taller than Hasani."

Nevina considered for a moment, the wine making her thoughts sluggish. "No, I don't think so." She lifted a finger, wagging it in Ajax's general direction. "But someone was following us on our way through the market square this morning. He was dressed as a King's Guard, but I didn't get a good look at his face."

Ajax made a contemplative sound, his eyes on his desk again. "I wouldn't worry too much about it." He nudged the single page of parchment that Nevina had glanced over back into its proper place with a careful touch. "You'll be back safely tonight, and Dars is making arrangements to have the man found and brought in for questioning." Ajax looked up at her again, his face brightening as his eyes met hers. "Why are you smiling? I just told you that someone had been wandering around the castle, masquerading as a King's Guard, looking for you."

Nevina hadn't realized that she'd been smiling. She nodded at the now perfectly stacked papers. "Has anyone ever told you that you're a bit too orderly?"

Ajax huffed, giving her a side glance as he turned his attention back to his desk again. "My sister makes a point to remind me whenever she can."

"I'm sure she relishes every opportunity to do so." Nevina picked up the stack of papers, sifting through them without so much as glancing at the writing. Ajax's nostrils flared in irritation, but the slight smirk playing on his lips told her that he was enjoying her company as much as she enjoyed his. "I know I look forward to …" Her voice trailed as her eyes found a page in the stack that was covered in something other than carefully looping lettering.

Ajax's eyes widened and his face paled as Nevina held a drawing up for him to see. "Is this supposed to be me?"

"That's … that's nothing. Just some silly sketching I did earlier."

Nevina twisted away from Ajax's reaching arm, looking more closely at the drawing in her hands. "It's beautiful, Ajax. I had no idea …" Her thought went unfinished as she stared at the page.

Ajax had captured her standing in the market square, surrounded by half-finished stalls and faceless Etritian citizens. He'd drawn her faithfully, and with surprising detail. She could even make out the small dimple in her cheek that she disliked so much, but that Ajax had managed to make attractive and perhaps a touch coy. He had given her an expression of exasperated anticipation, and her smile made her appear lovely and exhausted at the same time.

But the eyes were wrong. "You've given me the Goddess Imis's eyes," Nevina said, looking up at Ajax. "Why?"

Ajax's mouth twisted. "I've never seen your eyes. And I couldn't leave you unfinished."

Nevina held the page out for him to take, and he tucked it back into its proper place in the stack. "No one has ever drawn me before, Ajax."

"It was nothing. I'm sorry you saw it." Ajax carefully shuffled through the papers, checking each one. He stopped before reaching the drawing again.

"It's beautiful." She touched his arm lightly, and he seemed to relax under her hand. "I'm not sorry to have seen it."

Ajax gave her a sideways glance and a small smirk. "Then I'm glad." He set the papers back on their proper spot on the desk, taking a second to make sure they were perfectly straight.

"You know …" Nevina placed a finger on the same stack of papers, twisting the pile slightly askew. "There's nothing wrong with a bit of chaos."

"Just as there's nothing wrong with a bit of order." Ajax reached for the papers himself, but Nevina's hand over his stopped him.

"Just try it. Only for a moment." Ajax's eyes shifted from their clasped hands to her face. Her cheeks warmed again under his gaze. "Then it can all go back to the way it was before."

"Alright," Ajax murmured, leaning closer to her. The scent of him grew deeper, and his lips were on hers in an instant.

Nevina welcomed his warmth pressing so close to her, hands instinctively reaching up to feel his chest. His body was both solid and comforting, and she let him wrap his arms around her and pull her closer.

His kiss deepened, and she could feel the hunger in it. She wanted to give in, to give herself over to that longing she sensed. But a nagging feeling warned her to stop, some small alarm sounding silently in the back of her mind. She ignored it, letting Ajax hold her tight against him. But the feeling persisted, and clarity pierced the wine-induced mental haze long enough for Nevina to gently push Ajax away.

Their lips parted, and he looked down on her. "Is everything alright?"

"I can't do this," she whispered.

His hands fell from her waist. "Right." He turned away from her, eyes pained. "It was only for a moment." He straightened the papers with a shaking hand.

"Ajax, I'm sorry." She reached for his hand, squeezing it gently. It was warm and strong in her grasp. "I would say yes in an instant, if only—"

"If only it were your choice," Ajax muttered darkly. He kept his face turned away from hers. "You've said so before. But you're Matriarch now, isn't it your choice?"

Nevina was silent for a heartbeat. She was Matriarch, and it was her choice. *And I want to say yes, but ...* "It's not that simple, Ajax."

"Then explain it to me," Ajax pleaded, taking both of her hands, bringing her fingertips to his lips. "I'm going mad, always waiting for you."

She hesitated for only a moment. "I'm trying to give Areanath an heir," she admitted quietly. "Today was our last chance to do so."

Ajax let his breath out slowly, eyes shut. "I see." His hands held hers for a heartbeat longer before releasing them. "I didn't realize that Areanath was …"

"My infatuate, yes," Nevina whispered. "You need to understand, Ajax." She reached for him, cupping his face in her hands. "I care about you very much. And I want to be with you. But I love Areanath as well, and right now he needs me." She frowned, letting her hands drop to her sides. "Such is the way of the Coven."

Ajax nodded slowly. "I understand. I've always known that would be the case." He shrugged one shoulder, accepting her words. "I'll just keep waiting for you, Nevina."

She smiled sadly. "The Coven has always said that there is power in love. Sometimes I even believe it."

Ajax snorted softly, a small smile tugging at the corner of his mouth. "Perhaps next time, then?"

"Next time, Ajax." Nevina pulled at the ties holding her veil in place, letting the cloth fall away. "I promise."

The fact that she would probably never return to Etritia made her heart weak.

Ajax's smile deepened, and he leaned to kiss her forehead. "Your eyes are more beautiful than I could have imagined."

Nevina forced her own smile in return. With her veil pulled away, she could See Ajax more clearly. There was love in his eyes, of course, but there was also tremendous heartbreak. And loneliness.

Is that the present, or a future? She briefly thought of the future she had glimpsed for Silvana earlier, and hoped that both Sights meant nothing. "We should go, Ajax," Nevina said, replacing her veil with practiced ease. "I'll need to return to the Coven soon, and my girls are waiting for me, I'm sure."

Ajax nodded, crossing the room and opening the door out to the hall without another word, and they left the moment behind them.

He led her to the library, where Silvana was sitting with

the younger girls surrounding her, reading aloud from a storybook. Millie and Kall were huddled together at a small table, whispering in hushed tones and casting side glances at the pair of young knights standing nearby. Judging by the flushed face of one of the knights, Nevina could guess that her older students weren't as quiet as they thought. *Unless that's their intention, of course,* Nevina thought with a smirk. Layle, as studious as ever, sat alone by the fire, a book in her lap and a small stack of texts on the floor beside her. Hasani sat close to his wife, eyes never straying from her face as she read to the little ones. The sight pained Nevina, and for a moment she wished she could have the same kind of life that Hasani and Silvana would have.

That could be Areanath and I.

Or Ajax and I.

Nevina shook herself as Ajax leaned close to whisper in her ear.

"I keep sending the younger King's Guards down here." Nevina heard the smile in his voice. "I thought it might keep the older girls from getting bored. And it gives the men something to do."

She smirked, glad to know that Ajax's bitterness had been left behind in his rooms.

"'So the wolf turned to the princess, and said to her …'" Silvana glanced up, catching sight of her. "Matriarch." Silvana let the book fall to her lap as all eyes left her and shot to Nevina.

Arella leapt up, running barefoot across the library to embrace her. "Matriarch!"

Nevina took a knee to catch the girl. "Oh, Arella, I missed you. Were you a good little girl for the nice lady?"

Arella nodded her head vigorously, but Nala spoke up, snickering. "She tried to take her veil off for cakes. But Layle helped her keep it in place while we ate."

Layle was already on her feet, Arella's discarded shoes in her hand.

"Thank you, Layle, for helping her."

The girl inclined her head, kneeling to help Arella with her shoes. "We were all very well behaved, Matriarch."

"I wouldn't doubt it for a moment."

"Lady Silvana is really good at telling stories," Arella said, smiling broadly. "She does voices and everything!"

Silvana laughed, holding the book close to her chest. "It's easy to tell good stories when you have good listeners, Arella." She inclined her head slightly to Nevina. "You'll have to bring them back soon, Matriarch. I'm sure our little one would love to play with them."

Nevina forced a smile, returning Silvana's bow. "Of course, Silvana. You and Hasani have been generous, as usual. Thank you."

"Night will be falling soon, Matriarch. Are you ready?"

She turned, finding Ajax less than an arm's width away. "Yes, of course, Commander." Nevina already resented the way the titles sounded, wishing instead that Ajax would continue to use her name, despite their company. "Let's go, girls." She released Arella, beckoning for her to take her place in line. Instead, the little girl ran to Layle and took her by the hand. Layle said nothing, and stood hand in hand with her sister. Ajax offered Nevina his arm, which she took with a polite smile, and he led her through the castle, her girls trailing behind them, Hasani and Silvana taking up the rear.

At the great double doors leading to the main square, farewells were exchanged with the expectant couple, as well as promises for Nevina to return soon.

For her part, Nevina tried her Gift on Silvana and Hasani before they departed, but Saw nothing.

But the earlier vision of Silvana, heavy with child and wandering the darkness alone, wouldn't leave her.

With a final farewell, Ajax led Nevina and her girls out through the double doors and to the steps that led down into the empty square. The shops in the market below were closed, or nearly so, and lanterns had been lit and hung on long poles around the open space, the firelight casting long shadows in the fading sunlight.

"Where within the city are you staying?"

"We aren't actually." Nevina took the stairs slowly, the lingering effects of the wine still making her unsure of her footing.

"Understandable. It must be difficult to get a few moments of peace in the city as the Coven's Matriarch."

"There's a farm to the southeast, just off the main road. Beautiful rose bushes out front. You can't miss it." Nevina took another step, stumbling slightly.

Ajax was quick to catch her. He laughed, helping her to steady herself. "Are you alright?"

Nevina chuckled. "Areanath and I had a lot of wine." She gripped his arm tightly, leaning against him for support. "I'll be fine soon, I think."

He laughed again. "Don't worry, I'll get you home safe."

They proceeded slowly through the city streets towards the main gate. The roads were nearly deserted, and they only ran into a few people along the way. By the time they had reached the gate, the sun was beginning its final descent, slowly disappearing behind the wooded horizon in the west. They walked along the main road, following the curve of the city's walls, watching as the sky darkened.

Nevina stopped, admiring the deepening red sunset around them. "This is nice."

"What is?"

"The sunset. It's so beautiful." She sighed. "I never take the time to just enjoy the small pleasures in life."

"There's still time to start." Ajax stared out across the horizon.

Nevina shrugged. "I'm not sure that I want to bother with it anymore." Her voice was quiet, almost a whisper.

Ajax looked over at her, his brows pinched together slightly. "Is everything alright?"

She straightened her shoulders, taking a slow breath. "Everything is fine. It's just been a distressing day."

They finished their walk in relative silence until Nevina ushered the girls into their borrowed home. The girls left them without a word, though Arella dropped Layle's hand long enough to hug Ajax around his knees before disappearing inside.

Nevina turned to Ajax, whispering, "Thank you for coming with us. You didn't have to."

Ajax shrugged one shoulder. "Anything to spend more time with you." In a quieter tone, he added, "And you shouldn't have to be afraid to come to the castle, Nevina."

Nevina huffed, feeling foolish for her earlier admission. "It wasn't even needed. We saw no sign of Mothlenor along the way."

"It doesn't matter," Ajax insisted. "I can talk to Areanath, if you'd like—"

"No." Nevina raised a hand to stop his words. "Don't say anything to Areanath. Please."

Ajax sighed, frowning. "Alright. I won't say anything." He straightened, nodding politely to her. "Until next time, Matriarch."

Next time ...

"Of course, Commander," she said, smiling.

Ajax's lips curved into a smirk for only an instant, and he leaned to kiss her cheek. His breath was warm on her skin. "I'll keep waiting, Nevina."

Their eyes met as he pulled away, and Nevina Saw a hint of heartbreak and loneliness again.

"There's power in love, Ajax."

He nodded once, then turned and left.

Nevina's heart wrenched as he strode off into the quickly approaching night.

I'll never see him again, either. That will be our last memory together.

LAYLE

Layle started awake, eyes snapping open to see only darkness around her. It took a moment for the unfamiliar surroundings to make sense. *We're in Etritia, in a cabin Mother rented for us. We should be going home soon. Back to the Coven ...* Layle sighed, the thought of returning home relaxing her startled mind. *But something woke me ...*

There was a soft sniff near the foot of the bed, and Layle sat up to find the shadowy form of Arella. "Layle?" the girl whined, voice thick with tears. "I had a bad dream."

Layle sighed again, accustomed to her sister's nightmares and the crying that usually ensued. "Come on up, there's no need to be afraid anymore." Layle pulled the covers back, motioning for Arella to slip into bed next to her.

"But Layle, it was bad!" Arella cried, climbing onto the bed and clutching Layle.

"Can't you shut her up?" Millie moaned from the adjacent bed. "I'm trying to sleep."

Layle ignored the older girl's complaint. Millie was already asleep again—there was no point in saying anything. Instead, she clutched Arella close to her chest as the little girl wept quietly against her. "Hush, Arella, it's alright." Arella's veil was missing, as it so often was, and hot tears dropped against Layle's neck. She rocked the child gently, stroking her tangled hair and whispering comforts in her ear.

After a few moments, Arella quieted, only the occasional sniff coming from her.

Layle continued to stroke her head, knowing the motion soothed her little sister. "Do you want to talk about it?" Layle whispered.

"There was a scary man …" Arella began slowly. "He came for us and took us to the castle. There was a dragon, and it ate someone …" Arella paused as a hiccup caused her shoulders to jump. "The Matriarch was scared. She couldn't help us. The man hurt us. He hurt you." Arella looked up at Layle, and in the dimness Layle could make out the bright wideness of her blue eyes. "And then I died."

Arella's last words sent a chill over Layle, but she only pulled Arella closer and continued rocking her. "It's alright, Arella. It was just a dream."

Wasn't it?

Arella was prone to nightmares, and most of them were of the silly sort that Layle knew children had. But, every so often, there was one that Arella talked about that sounded more … real. Perhaps more prophecy than dream.

And sometimes, Arella's dreams came true.

Arella had once dreamed that the stray cat the Coven girls took care of had died, and sure enough, Kall and Layle had found the thing cold and dead in the bushes a few days later. Layle had buried it without telling Arella.

Another time, Arella told Layle that a girl following another Coven sister would break her leg, she'd had a dream about it. Later the same day, the girl fell and twisted her ankle. It hadn't been as serious as Arella had said it would be, but it had happened.

Arella's retelling had felt just as real as those dreams had sounded.

But a dragon? Eating someone?

The dragons were extinct. Even Arella knew that.

"Can I sleep with you tonight?" Arella whispered, her breath warm against Layle's chest.

"Of course you can." Layle turned to her side, depositing the girl in the bed beside her. Though it was cramped, Layle pulled the blankets over both of them and wrapped an arm around her sister, pulling her close to her body. "How's that? Good?"

"Mm," Arella murmured, already drifting off to sleep. Her tiny hand found Layle's and clung tightly to it. "Don't leave me, Layle."

"I won't, I promise." Layle kissed the back of Arella's head, settling down to sleep again. "Not until morning, anyway."

Arella said nothing, her breathing hitching as another hiccup shook her.

Layle listened for Arella's breathing to change as she fell asleep. The girl's grip on her hand slackened, but Layle didn't move.

A dragon? Was it possible?

Had Arella Seen a vision of her own death?

Finally, Layle fell asleep once more, her dreams filled with winged beasts and the sound of her sister crying.

19

NEVINA

Nevina was asleep when a small hand gently shook her shoulder. She awoke enough to wave the hand away, then buried her face deeper into her pillow. Another shake, this one rougher, more impatient. Nevina growled into her pillow and instantly regretted it. Her head ached, and she realized her stomach was very queasy. Then the covers were ripped off her, her pillow yanked from under her head, and several hands shoved her with enough force to send her rolling and squealing to the floor.

Nevina moaned softly as she lifted herself off the floor and forced her eyes open. She quickly shut her eyes again, wishing the light would stop making her head feel like a half-split melon. She laid her head gently on the bed, eyes still closed, too weak to actually get to her feet. "Who the hell did that?" Her voice was hoarse and her throat dry.

"I did." A girl's voice, much too loud for her sensitive ears.

Nevina opened her eyes again, surveyed the room in an instant, and shut them again just as quickly. The room was empty, save for one girl—Layle. There was no one else.

"Just you? You've been working on that spell I taught you. You seem to have mastered it well, though I'm not sure how intelligent it was to use it on me on this particular morning." To herself, she added, *If I ever see Areanath again, I might just kill him for making me drink so much last night.* Remembering Areanath pained her, and she regretted her thoughts.

Layle sighed. "I called your name and tried waking you, but you wouldn't answer."

"Please don't shout."

"I'm not shouting."

"Then please whisper."

Layle sighed again.

Nevina, still keeping her eyes closed, pulled herself back onto the bed, lying on her back. "Water." She held out a hand weakly, and Layle gently forced a glass into her hand and helped her guide it to her lips. She drank, but it wasn't water. The concoction was thick, with a bitter aftertaste, but it settled over her stomach and soothed her head almost instantly.

Eventually, Nevina opened her eyes. She looked down at the glass in her hand. It was still half filled with a milky liquid. "What is this?"

A light flush rose to Layle's cheeks. "It's the medicine I take when I have my woman's blood. I made it myself. I also added some of those leaves you sometimes use for migraines. I thought they might help. Is it working?"

Nevina took another sip of the formula. Aside from the taste, it was wonderful. She could feel the pain in her head melt away, replaced with a slight giddiness. "You might have used too many leaves, but yes, it's very good. You did well." She squeezed Layle's hand gently. "Remind me when we get back home, and I'll show you older girls how to fix it up a little better—perhaps make it taste a little less like medicine and more like a refreshment." Layle nodded, taking the empty glass from her. Nevina pulled herself up into a sitting position. "How are the other girls?" Her voice was still hoarse.

Layle hesitated before answering quietly. "Arella is fine, Matriarch."

Nevina frowned slightly. Layle was always able to see right through her. "She slept fine, then?" Arella was plagued with night terrors, and often woke in the middle of the night, screaming. Nevina and Layle were the only ones who could comfort her.

"Like a princess." Layle smiled, but Nevina could tell it wasn't entirely genuine.

She frowned again, setting the glass aside. Nevina gestured for Layle to sit beside her on the bed, and the young girl did so, her weight hardly disturbing the covers. "Thank you for caring for your sister so much. I know she can be trying at times, but she loves you, and she looks up to you." She brushed back a stray strand of blonde hair from Layle's face, trying to look through the girl's veil and into her eyes. Layle's eyes were such a piercing blue they could be glimpsed even through her veil at times. "And I appreciate all that you're doing."

Layle's cheeks flushed again.

Nevina sighed. "Now, was there a reason you woke me up so early?"

Layle frowned. "Sunup was a few hours ago, Matriarch. And there's a knight here to see you."

Nevina cursed and quickly rolled out of the bed. "Is he here, inside? How long has he been waiting?" She hadn't expected Ajax to come back after escorting them the night before. *Did I say something to make him come back?* She quickly rushed over to the small mirror leaning on the mantle, smoothing her hair and frantically trying to remember if she had invited Ajax to return in the morning.

"The other girls said he'd only just arrived a few moments ago. Millie and Kall are keeping him entertained."

Nevina groaned. Millie and Kall were her two oldest girls and were eagerly awaiting their chance to have their first infatuate. They were far too flirtatious for her liking when given the chance. She would have preferred it if Layle had been the one to keep Ajax distracted. But, she realized, the other girls probably asked Layle to wake her, since Layle was the least likely to hear a tongue lashing. She sighed, straightening her veil and smoothing some of the wrinkles out of her crumpled dress.

"Layle, have you seen my shoes?" She searched the floor, even crouching to look under the bed. *We should be gone already, on our way back to the Coven.*

"Here, Matriarch." Nevina turned to see Layle holding her shoes out to her, as she often did with Arella.

Nevina sighed, taking the soft boots from Layle and slipping them on. "I'll deal with the commander. You get everyone ready to go home. Our business in Etritia is done."

"Of course, Matriarch." Layle bowed politely, falling into step behind Nevina as she opened the door to the hall and made her way to the living area.

Nevina had barely entered the front of the house before she realized something was wrong. The five other girls in her retinue were all clustered together, sitting very quietly at one end of the room. Even Millie and Kall were unusually silent. At the opposite end of the room, a tall knight stood in full armor, staring silently at the girls. He had kept his helmet on, a strange piece that completely covered his face, leaving only a small slit for him to see through. He was most definitely not Ajax, Nevina realized, but was much too tall.

And just his presence unnerved her.

Nevina wondered if this man was perhaps the same one that had tried to pass himself off as a King's Guard the day before.

She paused at the entrance, unsure of what to do. The knight turned at her entrance, bowing slightly towards her. He said nothing.

"Can I help you?" she asked nervously. She wanted to kick

herself. The Matriarch of the Coven does not ask to be of service like a common barmaid. But the man before her was intimidating.

"The king requests your presence." His voice was silk, quite unlike what she was expecting. It made her stomach roll unpleasantly.

Nevina hesitated, looking between the knight and her girls. Areanath was still in the city? Had he decided not to go with his brother on the Last Hunt? Or was there some mistake he had made the night before, something he needed her help to fix?

"Very well," she said quietly. She turned back to the girls, all of whom were looking at her. Even with their veils in place, she could tell they were frightened. They huddled closely together, instinctively guarding the younger ones from the knight. It would be better for them to remain here until she returned, and they could all leave the city together. "We'll be leaving for the Coven as soon as possible, so I want you to stay here while I—"

The knight raised a hand in protest, cutting her words off. "The king requests all of you."

Now Nevina was sure something was terribly wrong. Areanath had warned her to get out of the city quickly. Had she already waited too long? Areanath shouldn't have need of her skills and those of the girls in her retinue. Nevina stood a little taller, hoping her false confidence would give the knight cause to hesitate. "Very well, then. Just let me get a few things."

Again, the knight protested. "There is little time. I have several men outside, ready to escort you all directly to the king. He is waiting for you."

Nevina's heart skipped several beats and her breathing hitched slightly, understanding the implied threat. She had waited too long. It was only midmorning. Areanath had only left a few hours ago. Was he already dead? He had said she might not be able to tell immediately, but she had hoped she would have a little more time to leave Etritia. Nevina's skills were formidable enough to fight this knight, no matter how large and frightening he seemed. She could even stand her own against however many men he might have waiting outside. If it was just her, she could escape. But her girls … Even with Layle's exceptional talents, there was no way to protect them all.

Her panic rising, Nevina hardly noticed the girls moving to cluster around her until Arella slipped her hand into hers. "It's alright, we can go with you." Her voice was quiet but firm, her tiny hand cool in Nevina's own.

Nevina looked around at her girls, slightly dazed. Finally, a flash of angry blue eyes under a white veil caught her attention. "Layle …" she whispered. "You don't understand …"

"We understand." Layle nodded slightly, her eyes softening from anger to sad resignation.

Nevina straightened slowly, taking a deep breath to steady her frayed nerves. "Very well, sir. We will go with you."

"Of course you will."

Nevina and her girls were roughly shoved through the cabin's door and into the arms of half a dozen other men. Heavy metal cuffs were quickly fastened around their wrists, and Nevina's panic grew at the sight of her girls standing calmly as their hands were secured. Even Arella was silent as a knight clamped the heavy steel around her tiny wrists. Nevina stared at the cuffs for a moment, bewildered. There was no chain to connect one wrist to the other, and the cuffs seemed to fit each of them tightly, despite their varying sizes. Nevina funneled arcane energy to one palm, intent on breaking the cuff free. No sooner had the energy started flowing to her hand than a sharp stinging sensation pierced her wrist. Startled, she stopped the energy flow, and the pain subsided.

"Careful, witch," the tall knight crooned, eyes on her. "Those aren't normal cuffs. And once they're on, only the king can take them off."

Nevina flexed her hand, watching her girls as they also tested their cuffs with similar results. *Arcane cuffs. Meant to leave us defenseless. Who could make such a thing?*

She knew the answer, and a heavy weight settled in her stomach at the realization. *Mothlenor. This is his doing.*

Nevina eyed the men around them. Many of them were dressed in full armor, including heavy headpieces that obscured their eyes, making it impossible for Nevina to use her Gift. One man, however, stood out. He was dressed in nothing more protective than a simple jerkin, and he didn't bother to hide his face. She could read his emotions plainly, even without using her Sight. The man was terrified, especially of the large man that led the party away.

As they were taken into custody, Nevina wondered if they might be escorted through the city and into the castle, using the same path she had used the day before. If so, surely someone would stop and question these knights, and they might be saved. She couldn't believe that Areanath could have been killed and usurped so soon. *Areanath would have made sure we had enough time to leave Etritia. He is still alive. He has to be.*

Instead of leading them directly to the main gate, their captors led Nevina and the others down a wide dirt road that led deeper into farmland and away from the castle. The road was empty; there was no one to help them, or to hear her if she cried out. Even the farms were set far enough away from the road to provide little hope of rescue.

As they walked, Nevina tried again and again to funnel arcane energy through the cuffs on her wrists, testing them for weaknesses. But with each attempt, sharp stabbing pains in her wrists and arms stopped her. She finally gave up when thin trickles of blood began to seep their way under the cuffs and down her red and swollen wrists. Magic would not be the answer.

Another way, then. There has to be another way.

But Nevina's mind was too panicked to think clearly. Was this the end for her? For her girls? Her daughters? The idea paralyzed her, and she could only walk nimbly in the direction she was led.

For some time they traveled south and slightly west, then turned up a second road to head north. It took several moments, but Nevina realized they were traveling in a large circle. They would eventually be led around to the back of the castle, which sat against the Northern Mountains. The sound of the Knife grew louder as they drew closer to the river. The terrain became rough, soft soil giving way to gravel and sharp rocks scattered among sparse trees. At one point in their quiet captivity, Nevina tripped over an exposed root and fell to her knees on the sharp gravel. The tall knight wrapped one large hand around her upper arm and yanked her to her feet effortlessly. She felt blood trickling down her shins.

"Careful, witch," he crooned again, mouth inches from her ear. The sound of his voice chilled her.

As they neared the western side of the castle walls, drawing closer to the base of the steep Northern Mountains, hot bile rose to the back of Nevina's throat. *What will they do with us now? There is nowhere for them to take us.*

She began resisting the shoves from behind that urged her forward, frantically trying to think of a way for them all to escape. Finally, one man, cursing her, kicked her behind the knee, sending her sprawling to the ground. She landed painfully on her knees again, the sharp pain of the stone digging into her flesh making her cry out. Behind her, Arella let out a matching cry, and Nevina turned to see the girl clutching at Layle. Layle was frantically trying to console the child, who had her face buried in Layle's side, mumbling incoherently.

"This is the place," the tall knight called, and the other men stopped shoving and prodding the girls across the rocky ground. The knight was staring at the empty expanse of limestone just in front of them, searching. The flat face of the mountain was only a few dozen feet away, dark and unwelcoming.

Craning her neck to look around the knight, Nevina saw nothing but smooth grey stone, cracked and broken with age and erosion. As Nevina stared at the stone cliff, searching for whatever had brought them to a stop, she spotted a series of carved lines in the cliff face. Studying them, as the tall knight seemed to study them, revealed the outline of a great dragon, the cuts made to blend with the natural cracks and markings of the stone.

Large wings, taller than her and nearly as wide, fanned out against the dark stone. The claws and legs were almost natural looking, carved from small outcroppings on the mountain's face, giving the stone dragon a terrible realness. The eyes were empty pits that seemed to stare at her where she lay in the dirt.

The dragon's mouth was open in a snarl, the snout protruding as if the beast might leap from the mountainside and snap at her. Four long teeth had been made from sharp stones, each as long as her forearm, a pair nestled into both the top and bottom jaws.

Behind her, Arella began to sob loudly, Layle's pleading voice doing nothing to calm her.

"The Dragon Door," the knight whispered. He hesitated, and Nevina dared to hope that he was questioning their capture, that he might free them after all. But a moment later he turned to look at the assembled men before him. "You." He gestured to the man in the jerkin. "Open it."

"M-me?" the man stammered. "Why me?"

"Consider it repayment of your debt to me," the knight answered coldly.

"What? B-but you asked me to follow them out of the castle. You said to find where the witch and her brats were hiding, and that we would be even. Please, my debt is paid." The man fell to his knees, begging.

"I gave you your life back. Following the Matriarch was not enough to pay for even your worthless life." The knight motioned to three other men standing nearby. "Help him."

The three knights seized the man, two holding him bodily, while the third used a long dagger to cut away one sleeve of his doublet, leaving the tanned arm beneath bare. They struggled briefly with him, dragging him over to the cliff face and shoving his naked arm into the mouth of the stone dragon. They held him there for a few seconds, waiting, and the hairs on the back of Nevina's neck rose as a wave of dread swept over her.

After a few seconds of waiting, the mouth of the dragon suddenly snapped shut, loudly crushing the bone it now held between its teeth. The man pinned by the great stone teeth screamed, and the others holding him jumped back. Nevina could see where the four long fangs of the dragon had each bitten completely through the man's arm. There was blood pouring liberally from the wounds, yet none of it was spilling into the earth at the base of the carving.

"A blood sacrifice," she whispered. "To open the door." She had no doubt that Mothlenor had somehow created this beast, though how something so terrible could be made she had no idea. She watched in horror as the man continued to grow paler as his life's blood was pulled from him. He slumped against the stone, his screams fading into whimpers. Finally, the dragon's mouth opened once more, and with a loud cry from the man, released its grip. The man fell to his knees, clutching his arm close to his body.

Behind her, Arella wailed, "The dragon ate him. It ate him."

The knight walked up to the man, tsking quietly. "It seems it's been too long since she was last fed. Mothlenor should take better care of his pets." The knight stood before the carving, arms crossed impatiently over his chest. A quiet rumbling permeated the air as the stone dragon began to move. Twisting in its spot, it slowly opened, providing a narrow opening for them to pass through. At last it came to a halt, the sound of grinding stone echoing around them. Where it had stood, a long and dark passageway had been revealed, and dank, musty air billowed over Nevina's face.

"My arm …" the man whispered weakly from beside the statue.

"I wouldn't be so worried about your arm. You've lost a lot of blood. I'd be surprised if you lasted another hour out here." The knight stepped around the wounded man, ignoring his continued pleas.

Someone pulled Nevina back to her feet, and she was half carried, half dragged through the passageway the stone dragon had revealed. As she passed the man lying on the ground, she caught his eyes for a moment. Nevina looked away quickly, afraid she might See something terrible in those eyes. On his arm, she saw four deep punctures, boring straight through the bone and completely through the arm. His arm was a mangled mess, and Nevina realized that the knight was right. The man wouldn't last much longer at all.

As the last of them filed through the narrow opening, the sound of stone grinding on stone told Nevina that the door was rotating back into place. She turned back just in time to see the rear of the dragon carving. It exactly mimicked the front, and in the quickly fading light, Nevina thought she could see blood glistening on the mouth carved on this side of the door. Then the Dragon Door closed completely, and they were thrown into darkness.

AREANATH

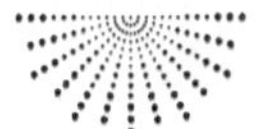

When Areanath made his way down to the kitchens, he wasn't altogether surprised to find his brother already waiting for him.

"There's a horse ready and waiting for you out by the eastern gate. I thought we could cut through the gardens to get there." Mothlenor's jaw tightened slightly. "Perhaps avoid the market crowds."

Behind him, Cookie stood silently at the oven, her back turned to them both.

"Alright," Areanath said, casting a quick glance Cookie's way. "I'll follow behind you shortly."

Mothlenor gave him a slow bow then left without another word.

Areanath waited for his brother's footsteps to fade, then called quietly across the room, "He's gone, Cookie. You can stop hiding in the corner."

Cookie snorted, turning to face him. "I wasn't hiding. I was staying out of the way." She wiped flour from her hands, shaking her head. "That brother of yours always seems so angry. I feel it's best to just make myself as scarce as possible when he comes around."

"It's his loss," Areanath said, giving Cookie a coy smile. "My brother has no idea what kind of pleasant company he's been missing."

Cookie snorted again, a faint blush rising to her already red cheeks. "Get out of here already." She handed him a linen-wrapped bundle. Areanath could smell baked apples, and the bundle was warm to the touch. "And take these with you. For the road."

"Thank you, Cookie." He bent and gave her a quick peck on one cheek. "I knew I came down here for a good reason."

"Oh, go on. Shoo!" Cookie flapped her flour-dusted apron at him, her whole face faintly red. "And come home safely, you hear? I'll have no one to steal my tarts from me, with you gone."

A hard lump formed in Areanath's throat. He couldn't trust himself to speak, not without his voice betraying the anguish he felt. So he forced a smile and gave Cookie a sly wink before darting out of the kitchen.

It wasn't half the farewell the woman deserved, but it would have to do.

Mothlenor insisted on leaving the hunting dogs in their kennels, arguing that they would be too difficult to control on the trail and that they could manage well enough without them. "This is a symbolic hunt, anyway. We could return empty-handed, and it would still mark the beginning of the harvest season."

"I suppose," Areanath reluctantly agreed.

The morning was still grey and cool, and from the garden Areanath could hear the bustling from the market square as shops were opened for the day. They walked in silence, Mothlenor taking the lead with his brisk pace, Areanath following more slowly behind, nibbling on an apple tart and taking in the scents of the garden for the last time. Every rose bush they passed reminded him of Nevina. The lump in his throat tightened, and he tucked the half-eaten tart back in with the others, appetite gone.

On exiting the garden, Mothlenor led Areanath to a small group of four riders, each on a dark horse. Mothlenor's own stallion, a mean thing with a penchant for biting stable boys, stamped his hooves impatiently nearby.

One of Areanath's favorite horses, a dappled mare he had known since her birth, stood apart from the rest, her reins held loosely by a tall, pale-skinned man that Areanath didn't recognize. He passed the reins to Areanath wordlessly, bowing and turning on his heel to head back to the castle.

Areanath watched him as he departed. "Who is that?"

Mothlenor, already in his saddle, cast a glance over his shoulder at the man. "Just another hired hand, I'm sure. Here for the summer, gone by the first snowfall, no doubt."

Areanath watched the man for a moment longer, then shrugged and climbed into his own saddle. Mothlenor was probably right, though Areanath would have preferred it if someone more familiar with their animals had prepared his horse for him.

"Are we ready?" Mothlenor asked.

"This is the whole party? Six of us?"

"Six should be plenty." Mothlenor's eyes narrowed. "As I said before, it doesn't matter if we return with anything or not. The Last Hunt is a symbolic affair."

Areanath frowned, unsure of what his brother's plans might be. "Then we're ready."

The weather was pleasant, and Areanath was content to let his brother lead their team through the woods. But the hours seemed to stretch much longer than normal, and every move Mothlenor made in the saddle set Areanath's nerves on edge. The sun was finally beginning its slow descent, and still his brother had not made a single move to harm him. In fact, after several hours of Areanath feigning annoyance at the lack of any actual hunting, Mothlenor had taken to completely ignoring his presence.

The four men with them rode slightly apart, huddled together several feet behind him. Areanath tried a few times to lure them into conversation, twisting in his saddle to do so, but they too ignored him. Finally, Areanath gave up and rode silently along.

The silence of the hunt, as the cool morning turned into a warm afternoon and finally a humid evening, began to eat at him. Even the horses seemed quieter, and the eerie sensation of four expressionless pairs of eyes staring at his back set his nerves alight.

There was something not quite normal about the men his brother had brought with them, but Areanath couldn't decide what it might be, despite the long ride to contemplate it.

They continued for some time, the sun continuing to lower as the day stretched on. Areanath watched the sky through the canopy overhead as it changed from brilliant oranges to darker purples, contemplating the possibility of egging his brother into a fatal altercation for the ease of his sanity, when Mothlenor suddenly stopped in front of him.

"This will have to do for the night, I suppose." They had reached a small clearing, which Mothlenor surveyed with obvious disdain. "Give me just a moment, Areanath, and I can have a tent ready for you. Then we can see to perhaps starting a small fire and having some sort of meal." From the back of his saddle, Mothlenor detached two large, rather heavy blankets. He threw one into the clearing, muttering under his breath. The blanket writhed in midair, twisting and turning until it landed quite nicely on the ground as a tent, apparently holding itself together without the aid of poles or sticks. Mothlenor repeated the motion with the second blanket, and a matching tent landed a dozen or so feet away.

Areanath barely contained a loud snort at his brother's theatrics. His knee smarted angrily as he left his horse to walk around the first tent. "Your abilities continue to amaze." He pulled the opening flap aside to peer inside. "It will hold itself together through the night?" He already knew the answer, but Mothlenor enjoyed showing off when he had the opportunity.

"Of course, my liege," Mothlenor said slowly. He carried a bundle of firewood under one arm, which he arranged in the center of the clearing with a careless throw and some whispered words.

Areanath let the flap drop from his hands. "I appreciate the help, Mothlenor. You know better than most how bad my knee has been lately."

"I live to serve," Mothlenor muttered. With a snap of his fingers, the wood caught fire. The sudden flare was almost explosive, and Areanath narrowed his eyes against the bright flames.

Areanath bit his lip, watching as the fire dulled to a warm red color. "You don't have to say that, you know."

"Say what?" Mothlenor hissed, pulling a pair of saddlebags down from his horse and dropping them to the ground.

"'I live to serve,'" Areanath repeated carefully. Mothlenor turned towards him, a mix of anger and surprise on his face. "There's no need for it," Areanath added slowly. "You're my brother, not my ... my slave." Areanath frowned.

Mothlenor's face relaxed. "I suppose you're right." He looked almost pleased.

A thought struck Areanath. *If I could reach out, make him see reason ...* He took a deep breath. "Brother?"

Mothlenor looked up from the bags at his feet. "Yes?"

"Do you still worry about the other races? The elves and dwarves?" Areanath wasn't sure how to steer the conversation, but needed to know his brother's thoughts.

"You know I do." Mothlenor's voice was flat.

"Why?"

Mothlenor abandoned the bags, straightening to face Areanath. He crossed his arms over his chest, looking Areanath over skeptically. He seemed a bit surprised by the question, one eyebrow rising for a moment as he considered his answer. "They're older than our race is. They think that makes them wiser and more powerful than we are." He hesitated, head tilting slightly to one side. "It's only a matter of time before they try to take back the known world, before they try to drive us back to the fringes of civilization." He frowned, eyes narrowing. "And we are not ready to face them."

"You're not at all reassured by the treaties they signed at the close of the Great War?"

Mothlenor snorted. "Of course not. They're just words on paper."

"They're promises," Areanath insisted.

"Promises are hard to keep."

Areanath hesitated, wondering if he should continue. *I've already come this far ...*

"I've written to the elven Elders of Thessala and Talemeca. And to their king in Vyris."

"You what?" Mothlenor snapped, rounding on Areanath.

"And to the dwarven king in Doldural Keep," Areanath added.

"Why?"

"I wanted to remind them of the treaties. To make sure they remembered the result of the Great War."

"And?"

"And they assured me that they kept the treaties well in mind. That they recognized the power of our race, and that they were content to only ever be our allies in peace." Areanath sighed. "We have nothing to fear from them, Mothlenor."

"They have tricked you, Areanath. They've fooled you!" he

growled, his face contorting with anger. "Just more words on more paper, more silly promises." His voice thundered, and for a moment Areanath thought his brother might attack him. "They are not to be trusted," Mothlenor finished in a low snarl.

"Perhaps." Areanath sighed again, watching Mothlenor as he tried to rein in his anger. There were occasions when Mothlenor's loss and regain of emotional control were both fascinating and terrifying to watch.

After a moment, Mothlenor's face was once more a stony mask of indifference. "You will kill us all with your inaction, Areanath."

Areanath shook his head, pulling a bedroll from his mare's back and turning his back on Mothlenor. "I'll see you in the morning, brother."

<hr>

Areanath forced himself to stay awake, not daring to drift off for a moment. The night was eerily quiet, the only sound the crackling of the fire. Mothlenor had set up a rather elaborate shielding spell over the entire camp, preventing anyone or anything from stumbling across them, and it blocked the usual night sounds of insects. Once again, the silence was unnerving.

Yet Areanath was hardly bothered by the idea of being attacked by something outside the camp, and was instead worried about the four men his brother had brought along. They all sat together, a few feet away from the fire, and kept watch as the night progressed. Areanath could see their shadowy silhouettes cast by the campfire framed against his tent, and they never seemed to move. They still managed to maintain their silence, and Areanath was increasingly disconcerted by their presence. As each hour passed, he grew increasingly paranoid that they would come together, slip into his tent, and slit his throat. But they sat the whole night through, unmoving.

Finally, in the early hours of the morning, Areanath quickly cast another shielding spell inside his tent, one that would prevent his movements from being heard. He rolled out of his covers and groped around on the floor of his tent for his pack. Once found, he reached inside and felt around until he felt a thin round metal handle among his spare clothing and utensils. He wrestled with the handle until he pulled out a plain hand mirror. He cast a Searching spell on the mirror, similar to the one he had used just a few nights before. He could only hope Nevina had taken his advice and was well on her way back to the Coven. After several moments of waiting, nothing happened to the mirror. He cast the spell again and waited. Again, there was nothing. He took it as a good sign, that Nevina was on the road, and away from any reflective surface that his spell could use to show her to him.

He cast the spell a third time, this time Searching for Hasani. Within seconds, the surface of the mirror rippled like water, and an image of Hasani lying in bed next to his wife appeared. From the angle of the image, it seemed he was looking down on the couple from across the room. He thought about activating a second spell, one that would allow him to speak to Hasani. He thought about waking his friend and taking the time to speak to him one last time. He briefly thought of telling Hasani everything his brother planned to do.

But he didn't. The less Hasani knew upon Mothlenor's return, the better. He pressed the surface of the mirror against his forehead, thinking intently. After a few seconds, he dispelled the Searching spell, satisfied, and slipped the mirror back into his pack.

He rolled over to slip back under his covers and jumped when he saw a figure standing outside his tent. His heart beating rapidly, it took him a second to realize it was one of the four strangers, standing right outside the opening to the tent. Areanath hadn't heard him approach, hadn't heard his footsteps crunching on the leaves and twigs filling the campsite. The man stood silently for a moment, facing the tent. Areanath was sure he was going to enter and kill him. The other three men remained where they had been the whole night, watching the fourth. They still said nothing.

Finally, the man turned and walked back to the other three and resumed his place among them. He walked so silently, so skillfully, that Areanath realized it was no wonder he hadn't heard the man approach.

After a time, Areanath's heartbeat returned to normal, and he slipped back under the covers of his makeshift bed. For the rest of the night, his eyes never left the four men sitting quietly by the fire.

HASANI

Hasani woke up to a gentle shoving and Silvana's voice. "Come on, time to get up."

Hasani shied away from her, grumbling under his breath.

Silvana slapped him sharply on his rear, making him grunt in surprise. "I'm sure there are some things you should probably be doing right now besides sleeping, Hasani."

"Not quite yet. I'm still sleeping," he mumbled into his pillow. He heard Silvana sigh, roll out of bed, and walk away. He started drifting away, nearly asleep again.

"Hasani." Silvana's voice was sharp.

"Not quite yet," he mumbled again, pulling the covers over his ears. *May Imis preserve me, I'm exhausted.*

"Hasani, come look at this. Now." Her voice was high and tinny, and the fear in her words instantly awoke him.

Hasani rolled out of bed, shuffling his way towards her as fast as his tired legs could carry him.

Silvana stood rooted to the center of the room, one hand pressed against the small bump of her pregnant belly, staring at the opposite wall. "Look, the mirror."

On the mantle above the fireplace sat a large mirror, a gift he had bought Silvana shortly after they married. The surface of the mirror was foggy, as if someone had breathed heavily on it. And written on the surface was a simple warning.

Leave.

While you still can.

"It's Areanath's handwriting." Hasani pulled the mirror down from the mantle for a closer inspection.

"Areanath? But he's out hunting. How did his handwriting end up on our mirror?"

"I have no idea." With a corner of his tunic, Hasani wiped the surface of the mirror, trying to clear the words away. But they weren't erased. He rubbed the mirror again, a little harder. Still the words remained. "It's not going away."

There was a knock at the door, and Silvana and Hasani both jumped at the noise. Hasani called out apprehensively, "Yes? Who is it?"

"It's me. Mind if I come in?" Ajax sounded anxious, much as Silvana had.

Both Hasani and Silvana breathed a sigh of relief, and Silvana opened to door to let him in.

"Have you seen Nevina?" Ajax asked after a quick kiss on Silvana's cheek.

"The Matriarch? No, of course not. Why?"

"I think she's missing. She mentioned that she would be leaving today to return to the Coven. I stopped by to see if she wanted some company on the way out of Etritia, but no one was there."

Silvana bit her lip. "Could she had left early in the morning?"

"The door was open, and their belongings were still inside."

Hasani rubbed tiredly at his unshaven chin. "I'd bet she was warned to leave as soon as possible."

"Warned?"

Hasani held the mirror up for Ajax to read, casting a

glance at his wife. Silvana looked anxiously between the two men, one hand rubbing absently at her belly.

"While you still can?" Ajax asked, brows furrowed. "What is this?"

"Look." Hasani rubbed the sleeve of his tunic over the surface roughly and handed the mirror over to Ajax. "It won't go away."

"Magic," Ajax grumbled. "Who wrote it?"

"I don't understand how, but it looks like Areanath's writing."

"You've got to be mistaken. Areanath is on the Last Hunt. And he doesn't use magic." Ajax shook his head in disbelief.

"I'm sure it Areanath's handwriting." Hasani hurried across the room to the chair at his desk. Across the back lay the vest he had worn the day before. Reaching inside, he pulled out the little book Areanath had given him. He flipped the cover open, holding it for Ajax to see. "Look here, see the E and A, in 'sea' and 'leave.' And the W in 'wings' and 'while.' And—"

"Wait, what the hell is this?" Ajax motioned towards the book.

"This?" Hasani closed the book, turning it over in his hands. "It's a book Areanath gave me to look after. Most of it is blank, but what he did write is fairly cryptic. And a bit poor in quality." Hasani would have chuckled if his nerves weren't so frayed.

"Let's see that first page again." Ajax gently set the mirror aside and motioned for the other two to join him in front of the fireplace.

Hasani obliged, opening the book again and offering it out for Ajax and Silvana to see.

Ajax read aloud:

"To destroy the Evil
The King's death brings.
Seek out the Beast with

Deep Sea Wings."

After a moment, Ajax sighed. "I have no idea."

Hasani snorted. "I told you, he's cryptic. It makes no sense. What 'beasts' is he talking about?"

"Not to mention, there are only so many kings. The elven king, the dwarven king, and Areanath himself. And last I heard, none of them has died recently." Ajax shrugged his shoulders. "Perhaps it's just another bad troubadour attempt on Areanath's part."

Hasani shook his head, frowning, "There's more to it than that. I just need some time to puzzle it all out."

"Puzzles and warnings … I don't know what Areanath is thinking, but I'll be glad when he returns and begins to settle back down again. I'm starting to miss the quiet days the summer months usually bring us." Ajax ran a hand through his red hair, glowering.

"When Areanath returns, we'll get to the bottom of this," Hasani said, nodding.

"So we aren't leaving?" Silvana asked warily, casting a glance back at the mirror.

"No," Hasani said. "We stay. And we figure out what this is all supposed to mean."

AREANATH

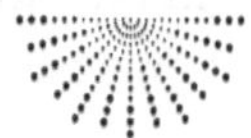

Once the sun had nearly risen, Areanath rose quietly and packed his belongings in silence. He cracked the hand mirror he had used during the night, breaking the thin glass as quietly as possible. He would no longer need it, he was sure, and, once broken, Mothlenor wouldn't be able to use it to trace who Areanath had reached out to. He didn't want Nevina or Hasani put into any danger should Mothlenor realize something was awry. As an extra precaution, Areanath buried it under a few inches of soft dirt. He left his tent to see Mothlenor brushing his hands over the dappled mare Areanath had ridden the day before. She seemed agitated, jerking her head around and scraping the ground anxiously with one hoof.

"Is she alright?" Areanath eased towards the mare, running a hand over her neck soothingly.

"Something in the trees spooked her, that's all." Mothlenor turned away from the horse, leaving her to Areanath. "I've already used a calming spell on her. She should be fine momentarily."

Areanath continued to stroke the horse gently. He could feel the power of Mothlenor's spell where his hand stroked her. He seemed to be telling the truth, for within a minute the mare was as calm and placid as ever.

They packed their camp as quickly as it had been made, Mothlenor using his skills to break down and refold their tents in little time. The fire was doused and covered, and Areanath and his brother were back in the saddle and ready to leave after only a few minutes.

"Where are the others?" Areanath searched the small clearing, surprised to realize that the four strangers had managed to saddle their horses and slip into the woods without his noticing.

"They've gone ahead. They'll find us again on the trail." Mothlenor clicked his tongue, urging his horse forward. "No worries, Areanath."

Areanath followed his brother, suppressing the wave of anxiety that rolled over him at Mothlenor's words. As Mothlenor led them back to the game trail, Areanath imagined one of the silent assassins appearing suddenly at his side and stabbing him while his brother looked on. But when the four men appeared a few minutes later, it was on the trail in front of them. Their horses stamped the ground impatiently and tossed their manes, but their riders held them fast and allowed Mothlenor and Areanath to pass before bringing up the rear once more.

The day continued to stretch on, the air around them becoming warm and heavy as the sun climbed. No one spoke. Areanath could feel the stares of the men at his back, and their silence continued to disturb him. Their horses continued to act out, whinnying loudly and stamping the ground. After some time, Areanath's horse became equally agitated, despite Mothlenor's calming spell. Areanath risked renewing the spell, but his mare continued to protest until Areanath could hardly control her anymore. Only Mothlenor's horse seemed unaffected by whatever was distressing the other animals.

Finally, his emotional exhaustion at its peak, Areanath called out to his brother. "Mothlenor, wait."

Mothlenor stopped, turning his horse to get a better look at Areanath.

Areanath took a deep breath, willing his hands to stop shaking on the reins. "If you're going to kill me, please just do it now. I grow tired of waiting."

Mothlenor was silent for a moment, an eyebrow raised in surprise. Finally, he gave a quiet chuckle. He turned his horse forward again, calling over his shoulder. "Just a little longer, brother. We are nearly there."

It had never occurred to Areanath that they were headed to a certain destination, only that Mothlenor was trying to put as much distance between themselves and the castle as possible. Knowing that there was a definite end to this journey caused his panic to rise further. He sucked in a lungful of air and craned his neck up to look to the sky. But this deep into the woods the trees grew too densely together, and what little sun peeked down through the treetops was not enough to calm him. His skin began to crawl, and his heart beat faster in his chest, the pounding growing louder in his ears. His palms grew sweaty, slipping on the reins. Bile started to rise in his throat as full panic set in. And still the four men behind him continued to stare at his back, their gaze making the hairs on the back of his neck stand. Areanath wondered if he might collapse from sheer panic right there.

Suddenly they were in a small clearing. Areanath took a deep breath, feeling the sun on his skin again, and a wave of comfort washed over him.

In the center of the clearing stood a long table, crumbling with age and disuse. Areanath instantly recognized it as an altar, though it had been years since he had last seen one. As he jumped down from the mare and stepped closer to the table, he felt the buzz of strong magic in the air. Most of it, he could tell, was old magic. It hung in the air like a heavy damp, and he could almost taste the ancient energy. But some of the magic staining the altar was much more recent, and the power of that newer magic covered the altar like an oily smut, darker than night itself. Areanath pulled his hand away from the altar, disgusted.

"So this is it, then," he said, wiping his hands on the inside of his robe. "This is where you will kill me."

Mothlenor did not answer, instead looking down on his brother from atop his horse. "Let's be honest with each other, shall we?"

Areanath nodded. "Sounds fair enough." The four men surrounded the clearing, remaining just inside the tree line. Areanath suddenly felt at a disadvantage. And yet, he always had been.

"Tell me," Mothlenor started, "how long have you known I was planning to kill you?"

"Since you asked me to go hunting with you."

"And you've feigned ignorance this whole time? Clever, brother. Perhaps you are not half the fool I thought you were. Although I must admit I'm surprised you came without a fuss." Mothlenor laughed.

Areanath was not amused. "If you want to kill me, it will happen. I suppose I knew there was really no point in fussing." He arched an eyebrow at his brother. "Now you can answer a question for me. Why wait so long? Why did you not kill me last night? Or last year? You've had many opportunities over the years, I'm sure."

"Perhaps I have a soft spot for my own flesh and blood. Or perhaps I wasn't sure I wanted you dead."

Now Areanath did laugh. "I thought we said no lies, brother."

Mothlenor eyed him for a moment before answering quietly. "I can be compassionate, Areanath."

Areanath had no answer. Perhaps Mothlenor believed it,

but Areanath couldn't be sure. It had been too long since he had seen his brother's compassionate side. He wasn't sure it could be found again.

Mothlenor jumped down from his horse and stood with his brother over the altar. He brushed away a layer of dust and dirt, his hand caressing the top almost lovingly. "It is beautiful, in a crude way."

"It is far older than the both of us together. No one has worshiped here in a long time. There have been no gods to worship since long before the Great War."

"True. The Great Ones have long been dead and buried, and even the bones of their last believers have gone to dust. I have only been here myself a few times. And I do not use it for worship. I use it for Calling." Mothlenor smiled, the first genuine one Areanath recalled seeing in a long time.

His brother's smile filled him with dread.

The dark power soiling the surface of the altar ... had that been his brother's doing? "Who have you Called, Mothlenor?"

Mothlenor motioned around the clearing. "I Called them."

Areanath followed his brother's gaze. The four men still stood guard around the clearing, silent as ever before.

"Wraiths. They're Shadows." He had a sudden realization. "This morning, my horse ... There was nothing in the trees, she was afraid of them. You've been using calming spells on all the horses. And you didn't want dogs with us because they would have given the wraiths away ..."

"Very good, brother." Mothlenor smirked. "But these aren't normal wraiths, or they would have faded from the land of the living long ago."

"These are the souls of those who died in battle. Souls of men who died in the Great War." Areanath shook his head in disbelief.

Mothlenor shrugged. "Perhaps. But you should know as

well as I do that a wraith can be made from the soul of any murdered man." Mothlenor made a small circle, eyes moving from wraith to wraith. "These do seem to be a bit more … voracious, so perhaps you are right."

"It has been so long, and yet there are still so many." Areanath was petrified, staring at each of the four wraiths in turn.

"Yes, and I would like to have a few more." Areanath turned to Mothlenor, confused, and his brother's eyes glinted cruelly. "You see, Areanath, I don't wish to kill you, unless needed. But …" he sighed, "if needed, I will take your soul, and fashion myself a new wraith. And then the five of you will feast on your corpse."

"You don't wish to kill me? What do you want then, Mothlenor? My throne?"

"It is not your throne I want, Areanath. Only your power. Your people trust you, and your men would follow you anywhere. With my skill, and your army, we could destroy those who oppose us, and take everything we could ever need for ourselves."

"Mothlenor, we are at peace," Areanath pleaded. "We have no one that opposes us. Not elves, not dwarves, there is no one."

"Then you will not join me?"

"No."

"Then you will die." With a movement almost too fast for Areanath to see, Mothlenor wrapped a hand around his neck, lifting him off the ground. Through bared teeth, he growled a spell while Areanath gasped for air. When nothing happened, Mothlenor tightened his grip and repeated the spell. Areanath felt the magic flowing through Mothlenor's fingers and into his body, searching. Again nothing happened. Mothlenor loosened his grip on Areanath's neck but did not let go. "My spell isn't working. What did that Coven bitch do?"

"Nevina … did nothing." Areanath struggled. "I did."

"You did?" Mothlenor laughed. "You can't light a candle with your magic, Areanath." Mothlenor tightened his grip again.

Areanath could feel his mind slipping away as his lungs burned and his vision faded. He summoned what energy he could and sent it radiating out around him. Suddenly, he could breathe, and when his vision cleared he found himself lying in the dirt in front of the altar. He sat up. The world was spinning around him, and spots danced in his eyes, but he found his brother. The blast had knocked Mothlenor back several feet and into a tree, but Mothlenor was getting to his feet much faster than Areanath was. Using the altar as a crutch, Areanath scrambled to his feet and turned to look at his brother.

There was blood flowing from Mothlenor's nose, but he paid it no attention. His expression was flat, his eyes shining with cruel light. "You can wield magic, Areanath? I have indeed underestimated you. Will you still not help me?"

"No, Mothlenor," Areanath managed through his bruised throat.

"You would still deny me? Our realm is growing weaker by the day, and you would sit back and let the heathens take what we men have fought for?"

"There are no heathens, brother. The races have lived together peacefully since the Great War, and they could continue to do so if you would just let them be." Areanath straightened himself, his weak knee almost buckling underneath him. "You would endanger the lives of my people, of our people, for a threat that does not exist. And what of the other races? How many of them will you need to eradicate before you feel you have achieved complete dominion? I am no fool. I know what you plan to do with my throne. And I cannot allow it."

Mothlenor smirked. "You cannot allow it? You will be

dead, and I'll no longer have to listen to your pathetic claims of peace and cooperation. You refuse to see the danger you have left us in. The dwarves would sooner knife us in the back than shake our hand, and the elves are even worse! They would say many a pretty word about 'trust' and 'diplomacy' to our faces, yet they plot to take our kingdom away from us behind closed doors. And still you remain blinded by your endless faith."

"You are the only one that is blind, Mothlenor."

"Very well. If I can have neither your help, nor your soul, I can still have your life." Mothlenor drew a long dagger from his robes. "Will you fight me then?"

"No. Just kill me. I am tired." Areanath sighed weakly, struggling to stay on his feet.

"Very well." Mothlenor's figure blurred, and suddenly he was standing in front of Areanath. In one swift motion, the dagger was plunged into his side, directly into his heart.

The bastard can manipulate time, Areanath thought.

Areanath fell to his knees, clutching the wound in his side. He felt the warmth of his blood for a moment, then a deep chill like nothing he had known before.

Mothlenor knelt, reaching for him, guiding him down to the earth. His brother's eyes never left his, even as his own eyesight began to go dark.

"Brother," he tried to say, but the sound he made was unintelligible to his ears.

"It's over now, Areanath."

He felt himself passing, each breath shallower than the last, and, as his last moments turned into his last seconds, one thought repeated itself over and over in Areanath's fading mind.

He can have my life. But not my soul.

He can have my life.

But not my soul.

othlenor spotted a thin, silvery wisp escaping from Areanath's lips and clutched angrily for it. "No, no. This is supposed to stay. If I cannot take it, it should stay. What have you done?" He looked down at Areanath, but his brother's eyes were already cold. Mothlenor growled, watching the silvery wisp float up from Areanath's mouth and disappear in the treetops. "What have you done?" he snarled. But his brother's soul was gone.

A moment passed. Mothlenor sighed, releasing the hand that Areanath had wrapped around his own and getting to his feet. "I seem to have broken my nose." The clearing was silent in answer. "I should get cleaned up. I have a rather pressing meeting with the Coven's Matriarch." He paused, looking down on his brother's body. Finally, he turned away. "Take care of this mess."

Mothlenor led his horse away. An eerie slithering broke the quiet stillness of the clearing and when Mothlenor chanced a glance over his shoulder, it was to see four long shadows sliding over the ground, rushing to cover Areanath's body in darkness.

23

NEVINA

Nevina's breathing came in ragged gasps, the foul air gagging her even as she struggled to fill her lungs. She was doubled over, the muscles in her throat working as she tried to scream. Hot fire lanced through her body, momentarily blinding her with pain. She was sure, for a moment, that her heart had stopped and that she was dying.

And then, in an instant, the pain was gone.

No lingering aches, no fading muscle spasms.

Just gone.

She tried to sit up, wiping spittle from her lips, but a wave of nausea sent her scurrying as far as her chains allowed her before she retched. She could taste blood, where she had inadvertently bitten her tongue. After a moment the nausea passed, and she crawled back to the wall she had been chained to.

What just happened?

The pain had been sudden and unexpected. One moment, she had been sitting on the floor of a dark and filthy dungeon, trying to slip her already chafed and raw hands through the cuffs they were in, and the next she was doubled over, spasms agonizing every muscle in her body as her blood turned to fire inside her veins.

And then it was gone, just as quickly as it had come.

Nevina sat against the wall, not daring to move, afraid that torturous pain might come back again. Had she activated some spell by trying to slip her bonds? She tried again to probe her surroundings, but was unable to perceive anything. She could tell there was magic in the dungeon, she could almost taste it, but the cuffs on her wrists blocked her arcane abilities. She was alone, defenseless, and chained to a wall in a filthy dungeon.

She could only hope her girls were better off.

After the Dragon Door had shut behind them, their captors had led them through a labyrinth of tunnels and hallways. Nevina had hoped that if they were to be held prisoner, they would at least be held together. But once they had reached the foul-smelling pits, Nevina was separated from her girls. She had fought, even kicked a man in the groin and had her arm around his throat, ready to squeeze the life out of him. But Layle called out to her, those blue eyes burning again in the torchlight, and had told her it was alright. She had told her to let them go. And with Layle's words, Nevina had felt utterly defeated. They already knew their fates. She could do nothing for them.

That had been some time ago. How long, exactly, she couldn't be sure. There were no torches, and no way to sense the passing of time. There was only darkness, her cuffs, and now the fear of that awful agony returning.

Nevina gathered her courage and tried again to slip her cuffs. After a moment, she stopped. There was no searing pain running through her body. Only pain from her wrists, which were now cut and bleeding again. It hadn't been a spell she'd triggered that doubled her over only moments before.

Fear settled over her, making her stomach roll with nausea again. Could the pain have been from Areanath's death? An effect not from a spell she'd triggered, but that he had? Areanath had said she might not feel his passing.

But magic is tricky.

She couldn't use magic to tell if her fears were true, not with the cuffs cutting into her wrists every time she tried to channel energy, but there was an emptiness in her soul that told her she was right.

The darkness seemed even heavier around her, and she wept.

Her first round of tears had only just dried when she heard footsteps echoing close by. Torchlight glowed dimly under the wooden door, and she could hear the unmistakable jingling of keys just outside. Nevina got to her unsteady feet, hoping against hope that someone had come to release her. Within seconds, the lock clicked and the door was shoved open roughly. Three men entered, including the tall knight that had led her captors. They'd taken off their helms, apparently satisfied that either the dimness or the cuffs would prevent her from Seeing anything about them. They might have been right, but Nevina was sure no amount of Sight would make her any less afraid of them.

"The king asked us to keep an eye on you. He'll be on his way back soon, I expect," the larger one said. His pale face was ghastly in the odd flickering of the torch he'd brought with him. "He did say he wanted you alive, which is a damn shame. He even said he wanted you to be left in good condition. But I think he and I might differ a bit on the meaning of 'good condition.'" He smiled, an evil smirk half cast in shadow. "And he said nothing about your girls." He shrugged. "Which is good, considering you're now two little witches short."

Nevina bit her lip, stifling a cry. Her heart skipped several beats. What had they done to her girls?

"The whole lot of us all had our turns with the little ones. But my friends and I, well ..." He smirked again. "I suppose our appetites are a little more voracious than most." He motioned to one of the men with him. This one pulled a long dagger out of his belt, his glittering eyes fixed on her. Nevina tried to run, but could only get so far with the chains digging into her wrists. And the man with the knife was faster than her. He grabbed her by the hair, slipping the dagger under her chin. She yelped at the cold touch of metal against her neck, but the man restraining her only chuckled in her ear. The larger one stepped in front of her. With one quick motion, he yanked the veil from her face, taking several strands of her hair with it. That sinister smile twisted his lips again. "Good for you that you're a pretty one." He took a half step back, untying the front of his breeches. "It'd be easier to get away with killing an ugly witch."

With only a quick glance from the larger man, the one restraining her pushed her into the wall, face first. Her forehead hit the stone with a jarring smack, and Nevina struggled vainly as the man stretched her chained arms above her head and touched the tip of the knife to her ribs.

"You just said you can't kill me," Nevina pleaded with him, turning her head until one cheekbone pressed against the cold wall.

His muddy brown eyes met hers. "I can make you bleed." His voice was reedy compared to the larger man's, but his words sent a cold chill down her spine.

The larger man kicked her feet apart, and she tried she break away as her skirt was lifted, but the tip of the dagger dug painfully into her flesh and she stopped writhing.

Nevina caught sight of the third man, silent and unmoving by the door. "Please. Don't let them do this." A drop of moisture fell onto her raised arm, and she realized that she was crying.

"Careful, witch," the larger man crooned in her ear. With a few tugs, he tore away her underclothes. "That one likes it when they beg."

And his weight suddenly pressed against her, pinning her against the stone wall as he forced himself inside her.

At first she fought, but each movement earned her a cut from the dagger or a punch to the ribs. She called on her skills again and again, but still she could not defend herself with her magic. Finally, too bruised and bloody to move, she stopped fighting, calling instead on the Great Ones to aid her.

But they could not hear her, so deep within the dungeons.

Layle sat alone in her cell, shaking hands draped in her lap. The room stank of blood, and the smell of it made her sick, but she could do nothing to rid herself of it. She could hardly be bothered to breathe.

They had separated the Matriarch from the rest of them soon after they had found themselves inside the dungeons. Layle knew even then what might happen, but she had urged her mother to go. She had already tried and failed to work spells around her cuffs, but had thought that they might still be able to fight back.

She had been wrong.

She and the rest of the girls had been led down to the far end of a row of cells before being separated into two groups and locked in adjoining rooms. The screams from the next room had been unearthly and terrifying. Arella had started to cry almost immediately, cowering behind Layle. Millie pounded on the wooden door, screaming for them to stop hurting the other girls. Layle tried using every defensive spell she knew, but the cuffs stopped her each time, their cold metal piercing and digging into her flesh. Millie screamed until her throat was hoarse, and her hands bled from splinters digging into the flesh of her palms, but the noises from the next room continued.

Finally, the sounds stopped.

The door to their cell was unlocked, and Millie threw herself at the first man to enter, but she was batted away like an annoying insect.

Arella was pulled from Layle's grasp, and Millie once again tried to intervene. She was once again batted away.

Layle tried again to call on her magic, hoping she could still save them. But nothing worked. She was powerless.

Arella was thrown to her back on the floor, and Layle was forced to her hands and knees close by. Her sister's terrified eyes locked onto hers as one small hand shot out to reach for her.

Layle grasped Arella's hand tightly, unwilling to let go.

She held on when a man fell onto her sister's frail body, covering all but her golden hair.

She held on while her sister was ravaged, Arella's grip tightening with every thrust.

She held on when the man pressed a knife to Arella's throat and cut it open.

She held on while her sister's grip weakened.

She was finally forced to let go when someone grabbed Arella's body by one ankle and dragged her from the cell, leaving a trail of wet blood. It was only then that Layle realized that Millie lay in a similar state nearby, the brown eyes always hidden behind her veil now dead and distant. She was also dragged from the cell, a second trail of crimson marking her path.

Only Layle was left, sitting against the door, staring at the trail her sister had left behind.

"Layle?" It was Kall's voice, coming from the hall. The girl must have pressed herself to the door to be heard.

"Yes?" Her voice was hoarse. Had she screamed too?

"It's Lilith. She's bleeding badly. I … I think they put a knife in her …" Kall's voice trailed.

"We can't heal her," Layle said numbly. "How is Nala?"

"She's in shock."

"And you?"

"Better than Nala."

For now, Layle almost said.

"How are Millie and Arella?"

Layle hesitated. But what use was it to lie?

"They're dead."

Layle could hear Kall beginning to cry, but she ignored it. She could only stare at the blood on the floor, hearing the sound of her sister screaming her name, over and over again.

With each remembered scream, Layle called on her magic again, relishing the pain the cuffs brought. Her own blood began to trickle down into her open palms.

She would find a way around them.

She would find a way to break her bonds.

For Arella.

2 5

HASANI

Hasani was once more in his rooms, Ajax and Silvana clustered around him by the fire. The mantle was still bare, though the mirror that had troubled them this morning was now blank. Silvana was uncomfortable with the idea of putting it back in its usual spot, and Hasani couldn't blame her for her unease. "Any sign of the Matriarch yet, Ajax?"

The worry lines in Ajax's face only deepened. "I still haven't found her, though a farmer not far from where she had been staying insisted that he saw her and her girls being led away by several men-at-arms. Which could mean one of two things—either she received the same warning you did, and found an entourage to lead her out of the city, or—"

"Or she has been taken captive," Hasani finished. "Something foul is afoot, and I don't like it. The timing couldn't be worse, with both Areanath and his brother absent." Hasani was silent for a moment, one hand ruffling his unruly hair. He turned to Ajax, whose eyes were swollen with weariness and worry. "As King's Regent, I have the power to call the King's Guard into action …"

"How many men can I send to search for her?" Ajax asked, sudden hope lighting his face.

"As many as you need." Hasani sighed, rubbing at his face with one hand. *Great Ones take it, of course this had to happen while Areanath was away.* "Etritia can do without the King's Guard for a short time."

"I'll start gathering my men," Ajax said, turning on his heel and heading for the door. "I'll devise a plan, and we'll set out within the next hour."

"Leave the planning to me, Ajax," Hasani called to his brother's back. "You collect the men and meet me in the Great Hall in twenty minutes. We'll be out there searching for the Matriarch faster that way."

Ajax turned and gave him a curt nod before disappearing into the hallway beyond.

"You're not planning on going out to search with them, are you?" Silvana's voice had lost most of the timidity the morning's scare had given her, but her eyes were still wide, and her hands clung tightly to his when he took them.

"If Ajax asks me, I will go." Hasani pulled Silvana's hands to his lips and kissed her fingertips. "I want to make sure the Matriarch is well, and I have a duty as King's Regent to do what I can for all of Etritia."

The answer didn't seem to please her, but his wife nodded and gave him a gentle kiss on one cheek. "Be careful, Hasani."

Hasani made for the Great Hall, concern for the Matriarch making his footsteps hurried. Had anything like this happened before? Men leading the Matriarch through Etritia's farmland? Ajax and Areanath had both failed to convince Nevina to allow an escort of King's Guards to lead her through Etritia. Nevina was just as stubbornly inflexible on that subject as her predecessor had been.

Yet now she had half a dozen men surrounding her and her followers?

Hasani sucked in a sharp breath as his steps quickened further. He should have acted sooner. *Areanath would have acted sooner.*

Hasani made only a single stop on the way to the Great Hall. There was a small archive room, little more than a study lined with shelves of books and rolled parchments, not far from his destination. The small room did little to rival the great Azimar Archives, with its huge halls filled with the whole history of Azimar herself, but there was still a great deal of important knowledge tucked away in that little room.

A few quick words exchanged with the old man inside, a servant by the name of Kas, and Hasani left with a long parchment rolled and tucked carefully under one arm.

Hasani didn't have to wait long for Ajax to reach the Great Hall.

Armed King's Guard were already there when Hasani opened the door and made his way to the front of the room, close to the stepped dais that supported the throne, and more men trickled in with each passing moment. Some wore heavy armor, having been pulled from their posts, but most wore the long black cloak of the King's Guard and a belted sword over lighter clothing. They looked serious, even the younger ones, their faces lined but unafraid. Hasani tried to count the faces he saw, but lost track as more men entered.

Ajax intends to leave no stone unturned ...

The door opened again and First Knight Dars entered, Ajax a long stride behind him. "Attend!"

The knights in the room snapped straight, left hand on the swords at their hips, right arms crossed over their chests, fists over their hearts. Hasani found himself standing a little straighter, catching Ajax's eye.

"Let's hear your plan, Hasani."

With a snap of his wrist, Hasani unfurled the map Kas had found for him. He pinned one corner with a hand, Dars catching the other and pinning it with a tankard of ale a passing servant girl offered him. Near the northern edge of the map was the castle, pressed against the Northern Mountains. Bold letters marked the empty space beyond the mountains as the 'Unknown Lands.' To the south, desert for more than a hundred miles, then the Free Cities, and finally the coast. The Felgar Woods and Mountains were to the east, land shared between the woodland elves and men. And to the west, the Knife, the river that marked the end of Azimar and the beginning of the strange land of the Vyris, where the high elves lived.

Hasani's gaze roamed over the Etritian lands on the map. "Where was the Matriarch staying?"

Ajax brought his finger down on a spot to the southeast, along the main road that led from the farms to Etritia's main gate. "Here."

"And they were headed in which direction?"

"Southwest." Ajax traced a line on the map—the main road, headed away from the castle.

Hasani cursed, taking up where Ajax had stopped and following the curve of the main road as it continued southwest. "To the King's Bridge?"

Ajax made a sound like an angry grunt, turning his back on the map and pacing a few feet away.

Hasani turned his attention to Dars, "How many men have you called for?"

"Sixty. There will be a few stragglers, but the bulk of them are here."

Sixty men … "Shall we split in half, then? Send thirty to the King's Bridge, another thirty to search the farms to the south?"

Dars nodded. "A good plan and simple enough. But the Knife is not so deep this long into the dry months. It could be forded anywhere between the castle and the King's Bridge. Best to split into thirds, and send the last twenty to search the Knife."

"As you say, First Knight."

Ajax stopped his pacing, turning back to Hasani. "And if

she is on the other side of the Knife? If she is being led into Vyris?"

Hasani let out a sigh, considering. Finally, he met Ajax's worried stare. "Areanath and the Vyrisian king are good friends. I do not think our elven neighbors would be too upset by our intrusion into their lands, so long as we remain friendly and explain ourselves to any elf we might meet." Hasani chewed on his lip, hoping he wouldn't regret that choice. "Areanath would do the same, I think."

But sending a party of armed knights into Vyris? Even twenty might be mistaken for a show of force ...

"Then we'll move out." Ajax turned to Dars, "First Knight, you take the party searching the Knife. I will lead the men searching the farmlands. Hasani—"

"I will go with the knights heading for the King's Bridge," Hasani finished for him. Ajax didn't say it, but Hasani knew why he had left those men to him. A party of armed knights led by the king's adviser would be much better received than one led by the commander or First Knight.

"Then we leave now. Let's go." Ajax turned back towards the doors to the hall, his men moving to follow him out.

"That would be unwise."

He had slipped in unnoticed, and only now stepped out of the shadows to be seen by the gathered men. At the sight of him, hushed whispers flurried through the hall. Hasani could tell his nose had been broken, and his riding cape was torn. His clothes and boots were caked in dust and dirt, and several scratches covered his hands and face. "Mothlenor? You've returned so soon? What happened?"

The gathered King's Guard made way for Mothlenor, who walked briskly through the hall towards Hasani and Ajax. He was visibly angered, his dark eyes flashing, each hurried step reverberating in the hall as a furious beat. "We were ambushed."

A few men gasped; more whispers filled the hall, angry

now. Mothlenor rounded the end of the long table and came to a stop at the foot of the dais.

Hasani was stunned. "Am-ambushed? Where is your lord brother?"

At the mention of Areanath, Mothlenor crumbled. His angry eyes softened and his shoulders slumped, his face pallid. "Areanath is dead."

A ripple went through the gathered crowd as each man looked to his neighbor. There was a crash from the far corner of the room, and several heads turned to see two serving girls collecting broken mugs from a dropped tray. One of the women was staring at Mothlenor, open-mouthed and wide-eyed. Whispers rolled through the assembled knights, growing louder with each passing heartbeat.

Hasani caught Ajax's eye. *Areanath, dead? Surely it couldn't be true ...*

Ignoring the noise, Mothlenor continued. "My brother fell ill on the first evening of our trip. I tried to help him, thinking it was just some food illness." He took a slow step towards the throne, the sound of it echoing around them. "When he did not recover by the following morning, I realized it was something much more serious. Someone had poisoned him." Another step. "I did not have the necessary ingredients for a curative, so we doubled back." Mothlenor took a deep, shaky breath before continuing. "Not long after, we were ambushed by several ... demons. Monsters summoned through dark arcane crafts. They were terrible, and terrifying. We tried to defend ourselves, but weapons did nothing to hurt them. My own magic only angered them more. I tried to protect my brother, but I was knocked from my horse." He had reached his brother's throne, which he collapsed into. "I watched my brother fall and I could do nothing. The other men with us died as well. I barely managed an escape." He took another shaky breath. "King Areanath is dead."

The men were silent. Hasani was stunned, his mouth working wordlessly. It was Ajax who managed to voice what they were all thinking. "Who would do such a thing? Summon dark creatures to kill our king?"

"It was that Coven witch, Nevina!" Mothlenor shouted angrily, pounding a fist on the arm of the throne.

More angry whispers went through the crowd. Hasani heard Ajax curse next to him, saw his friend stiffen in anger and glare at Mothlenor. Hasani moved to block Mothlenor from seeing Ajax's angry response to the accusation. "How can you be sure it was the Matriarch? She and Areanath are friends, and she doesn't seem a witch to me."

"She is a witch, just as her predecessor was. And she is a powerful one. That is why she was made Matriarch. And she came here not to reaffirm the treaties between the Coven and the king, but to kill my brother and myself so that the Coven might take over our kingdom. She was with him the night before our parting, was she not? You and the commander escorted her to my brother's chambers yourself, or have you forgotten?" Mothlenor glared accusingly down on Hasani and Ajax.

Hasani turned to his friend. Ajax's anger had subsided to confusion and regret. "I'm sorry," Hasani whispered. "We did not know."

"Nor did I, and I offered to announce her to my brother and to lead her safely back to her quarters after their meeting. If you are to be named an accomplice, then I should be as well." Mothlenor stood. "Any and all blame for my brother's murder is to be placed on the Coven witch. I understand she has conveniently gone missing?"

Hasani spoke up. "We've heard it said from a farmer that she was being led southwest by a retinue of armed men. We had assumed she was being taken captive, but under the circumstances, it seems that she was instead being escorted home."

"We were about to head out on a search party. They're likely headed for the King's Bridge," Ajax finished.

"Good. How many men are going with you, Commander?"

"These sixty here with us."

"Take thirty of them. The rest are to search the woods to the southeast. I have little hope that my brother's body can be found and returned to me, but there may still be some small miracles to be had in this dark hour. Now go."

Ajax and his men turned to leave the Hall, but Hasani lingered for a moment more. "And what of me? What would you have me do?"

"Spread the news of my brother's death. And prepare for his funeral … and a coronation."

"A coronation?"

"My brother is dead with no sons of his own. As of now, Hasani, I am your king."

Ajax rode quietly down the main road to the castle, mind whirling. It had been nearly a full day since Mothlenor had announced Areanath's death and had accused Nevina, but the Matriarch and her troupe of young followers had yet to be found. Ajax had hoped that riding with the party that had searched along the Knife would give him the chance to speak with Nevina again. To figure out why she had done what Mothlenor was accusing her of. Or even *if* she had done it. He tried to reconcile Mothlenor's accusations with his knowledge of Nevina, but it only left him confused.

Their beloved king was dead, his body missing, and the king's brother attested that Nevina was a witch, capable of summoning the demons that had struck him down.

But Ajax loved Nevina and couldn't bring himself to label her a murderer. Nevina also cared for Areanath. She had confessed to him that she and Areanath were trying to conceive an heir together.

And she promised me ... She wouldn't have made that promise if she had no intention of returning to the castle. Would she?

But until the Matriarch was found, Ajax only had Mothlenor's word. So he continued the search, even after sending his men away to join the other party still searching for Areanath's body. Conflicted, he argued back and forth with himself. Mothlenor was no doubt cruel, but he was the king's brother, and would have fought to protect Areanath against the arcane ambush. Nevina was loving and kindhearted, but there had been moments when her smiles seemed forced, and her laugh sounded hollow. He suspected she had known something about Areanath's death, even if she had not been the one to send demons after him.

Finally, as the sun began to set again, he made his way back to the castle.

He passed the farm of the little old man that had told him where Nevina had been headed, and continued up the road towards the castle. But he stopped when he heard a far-off shout behind him. Turning in the saddle, he saw the farmer rushing across his fields towards him. Ajax jumped down from the saddle and picked his way around rows of tall vegetables to meet the man.

"I'm sorry, sir, to cause you trouble. I wasn't sure you would come back this way again." The old man was breathing heavily and sweat stained his face and stuck his shirt to his chest.

"It's alright. What do you need of me?"

"Well, we'd heard some rumors. And now my wife is upset—I can't get her to stop crying. Is it true what they're saying … that the king is dead?" His small face was creased with wrinkles, and his dull eyes filled with sorrow.

"I'm afraid the rumors are true. He died while hunting." Ajax couldn't bring himself to mention the circumstances of Areanath's death, holding on to some hope that Nevina was innocent.

The old man grimaced, shaking his head. "The wife certainly won't be happy about this. He was a good king and well loved. And what of the Matriarch? Have you found her yet?"

Had word of Nevina's involvement circulated too? "No, the Matriarch is still missing."

The old man shook his head again. "Not good at all. My wife and I were lucky enough to be in the market when she came through with her girls to see the king. It was an amazing sight." The old man smiled, his sun-weathered face beaming. But his smile quickly faded, replaced with anxiety. "My wife is worried about them. When I told her about the Matriarch and her girls being bound and led away—"

"Wait." Ajax's heart skipped a beat. "Did you say they had been bound?"

The old man stammered, "Y-yes, they were bound. Big metal cuffs round the wrists of each one." The man lifted both arms, fists balled for emphasis. "Did I not say so before?"

Ajax cursed. So they had been taken captive, not escorted away. The old man was apologizing profusely, even falling to his knees to beg forgiveness. Ajax hushed him with a wave of his hand. "Please, no more apologies. Just help me understand. They were bound, taken captive, and led to the Knife?"

The man shook his head vigorously. "No, no, no. Not to the Knife. To the castle."

"To the castle? You said they were headed southwest. The castle gate is to the northeast of here." Ajax was frustrated, angry now that perhaps the man was making a fool of him.

The man shook his head again. "No, no. The main gate to the castle is to the northeast of here." He pointed in the direction in which Ajax had been headed a moment before.

"Yes, but you said they were headed southwest, back where I came from. Back to the Knife."

The man sighed, apparently just as frustrated as Ajax was. "Sir, they wouldn't call it the main gate if it was the only one.

There are others, dotted along the castle walls. To get to those you got to follow the main road, headed southwest."

Ajax cursed again. The man was right. He turned towards the castle, staring at the walls. The castle sat with its back against the sheer mountain face, the walls encircling both the castle and the surrounding city. He had only ever used the main gate, which stood along the northeastern section of the wall, because it was closer to both the castle and the tower of the King's Guard. But directly to the north of the old man's farm was another gate, sitting on the southern curve of the wall. Ajax eyed the curve of the castle wall, first southwest, then back up to the northwest, where he knew a third gate could be found. Those gates were seldom used, as they both now opened directly into the housing district. But they were still there. He turned back in the direction he had ridden from. The main road continued southwest, to the Knife, where they had all assumed Nevina had gone. But, sure enough, there was a fork in the road, one that led northwest, to that third gate. He had ridden right past it without giving it a second thought.

"They didn't go to the Knife. They went back into the city." He turned back to the farmer who was still kneeling in the dirt. "Have you told anyone else this?"

"No, no, sir."

"And you were not seen by the men that took the Matriarch?"

The old man shook his head quickly. "No. I was here, in my vegetables, harvesting. My own wife can't find me most times, and she knows where to look."

"Good." He helped the man to his feet then untied a leather pouch from his belt. He pressed it into the man's hands, adding fiercely, "If anyone comes asking, you tell them you saw them heading directly for the Knife. Do you understand me?"

The old man stammered, "Y-yes, sir." He held the pouch

out for Ajax to take again. "We don't need the money, Commander ..."

"Keep it," Ajax said, thoughts already on his next steps. "Keep it, and remember me, should I need your help again."

"Of course, Commander," the old man said quietly. "The name's Martyn," he said, bowing to Ajax. "The wife is Darla, though most around here call her Nana, myself included." He clutched the leather pouch close to his chest. "You call on us if you need anything, Commander."

Ajax nodded, already stepping around plants to make his way back to his horse. "Thank you, Martyn. I will."

Ajax could feel Martyn's eyes on him as he climbed into the saddle and took up the reins again. He could only hope that the old man would keep his word. For now, his thoughts were focused only on finding Nevina, before anyone else did.

27

NEVINA

Nevina lay on the floor, her cheek pressed against the cold stones. Her body was cut and broken, and her stomach ached with hunger and nausea, but she was thankful to still be alive. After being ravaged by the three men who had come to visit her, she had drifted into a dreamless sleep, where the pain of her wounds could not reach her. Perhaps it was the shock, or simply her body shutting down to begin healing, but Nevina was grateful for those few hours of death-like slumber.

On waking, she found herself once more alone, and tried to make sense of her injuries. The front of her dress had been torn to ribbons, her chest completely exposed. Her thighs, arms, and stomach were covered in cuts, some long and shallow, some deeper. The floor was slick with blood and seed, the smell of it filling her nose. She couldn't move without searing pain coursing over her body. They had left her lying on the stone floor, and she had hardly moved since, only rolling from her back to her side. Her body was too weak, and her heart was too broken to care. After some time, she gave up, lying limply on the floor, secretly praying for death.

I could be with my girls, she thought, mind drifting. *I could be with Areanath. And the pain would stop.*

When she awoke again, it was to the sound of the heavy door to her cell creaking open. Two women entered, servants by the look of them. One carried a tray laden with a steaming kettle, a bowl, and a stack of neatly folded linens. The other woman, the older of the two, carried a torch in one hand and a small wooden tub in the other.

Nevina sat up, propping herself up with both arms, and watched the two women. The older one hardly moved, only slamming the door shut and setting the torch into a sconce on the wall. The younger one slipped closer to where Nevina half sat on the floor before setting the tray onto the ground and holding the bowl out for Nevina to take.

She hesitated, looking between the women before carefully taking the bowl. She caught the faint scent of winterberries and creeping wort. *Common ingredients for potions of persuasion ...*

"Drink it." The older woman's voice was sharp and demanding. The younger woman said nothing, shifting her gaze away from Nevina and quickly backing away towards the door.

Nevina drank. She almost gagged on the brew. Though it had been mixed with a thin broth, there was no mistaking that it was a potion. But the liquid was warm, and her stomach ached with hunger. Whatever these women wanted to do to her, she had already been through worse.

When the bowl was empty, Nevina held it out for the younger woman to take. The cuffs chaining her to the wall were undone, the small key disappearing into a fold of the older woman's dress. She continued to hold her arms out to the women, hoping the arcane cuffs might be removed as well, but the older woman sneered at her.

"Not those. Once those are on, only the king can remove them."

Nevina let her arms drop back to her sides, the heavy potion already making her docile and weak-minded.

She was led to the tub and helped into it. There was hardly enough standing room in the bottom of it, and the sides came up only to her knees, but it was suitable enough for a simple bath. The women stripped her of the remaining rags of her clothing, then the older woman promptly dumped the contents of the kettle over Nevina's head. The water was hot, and Nevina cried out in pain as it ran down her body. The women said nothing, each taking a rag and scouring at her tender flesh.

The younger woman started with her face, rubbing gently at the smears of dirt and tear streaks Nevina was sure were there. In the firelight, Nevina could catch glimpses of the girl's eyes, and they seemed red and swollen from crying.

"Please," Nevina asked, "can you tell me if Areanath is dead?"

The girl opened her mouth to answer, but the other woman spoke first. "Don't speak to her, Ishta." The older woman had Nevina by one arm, and her fierce scrubbing suddenly grew more intense, until the tender scabs and cuts on her upper arm burst open again, and Nevina had to bite her lip from whimpering. The girl, Ishta, turned her attention back to gently scrubbing Nevina's neck and chest, refusing to look her in the eye.

Nevina remained quiet as the women continued their work. They scrubbed her from the top down, leaving nothing untouched. The older woman seemed to take a small amount of pleasure in savagely scouring the raw recesses between Nevina's thighs and buttocks, perhaps knowing what she had endured and wanting to inflict further pain. She bit down on her lip until she tasted blood, but it still did not stop her from letting out a shaky whimper at the woman's cruel touch.

When she was cleaned to the older woman's satisfaction,

they wrapped Nevina's deeper cuts in clean strips of linen and dabbed the shallower ones with a foul-smelling ointment. Her wrists were bandaged where the chained cuffs had rubbed them, but not where the arcane cuffs dug into her flesh at each attempted use of magic. Her hair was braided and pinned against her head, and she was quickly dressed in a simple white shift. With a final painful tug, a veil was fastened around her brow, once more concealing her face.

As the youngest one gathered the discarded rags, wet and stained with blood, the other woman refastened the chained cuffs to Nevina's wrist. She took the torch from the sconce on the wall and opened the cell door for the younger girl to leave. She looked Nevina over, eyes narrow behind the glint of the torch. "The king has called for your execution tomorrow morning. He wanted to make you presentable." The woman huffed lightly. "I don't see the point, but then I am not king." She started through the door again, then paused and looked back. "I'll be sure to spit on your corpse, for Areanath's sake."

And then Nevina was once more alone in her cell. The sound of the lock fastening on the other side of the door echoed off the stone walls around her.

Ajax walked through the castle corridors to his new king's chambers. The hallways were unusually quiet and empty. Etritia was in mourning, and Ajax was no different. But he at least had the search for Nevina to keep his mind from dwelling on Areanath's death. The rest of Etritia was not so distracted, and the heavy silence choking the castle was a grim reminder of Azimar's loss.

Mothlenor had refused to take up residence in the same rooms his brother had used, for which Ajax was oddly grateful. Instead, Mothlenor had decided to stay where he had resided for all of Areanath's rule. The Old Tower sat on the northwestern side of the castle, oddly dark and ominous in the shadow of the Northern Mountains.

Ajax had always ignored the whispers about Mothlenor's curious residence. Some of the older townspeople insisted that it was haunted, some going so far as to say that Mothlenor would anger ancient spirits by residing there. The less superstitious Etritians were still unnerved by the arcane arts that Mothlenor practiced in his seclusion, and did little to quiet the more absurd rumors. Thus the Old Tower had grown to be associated with the mysterious and unknown, perhaps even with things better left unsaid and unstudied. But Ajax had never been shaken by what the townspeople said. The Old Tower was strange because it was old and needed tending, much like the other older parts of the castle. And Mothlenor, while odd and often rude, was another Etritian citizen, and their king's brother.

Ajax's steps faltered on the first steps of Mothlenor's tower.

Not the king's brother.

The king.

Ajax continued his climb, a weight settling in his chest.

As Ajax ascended the winding stairs of the tower to the chamber doors, he wondered if perhaps some of the whispers about the Old Tower were correct after all. The curving stairs were drafty, and the walls bare of any decoration, unlike the rest of the castle. The air was heavy and stale, and there was something else … something Ajax couldn't quite put words to. It felt as if the tower was alive and full of energy. As if he was an unwelcome guest, facing the scrutiny of unseen beings all around him. The sensation of being watched by unknown eyes made his skin crawl. But he continued to climb, the air growing fouler with each step, until he finally faced the door to Mothlenor's chambers.

He could hear voices on the other side of the heavy wooden door, and Ajax found himself hesitating, one hand raised to knock.

"You were seen with her! If I had wanted her to be seen, I would have paraded her through the city myself."

"Forgive me, my lord."

The first was Mothlenor's voice, undoubtedly, but Ajax couldn't recognize the other man. His voice was smooth and rich, and there was an unsettling quality to his voice that Ajax couldn't place.

"I ought to dismiss you for your foolishness, especially

after learning of your … actions, but I need your skills," Mothlenor said venomously.

"Thank you, my lord, for your kindness, and for your forgiveness," the other man began. "But it was not specified—"

"That you were to leave her be? You are right. I thought I might reward you with a bit of amusement. But you grossly overstepped what I might consider 'amusement.' From now on, you are forbidden from laying your hands—or any other part of your person—on her again. There are whores plenty enough in the city. Perhaps you can find one that is willing to put up with your … tastes."

"Thank you, my lord, and I—"

"Go on, do as I've asked and leave me."

There was a mumbled reply followed by silence on the far side of the door. Ajax knocked sharply on the door, not sure who might be waiting just beyond. *Who could Mothlenor be meeting with? And what woman were they discussing? A favored bedroom companion of his?* Ajax had never known Mothlenor to visit the brothels of Etritia, but every man had his needs.

The door swung open on its own, and Mothlenor waited behind an ornate workbench cluttered with papers, books, and other odd assortments, some of which Ajax couldn't put a name to.

"I summoned you nearly an hour ago, Commander." Mothlenor's voice was hard, and he frowned across the room at him. "Come in. No need to sit, this will not take long."

Ajax entered the large room, his eyes roaming about the place in awe. "I'm sorry to keep you waiting, my lord." All along the walls were piles of books and papers, as well as rather questionable odds and ends. Indeed, there was nowhere to be seated, aside from the chair Mothlenor already occupied. There were books of various sizes and thicknesses, as well as carefully handwritten notes in a script Ajax couldn't read. Balanced atop one rather precarious stack of papers was an ugly, misshapen chunk of gold, large enough to make any merchant envious. And standing in one corner was a small water basin, seemingly out of place. Other than an odd assortment of arcane trappings and Mothlenor himself, the room was empty. There was no one else present for Mothlenor to argue with.

"It has come to my attention, Commander, that you have been shirking on the duties assigned to your station." Mothlenor's dissatisfied stare settled on Ajax. "Where have you been the last several hours? You returned much later than the rest of your retinue last night, which I took as a sign of your devotion both to myself and to my brother. And yet you chose not to resume searching with everyone else this morning."

Ajax straightened, fastening his hands together at the small of his back. "My apologies, my lord, but I was attending to other duties in preparation for your upcoming coronation. I was unable to attend the continuing manhunt."

"These duties, they took you to the housing district of the city?" Mothlenor asked slyly.

Ajax was a little surprised that Mothlenor knew he had spent the better part of the day in the housing district, but he was not wholly unprepared. "Yes, my lord. As I understand it, it is customary practice to perform a census when a new king is crowned. I was only doing my duty as a member of the King's Guard. I knew that not many men could be pulled from the search for the Coven Matriarch for this task, so I took it upon myself to do it." Ajax dipped his head in a low bow. "I beg your forgiveness if this has upset you."

"I suspect, Commander, that a census is not the only thing that brought you to the housing district." Mothlenor's eyes glinted, and he crossed his arms over his chest, pulling his robe tighter around his frame. "Am I right to assume that you suspected, just as I did, that my brother's murderer had managed to sneak back into the city unnoticed?"

Ajax hesitated, unprepared. *How did he guess it so easily?* "You are correct to assume so, my lord," Ajax spoke slowly, weighing his words. "My men and I searched the Knife thoroughly, and there was no sign of their passing. My men suspected that witchery was involved, to hide their tracks so well. But I started to question if she had ever crossed the Knife at all, and might have instead doubled back to enter the city unnoticed. I suspect she may have further plans that require her presence within the city walls." It pained Ajax to speak ill of Nevina, but he continued. "I went into the housing district under the guise of conducting a census for your reign, my lord. But my true intention was to discreetly search the homes I entered for any sign of the Matriarch." This was true enough, although if he had found Nevina and her girls, he wasn't sure he would have released them to Mothlenor.

Mothlenor seemed intrigued. Impressed, even. But even this did not ease the disfavor or hatred in his voice. "And?"

"And I found nothing," Ajax answered. There had been no sign of the Matriarch, and Ajax had spent the day growing increasingly worried for Nevina's safety. "I have failed, my lord. Please accept my deepest apologies."

Mothlenor shook his head, his frown deepening. "While I admire your thinking and your ingenuity, Commander, I cannot forgive you for your clumsiness and lack of discipline."

Ajax frowned. "My lord?"

"You are the Commander of the King's Guard. Your men answer to you, and you, in turn, must answer to me." Mothlenor bent in his chair, reaching for something Ajax could not see. When he straightened, Mothlenor held a palm-sized orb, perfectly round, resting on a pillow of the finest silk. It looked to be made of dark stone, polished to a sheen. Mothlenor set the pillow onto the empty space directly in front of him, and when his fingers laced around the stone, it seemed to come alive, responding to his touch by swirling with bright colors. Reds and yellows, blues and greens. There was no discernible pattern to the colored whirls, but the sight mesmerized Ajax.

"If you had come to me with your concerns and suspicions, Commander, then perhaps we could have worked together to find my brother's murderer. Instead, I had to rely on others to perform your duties for you."

Ajax continued to stare at the stone, his mind making little sense of the display. He watched the colors swirl and dance, and thought he could see images forming from within the stone. He caught a glimpse of Silvana's face before it dissolved. The image reformed, and he saw Hasani's dark eyes staring at him from the stone. The image dissolved again, and after a moment, another image formed. Here he saw the unmistakable face of Areanath, his eyes glassed over in death. The last image dissolved, and Ajax jolted out of his reverie, quickly looking away from the stone. Mothlenor was staring at him.

"Do you like it?" he asked, indicating the stone. Ajax refused to look at it again. "It can help me see things. Or people." Mothlenor smiled. "I used this to track the Matriarch down. She has been found."

"You found her, my lord? Where was she?" Ajax asked, relieved.

Mothlenor raised an eyebrow. "Eager, aren't you?" He didn't wait for Ajax to reply. "I found her hiding within the housing district, as you suspected. And tomorrow, following my coronation, she will hang from the gallows."

Ajax bit back an angry outburst. *Hang her? For a crime she would not have committed?* "I'd like to see her, talk to her, if possible."

"Why?" Mothlenor's voice was flat, but his eyes shone with a furious glint.

Ajax took a hesitant breath. "I'd like to know why … or if … she killed Areanath."

Mothlenor huffed, giving Ajax a disdainful glare. "That won't be necessary. The witch had already confessed. As for why she killed my brother—why are kings ever killed?" His eyebrows were raised, the whites of his eyes showing as he stared across the table at Ajax. "For power."

"Confessed?" Ajax's voice caught in his throat. Pieces of the conversation he had overheard were falling together. Was Nevina the woman Mothlenor had mentioned? What had they done to her? *Did she really kill Areanath?*

Mothlenor frowned. "Are you not pleased?"

"Of course I am pleased, my lord. It is a righteous end. I am only sorry I was not there to help you." The words were difficult to say, but he tried his best to sound sincere.

"Perhaps it would do you well to remember that the next time you go off on your own, you fool," Mothlenor hissed. He dropped the stone back onto its silk pillow and took a deep breath, collecting himself. After a moment, he added, "Not that your assistance will be needed any longer."

"My lord?"

Mothlenor straightened in his chair, hawkish eyes fixed on Ajax. "Effective immediately, Ajax, you are no longer Commander of the King's Guard."

Ajax's knees nearly buckled. "W-why?"

"Because I do not need men who cannot follow orders, Ajax." Mothlenor's eyes narrowed. "These are dangerous times, and I need men I can count on." He folded his arms across his chest. "Don't worry, you won't be leaving my service completely. You will be leading the Peace Guard, and you will be reporting to the new Commander of the King's Guard, Commander Ferrand."

Ajax felt his jaw clench, but he managed to keep his words civil. "And what is it that the Peace Guard will be doing, my lord?"

Mothlenor sneered, one corner of his mouth curling up at Ajax's question. "For too long, the King's Guard has seen to the petty problems of Etritia. They have stayed within the castle walls, growing soft from lack of battle, and growing idle from lack of discipline." Mothlenor paused, eyes staring darkly at Ajax. "From now on, these little concerns will be granted to the Peace Guard, who will help to maintain conformity and peace within the city and the outlying vicinities, and indeed, within all of the kingdom's ever-growing boundaries."

Ajax's eyes narrowed. *Ever-growing boundaries? The kingdom of men has had set borders for hundreds of years. What is he talking about?*

"And from now on, the King's Guard will take up the tasks originally appointed to them long ago. They will once again become the spearhead for the army of this kingdom, an army my brother was too lax in maintaining. We have long gone unprepared, and wholly undefended. I will not make the same mistakes my brother did."

"Where am I to find men for this new group?"

Mothlenor's smirk deepened. "Recruitment will be unnecessary for some time. Even now, certain … unfit members of the King's Guard are being stripped of their honors and titles and are being prepared for their new role as a Peace Guardian. You should find them outside, in the market square." With a wave of one hand, Mothlenor dismissed him. "That will be all, Ajax."

Ajax gave a quick bow before turning and walking calmly from the room. Once the door shut behind him, however, he bolted down the steps two at a time, racing towards the square.

2 9

HASANI

Hasani found Ajax right where he expected to. He stood alone, off to one side at the bottom of the front steps, watching the formation of the new Peace Guard. There were roughly twenty members of the King's Guard standing in a long row in the market square. Hasani watched for a moment as they removed helms, chest plates, and even weapons, dropping them at their feet to be collected by a half dozen or so boys. Just yesterday, this morning even, those boys had been recruits, and Ajax had been commander. Now they were knights, and Ajax would be taking orders from them instead.

Hasani descended the last of the steps to stand beside his brother. "I'm sorry, Ajax. I would have tried to stop it, but I only just found out."

"It doesn't matter," Ajax muttered. He held a black surcoat in his hands, the sigil of Etritia carefully stitched into the cloth, a pair of crossed blades over a single tower standing in contrast on the dark fabric. "This is the dawn of a new age, Hasani."

Hasani was quiet for a moment, watching as a thin knight in King's Guard regalia read aloud a public notice to the assembled onlookers. "Have you heard about the Matriarch?"

Ajax nodded once, eyes never leaving the row of former knights below him. "She was captured in the housing district, and has confessed her crimes."

"I'm sorry," Hasani repeated. "I know you cared for her."

"Don't be sorry about that, either." Ajax turned and gave Hasani a hard look. "I'm not sure I believe it. Nevina would never kill Areanath."

Hasani frowned. "Ajax …"

Ajax shook his head, turning back to the activity below. "I know it sounds mad, but I knew her better. I know she wouldn't have killed him."

Hasani said nothing. Perhaps this was Ajax's way of grieving for his king, and for the woman he loved. *In time, he'll come to realize that maybe he didn't know her very well at all.*

At the sight of Ajax and Hasani, one member of the newly formed Peace Guards broke from the cluster of black-clad former knights and climbed the steps to meet them. Hasani recognized him immediately, though he looked different without his King's Guard regalia. "Commander. Hasani." He dipped his head. "Care to tell an old fool just what the fuck is going on here?"

"Dars …" Ajax groaned. "They pulled you, too?"

"Yeah, they did." Dars spat a wad of phlegm onto the steps to the castle. He sighed, adjusting the front of his surcoat. "Told me the commander had seen fit to relieve me of my duties. Knew then there was trouble afoot. You'd never let me leave the Guard, Ajax." Dars sighed, turning to watch the continuing dismantling of the King's Guard. "I always thought I'd be on my deathbed and still yelling at little shits trying to be knights."

"Has anyone met this new commander?" Ajax asked. "What's his name?"

"It's Ferrand," a rich voice called from behind them. The

three of them turned as one, catching sight of a tall and broad-shouldered man descending the steps to meet them. "You had better remember that, Ajax."

"You," Dars growled. "You're that slimy bastard that tried to slip into the king's chambers while he was meeting with the Matriarch."

Ferrand smirked. "And you *were* the First Knight of the King's Guard. And now you are just another errand boy." Ferrand's attention shifted to Ajax. "I'm here to relieve you of your helm."

Ajax obediently passed the plumed helm from the crook of his arm to Ferrand.

"And your armor."

Ajax scowled, but undid the belt holding his sword, which he handed to Hasani, then unbuckled the sides of his chest plate and pulled it off, tossing it at Ferrand's feet. Hasani had seen Ajax with his chest plate off more often than with it on but, for some reason, he looked particularly small and defenseless at that moment.

Ajax had just started tying his sword belt back around his waist when Ferrand eyed it. "Your sword, too, Ajax."

"This is my personal weapon, not the property of the King's Guard," Ajax objected.

Ferrand smirked again, eyes glinting. "Peace Guardians go unarmed, Commander. You must surrender your weapon."

Ajax opened his mouth to object again, but Hasani stepped in. "Peace Guardians may go unarmed, but there is nothing to say that the king's own adviser must also. I will take the sword, Ferrand."

Ajax looked at Hasani, his expression almost grateful, and silently handed the weapon back to him. Ferrand scowled, his dark eyes flicking between the pair of them. "Very well." He nodded to Hasani, sneered at Ajax, then turned and walked away, ignoring Dars completely.

Hasani watched Ferrand leave, waiting for him to walk out of earshot. "I'll bring the sword by your quarters later, Ajax."

Ajax sighed. "Don't worry, Hasani, it is yours now."

Hasani was troubled by his friend's complacency but said nothing.

Ajax's eyes narrowed, his gaze far off and unfocused. "I overheard him talking with Mothlenor in the Old Tower."

"So you've met already?" Hasani asked.

Ajax's head tilted. "Ferrand wasn't in the room. Mothlenor was talking to him using magic, I think."

"Sounds convenient. That would have been a handy trick to have with Areanath." Hasani considered for a moment, remembering the night Areanath had slipped into his rooms without him noticing. "Perhaps not, on second thought," he added quietly. Thinking of Areanath hurt.

"I think they were talking about Nevina." Ajax may as well not have heard him at all.

"The Matriarch?" Dars asked. "What about her?"

Ajax turned to look at them. "Mothlenor was upset by something Ferrand did to her." He turned away again. "I think he might have raped her."

Hasani and Dars exchanged a brief look. Dars looked as unsettled as Hasani felt.

An uncomfortable silence fell between the three of them, but Hasani wasn't sure Ajax noticed the effect his words had.

Together they stood, watching the commotion before them.

"You do realize which men they have picked to become Peace Guardians, do you not?" Ajax asked. At the question, Dars snorted and nodded once.

Hasani looked around. He recognized several of the faces, and could even put names to a few of them. But he could find no discernible pattern among the men. "I have no idea. Why these men?"

Ajax turned towards him, and it was only then that Hasani could see the sadness and despair in his eyes. "These men were the most loyal to me, and they trusted me as their commander. These are the men that would question the motives behind an order, instead of blindly following it. They are not just fighters, blindly running into combat just for the sake of the fight. They are freethinkers, and men of valor and honor, and courage. And Mothlenor has reduced them to little more than commoners, here only to break up fights in taverns and take complaints." His voice had a hint of bitterness to it.

Dars snorted again. "These were the best fucking knights we had."

"It is because he fears them, Ajax." Hasani put an arm across his brother's shoulder. "And you, too. Men like you would question and argue with Mothlenor, and you have these men to follow in your stead. He fears that power, so he has tried to strip you of any chance you might have to use it."

Ajax sighed. He was silent for a moment, looking out over the gathered crowd of newly appointed Peace Guards as they donned their black surcoats. His voice was soft when he finally spoke. "I fear for what this new age may bring."

MOTHLENOR

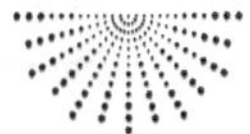

Mothlenor's footsteps were light and quick as he walked the halls of the castle. The normally busy corridors were nearly empty, save for a handful of young King's Guards milling around the Great Hall and the odd servant or two. The knights, barely out of boyhood, looked awed and a little lost. They had probably never been inside the castle proper, and it showed on their boyish faces. As for the servants, mostly women, they walked around in silent shock, their eyes red-rimmed and expressions grim. Mothlenor was pleased with the quiet air Etritia had taken on, but he felt the atmosphere could do with an adjustment.

He rounded a corner, nearly knocking over a slim woman in the process. He caught her elbow, preventing her from falling, but only just.

It was another servant girl, this one carrying a metal oil decanter, its long neck curved slightly, and a small flint striker. The lamp above their heads was unlit, but a drop of fresh oil clung to the outside of the thick glass.

Evening already?

The girl let out a startled gasp, stepping away from him

quickly. "My lord, I-I'm sorry. I didn't hear your approach or I would have—"

"It's alright." Mothlenor raised a hand to quiet the girl. "No harm was done, though we might be in a spot of trouble if that oil had spilled."

The girl didn't meet his eye. "Of course, my lord."

He looked her over again. She seemed familiar, though he couldn't quite place a name to her face. Ishra, or Ishka, or something similar. One of the cook's daughters, no doubt. The whole family worked in the castle in some fashion. He pointed up at the lamp, and her gaze followed his hand. "May I?"

She nodded, her short supply of verbosity apparently spent.

When she held the flint striker out for him, he nearly laughed. "That won't be necessary."

With a snap of his fingers, loud in the hall around them, the lamp was lit, flaring to life in a soft whoosh.

If she was startled, she did not show it.

"Thank you, my lord." She dipped her head low, her eyes still not quite meeting his.

"It was nothing." With the added light of the lamp, Mothlenor could see the finer angles of the woman's face. She wasn't altogether unattractive. Almost pretty, even, in a plain sort of way.

And much too young.

"Take care in the future, please." Mothlenor smiled at her, keeping his tone light. "I can't have all my people bumbling around, injuring one another. It just wouldn't do."

She bowed again, this time a little more stiffly. "Of course, my lord. Please excuse me, there are more lamps to be lit." She stepped around him nimbly, eyes downcast, and slipped around the corner.

The rest of his walk was less eventful, though Mothlenor did pause at the next large window he passed, dismayed to see that the sun was already descending. *Another day gone before I was able to steal myself away long enough to check on my greatest acquisition. And tomorrow, the hanging ... Then the real work begins.*

When he at last found the large double doors he wanted, he found it guarded by two young King's Guards. They looked up at him, eyes wide and shocked, as he came to a stop not three feet from them.

A second passed; one boy cast a quick glance to his neighbor. They said nothing and made no move.

"Well," Mothlenor said with an exasperated sigh, "aren't you going to open the doors for me?"

This time they looked at each other.

"My lord," one began. He looked to be perhaps a year older than the other, but his voice was still a bit high and weak. "This is the treasure room ..."

Mothlenor sneered. "I'm quite aware that this is the treasure room. Unlike the two of you, I've lived in this building my whole life. Now open the damned doors."

The boy opened his mouth again, but Mothlenor cut him off with a sharp motion of one hand and a hiss of breath between his gritted teeth. "If you are about to tell me that only the king is allowed to enter the treasure room, I will once again remind you that I am well aware of that little rule. I understand that I will not be officially crowned until tomorrow morning, but there is something in there that I need tonight." He lowered his voice, glaring at each of the boys in turn. "And if you do not open those doors right this instant, I swear on the bones of the Great Ones that I will have you stripped of your weapons and sent south to find whatever work a foolish Etritian exile might find."

One last look between them, then each of them scrambled to pull a heavy metal key from under his mail shirt and hastily shove it into the large keyhole set into each of the double doors.

As he waited, Mothlenor fumed quietly. *Why did Ferrand feel the need to remove* all *the proper knights? These imbeciles will take months yet to train properly, and longer still to mature into intelligence, if the Great Imis saw fit to bless them with any.*

The door was opened, and Mothlenor stepped through, giving each of the young men a glare as he passed. He could have magicked himself inside the room, bypassing the fools stationed to guard it, but the room was surrounded by a good twenty inches of stone wall on all sides, and that much stone would have been difficult for even him to magic through. And it was better to make his presence known to all that he could, even the stupid boys Ferrand had chosen to bring into the King's Guard.

"Shut the door behind me. I need privacy." He didn't wait for their response, instead stepping into the darkness of the treasure room and whispering a word under his breath.

As his low voice echoed around the room, a dozen oil lamps lit themselves in quick succession, bringing the treasure room into full view. He had expected piles of gold coins spilling across the floor, gems and precious stones, perhaps artwork or other pageantry. But it was not at all what he had imagined.

There was plenty of coin, of course, but it was carefully organized into chests, not spilled haphazardly across the room. There was a low table lining one wall, with a long row of velvet bags. Opening one revealed rough-cut sapphires, another diamonds. There were weapons, as well. Carefully, artfully crafted weapons, likely dwarf made. *Very like Areanath to collect dwarven weaponry.*

There was some art, covered by sheepskin cloths to protect it. There was even a gold harp in one corner, its neck and strings curiously free of dust. Areanath brushed a hand over the neck, careful not to disturb the strings. He could feel a pleasant, half-familiar buzz of energy under his fingertips. Mothlenor considered it for a moment, letting his hand rest on the instrument. *Areanath's magic?* It felt very similar to his own, which did not surprise him in the slightest. They had been twins, after all. But the energy was already beginning to fade; the one who had cast it was no longer able to continue feeding energy into whatever spell had been woven over it.

The large bulk of the treasure seemed to be in books, which Mothlenor realized with a snort he should have expected from his brother as well. One of the walls adjacent to the double doors was lined with several matching shelves, their wood stained dark to complement the walls around it, and there were perhaps a thousand volumes carefully tucked into the shelves. Only the very bottom of the last case had any empty space, about enough for another dozen books or so. Mothlenor traced the line of spines just above his eye level, not truly interested in the collection. Until, that was, he stumbled across a thin volume bound in green leather, with a curiously detailed spine depicting some sort of vegetation. Mothlenor pulled it out, opening the cover to the first page. Handwritten text in a delicately curling script filled the page, and with a grimace Mothlenor recognized the flowing text as ancient elvish. He snapped the book shut, shoving it back into its place with a low growl.

He continued his quick inspection of the remaining books, pausing again when his hand found another buzz of arcane energy. This was decidedly not his brother's craft work, but the short touch of Mothlenor's hand against the spine brought the coppery taste of blood to his mouth and made his skin crawl and itch unpleasantly. He pulled his hand back instinctively, and the sensations faded. He stared at the book for a long moment, but the spine revealed nothing. The book was bound in black leather, though Mothlenor thought he could spy reddish tinges around the edges and in the soft cracks of the binding. It was also thick, much thicker than the books surrounding it.

Mothlenor reached out a hesitant hand, fingers wrapping

around the spine with an anticipatory grimace. But the strange arcane flare he had sensed a moment before did not return. He pulled the book out gently, cradling the heavy tome in both arms. The title was embossed in thick silver on the front of the cover.

"*Daemonica*," Mothlenor breathed. He had heard of the book, but had never seen a copy, or even truly discovered if the thing existed at all. But here it was, in his hands. *And Areanath had hidden it from me.*

Still, he had it now, though he was not entirely sure the deeper study of demonology would be necessary at this point in his life. He had mastered the art of Calling. What higher knowledge was there?

Yet its presence gave Mothlenor reason to inspect the remaining shelves more critically. He found half a dozen titles that Areanath had likely pulled from Etritia's library, or perhaps even the Azimar Archives, to hide away in his little treasure room. None of the other books gave him that unsettling arcane shock, but they all had titles that piqued his curiosity.

Finally, after wasting more time than he had intended to, he placed the stack of books on the table of gems, brushing the velvet bags aside to make room.

Brushing dust from his hands, he looked around the room once more. "It has to be here, somewhere."

But the room was small, disappointedly so. There was no other door leading to a second, perhaps larger room.

So, gritting his teeth in annoyance, Mothlenor took to opening chests and crates, searching for the item he wanted.

Most of the chests were filled with coins and trinkets. There was one crate full of old bottles of elvish wine. Not Vyrisian red, but a colorless and thick liquid. Each bottle was stamped with a wax seal of a great tree. Mothlenor made a note to burn the whole crate at a later date.

None of them held what he wanted.

Finally, angry and ready to burn the whole room down, save for the money and the few books he had found worth saving, he spotted a small chest tucked between two tall canvases, its top hidden by the thick coverings on the art. He lifted it, surprised by the light weight of it. Setting it next to the books he'd found, he immediately tugged on the lid.

It wouldn't open.

He cursed it then growled a word of power and a bit of energy discharged from his open hand.

The chest jumped slightly on the table, and stilled.

Mothlenor tried the lid again; he was not surprised when it still wouldn't open.

He took a long breath. *This is it.*

Reaching into a pocket of his robe, he pulled out a long silver chain. There was a tiny silver key dangling from it with a small sapphire set into the top.

The only thing left of my brother.

He was suddenly glad he had stayed to watch the wraiths as they had slowly consumed his brother's body, or he might have missed the tiny glint of silver around his brother's neck. It might have been a sentimental thought that scooped the chain up from the bloodstained grass, but the act might have saved his plans for his greatest inheritance.

He slipped the key into the chest's keyhole, giving it a gentle twist. With a gentle click, the clasp opened.

Mothlenor took a slow breath, calming his sudden excitement. *This is not a moment to rush through.*

After a quiet moment, he lifted the lid.

The scent of burned arcane energy wafted up to his nose. There was a slightly stale aspect to it as if it had been trapped inside the chest for a few days, only now free to escape into the fresh air. And again, Mothlenor had a sense of half familiarity as the energy dissipated through the room.

The inside of the chest was lined with velvet, deep blue in color. The bottom was plush, stitched carefully to form a thick pillow. There was an oddly shaped depression in the velvet.

Mothlenor traced the shape of it, fingers moving slowly. The chest was empty.

He flung the chest across the room, moving without thinking. It crashed into a stack of covered paintings, breaking through one and knocking the others to the floor.

He stalked a few steps back towards it, but turned on his heel and shoved the golden harp to the floor, fingers nearly catching between some of the strings. The harp fell with a crash of discordant notes and metallic thuds. The spell woven over the harp broke instantly, the smell of acrid arcane energy once more filling his nose. The harp seemed undamaged, despite the fall, so Mothlenor sent it skittering across the floor with a hissed word. Several of the strings snapped, and when it finally came to a stop against the far wall, the shoulder and crown of the harp were both bent.

"Areanath," he growled. "What have you done?"

Mothlenor fumed for a few more moments, staring at the bent and ugly harp lying broken on the floor. *What to do, what to do ...*

A thought struck him, and he searched the room once more for a mirror, or anything remotely reflective. He considered using a dwarven blade, but decided against it, though any one of them would have worked well enough.

Finally, he settled on a large diamond, larger than his eye and flawless.

If Ferrand was disconcerted by seeing his master's face cut into odd angles by the diamond's surface, he made no show of it. "Yes, my lord?"

"Listen closely, Ferrand. I have a task for you."

FERRAND

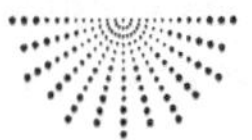

Ferrand grimaced at the noise of the bar, eyeing the farmers and other common filth around him with distaste. Somewhere close by, a pair of drunks were belting out a funeral dirge for the fallen king, but had made the tune lively and spirited. The song, both the words and the tune, made Ferrand's teeth grind together. It was hard to like a rowdy bar filled with poor degenerates, but Mothlenor had given him a job to do, and this would be as good a place as any other filth hole in the city. And besides, there *were* reasons to be drinking, though it wasn't the upcoming harvest or Great Ones only knew what the farmers were laughing and spilling ale on themselves for.

Ferrand had better reasons to celebrate than the vermin of the fields and sewers.

There were drinks, there were several of his men, now members of the King's Guard, and there were plenty of women. There was one woman in particular that Ferrand was keeping his eye on, and he sipped lightly at his watery ale as he watched her weave her way through tables and around drunk men to fill and refill mugs of beer. One fat farmer slipped his hand up her skirt to her thigh, and she let him for a moment, casually chatting up the whole table while he wrapped his meaty fingers around her leg and looked her up and down hungrily. But she walked away, giving the man a smile and a wink as she did so.

Finally, she started walking his way. As she grew closer, Ferrand noticed that her breasts were larger than he would have liked. Her hair was stringy and a shade too dark, and her face held on to the last remains of youthful roundness. Her eyes were brown instead of the icy blue he wanted. But from far away, she looked exactly like what he needed. She approached his table, a pitcher of ale in her hand, hips swaying seductively. "Can I top you off, darlin'?" She paused, leaning slightly to reach for his mug. Her corset was loose at the top, leaving just enough covered to not seem intentionally immodest, but to still leave a man eager to see more. Her voice was high pitched and a little grating, but he could ignore it for now.

He smiled, sliding his mug towards her. She promptly refilled it and came around the table to hand it back to him. As she set it down on the table in front of him, he wrapped his hand around hers. "Won't you sit with me, lovely? I haven't had much company all night, and I have some celebrating to do." He slid his chair away from the table a bit and pulled her towards his lap.

She obediently sat, straddling him, her skirt bunched up to her thighs. "Some celebratin'? What are you celebratin' tonight?" She put the mug to his lips, and Ferrand took a small sip. She had a bit of a drawl to her voice, a pretty common thing found among the filthy vermin of the city, but he could ignore that too. Besides, a voice like hers couldn't be heard through a gag.

"I was made Commander of the King's Guard today." *She probably thinks I'm quite the catch. I'm not falling-down drunk, and I'm not some sweaty overweight bastard trying to catch a peek at her underclothes.* He slipped a hand under her skirt and felt his way up her thigh.

She smiled. "Commander? Well, that *is* a reason to celebrate." She took a long sip from the mug and quickly refilled it from the pitcher. She giggled as his hand wandered further up her thigh. "And how do you plan on celebratin', Commander?"

"I'd like to celebrate with you." He tucked her hair behind her ear and stroked her cheek. "You are very beautiful. What's your name?"

"Lisbeth. And what's your name, Commander?"

"Ferrand." He fingered the lacing on her corset. It tied in the front, and the knot was at the top, all the easier to quickly take off. He pulled slowly at the string, undoing the knot. "Aren't you a little young to be running around in a tavern like this? Where is your family?" She was young, Ferrand realized, not even a woman fully grown. That might be a problem, but he was sure it could be ignored, too.

The girl sobered up a little, but lost none of her charm. "My family lives in a village to the east. I came here to find my own place in the world." She smiled again, a dimple forming in one cheek. "And I'm not that young. I know what to do with *this*, after all." Her thin little fingers had found a gap in the lacing of his breeches, and she stroked him slowly, eyes glinting. Ferrand could feel calluses on her hands.

He smiled, letting her think it was her he was craving. Mothlenor had suggested that he search the taverns for women that could appease his appetite. Perhaps this one would work for both of them. "Do you have any rooms left?"

The girl pouted a little, her bottom lip thin and bright with red lacquer. "No, there aren't any rooms left."

Ferrand tsked. "Pity, I would have paid very nicely for a little bit of privacy to enjoy with you."

At the mention of money, the girl's eyes lit up. She stirred up her charms again, giving him a sly little smile. "If it's privacy you're wantin', I know a little place not far from here. A quiet little barn, not often used. It's just around the corner."

Ferrand smiled and nodded, and the girl slipped off his lap and led him out of the tavern by the hand. Ferrand turned back as he walked out of the door to see two men rise from their table to head after them.

The girl led him around to the back of the tavern and down a little alleyway. Sure enough, there was a quiet little barn off to one side of the alley. Off in the distance a bit, the western gate into the city could be seen. At the sight of the barn, the girl ran ahead and heaved open the door. She took his hand, leading him just inside. With her back to him, she stepped a little further in. "I think it used to belong to a farmer or somethin'. But I've never actually seen any animals in here." She was fumbling with the lacing on her corset, he could tell. He quickly untied his breeches as she continued talking. "But it's warm, and no one really bothers to come by. I think it'll be perfect for us."

She turned, tossing her corset aside, her blouse barely concealing the breasts underneath. The smile on her face quickly faded. "Oh, I didn't realize you were bringin' friends." Ferrand took a few steps towards her, as did his two comrades. She smiled again, but it was faltering a little, and her voice cracked as she spoke. "That won't be a problem, but you'll understand if I charge for each of you."

"We don't actually intend to pay, darlin'." He mimicked her drawl, delighting in the way her eyes widened at his words. Ferrand took a few more steps towards her. She looked scared, her dark eyes wide and one arm wrapped protectively around her chest. She took a step back, but her reaction was too slow. Ferrand backhanded her hard, sending her sprawling to the dirt. She was motionless for a moment, which gave the other two men the chance to pounce on her. The bigger one, Dirk, ripped the front of her blouse open, exposing her breasts, grabbed both of her wrists in one hand and clamped his other hand over her mouth. The faster one, Clay, stripped her first of her skirt, which he tossed to one side, and then of her underclothes. She came to at that moment and tried kicking Clay in the head. Her muffled scream could be heard even through Dirk's hand. Clay dodged the kick; he wadded up her underclothes and shoved them into her mouth as a gag, and Dirk clamped his hand down on her mouth even harder.

Clay straightened up, looking up at Ferrand. "Do you need me to hold her legs down?"

Ferrand shook his head. "No, she won't be a problem." He leaned over to look her in the eye. "Will you?" In answer, the girl aimed a kick at his knee, but missed. Ferrand scowled, kicking her hard in the ribs. She cried out, but the sound barely made it around the gag and Dirk's hand. She rolled over a little onto her injured side, and Ferrand heard her struggling to refill her lungs. "You won't be a problem, will you?" Ferrand repeated. The girl was unable to answer, but she didn't move her legs.

Ferrand turned back to Clay. "If she kicks or fights a little too much, just kick her again. No need to be gentle. As long as she makes it through the night, it won't matter. She'll be dead before the end of tomorrow." The girl whimpered, and as Ferrand slid himself inside her, he could see the tears running down her face. It made him harder, seeing them, and with each whimper she gave, he rode her a little faster and a little rougher. She fought a little, trying to wrangle her way out of Dirk's grasp, but the man held her tightly. It took a little while, but he finally finished. He stood, pulling his breeches up, and motioned to Clay, who smirked and untied his breeches, getting to his knees. The girl suddenly brought one knee up, her aimless attack catching Clay in the thigh. Ferrand gave her another boot to the ribs, and she quickly became more manageable.

By the time Dirk's turn had come around, the girl was

limp and unmoving. Clay insisted she was still alive, just unconscious, and after a little while, even Dirk finished. The girl remained limp on the ground, and Ferrand used a foot to roll her over onto her stomach. The other two men smirked at him, knowing what was coming next. Ferrand undid his breeches once more before positioning himself. He pinned her hands down to the ground, using them as leverage. Her hair had fallen over her face. From this angle, he realized as he forced himself into her that he couldn't feel the calluses on her hands, couldn't see that her breasts were a little too large, and her face a little too chubby. The moonlight even shone on her hair, making it look a shade lighter than it was. At this angle, she looked just like that Coven bitch that Mothlenor had forbidden him to touch again. He imagined it was her he was thrusting into and, for a while, he could ignore everything else.

NEVINA

"Wake up, Nevina." Areanath's voice called out to her, piercing the heavy veil of sleep. But his voice was wrong, too coarse and deep.

And Areanath is dead.

Nevina's eyes snapped open, her heart already pounding. On instinct, she lifted one hand to cast a shielding spell, but before the spell could be activated, pain lanced through her wrists and halted her.

"Ah, I supposed I shouldn't have startled you. Would you like some ale to calm your nerves?"

It was Mothlenor's voice she heard, and she could see him through a haze of thin smoke surrounding them.

Not smoke. Steam.

Nevina blinked away her confusion, taking in her surroundings. She was in a bathhouse, up to her neck in deliciously warm water. Mothlenor sat across from her, on the lip of the great tub, bare legs dangling in water up to his knees.

And I'm naked.

She wrapped her arms around her chest and curled her legs together.

"What do you want?" Nevina snapped.

"Only to talk, Nevina." She could feel his eyes on her as her own gaze roved around the room. "I must say, it's nice to finally see your face. Would you like some ale?" Mothlenor motioned to a spot next to her, and Nevina turned to see a small tray with a glass of amber liquid. The glass was filmed in a light layer of frost. Nevina was sure the tray hadn't been there a moment ago.

"I'm not the kind of woman that drinks ale, Mothlenor," Nevina spat. "How did I get here? Where are my clothes?"

Mothlenor tsked, shaking a finger at her. His robe fell open slightly as he leaned towards her, and she could make out a hardened chest covered in greying hair. "Be kind, now. We're here to have a nice discussion." He leaned away again, surveying her. "What do you prefer to drink, Nevina?"

Nevina answered without hesitation. "Vyrisian wine." The words came to her without thinking, but they sounded right. She smirked at the look of distaste on Mothlenor's face.

Mothlenor once again gestured to the tray, where the ale had been replaced with a crystal glass of red wine. Clearly not Vyrisian, but Mothlenor would never allow himself to enjoy anything elf-made. Nevina took the glass in hand, sniffing delicately at it.

"No potions or concoctions this time, you have my word, Nevina," Mothlenor said solemnly.

"Your word is worthless to me." She took a small sip of the wine. "And stop saying my name. It sounds foul, coming from your mouth."

Mothlenor frowned but said nothing.

Nevina surveyed the bathhouse once more. "This is an impressive illusion, Mothlenor. But just an illusion. Why did you bring me here? And how?" *And where are my damned clothes?* But that last one was pointless. The room was completely empty, save for the two of them.

"I used magic, of course." Mothlenor smiled, teeth glinting. Nevina hated the way it looked so much like Areanath's smile. "I wanted to discuss my brother with you."

Nevina snorted into her glass, which seemed to be refilling itself even as she drank. "What is there to discuss, Mothlenor? You killed him, and you'll have my Coven and I hang for it."

"I don't plan on hanging you. Not unless I need to." His voice had grown colder, threatening.

"Do it anyway." She sneered. "If you don't, I'll kill you." Her anger and hatred were returning, writhing hot in her stomach. She downed another gulp of wine, her hand shaking around the glass.

"You can't kill me, Nevina." Mothlenor's voice was still cold and quiet.

"Take off these cuffs, Mothlenor. Or are you afraid of the big bad witch?" She set the glass on the lip of the pool, fingering the stem. "And stop saying my name."

"I want your help undoing my brother's spell." Mothlenor glared down at her, his voice growing more annoyed with each passing moment.

Good.

"Great Ones take your wants, Mothlenor. I won't help." His gaze unnerved her, and she found herself staring into the redness of the glass.

"Then tell me where the Coven is."

Nevina choked out a small laugh. "I couldn't tell you if I wanted to." She tapped a fingernail against the glass in her hand. "The women of the Coven are spelled to prevent them from sharing the Coven's location. And I won't help you," she repeated.

"I would spare your life."

That caused her to look up. "Spare my life? And what of the lives of my girls?" Nevina snapped.

Mothlenor's brow pinched. "Girls?"

Nevina flung the glass at him, but it only bounced off the arcane shield around him and shattered against the bath-house floor, wine spilling across the stones. "I came here with half a dozen Coven daughters. *Your* men took us to *your* dungeon, then abused and raped them. All I know of them is that two of them have been killed." Nevina took the tray in hand and hurled it through the air, knowing it would only crash against his shield again. "And you want me to help you, you, monster?"

Mothlenor didn't flinch as the objects clattered around him. His brow pinched deeper. "I didn't know."

Nevina sniffed, eyes watering. "I don't believe you." She sighed, her shoulders dropping. "Release me from this illusion. Let me go back to my cell and await my death."

Mothlenor straightened, considering her for a moment. "As you wish, Nevina."

Nevina's eyes snapped open once again, and she found herself in the dim darkness of her cell. Mothlenor was gone, as was the pool. The only thing with her now was a small pitcher of water that the younger servant girl—Ishta—had brought her. There was no light, and the air was stale and cold. She was still naked, her clothes in a crumpled pile beside her, and her skin was damp. There was a lingering warmth in her body, and the ends of her hair were wet. She licked her lips, tasting wine. *No illusion, then.*

Nevina dressed quietly, forgoing the veil when one strap broke away from the ensemble. *It doesn't matter,* she told herself. *My face has already been seen by the only person I wanted to never show it to.* She sat in the darkness for a few moments, her arms wrapped around her knees, her head hanging low. And she wept. For Areanath, and for the two girls she knew she had lost. She still didn't know which girls were gone, but the pain of losing them to Mothlenor's men was still too much to bear in silence. *Had Mothlenor truly not known?* She didn't want to believe it, but Mothlenor rarely left his tower, and the only time she had seen him, she had been without her girls. *But he wouldn't have done any different, if he had known. It would all be the same.*

She argued with herself, hated herself for her inability to protect her girls. She thought she heard a voice in the dark, but she ignored it. *Mothlenor and his tricks again ...*

"Nevina?" Layle's soft voice echoed in the dark around her.

"Layle?" Nevina lifted her head tiredly, searching. The cell was still empty.

"Nevina!"

"Layle!" The girl's voice was coming from the pitcher. She scrambled over, peering into the depths. Inside she could just make out Layle's face. Her veil was missing, and her eyes swollen from crying. Nevina could just barely tell that the neckline of her dress had been torn to rags. "Layle, what happened?"

"They separated us. Millie and Arella were in here with me. They're dead. They killed them."

Nevina's breathing stopped, eyes suddenly burning. She had known. Two of her girls were dead. But she had never for a second thought Arella would be one of them. Arella, the littlest one, who had just come into her Gift. Arella, her own flesh and blood.

"We heard screaming from the next room," Layle was saying. "I knew what they were doing to the others." Layle was crying, her breath coming in ragged gasps. "They came to us, all of them. Millie tried to protect Arella. But they got Arella, and they pushed her to the floor, and they ..." Layle struggled to speak around the sobs that shook her. Nevina didn't want to hear it; she already knew what Mothlenor's men had done. "They slit her throat. They did the same to Millie." Layle buried her face in the crook of her arm.

Nevina couldn't speak, couldn't think.

"It should have been me," Layle continued. "I should have died, not her. She was my sister."

"No, Layle," Nevina cut in. "You need to survive. You ..." Nevina stopped, a sudden realization hitting her. "You're doing this. How are you doing this? Did they take your cuffs?"

Layle sobbed in frustration. "No, I still have the cuffs. I could have saved them, if not for the cuffs."

"But I can't do magic. How are you able to?"

Layle lifted her arms weakly, showing the cuffs and her forearms to Nevina. "I forced my energy through them," Layle said tiredly. Her hands were red and slick, and blood trickled down her forearms. As Nevina watched in horror, a drop of blood spilled from Layle's elbow and into the pitcher she was scrying from.

"Layle, you're bleeding."

Layle sniffed, or it might have been a snort. "It took a long time, and it was painful, but I made it through the cuffs. I can make them pay for Arella's death."

Nevina's heart skipped a beat. "No, Layle," she said again. She couldn't bear the thought of finding Layle again, only to have her rush to her death. "You need to find a way out. You can leave, warn the rest of the Coven."

"It should have been me," Layle said quietly, staring into her bloodied hands. "It should have been me that died while Arella lived. You love her more than me."

Nevina's heart sank. She was silent for a moment. "That's not true. Arella needed me, so your grandmother let me care for her. But I wanted to care for you because I know you're stronger than the other Coven sisters. And I wanted to help you." She looked into Layle's eyes. They had grown ice cold again, the bright blue irises darkening. And even without Seeing, she knew. "You would have been the next Matriarch, and you would have been the best Matriarch the Coven has ever seen."

Layle shook her head and was silent for a moment. "I can't hold this much longer."

Nevina nodded. "You should rest if you can. Save your strength." She watched as Layle wiped tears from her cheeks, smearing blood across her face in the process. "I love you," she blurted, knowing there would never be another chance for her to say it again.

Layle's eyes widened. Nevina was sure that Layle had never heard those words from her before. "I love you too, Mother."

MOTHLENOR

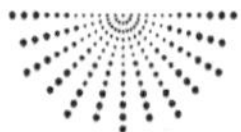

Mothlenor stared at the spot the Matriarch had occupied a moment ago. The spell he'd woven to bring her to the bath had not been an easy one, and the effort had left him tired, but seeing the annoyance and anger on her face when she saw him had made it worth it, as had the indistinct glimpses of her body beneath the water's surface. *And when she realizes it wasn't a mere illusion ...* It was a shame he would miss that.

Still ... what she had said about her girls being ravaged in the dungeons bothered him. He knew that it was customary for each woman of the Coven to teach and care for a group of younger members. He had seen as much himself when Nevara used to visit the castle with a younger Nevina in tow. But Nevina herself had never brought her girls to the castle before. *Why would she do so now?*

Mothlenor dressed in silence, discarding the robe he'd worn and pulling on the more comfortable heavy silks he was accustomed to wearing. His visit with Nevina had not gone as planned, but he should have expected as much. He couldn't just put on his brother's clothes, bring her to his brother's private baths, and expect her to treat him as she would his brother. To her, he was only a murderer. But he could be more.

He left the heavy damp of the bath behind, exchanging a few short words with the knight waiting outside the door. His steps carried him to the foot of his tower, though his mind was still with Nevina. Her anger had been expected, even the tantrum and wine flinging could have been expected. She had asked him for Vyrisian wine, knowing he wouldn't supply it. That, too, could be expected of her. But still, there was something to Nevina that he could not place, could not decipher. Hers was an unfinished portrait. And he loathed half-finished work.

His thoughts were still on Nevina when a knock sounded on his tower door.

"Come in," Mothlenor growled, straightening to greet the visitor.

Ferrand opened the door, stepping over the threshold and into Mothlenor's study. He looked like a proud young buck, with his black King's Guard cloak and plumed helm. *But even the strongest bucks can be brought down, Ferrand.*

"You asked to see me, my lord?"

"I just had a rather interesting visit with the Matriarch, Ferrand." Mothlenor watched his commander carefully for any reaction.

"Oh?" Ferrand's eyes narrowed at the mention of Nevina, but nothing more.

"You did not tell me that she had other members of the Coven with her," Mothlenor said slowly. He leaned back into his chair, eyes still on Ferrand.

"I didn't think it mattered."

"When you took them to the dungeons," Mothlenor began, feeling his anger rise, "how did you treat them?"

"About the same as the Matriarch." Ferrand gave a half-hearted shrug. "I didn't think it mattered."

"They were only children, Ferrand. You should have let

them go," Mothlenor snarled. "Instead, you beat and raped them. You murdered two of them."

"They were Coven children," Ferrand said quietly.

Mothlenor considered his words for a moment. "They could have been turned from the Coven. They could have been useful." He frowned, glaring at Ferrand. "Not now."

"They were Coven children," Ferrand repeated, his voice smooth and low. "They would not have been turned."

Mothlenor sat in silence for a moment. Perhaps Ferrand was right. The idea of harming an innocent child was abhorrent. But an elf child would grow to be an elf, and a dwarf child would grow to be a dwarf. "A Coven child would grow to be a Coven witch," he murmured.

"My thoughts as well."

"Perhaps you did well after all." Mothlenor sighed. "The cuffs, did they work well?"

"They worked splendidly," Ferrand replied with a nod. "If possible, I'd like to request more to be made."

"More?"

"We only have a few sets left, after bringing in the Matriarch and her ilk. If we are to take the Coven—"

Mothlenor waved a hand to silence him. "They are easy enough to make. I'll see to it that you are equipped with more."

"Thank you, my lord."

"And the other task I left to you? Have you found a suitable replacement?"

Ferrand smiled, his eyes glinting. The expression was strangely unnerving. "Yes, I have."

Ajax tugged absently at his new surcoat, eyeing the swelling crowd nervously. News of the Matriarch's confession to the king's murder had spread quickly throughout the city, and the people's anger at the Coven was nearly palpable. There had already been a near riot this morning, prior to Mothlenor's ascension as king, and Ajax and his men had been woefully unable to quell it unarmed. It had only quieted for good when Mothlenor himself stepped out onto the balcony overlooking the market square and had promised vengeance and retribution for the Matriarch's deeds. Ajax almost found himself questioning whether he was right to be skeptical of the new king.

Almost.

The market square was beginning to fill again as those who had left after Mothlenor's coronation returned to witness the first public hanging in several years. A hastily constructed gallows surrounded by wooden barricades waited beneath the same balcony Mothlenor had stood on earlier, but far enough away from the castle wall to give the king a decent view of the proceedings. It was the job of the Peace Guard to prevent anyone from slipping from the crowd and reaching the gallows, and Ajax could feel his stomach tighten with each passing moment.

Nevina ... I'm sorry. But you confessed ... Why did you confess?

He took his post directly in front of the noose, making sure he was close enough to hear the sentence being carried out but angled so that he wouldn't have to see it happen. Ajax was just as upset by Areanath's death as everyone else present, but he couldn't bring himself to believe that Nevina was responsible. And he couldn't watch her die.

A young man approached Ajax, eyes bright with anticipation or anger, Ajax couldn't tell for certain. "When will the show be starting, Commander?"

Show? Is that what they think is happening? Ajax frowned down on the young man, dropping a hand to rest on the pommel of his sword, forgetting for a moment that it was no longer on his hip. "The sentence will be carried out at the mercy of our king," Ajax answered stiffly. But the young man just stared blankly at him. Ajax grimaced. "It will happen when it happens. Now step back. And I'm no longer the commander," he added. His words had a bitter bite to them that he wasn't fond off, but he didn't apologize as the man turned and walked away.

The young man had hardly stepped back into the crowd when Ajax heard the slam of a heavy door behind him, and several members of the waiting horde cheered loudly. Ajax turned to see the new commander leading a small entourage of fresh King's Guards from the entrance of the guard tower. Between them staggered a woman, bound at the wrists and head covered with a black bag. She was led up to the gallows steps by the elbows, and Ajax quickly turned away as Ferrand started to pull the bag from her face.

The crowd cheered again, and Ajax heard a muffled cry behind him. *Did they gag her?* he wondered, but he couldn't bring himself to turn and look. A middle-aged man stepped forward, arm poised to throw the sizable rock held in his fist.

Ajax reacted without thinking, shoving the man back as he threw. The rock skittered to the ground a few feet away, and the man scowled up at Ajax as he picked himself up from where he had fallen.

"Stay back!" Ajax bellowed, his voice carrying out across the jostling crowd.

Commander Ferrand began to read aloud the charges brought against the Matriarch. Ajax didn't want to listen. He tuned them all out. Ferrand's reading, the shouts and jeers of the watching crowd. He went deaf to them all.

The crowd obediently stayed an arm's reach away from Ajax and his men, the sole exception being an old woman who hobbled forward at a shocking speed to spit on the ground before the gallows. Ajax let her. He couldn't stop an elderly woman. But the man next to him, Mirn, stepped forward to take the woman's arm and escort her back to the crowd. The woman smacked his hand away, cursing him. Then she turned once more, raising a shaking fist to the gallows. Her cheeks were wet. She returned to the crowd and melted into it again. Ajax looked at Mirn, who caught his eye before turning away. He looked like he was going to be ill. Ajax felt the same, his stomach roiling.

Oh, Great Ones, Ajax thought, fighting the rising bile in his throat. *Is this the worst of it all, or is this only a small taste of the darkness to come?*

As if in answer to his prayer, Ajax heard the trap door to the gallows collapse, and the snap of the rope as it went taut.

The crown went frantic, erupting into loud cheers. They tried to press in closer, and Ajax and his men fought to keep them back. One man slipped under Ajax's arm and made a run for the gallows. Ajax turned, grabbing the man and pulling him away. But at that moment he saw the face of the woman hanging from the gallows. She was swaying slightly, but she had thankfully died with her fall. Her mouth had been gagged, as Ajax had thought, and her neck was twisted at an angle that made his breath catch.

With a hasty shove, he pushed the man back into the screaming crowd. His gut was in turmoil at the sight of a broken woman hanging for all to see. But his heart was elated, pounding in a rapid staccato in his chest.

It was not Nevina's face that he had seen.

35

SILVANA

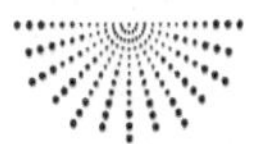

Silvana watched her brother from the corner of her eye as she finished a bit of mending on one of Hasani's shirts. He sat in the hard-backed chair at Hasani's desk, elbows propped on his knees, head hanging low. He looked almost repentant.

As he should.

Silvana sat across the room in her favorite cushioned seat, work spread over her lap. She tried desperately to seem unconcerned by his presence, by his change in demeanor, but she couldn't help but glance his way every handful of seconds.

"Silvana—" Ajax started.

"Not yet." Her words had an angry bite to them, and she thought she might have seen Ajax recoil slightly. She considered softening her words, perhaps apologizing, but didn't.

After his last visit, no one could blame me for a little anger.

The Matriarch had been hanged over a week before, and this was Ajax's second visit to her. The first time he'd come was only hours after the hanging, and he had been drunk. Ajax had raved, mostly incoherently, and had seemed simultaneously furious and elated. He'd cursed the new commander, smashed the mirror Silvana had finally returned to the mantle, and had insisted that the Matriarch was still alive. And finally, after a good half hour that felt more like a week, he had collapsed into a drunken sleep on the floor in front of the fireplace.

When Silvana awoke the next morning, Ajax had gone, and a note had been penned in his immaculate script.

"I'll be back.

We need to talk about Nevina."

Silvana had dared to hope that sobering up had given him the clarity to admit that the Matriarch was dead. But when he knocked on her door not an hour ago, the first words out of his mouth when she opened it had been a rushed apology, followed by, "Nevina is alive and I have to find her."

Silvana made her last stitches slowly, counting out a quiet second or two between each. Finally, she knotted the thread and bit it off. "There. All done. Now what did you want to talk about, Ajax?"

Ajax sounded bitter. "You know what I want to discuss. Nevina is—"

"Nevina is alive, yes, yes," Silvana snapped. "Anything else you care to discuss? Dragons have been spotted along the southern coasts, perhaps? The Great Ones have returned in a shower of light and thunder?"

"Silvana—"

"We saw her hang, Ajax," Silvana pleaded. "I know you cared for her, I'm no fool. But she confessed to murdering Areanath, and we watched her die."

"I know, I know," he growled, standing to pace in front of her. "But you weren't close enough to see her face. Those weren't her eyes that I saw."

Silvana snorted. "You've seen Nevina's eyes, then?"

Ajax's step faltered slightly, almost imperceptibly. But she caught it. "Yes."

"Through her veil?"

"Yes." His voice was quiet, somber.

"Ajax—"

"She showed me her face." Ajax halted, turning to face her.

Silvana looked up. "What?"

"Before she disappeared, she took off her veil for me."

Silvana's voice caught for a second, and she could only stare at her brother. *A Coven sister, removing her veil? It was nearly unheard of ...*

Ajax knelt beside her, taking one of her hands in his own. Finally, Silvana choked out, "Why?"

"Because she loves me. And I love her. And because it was a promise. That she would come back."

Silvana searched her brother's eyes. There was a pain there that she had never seen before. He was the older sibling, always there to comfort her, and now he was the one that needed comforting. And she had intentionally needled him, out of anger. "You've seen Nevina's face, then?"

"Yes," Ajax muttered.

"And those weren't her eyes?"

"No." Ajax sighed. "I was close enough to see that woman's face, and it was not Nevina. The woman they hanged was too young. She had brown eyes, large and frightened."

"And Nevina's?"

Ajax's lips turned up into a small smile, and he stared vacantly down at the floor between his knees. "Nevina's eyes are like ... sapphires. Icy sapphires."

"Ajax ..." Silvana dropped her needlework, tossing one arm around her brother's neck, the other smoothing out his unruly hair. "You're sure? Very sure?"

"Yes." Ajax's eyes stared into hers. There was so much pain within them, the sight of them crushed her. "She's here, somewhere in the city."

"Why would the king lie? Why would he hang an innocent woman?"

"I don't know." Ajax closed his eyes, his shoulders slumping. After a moment, his gaze met hers again. "You don't believe me."

Silvana couldn't answer. She wasn't sure what to believe.

"Go and talk to the farmer Martyn. He and his wife live outside of town, along the southern section of the main road. There's a stable in the front. He'll be outside, I'm sure. Tell them I sent you, and Martyn will tell you what he saw."

Silvana shook her head. "Ajax, I can't—"

He took her hand in his, squeezing it painfully. "Please. Tell him I sent you."

His gaze held her more than his grip on her hand. *So much pain in those eyes* ... "Alright, I'll go."

His grip slackened and he pulled her close, wrapping his arms around her swollen waist. "Thank you." His voice was almost a sigh.

It was almost another week before Silvana could make her way out to the farm Ajax had described. The wind had turned, bringing with it a chill from the north. But Silvana had bundled herself and her swollen belly, which seemed to grow larger with each passing day, and made her way out of the city proper and into the farmland.

She traveled on foot, as the king's horses could no longer be borrowed by anyone other than King's Guards now. The walk was smooth, but her pregnancy made her tire easily, and she stopped for small rests along the roadside. She passed no one, though she had heard that patrols of the farmlands had increased dramatically since Ferrand had been given command of the King's Guard. Silvana briefly wondered where the guards on patrol might be, wondering if she could ask for assistance if one passed by.

But the road remained empty and quiet, and Silvana continued on her way.

Finally, shortly after the lunch hour, she came to the farm that Ajax had described. The house was small, though well loved, and the stable stood close by to one side, the smell of animals wafting on the cold air. And, as Ajax had predicted, an old farmer emerged from the stable to greet her.

"Can I help you, lady?"

"A-are you M-Martyn?" Silvana stammered around chilled lips.

"Yes, yes." Martyn shuffled forward, taking her around the shoulder. "Imis bless you, you're half frozen. What are you doing out here?"

"My name is Silvana. M-my brother sent me. Ajax?"

"The commander?" Martyn dropped a hesitant arm around her, guiding her towards the house.

"Yes, though he would insist that I tell you he's no longer the commander," Silvana answered, letting him pull her gently along beside him. "He wanted me to ask you about the Matriarch."

Martyn opened the door for her, ushering her into the warmth of the farmhouse. "Nana, we have a visitor," he called into the depths of the house. Turning back to Silvana, he asked, "The Matriarch? What about her?" His voice was hesitant, or perhaps just lilting with age.

Silvana glanced around the front room, finding the gentle wear of the place soothing. "He said you could tell me about what happened to her." In the light of the fireplace, Silvana thought she could make out an old bruise under one of Martyn's eyes.

"What's this about the Matriarch, Martyn?" A plump woman had come from the adjacent room, dusting her floured hands on her apron as she entered.

"Ah, Nana, this is Silvana, the commander's sister, she's been sent to ask us about the Matriarch."

"The commander's sister?" Nana asked. "He's a good one, your brother. Ever since the king made him into one of those Peace Guards, he always finds the time to stop by for a chat when he's out on patrol." Silvana held her hand out in greeting, and Nana shook it. "Oh, Great Ones be blessed, you must be freezing!" Nana said, taking both of Silvana's hands in hers and clutching them close. "Did you walk all the way here? And with a child coming, no less?" Nana tsked, rubbing warmth into Silvana's chilled fingers. "I have some cakes cooling in the other room. How about I make some tea, and we'll get you warmed and fed before we talk about the Matriarch, hm?"

"Thank you," Silvana managed, taken aback, "but I don't want to be a bother."

Nana tsked again, already turning to bustle back through the open door. "It's no bother, dear. I'll just be a moment."

Martyn pulled a chair close to the fireplace, motioning for Silvana to sit. She did, noting the pair of hand-carved icons standing side by side on the mantle. He sat opposite, a small table between them. "How is the castle these days? Nana and I haven't been since the weather began to turn." He rubbed his gnarled hands together, warming them as Silvana warmed her own hands. "Too hard going on our old bones, though you'll never hear Nana admit it."

"It's … different," Silvana said hesitantly. "Since Areanath's death."

Martyn nodded. "Most things are."

Silvana's eyes drifted to the pair of icons on the mantle, and she lifted a chilled hand to point at them. "May I?"

Martyn leapt to his feet with a grin, reaching for the carved figures and passing them to Silvana. "They're not so nice as what you might find in Etritia proper, but we're very proud of them."

Silvana turned each one carefully over in her hands. One was definitely female, with long flowing hair and a pitcher tucked under one arm. Her face was the most carefully carved part of her, with gently curving cheeks and a small nose set below large, round eyes. The other was more masculine, with the hilt of a sword held between both hands, the point thrust into the flat base of the carving. The lines of his face were sharper, with thick brow lines carved over large eyes. "Imis and Elir," Silvana muttered. She held them out for Martyn to take. "Did you make them?"

"I did." He returned the wooden gods to their place on the mantle, his hands lingering on each one. "Elir for the protection of our house and lands. Imis for the caring of our souls, both now and in death."

Silvana wanted to shudder, but Martyn's reverent tone stopped the unconscious tremor his words otherwise might have given her. She had never cared much for the Great Ones, but there were so many in Azimar who still did. *Areanath included,* Silvana reminded herself.

So instead she only nodded, letting Martyn settle himself back into his chair.

"That walk didn't upset the baby, did it? It's not an easy going, in this chill."

Silvana frowned, warming one hand against the heat of the flames, the other absently stroking her stomach. "It was bearable. The baby is fine." She smiled, looking down at her growing belly. "He seems to be fairly resilient."

"He?" Martyn asked with a smile. "You're hoping for a boy, then?"

Silvana chuckled. "My husband is. I keep hoping that maybe we'll have a little girl instead."

Martyn frowned, shaking his head. "Awfully brave, hoping for a little girl in a time like this."

Silvana tilted her head, turning slightly to warm both hands against the fire. "What do you mean?"

Martyn sighed, glancing back towards the open doorway. His eyes met hers briefly before he looked away. "There have been … attacks. By the new King's Guards."

Silvana's brows shot up. "Attacks? Have you complained to Commander Ferrand?"

Martyn scoffed. "A lot of good that would do. Ferrand is leading most of them."

"Martyn," Nana snapped from the doorway. She crossed the room in a handful of strides, setting a tray laden with sweet cakes onto the table in front of Silvana. "That's nothing to gossip about, dear."

"But, Nana—" Martyn started.

"No," Nana barked, giving her husband a harsh look. She hung a small kettle on a hook in the fireplace to warm. "That's not what the lady here came to discuss with us."

Silvana opened her mouth to protest but closed it. If Nana wanted help, she would ask for it. *Still … it might be worth mentioning to Ajax. Perhaps he can do something …*

"Now, darling, what did you want to know about the Matriarch?"

Silvana hesitated, not sure how to begin. "My brother …" She paused. *He what, exactly? Believes that Nevina is still alive? That would spread like wildfire.* "My brother seems to think that there was something odd about the Matriarch's disappearance and capture," she began again. "He says that talking to you will convince me of the same."

"It was odd enough, alright," Martyn said with a snort. "They were staying just up the road a bit, towards the main gate. You must have passed their cottage on the way down here, though I'm not sure which it was."

"Martyn was working in the field when he saw them being led away," Nana interjected, leaning against her husband's chair. "As soon as he could, he ran inside to tell me what he'd seen. Those poor little dears must have been terrified."

"Who?" Silvana asked, a knot suddenly forming in her stomach. "The girls?"

Martyn nodded. "Those men had them all trussed up in some sort of strange cuffs." Martyn shrugged a shoulder, staring vacantly for a moment. "No chains between them, like you might have seen before. Just the cuffs, one on each wrist." Martyn held his arms up, fists closed, to demonstrate. Silvana thought she could make out faint bruises on his knuckles. "And the littlest one, she couldn't have been taller than my knee—"

"Arella …" Silvana muttered.

"Well, she was wailing up a storm. Kept saying that she was going to die." Martyn shook his head. "It was painful to hear. She sounded so sure …"

A log in the fireplace collapsed and Nana hurried to add another, pulling the steaming kettle down as she did. Silvana jumped at the sound then drew a steady breath, willing the shaking in her hands to stop. "And they were taken to the castle? Through the residential area?" Martyn nodded and Silvana shrugged a shoulder. "Why does it matter? Mothlenor had declared the Matriarch a murderer, and had ordered her to be brought in for a trial. They were taken from the cottage for that reason, weren't they?" *Though it didn't seem to explain why the girls were taken, too.*

Martyn shook his head, leaning forward to rest his elbows on his knees. "You don't understand. The Matriarch was captured and taken into custody *before* the king was murdered. They were taken only hours after the king left with his brother. It wasn't until the next day that Mothlenor made his declaration, and the Matriarch was already in his custody by then."

Silvana opened her mouth to speak, but the sound of a horse whinnying down the road drew their attention towards the door of the farmhouse.

"He's back," Martyn said, standing with a bit of effort.

Nana took a deep breath, seeming to calm herself. She reached out to take Silvana's hand. "Come along, dear, you shouldn't be found here."

"Who's back?" Silvana asked.

Nana grabbed her hand in a surprisingly firm grip. "Never mind who. We just need to get you into a safe spot where you won't be seen." She looked Silvana up and down. "I'm afraid you're a bit too large for the larder, darling. It'll have to be the bedroom."

"Nana …" Martyn's voice was strained, and he watched her with thin lips pursed together.

"It can't be helped, Martyn. Better she not be seen, for the baby's sake."

Martyn nodded once, hesitantly. "I'll keep him distracted, then."

"Nana, what's going on? Who is out there?" Silvana asked as she was pulled firmly through to the opposite end of the house towards a closed door that could only be the bedroom. "One of the King's Guards?"

"Not if we're lucky," Nana whispered back, face drawn. She pulled Silvana towards the far wall of the bedroom, against which stood a tall wardrobe. "In here, darling, and you must not make a sound."

Silvana could hardly survey her surroundings before Nana tucked her hastily into the wardrobe and closed the doors against her. Silvana was thrown into darkness, surrounded by clothing she could not see.

Nana stood on the other side of the door, leaning against the wood and whispering. "Don't make a sound. Don't let him know you're in there."

Silvana could hear voices in the next room. Martyn's soft placating tone sounded weak against the muffled thundering of a voice Silvana thought she recognized. "Nana, what's going to happen?"

"Just stay in there, darling," Nana insisted. Silvana

thought the woman might be holding back the urge to cry. "No matter what you might hear, don't come out, and don't make a sound. Or he'll hurt you, too."

There was a cry from Martyn, and a heavy thump in the next room. Nana made a sound like a soft sob, and her light steps hurried away. Silvana heard the bedroom door open, and Nana gasped.

"Ah, Nana, you're already in here. Were you waiting for me?"

"Commander," Nana whispered, and Silvana recognized the smooth voice as Ferrand, the new Commander of the King's Guard. "What have you done to my husband?"

"He's just got a nice bump on the head. He'll be fine, Nana."

Silvana remembered Martyn's words. *There have been ... attacks.* And the bruise on his face? Had Ferrand done that?

"These cakes of yours are amazing, Nana. I should come by more often to sample them." Ferrand's heavy footsteps fell deeper into the room, and Silvana felt her heart pound with his every step.

"Th-thank you, Commander."

"No, thank you, Nana. How do you do it? They're so soft and plain on the outside, but the inside is so warm and delicious." Another footfall, and Silvana could almost sense Nana stepping away from him. "I really must know your secret, Nana." The sound of the door shutting was eerily loud.

"I'm flattered, Commander." There was a pause, broken by the sound of something scraping against the wooden floor, followed by a heavy thud. "What are you doing?"

"Just making sure your husband doesn't bother us while I thank you properly, Nana."

"Please, just leave us—"

There was the sharp sound of a slap, and Nana cried out in pain. Silvana had to cover her mouth to stop a sob from escaping. She clung to the soft linens surrounding her, burying her face in them.

"Come now, Nana." Ferrand's voice was still as silky as ever, and there was a soft thump and another cry from Nana. *Had he tossed her onto the bed? Hit her again?* "You should understand by now how this will work. But I can give you another lesson, if you would like."

"No, please, just … do as you must." Nana was sobbing, relenting. Silvana had to bite down on her lip to keep from crying out.

There was the sound of tearing cloth, and Nana's quiet whimper. On the other side of the room, Martyn could be heard pounding against the closed door. His muffled cries echoed through the room, and Silvana buried her face deeper into the cloth in her hands.

Ferrand grunted loudly, and Nana cried out again.

Silvana could only stifle her tears, and remember Nana's words.

Don't come out.

Nana's cries dissolved into sobs, punctuated by the occasional grunt from Ferrand.

Don't make a sound.

Martyn's pounding on the door grew more frenzied, and his shouts louder.

Or he'll hurt you, too.

After a time, it stopped. Nana continued to sob as Ferrand's heavy footsteps crossed the bedroom once more. Silvana heard something scraping against wood again, and when the door opened, it was with a thunderous crash.

"I'll kill you!" Martyn's voice was hoarse from shouting. "Elir guide me, I'll—" His words ended in a strangled gasp, and Silvana could hear a weak struggle.

"Martyn, no!" Light footsteps rushed across the floor, but a loud smack abruptly stopped them. There was a loud thud and a cry of pain as someone fell to the floor.

Ferrand's steps receded, and with him went the strangled cries of Martyn.

From the next room there came a crash, and Silvana's heart went to her throat.

Ferrand's voice was silk in the silence. "Touch me again, you piece of filth, and *I* will kill *you*."

The door to the farmhouse was opened then slammed shut again.

There was a moment of absolute silence, then Nana's weak voice called out, "Silvana, he's gone. You can come out now."

Silvana rushed out, wiping tears from her eyes and falling to Nana's side. She was propped up on the floor, one hand clutching the ruins of her dress and apron to her chest.

Silvana held a hand out for her, but Nana shook her head. Her hair was a tangled disarray around her tear-streaked face. "Martyn, please …"

Silvana nodded, and stepped around the prone woman to make for the adjacent room. There was a chair in the hall-way, perhaps dragged there during the struggle. Silvana righted it numbly, and hurried on.

In the next room, Martyn was finding his feet, one hand pressed to a cut on his head. The chairs by the fire had been knocked over; one had a splintered leg. Faint bruises were already flowering around Martyn's neck, and he looked at her with wide-eyed confusion. "Nana?"

Silvana pointed behind her, and Martyn stumbled away.

She watched him go, catching glimpses of his wife beyond him. They clung to each other, sobbing quietly and whispering words of comfort she could not hear.

Silvana righted the still intact chair, setting it close to the fire. The kettle was still sitting on the hearth and Silvana hung it in the fireplace to warm again. The wooden icons of Elir and Imis had fallen over on the mantle. Silvana sat them upright again, her hands lingering over each one. Her body moved of its own accord, her mind still back in the bedroom, still hearing Ferrand's smooth voice.

The sobs from the next room quieted, but the whispered words continued. Silvana could only wait, too afraid to leave, worried she might come across another King's Guard on the walk back to the castle.

She waited, watching the flames as they heated the pot of water, and tried to find her own comfort to ease the horror she had heard.

Ajax sat alone in his room, a book lying open across his lap and the fire across from him eating away at the chill in his body. The weather had turned cold quickly, and Ajax suspected the coming winter would be a tough one. It was as though Areanath's death had caused all the warmth in Etritia to slowly bleed through the cracks and crevices of the city's walls.

Ajax pulled his gaze from the fire and tried to recall his place in his book. He read the last several lines over again, unable to concentrate; his mind kept drifting to thoughts of Nevina. He was sure she was in the city somewhere, but he had searched all over for her. *Where is she? Where are her girls? And what did Ferrand do to her?*

A heavy pounding on his door pulled his gaze away from the fire again. Startled, he stood and hurried for the door just as whoever stood on the other side beat against the wood a second time. Ajax opened the door just a crack, not sure who might be waiting on the other side. He certainly wasn't expecting the flaming hair and red-rimmed eyes that stared at him from the hall.

"Silvana, what are you doing here? What happened?"

"Did you know?" Silvana asked, her voice low and hoarse. "Did you know what Ferrand was doing out on the farmlands?"

Ajax's gaze flicked down the hall, but it was empty. He opened the door wider, ushering his sister inside. Shutting the door firmly behind him, he turned to see her standing only a few steps away, angry eyes watching him. "Tell me what happened." Ajax sighed. He looked his sister over more closely as she stripped off her outer cloak and stood to warm herself by the fire. Her cheeks and ears were red, and her hair had been whipped from the neat plait she kept it in. Most disturbing was the tear-streaked face and the vacant way she stared into the flames. He handed her his own glass of wine, warmed from its time by the fire, and she took it in shaking hands.

"Ferrand has been attacking the farmers." Silvana brought the wine to her lips, sipping at its warmth eagerly. "I went to Martyn, as you asked, and they told me about the Matriarch." She fell into Ajax's chair, one hand nervously smoothing her hair.

Ajax took a knee, working on the lacing of her fur-lined boots. Silvana gave him a grateful glance, and he nodded for her to continue.

"I had only been there for a few minutes when we heard a horse on the road." Her gaze returned to the hearth, as Ajax's had been drawn only moments before. He knelt beside her, hands wrapped around one of hers. Her fingers were cold, the tips a dull shade of blue.

Silvana's voice continued in a low monotone, and she paused periodically to sip from the warmed wine. "Nana took me by the hand and led me through the house. She hid me in the wardrobe in their bedroom. She was frightened, though she tried so hard to hide it from me. Martyn stayed in the front room and welcomed the knight that had called on them. But he hit Martyn over the head, knocking him unconscious. Martyn told me later that the knight had come to the house with only one thing on his mind, and was already prepared to beat Martyn to get it."

Silvana downed the last of the wine, sitting up as if to fill it again, but Ajax took the empty glass from her trembling fingers and filled it for her, nodding again for her to continue talking. He was sure he knew where her tale would lead, but she needed to unburden the story onto someone else. And he wanted to better know the monster that was the new commander.

"The knight came into the bedroom, and I recognized his voice then. Ferrand hit Nana, tossed her onto the bed, and …" Her voice wavered and she pulled her hand from Ajax's grasp to wipe at her cheeks.

"Silvana …" He slid closer to her, wrapping his arms around her shoulders and pulling her tight against him. "You don't have to say it."

Silvana sobbed into his shoulder and he stroked her hair, murmuring to her as she wept.

She lifted her head after a moment, watery eyes finding his. "You're not surprised."

Ajax shook his head. "Dars has given me reports of similar incidents within the city in the last week. It seems Ferrand and his men see themselves as being above the law."

"You have to tell the king," Silvana insisted, her voice thin and hoarse. "He has to remove Ferrand from the King's Guard."

"I've been requesting an audience with him for days, Silvana. He refuses to see me."

"Ask Hasani. He'll make sure you can get an audience," Silvana pleaded.

Ajax sighed. "I haven't seen Hasani in several days, either. I keep trying to meet with him, and he with me, but our duties keep us apart." *On a suspiciously regular basis.*

"I'll talk to him. I'll tell him what I saw today and that you have more reports of the same. He'll get you an audience with Mothlenor, and you can convince the king to remove Ferrand."

Ajax nodded slowly. "I can try."

Silvana wiped absently at her face, staring once more at the fire. "You'll have to do more than try, Ajax." She turned to look at him again, her expression pained. "If you don't, who will protect us from our protectors?"

Who indeed?

But Ajax only nodded.

It was almost another week before he finally received his summons to meet with Mothlenor. Dars was the one to bring it to him, along with another report of Ferrand and his men coercing a tanner in the residential area into giving his daughter over for Ferrand to abuse. In exchange for his daughter's virtue, the tanner received a delay on paying the increased taxes Mothlenor had ordered in the days before. And, presumably, the tanner was allowed to keep his life, though that fact would never be found in any official report.

Dars followed close behind as Ajax hurried through the castle to Mothlenor's tower. "Have you found anythin' new about the Matriarch?" Dars asked in a low voice.

Ajax's gaze darted around their surroundings, but they were alone. Dars had surely done the same before asking the question, but it was only too wise to stay alert. "No, nothing yet." Ajax's voice was just as low and quiet as Dars's, and a small part of him was unnerved by the treasonous tone it gave his words. "I've searched the residential area and most of the farmlands, and I've combed every inch of the jails, but there's no sign of her."

"What about the dungeons?"

Ajax's step faltered, and he waited as another Peace

Guard passed them before answering. The Peace Guard gave them a strained nod as they passed, and Ajax and Dars both returned it. *Vayle, King's Guard for over ten years. Another faithful man reduced to nothing.* But he said nothing and waited until Vayle was out of earshot before speaking. "The dungeons were closed off over a hundred years ago, Dars. She wouldn't be down there."

"They *were* closed. Might not be closed any longer," Dars grunted. "And the entrance is below Mothlenor's tower. Awfully convenient, if you ask me."

Ajax considered his words. "I'll look into it. Thank you, Dars." He slowed as they neared the tower. "How have you been? It seems that our paths rarely cross anymore. How is your wife?"

"Gone." Dars' voice had a bitter bite to it, and it pulled Ajax to a stop.

"What do you mean?"

Dars frowned, a muscle in his jaw twitching. "I sent my wife and son south. Last week. She's got family down there still. I don't want them to see what this place will become."

"I …" Ajax hesitated, unsure. "I'm sorry." The words seemed terribly inadequate, but they were all Ajax had to offer. "You didn't go with them?"

Dars shook his head. "I want to be here. I want to help, as much as I might." Dars continued down the hall, leaving Ajax to wait at the base of Mothlenor's tower. "If you were wise, you'd get your sister out of the city, too. Ain't no sense in bringing a baby into this world."

Ajax could only watch his old friend depart, looking older and frailer than Ajax could ever remember him. Ajax considered what Dars had said for a moment. *Perhaps he's right. Silvana might not be safe in the city any longer. But she would never leave without Hasani, and he will be hard to convince.*

Ajax shook his head as Dars turned a corner and disappeared. *This is their home as much as it is mine. They'll want to help the people here in whatever way they can.* Ajax pulled open the heavy door that opened onto the curved stair to Mothlenor's study. *But the world has changed in the last month, and it will only continue to change as Mothlenor's reign continues.*

He climbed the stairs to Mothlenor's study slowly, the eerie sensation of being watched once more sending his skin crawling. It unnerved him to make the climb, but if he could convince Mothlenor to remove Ferrand from service, then perhaps the city and surrounding farmlands would be that much safer.

The door to Mothlenor's study was shut firmly, and Ajax rapped twice on the door to announce himself. There was a chill to the Old Tower, and Ajax waited silently on the drafty stairs until Mothlenor called him in.

Shutting the door behind him, Ajax bowed low to Mothlenor. "Thank you for agreeing to see me, my lord. I have some urgent news I'd like to discuss with you."

Mothlenor's eyes never left the pages of the book he was studying. "I normally wouldn't agree to meet directly with someone of your station, Ajax, but your sister's husband seemed rather adamant about it. Hasani's turned himself into a chittering little pest." Mothlenor's cold green eyes flicked up to meet Ajax's just for a moment. "I don't like pests, Ajax."

Ajax nodded, hearing the threat and not truly knowing how to reply.

"What was it that you wanted to discuss, Ajax?"

Ajax took a half step closer, but a glare from Mothlenor over top of his book stopped him. "It's Ferrand—"

"Commander Ferrand," Mothlenor corrected.

"Commander Ferrand, then." Ajax couldn't bite back the disgust he felt at using the title. "He's been behaving very poorly for someone of his rank. Frankly, if he were any other man, I would have had him arrested and spending the rest of his life in a cell weeks ago. He's—"

"I know full well what the commander has been doing,

Ajax." Mothlenor's voice was low and angry. "You don't need to tell me."

Ajax's brows raised. "Then you know that he has been raping women and girls here in the city? That he's been going out to the farmlands, beating old men and abusing their wives?"

"What the commander does is none of your concern, Ajax. He is bringing order to the city, he is—"

"He is using his title and your name to abuse your people. They are frightened of him, and fear does not inspire loyalty for long, my lord." Ajax spat the last words out, and Mothlenor finally let his book drop to his desk, eyes boring into Ajax.

"What would you have me do, Ajax?" he asked quietly.

Ajax hesitated, surprised by the question. "Strip him of his title and put him in jail. He's proved himself incapable of wielding power well, and your people would be better off if he never saw daylight again."

Mothlenor paused for a moment then shook his head. "I can't do that."

"Why?" Ajax asked angrily.

Mothlenor stood in a flash, leaning over his desk, both hands braced against it. "Because I am only one man, and I cannot control all of Azimar on my own!"

Ajax fell back a step, surprised by Mothlenor's outburst. *Your brother could,* he wanted to say. Instead, he half whispered, "You don't have to do it on your own."

Mothlenor made a sound that could have been a scoff or a laugh, and he fell back into his chair, seeming for a moment so much like Areanath. Ajax noticed faint burn marks like hand imprints where Mothlenor had braced his weight against the top of his desk. "Forgive me, Ajax, but you sound like my brother."

"I take that as a compliment. Your brother was a great man."

"Yes, he was …" Mothlenor said softly, eyes vacant.

For a moment, Ajax could almost feel sorry for him. But not quite. "You could put your trust in those who care about you—they can help you be the great man your brother was."

Mothlenor turned towards him, angry. "And end up like my brother? Frail and dependent on others? Murdered by someone I thought loved me?" He snorted, eyes flashing. "I won't be putting my confidences in anyone, least of all you, Ajax."

Ajax wanted to shout at Mothlenor then, but he kept his voice low. "Perhaps you could consider the idea of removing Ferrand from his role."

"There is nothing to consider," Mothlenor snarled. "*Commander* Ferrand will remain as he is." He paused for a moment, watching Ajax. Ajax crossed his arms over his chest to hide the clenching of his fists. "However," Mothlenor continued, "I will make tax collection and other such duties the responsibility of the Peace Guard. That should limit his need to go to the residential areas some, and will therefore hopefully force him to curb his appetite."

Ajax sighed, his arms dropping. "Thank you, my lord."

"I've also been entertaining the idea of closing the gates to all but the King's Guard and, I suppose, the Peace Guard. Those who wish to remain in their homes on the farmlands will be barred from entering the city."

"Th-that's madness!" Ajax balked. "The people here will starve!"

"They will not starve, Ajax." Mothlenor sighed. "Things will continue as they normally do, but with restrictions on who may enter and leave the city." Ajax remained silent, staring at Mothlenor, who sighed and continued, head shaking. "It's a necessary step, to protect ourselves from any outside threat. And one that I'm not fully prepared to make just yet. There will be time for the people to prepare."

"I don't understand," Ajax said. *There is no outside threat.*

"I don't have the time to explain it to you. Go, find the commander and tell him that his duties in the residential area have changed." Mothlenor picked up his book once more and waved Ajax away. "I won't discuss any of this with you again, Ajax. And tell your brother that we have spoken and that he should quit his pestering if he wants to keep his title and the comforts that come with it."

Ajax bowed stiffly, though Mothlenor didn't see it, and left the study, shutting the door a little more firmly than necessary on the way out. He took the stairs down two at a time, hurrying to find first Ferrand, then Hasani. Reaching the landing that opened back into the castle, he paused, recalling Dars's words.

What about the dungeon?

Ajax eyed the spiral stairs that continued down into the darkness. The old dungeons were down there, though the entrance was supposedly sealed off long ago. Ajax took a faltering step further down, leaving behind the door back into the castle. He took another step, curiosity and his desire to finally find Nevina getting the better of him. Another step, then another, until he had gone around the curve of the tower and the light from the torch hanging above the door was beginning to fade.

Before him loomed a stone wall, abruptly putting an end to the descent. Ajax's heart fell. He had hoped to find the entrance unsealed, and the way down to the dungeons open. He put a hand against the wall, testing its strength. Solid, cold stone met his palm. He dropped his head against the stone, forehead pressing against it.

"Nevina …" he whispered. "I'm sorry. I thought I might find you here. But it's just another dead end."

A light draft tickled the skin of one cheek and Ajax lifted his head, hopeful. *Perhaps it's a hidden door …*

Ajax ran his hands along the wall, and along the edges where the wall joined the curved walls adjacent to it. But

he found no hidden trigger to press, no secret handle to
pull.

After several fruitless moments, he beat his fists against
the stone then let his head drop against the wall once more.

"This whole damned tower is drafty. It was just my imagination, nothing more."

Ajax turned away and climbed the dozen or so steps back
up to the door that opened onto the castle proper, and began
his hunt for Ferrand.

But his thoughts turned back to Nevina, as they often did,
and his steps slowed.

I'll find you eventually, I swear.

3 7

FERRAND

Ferrand untied his breeches, motioning for the young girl with him to drop to her knees. She did, eyes wide and terrified. Ferrand could feel himself grow a little harder at the sight.

"Do it properly," he crooned to the girl, "or your family will regret it."

"Y-yes, sir."

Ferrand watched as she began working. She wasn't great, but this was an easy enough thing to teach, given more time. *In a few more weeks, a month perhaps, and she could be the best on this street.*

He twisted his fingers through her hair, wishing it were lighter. His touch startled the girl, but she never stopped.

She gagged at the end. Ferrand could feel the muscles of her mouth and throat working as she tried to keep from vomiting. But he held her close, dragging her too-dark hair to keep her from pulling away.

"Swallow," he commanded, voice low.

She did as she was told. They all did, eventually.

He released her and she immediately stood and bolted from the room. Ferrand followed her out, fastening the lacing of his bottoms once more. He could hear voices from the next room, and when he entered he saw the girl curled up against her mother, who held both arms around her protectively, staring at Ferrand with a delightful mix of anger and fear. And the father … Ferrand let out a low sigh at the sight of the father standing just inside the doorway with Ajax.

"Ajax, I wondered when you might start sticking your nose in places you shouldn't."

Ajax's eyes narrowed on spotting him. "Ferrand. I'd heard you were running over this area of the city." His glance shifted briefly to the girl, who was sobbing loudly into her mother's shoulder. "Here to coerce another man into giving over his daughter to you?"

Ferrand smirked. "I do not coerce, Ajax. I simply offer an alternative that they would not normally consider." The father shifted uncomfortably, fists clenching rhythmically. Ferrand looked him over; he was weak limbed and doughy around the middle. "I'll return tomorrow for the money you owe." He made for the door, but Ajax stepped into his path.

"How much do they owe?"

Ferrand smiled, glancing from Ajax to the father. "Seven gold pieces."

The father instantly protested. "Seven! You said moments ago that it was five!"

Ferrand sighed, eyes falling to the weeping girl. "Your lovely daughter managed to convince me otherwise."

The father balked, stuttering curses. But Ajax only reached out and slapped a small handful of coins into Ferrand's hand. "There's five."

Ferrand closed his fingers around the money, once more looking between father and daughter. "I'll return tomorrow for the rest." He stepped around Ajax, moving for the door once more.

"No, you won't." Ajax's hand tightened around Ferrand's

upper arm, and Ferrand stopped to look the former commander over. "I came to tell you that tax collection is now a duty of the Peace Guard. You will have no business at this home tomorrow, or any other day, Ferrand."

Ferrand took a slow breath, fighting the urge to snap Ajax's wrist. He looked from the former commander to the father, who stood motionless in the doorway, then to the wife and daughter behind him, huddled together like a pair of rats in winter. "Very well." He pulled his arm free of Ajax's grasp and turned his back on the family. "Come back to the barracks and have a drink with me, Ajax."

"I'd rather not." There was a derisive tone to his words that did nothing to please Ferrand.

"It wasn't a request," Ferrand called over his shoulder. He continued walking, and after a few silent seconds, Ajax growled and followed.

The barracks were close by, only a few hundred paces away, across the nearly empty square that stood at the end of the street.

Ajax followed in silence for only a few seconds then matched pace with Ferrand and snarled at him. "She was just a little girl, Ferrand. You should have let her be."

Ferrand smirked, not looking at the man beside him. "The younger they are, the better they can be." He fingered the pommel of his new sword, enjoying the weight of it on his hip. "What is it they say? You can't teach an old bitch new tricks?"

"May Elir damn you, Ferrand," Ajax snarled.

"Come now, Ajax. I'm sure, given the opportunity, you would agree." Ferrand motioned towards the barracks, now looming before them. "Let's have a drink together, and we can discuss matters further."

Ajax begrudgingly opened the door to the barracks, and Ferrand pointed towards a pair of empty chairs at a table just inside the door. Ajax obediently fell into one of the chairs, still glowering at Ferrand. This room of the barracks was nearly empty, save for a Peace Guard hurriedly shoveling down his lunch. At the sight of Ferrand, the man stood and left, taking the last of his bread and cheese with him. From the corner of his eye, Ferrand saw the man give a curt nod to Ajax before he slipped through the door. The sight annoyed Ferrand. Even disgraced as he was, Ajax commanded more allegiance than Ferrand himself did. *No matter ... All will be forgotten, in time.*

"Do you have a favorite drink, Ajax?" Ferrand asked, heading for the cupboard on the far wall.

"It's not the drink I normally care about, Ferrand," Ajax answered in a low voice. "It's the company."

Ferrand snorted. "Spoken like a true man of the people." He pulled down a chipped mug and a crystal wineglass from the cupboard. The first he filled with ale from a nearby keg, the liquid warm and pale brown. The second he filled with red wine, poured from a fresh bottle Ferrand had purchased the day before. He placed the ale in front of Ajax and sat opposite him, sipping the wine.

Ferrand lifted the wineglass to the light, watching the way the sunlight from the open windows played on the glass. From the corner of his eye, he could see Ajax watching him, his drink untouched. "I find, Ajax, that women can often be compared to alcohol."

"Oh?" Ajax's tone was unamused. He wrapped his hands around the mug, but still he did not drink.

"The comparison is a quite simple one, actually. I think even you might understand it." He set the glass down on the table, delighting in the way Ajax's eyes narrowed at the insult. "You see, most women are like that ale you have there. Nothing special, easy to make, but when you want a drink—" Ferrand shrugged a shoulder, leaning back in his chair to watch Ajax. "It'll work. It's better than nothing, anyway."

Ajax said nothing, his hands dropping from the mug to rest, palms down, on the table.

"I prefer white wine, myself," Ferrand continued, eyes on Ajax. "It takes talent to make white wine. In the end, you have something sweet, delicate, so easy to enjoy to its fullest. But, for some reason, it's so hard to come by." Ferrand frowned, tracing a finger along the rim of his glass, making it hum nicely. "And then there are the reds."

Ajax only scowled at him.

"Not quite so good as white wine, but still far better than a regular old ale." Ferrand smirked, amused by the mixed expressions of disgust and hatred on Ajax's face. "A good red wine can be delightful. They're tart, yet palatable …" Ferrand paused, watching Ajax. "And full bodied."

Ajax stood in one quick motion, knocking his chair to the floor. Ferrand only stared at the man as he glared down at him. There was a quiet moment where the only movement was Ajax's jaw working as he bit back whatever words came to him. Finally, Ajax dipped in a bow to Ferrand, who smiled at the motion.

"Thank you for the drink, Commander," Ajax said. "But the taste has gone sour, and I should be going." Ajax turned, reaching for the door.

"Ajax," Ferrand called, and the former commander stopped, hand on the door. "Tell your sister I said hello, would you? It's a shame I rarely see her. I might need to remedy that before the baby comes."

Ajax stormed through the door without a word. Ferrand smirked, sipping once more from his glass of red wine.

3 8

MOTHLENOR

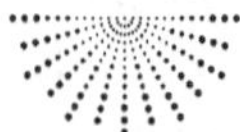

Mothlenor was deep in his research when the shouting first reached his ears. There was a woman's voice, high and quavering with age, growing nearer very quickly. Following it was the pleading mewl of Hasani.

"I will go wherever I damn well please, young man, and right now I want to have a word with your so-called *king*! Anna! Push him down the stairs if you must, but get me up there!"

The voice sounded familiar, and Mothlenor slowly closed his copy of *Daemonica*, contemplating where he had heard it last.

"I'm sorry, but you have to request an audience—"

"Your requests be damned!"

Mothlenor smirked; he recognized the voice as the door to his tower burst open.

In the open doorway stood an elderly woman, her face flushed and her grey-gold hair in disarray. She clung to the arm of a much younger girl, who paled instantly at the sight of him. The older woman's clouded eyes scanned the room, searching for him.

"Navara, is that you?"

At the sound of his voice, her eyes locked on to his figure, but Mothlenor was sure she could not actually see him. She took a hurried step forward, but the young girl pulled her back before she could walk into a pile of books just in front of her. "I want my daughter and her girls returned to me, Mothlenor."

Mothlenor glanced at Hasani at the mention of Nevina. The man's eyes widened, but he said nothing. Mothlenor turned back to the women, ignoring the demand. "I've never seen you without your veil, but I could recognize the screech of a withered old Matriarch any time, Navara."

"And I can recognize the stench of a fresh pile of horse dung, and it's nothing compared to your filth, Mothlenor."

Mothlenor frowned at the insult, choosing not to reply. The old hag could keep up with him better than anyone, except perhaps Areanath. He was surprised to realize both women were wearing plain tunics and pants, paired with old riding boots, choosing to skip the more traditional white dress. And the younger woman was also without her veil, though she seemed thoroughly unsettled by its absence. Her hands kept creeping to her face as if to adjust the missing veil, and her gaze never left the floor or Nevara's face.

"Hasani, in case you haven't realized it, we are in attendance with the former Matriarch of the Coven. I suppose you ladies had to sneak into the city? Hide yourselves among the peasants? You must have realized that you would have been beaten and left for dead if you had shown up in your proper attire. Since, after all, your daughter killed my brother not long ago." He opened his book again, scanning the page to find where he had been interrupted.

"Nevina did not kill Areanath! She loved him!" Navara slumped against the younger girl, Anna. "We all loved him. He was a good man."

Mothlenor's anger flared at her last words and he hissed at the old witch. "My brother is dead. Your daughter has been punished for it. Now leave, before I have you arrested and tried as well."

Navara lifted her chin, her dead eyes seeming to stare straight into him. "Nevina is not dead. I know it. I would have felt her passing." Her eyes narrowed. "I want my daughter returned to me, and her girls as well."

Mothlenor looked up at her, glaring. "Nevina *is* dead. And her girls. They were all tried, Nevina was hanged in the square, and the girls were left to starve in their cells." He had no idea what had become of Nevina's girls after Ferrand's abuse had left two of them dead, but that was an easy enough thing to find out. Out of the corner of his eye, he saw Hasani's shoulders slump. The man was too soft. He wouldn't do as an adviser for much longer. "It's been long enough now that the only thing I could return to you, Navara, would be their rotting, maggoty bodies. Would that please you enough to leave my tower?"

Navara's eyes widened, but she continued to glare at him. "You are lying. I know it." She began weeping silently. "I know it." She wiped frantically at her face, pushing Anna away when the woman tried to comfort her. "I hope you realize that at least one of the girls with Nevina was your brother's daughter. You've killed your own kin, Mothlenor."

He frowned. So his suspicions had been correct. Areanath had been Nevina's infatuate. "Which one?" he asked, interested.

Navara smiled ruefully at him. "I never knew. Nevina wouldn't tell me. Hell, all of her children could have been his, I have no idea. But now you've killed them all." She wiped her face again. "You monster."

Mothlenor's anger flared again. "Hasani."

The man jumped at the sound of his name. "Yes, my lord?"

"Escort these women outside the city then shut all the gates. We will be moving forward with our plan to shut down traffic into and out of the city. These two will be the last civilians to walk through those gates."

"Yes, my lord."

Mothlenor turned to the women. "Go home, Navara. Run back to your Coven. Enjoy what little time you have left with them, you old witch."

He watched as Hasani took Navara by one elbow, Anna taking the other, and together they escorted her through the doorway and down the first steps. As soon as they cleared the doorway, Mothlenor flicked the fingers of one hand and slammed the door on their backs. He paused, listening to their retreating steps, and an idea struck him.

He carefully pulled open a drawer in his desk, pulling from its pillowed spot the precious Dragon's Eye. He had barely framed the thought when the eye flashed brilliantly, and he spied Nevara in its depths. She was walking down the steps to his tower, mere yards away. At her sides, he could clearly make out both Hasani and Anna. Smiling, he let the image die and tucked the stone back where it belonged.

So, the stone didn't work before because I had never seen Nevina's face. Never looked into her eyes.

But it will work now.

NEVINA

"Wake up, Nevina. We have much to discuss."

Nevina sighed, eyes still closed. "Great Ones take your wants, Mothlenor." She slowly opened them, taking in the sights of the bathhouse once more. She was once again naked, the warm water soothing on her skin. The room was still empty, save for a glass of red wine sitting on the lip of the bath, already waiting for her. And Mothlenor was sitting in the pool with her, just out of arm's reach. "Do you have some odd fascination with summoning helpless women to you, naked and alone?"

Mothlenor smiled, though it seemed forced. "It's not my preference, actually. Just how the magic works."

"Blood magic," Nevina murmured. "I guessed as much, after last time. You used the rags your servants collected when they bathed me, am I correct?" Mothlenor nodded slightly, eyes on her. "And I'm actually here, in the bathhouse. This isn't an illusion." Another nod from Mothlenor. "I thought you were going to kill me. I was ready for it."

"Another was executed in your place. A woman with light hair, like yours, and with a similar build. To the rest of Azimar, you are dead."

Nevina nodded; the thought of an innocent woman dying in her place was unsettling to her. She picked up the wine glass, fingering the stem. "Red wine." She had been flattered when Areanath remembered the small things she enjoyed, but then Areanath hadn't caused the deaths of so many she cared for.

"It's an easy enough thing to remember." Mothlenor moved suddenly, and Nevina's eyes flashed to him as he did, but he only grabbed a matching glass of wine and sipped from it before setting it aside once more. "I heard you lost another two girls since we last spoke."

Nevina wanted to curse at him. But she couldn't find the energy to do more than answer numbly. "Lilith died a few hours after I was here last. Your men shoved a knife into her, and the wounds couldn't be healed with these damned cuffs on." Nevina shook one arm weakly, the cuff holding fast to her wrist. "Nala apparently went into shock after being raped. She never snapped out of it. She wouldn't eat, wouldn't drink. She wasted away, and Kall could only watch her as she died." She sipped her wine, the alcohol working its way around the lump in her throat. "Your servant has been kind enough to keep me updated. She seems to find joy in knowing that I am powerless to protect my girls."

"I'm sorry." Mothlenor sighed. "I didn't mean for it to happen this way."

Nevina snorted, eyes welling with tears. "Don't lie, Moth-lenor." She rubbed at a spot of dirt on her arm, trying for a moment to forget the cell waiting for her.

"I am not lying, Nevina." Mothlenor's voice was low, but unusually soft. He almost sounded like his brother, and the sound of it pulled Nevina's gaze up. "I only wanted you here," he continued, his eyes never leaving hers. "I still only want you. It was not my idea to bring your girls to the castle, and it was certainly not my idea to rape and kill them."

Nevina's gaze narrowed. She could nearly believe him,

and that frightened her. "Then let them go." Her voice was firm, far stronger than she actually felt.

Mothlenor nodded. "That is what I brought you here to discuss."

Nevina said nothing, not wanting to betray the sudden hope she felt.

"The former Matriarch came to visit me a few days ago. She told me something interesting about you and my brother."

Nevina's heart raced. *Nevara, here? Why would she come?*

Mothlenor continued, frowning at her silence. "She said that one of the girls you brought with you was my brother's daughter." His head tilted, lips thin. "Is that true?"

Nevina thought of Layle, and with a stab of sorrow she thought of Arella. "Yes."

Mothlenor stood, and Nevina quickly looked away, not wanting to see his naked body, sure it would resemble Areanath's too much. A few steps brought him next to her, where he settled himself, facing her. Nevina wrapped her arms more tightly around her chest and pressed herself into the wall of the bath.

"Has she died?"

Nevina thought of Arella, tiny hands clutching hers at every chance, running barefoot across the library floor to embrace her. "Yes," she choked out with a sob.

Mothlenor was silent for a moment. He didn't touch her, but Nevina could feel the hunger in his gaze as he watched her. She couldn't bring herself to look at him, and kept her gaze locked on the spot where he had been sitting before.

"When you came to see my brother …" Mothlenor started, his voice soft and low, "did you try to get with his child again?"

Nevina said nothing, eyes locked on that now vacant spot of the bath.

"You did, didn't you?"

Still, Nevina did not answer.

"Did it work?"

Mothlenor's hand crept across her stomach, and Nevina flinched. She grabbed his wrist, squeezing it in warning. "No, it didn't." She couldn't bring herself to meet his gaze.

"So my brother has no heirs?"

Nevina thought of Layle again. Technically not an heir, but if she had a son … "No." Her voice was hard and bitter.

Mothlenor pulled his hand away, turning to lean his back against the wall of the pool. "That's a shame, really."

Surprised, Nevina turned to him. "What are you saying? You wanted Areanath to have a son?"

Mothlenor shrugged, eyes vacant. "Considering the circumstance, it would have been easier." He sighed. "I've never thought of having children of my own. I never wanted to be a father."

Nevina wanted to laugh, but she could only stare at Mothlenor. *What is he saying?* "What do I care what you want?"

"Before my brother's death, I often found myself wondering how things might have happened differently, if I were the elder brother and Areanath the younger." Mothlenor crossed his arms over his chest, eyes gazing off into some distant spot. "I believed that things would have been better if I had taken the throne after our father. I could have made Etritia better. Azimar, even. My brother was foolish, and I was sure that I would not have made the same mistakes he did."

Nevina turned away from him, swallowing the words she wanted so badly to spit at him. But he was too calm, too hard to read. Any word might be enough to provoke him. *Who knows what he could do to me if he wanted?*

Mothlenor continued, unperturbed by her silence. "The injustice of it angered me no end. Five tiny minutes separated us, and yet it was enough to make him king." He turned sharply to look at her, and Nevina jumped at the movement. "What if we had been switched at some point, as infants? What if he were actually the younger twin, the less important brother?"

Nevina didn't answer. She only chewed her lip, clutching her arms tighter around her breasts.

"Now that Areanath is dead, I'm not so sure it mattered." Mothlenor took a sip from another wine glass procured from nothing. "I'm almost certain that if I had been king and Areanath the younger brother, I would have made all the same choices he made in life. And he would have made the same ones that I did."

Nevina snorted softly. "Including the choice to kill you?"

Mothlenor's eyes found hers, and Nevina was surprised by the softness in them. "Yes. I think so." He turned away, once more staring off into some unseen spot. "It would have all been the same, I think. It would have been me that you loved, and Areanath would have been the one to lust after you, never quite understanding why."

Nevina pulled her arms tighter around her. He nails dug crescents into the flesh of her upper arms, but she hardly felt it. His words had sent an eerie chill over her, and his distant gaze unnerved her. "What does any of this have to do with my girls?"

Mothlenor nodded slowly, seeming to realize that Nevina was not following his line of thought. "Here is the deal I am prepared to make with you." His eyes met hers, and Nevina was once more disquieted by the unusual tenderness in them. "I will let your remaining girls return to the Coven. I will even remove their cuffs, so long as they promise never to return to Etritia. The Coven will live as long as they might, hidden away from the rest of the world."

Nevina scowled, understanding his intentions. "And I will stay with you?"

Mothlenor nodded. "Your cuffs will remain. For the

remainder of your life, if necessary. You will help me undo my brother's spell. And you will bear my children."

Nevina's first instinct was to laugh at him, to call him a murderous fiend, to tell him she would never willingly let him put a child on her. But then she thought of Layle, and the words died away. There was Kall to consider too. She could return to the Coven and live out her days in relative safety. She might not live, otherwise.

"Do you need time to consider?"

Nevina could only nod, too confused to speak.

"Very well. Don't think on it too long."

And with those words, Mothlenor's face melted from view, replaced with the darkness and filth of her cell.

40

LAYLE

Layle tried once more to scry on her mother, her wrists already aching and oozing blood from the effort.

There was no response.

Layle sighed, setting the half-empty pitcher of water to rest on the stone floor of her cell. *Perhaps she's sleeping.*

Though if she had been simply sleeping, Layle would have still gotten a nice look at whatever the water in her mother's pitcher was reflecting.

Instead, no image had formed on the surface of her own pitcher, and Layle's magic had simply been blocked by something other than the arcane cuffs that lanced her wrists with every spell.

Mothlenor, Layle realized. *She must be with him and he is blocking my magic.*

Layle pushed the images of Mothlenor abusing her mother out of her mind, rubbing nervously at her aching wrists, smearing blood along her arms as she did.

It was time to try again. The spell was difficult, the most difficult one that she had ever done. But the Matriarch had promised that if she could master it, Layle could use it to

252

leave the castle. It was possible to even help Kall and the Matriarch escape the dungeons with her.

Layle focused, sending energy coursing through her body to rest at a spot just above her wrists. It was safer to store energy in the hands, where it could be controlled and directed easier, and where it was less likely to escape the body in unpredictable and dangerous ways. But directing the energy to her palms activated the cuffs, and she didn't want to bleed out while trying to master such a difficult spell.

Layle cast a quick glance around her cell, arms already tingling with the buildup of energy. Closing her eyes, she pictured the cell in her mind's eye. She had done so enough times that she could count the number of stone blocks that encompassed the floor, just from memory alone. But a good memory wouldn't be enough.

Her arms ached with the energy she had accumulated. Her bones felt like they might splinter with the slightest movement.

With a quick prayer to the Great Ones, she dumped the energy from her arms through the cuffs to her hands and activated the spell she held firmly in her mind.

Pain seared through her wrists, causing her to gasp.

But for an instant, she was gone.

She collapsed to the floor, hitting her knee against the hard ground.

"Fuck," Layle cried, rubbing her injured knee and smearing fresh blood across the ragged remains of her filthy dress.

"Layle?" Kall's voice was weak and tired, barely audible from the adjacent room. "Did it work?"

Layle stood, stepping gingerly on her injured leg. It was fine, but she would have another large bruise soon. "I came out too high." Layle frowned, rubbing her wrists. "Again."

"But it worked?"

Layle surveyed her surroundings once more. Still the

same cell, the same number of stone blocks lining the same floor. But she was a good three feet closer to the door than she had been a moment ago. "Yes, it worked."

"Good."

"And you? Are you alright?"

"I'll be fine," Kall's soft voice returned.

Layle shook her wrists, flicking small droplets of blood to the ground. "Alright, I'm going to try again." The first few days she had practiced the spell, she had always tried to stop the bleeding to her wrists before starting again, but she'd quickly realized that it was a wasted effort. They would just bleed again soon enough, so why bother spending precious time stopping it between attempts?

Layle focused again, once more drawing energy and focusing it into a point just above the arcane cuffs. Her arms still ached from the last attempt, but she pushed more energy into them, despite the nauseating sensation that crept into her body.

"You know, Millie and I were always jealous of you."

Layle bared her teeth in a snarl. Kall always chose the wrong moments to get talkative. But the distraction was helpful, in a way. Layle might need to use this spell with knights rushing her, swords drawn. A little distracting banter was nothing.

Layle took a steady breath, relaxing her shoulders as she exhaled. "Oh?"

"You were always so close with the Matriarch. Everyone could see it. She favored you, even though Millie and I had been with her longer." Layle thought she could hear a hint of frustration in Kall's words, but perhaps it was her own frustration she sensed. "Why was that?"

Because she's my mother.

"Perhaps I remind her of herself when she was younger." Layle's arms were heavy with unspent energy. She was nearly ready again. "Besides, she favored Arella more than me."

Layle closed her eyes, pushing the energy from her arms to her hands once more.

Pain.

Gasp.

Layle hit the floor, though not as hard as she had before. In the instant before she fell, she was sure the toe of one bare foot had grazed the cold floor, but she couldn't be sure.

"Damn it all," she muttered.

"Still too high?"

"Still too high."

Kall laughed, the sound weak. "Better to be too high than to be too low, I would think."

Layle sighed, flexing the fingers of her hands to stimulate blood flow again. Kall was right.

She sat against the wall, leaning her head against the stones. "I need a few moments, then I can try again." She was weak, what little energy her body could channel already spent.

"Layle?" Kall sounded so tired. Layle briefly wondered if she might also be trying to work magic around her cuffs.

"Hm?" Layle's eyes had drifted shut. It was so easy to sleep after even a couple of attempts at such a large spell.

"I just wanted to apologize. I should have been a better sister to you."

Layle lifted her head from the wall, blinking away the sleep that had come to take her. It wasn't like Kall to apologize for anything. And there had been a hint of … something … to her words. "Are you alright?"

"I'll be fine soon. Don't worry about me."

Layle's breath held for a moment, her mind working hard to combat the exhaustion she felt. "Kall?"

"Yes?" Her voice was too soft.

"What did you do?"

Kall sighed, and Layle's heart dropped to her stomach. "I

broke my pitcher. There was a nice, sharp piece in all the mess …"

Layle struggled to her feet, forgetting the weakness that had almost overtaken her a moment before. She turned to face the wall separating her from her Coven sister, hitting it with one open hand. "Kall, don't! Leave it alone! I just need more time!"

"It's already done … while you were trying to scry on the Matriarch … I just wanted to apologize, Layle."

Layle drew on the last of the energy she could, pulling it all together. "Kall … Please …" She wiped at her face, smearing warm blood onto her cheek. "Don't leave me alone."

Silence from the other side of the wall.

Layle pounded on the wall, gathering more energy to her arms. She called for Kall, with no answer, and beat against the stones separating them. Finally, after a few painful moments, she had taken nearly every bit of energy left within herself. She closed her eyes, hoping that Kall was still alive on the other side of the wall, and pushed the energy through to her palms.

Pain, and a dizzying sense of disorientation.

She fell, colliding with something warm and soft.

"Kall!" Layle grabbed the older girl by the upper arms, shaking her frantically. Half a dozen deep cuts ran up the inside of her arms, the edges jagged and raw. A broken bit of pottery lay to one side, the sharp edge bloodied. Blood had trailed down her sister's arms to pool on the stones around her, and Kall's skin was pale and clammy.

"Kall, please! Please be alive!"

But Kall's eyes were already glassy and vacant. Her head lolled as Layle shook her until she fell over to one side. Layle pulled her upright again, holding her close and weeping into her hair.

Kall had swirled her fingers through the pooling blood

around her, and Layle's stomach turned when she realized what Kall had written.

The letters were smeared and unsteady, but Layle could still read the names.

Millie

Arella

Lilith

Nala

Kall.

Layle's shoulders shook as she stared at the list.

I am alone.

Layle wept into her last sister's shoulder, too weak and too anguished to separate herself.

She stayed with Kall until the girl had grown cold and her body had begun to stiffen.

She once more filled her sore arms with energy, the process easier now that she had rested.

With a blink, she was back in her cell, her feet landing firmly on the stone floor.

Layle went back to the pitcher, pulling into her lap and scrying on her mother.

"Layle." Nevina's eyes were red. She had been crying, just as Layle had. "Mothlenor came to see me, and he made me an offer."

"Oh?" Layle whispered, her voice sticking in her throat. She had been right. Mothlenor had blocked her from scrying on the Matriarch. "What did he say?"

"He killed a woman in my place, some time ago. All of Azimar thinks I am dead." Nevina gave a watery snort, gaze unfocused. "He'll grant you and Kall freedom, as long as I stay with him and be his infatuate."

"Don't do it," Layle said bitterly.

"Layle, he'll take your cuffs off. You and Kall can return to the Coven, you can—"

"Kall is dead." *And I cannot return to the Coven.*

Nevina was shocked into silence for a moment, eyes blinking. "H-how? When?"

"Not long ago," Layle answered, wiping her face once more. "She cut her arms open on a bit of broken pottery."

Nevina said nothing, covering her face with her hands and weeping loudly.

"I've learned the transportation spell you taught me, though it takes time to get it ready." Layle's voice had a broken quality she didn't like to it. "I can leave this place. I can take you away from here, too."

Nevina pulled her face from her hands, head shaking. "No, it's a different thing entirely to drag someone along with you. It was foolish of me to suggest it in the first place." She wiped a few errant tears from her face. "I'll take Mothlenor's offer. I can still save you. I can still save the Coven."

Layle shook her head. "It would do nothing. He won't let me go." Saying it out loud made her stomach turn. "And even if he did, he would still find the Coven eventually. He would follow me. He would find me. You can't trust him. You know that."

"Then you'll just need to go on without me. Warn the Coven if you can, or find a new life somewhere."

"What about you?"

Nevina sniffed. "Mothlenor will keep me alive for as long as he wants. I can look for a different way out."

There will be no other way out.

Layle met her mother's gaze. "I'm sorry."

Nevina smiled sadly, her eyes seeming to bore their way into her. "I am too."

"I'll leave in a few days, I think. Maybe a week. Give myself more time to practice the spell, and to rest."

"Don't waste your energy scrying on me again. Save it for the spell."

Layle hesitated for a moment. *This will be the last time we speak to each other.* But, after a moment, she nodded. "Alright."

She ran a hand over her cheeks again. "I love you. And I'll miss you."

"I'll miss you too, Layle. And I will always love you."

There is power in love.

Layle broke the spell, shaking as a new wave of sobs broke from her.

Warn the Coven if you can, Nevina had said.

Layle's hand crept to her stomach, which had begun to swell, despite how little she had been given to eat.

Or find a new life somewhere.

41

AJAX

Ajax stood in the middle of the road, eyes fixed on the broken door of the farmhouse in front of him. The house was empty, the interior dark and quiet. The former inhabitants had left, just as so many others had left when Etritia shut her gates. The squawks and clucks of hens were gone, the few unharvested plants now rotting in the small field. But Ajax could still remember the warmth of Nevina's body as she walked beside him. He could hear her laugh on the chill wind that blew in from the north. He could still feel the touch of her skin against his lips …

Ajax turned away from the little farmhouse Nevina and her girls had borrowed, but he could not seem to leave it behind him. Would their things still be inside? Tucked in a room or a corner somewhere? Or did the owners burn their belongings after the Matriarch had been declared guilty of murdering the king?

In the weeks and months since Nevina's disappearance, Ajax had found himself standing in that exact spot more times than he could count, and he often asked those same questions of himself. It was the only constant in his life, that house and the few memories of Nevina it gave him. Hasani had grown sullen and quiet, often missing meals and returning to his quarters late in the night. Silvana tried to remain optimistic. Hasani was busy, she would say, making the new world a better place. But as the weeks passed, and she grew larger and larger with child, Ajax caught tears in her eyes more often than not, and even her cheery smile darkened. Ajax had warned her of Ferrand's veiled threat, urging her to remain in her rooms as often as she could. And she did. It hurt Ajax no end to see his little sister trapped in a gilded cage, with a husband whose sole job was to help a man he mistrusted to rule a city of starving and angry people.

Their only other choice was to flee, and leave the people they cared about to flounder in turmoil. Ajax was sure the turmoil would spread, eventually.

And there was Nevina to find, if she was still alive.

Ajax's boots crunched against the frosted ground as he trudged back up the road to the gate. His duty was complete, as much as it could be. There were no farmers trying to sneak into the city to sell their wares. There were no hungry city dwellers scrounging among the rotting vegetables for treasured food. There was no one. The farmlands were as dead and still as the forgotten vegetation in the fields.

Ajax had taken no more than a few steps back along the king's road when the wind suddenly picked up, chilling him to the bone. He felt the hairs on the back of his neck stand up and he paused, looking around anxiously.

Not more than a hundred feet in front of him, the air shimmered slightly. Ajax briefly wondered if it was an odd pocket of warm air, or if his eyes were playing tricks on him. But the shimmering intensified, and a woman appeared in midair a few feet above the ground. She seemed to float for just a moment, her dirty hair and ragged clothes caught in mid-motion, before she fell hard to the ground. The shimmer abruptly vanished, leaving nothing but the odd scent of something like incense.

Ajax could only stare, rooted to the spot.

The woman stirred, slowly climbing to her feet and muttering curses under her breath.

"Hey!" he shouted, startling even himself. His breath hung in the air, a puff of white on a grey morning.

The woman looked up, catching sight of him and leaping to her feet to run off.

Ajax started to pursue, each crunching step painfully loud. "Wait, wait, I can help you!"

The woman skidded to a halt and turned to face him, arm raised to throw something at him. But her hand was empty.

Ajax stopped short, realizing that this woman meant to curse him, or worse, kill him. He slowly raised his arms, surrendering. "I can help you, if you need it."

The woman paused for a moment then lowered her arm. "Ajax? Is that you?"

Ajax's heart skipped a beat. The voice was so familiar. He heard it in his sleep every night. "Nevina? Great Ones—"

"No," the woman said flatly. "Not Nevina. Her daughter, Layle."

And suddenly Ajax recognized the slight difference in timbre and the roughness to her voice. And the woman before him was much too small, hardly more than a child. "Layle," he repeated, recalling the dutiful girl he had met before. "But how did you …" He waved one hand around them, indicating her sudden appearance.

"My mother is very gifted in the arcane. What do you think she was teaching us?" She stepped closer to Ajax.

"The Matriarch. Nevina … is your mother?"

Layle only shrugged a shoulder. "The Coven's secrets don't matter to me any longer."

Ajax watched as she drew near, finding the similarities between mother and daughter easily. He noticed her clothing then, how torn and dirty it was. There were several rips and tears in some inappropriate spots, and there were rusty stains that Ajax recognized with a shudder as old blood. She wore no veil, and her incredibly bright eyes scanned the area around them. Her eyes bore the strongest resemblance to Nevina. "And how are your other … sisters?"

"They're all dead." Layle seemed very young for a moment, just a scared child, all alone. Her voice shook. "It's just me now. And Nevina, but I don't think she'll last for much longer."

Ajax's heart tightened in his chest. "Where is she? I've been searching—"

"You have?" Layle's brow shot up. "You knew she wasn't dead?"

Ajax hesitated, not sure if he should answer.

His hesitation seemed to speak for him. Layle's face softened, the bright blue of her eyes dimming slightly. "You know her face?"

"Yes," Ajax said with a sigh. "And that girl they hanged was not her. I knew then that she was still alive." He realized he was pleading with Layle, and her hand was still half raised in threat. "Please, I've searched everywhere. Where is she? Where were you taken?"

Layle's gaze left him as she considered the question for a moment. "The dungeons, I think. There was a door, at the foothills of the mountains …" She shook her head, dropping her hand. "I didn't see much of what happened."

Ajax frowned, looking Layle over again. "The dungeons are still sealed. I've checked already."

"Are you sure?" Layle shivered suddenly, wrapping her arms around herself.

Ajax cursed himself silently, removing his belt and pulling the black surcoat he wore off. He dropped the surcoat over Layle, though she wrinkled her nose at the sigil. "There was a draft. I couldn't find the source. I thought it might have been a hidden door, but I found no way to open it."

"It could have been an illusion." Layle frowned as Ajax

knelt to fasten the belt around her waist. It had to be looped around her frame twice, but it held the surcoat on well enough. "An illusion will seem real enough until you know it's not."

Ajax straightened, frowning at her bare feet. "At least the coat will keep some of the chill out. And I've grown tired of wearing it."

Layle stood before him, dirty and thin. Except for her stomach … With the surcoat on, it was easier to see, but Ajax was surprised he had missed it. "Layle, are you—"

"Yes, I am." Layle folded her arms over her chest, glaring up at him. "It's too late to stop it, not that I know how, or even could with these cuffs on." Her voice trembled as she shook a fist at him. A thick metal band was wrapped snugly around each wrist, and Ajax could see dried blood along the edges. "Just let me go. I need to leave before Mothlenor finds out I've escaped."

Ajax wrapped his hand around her upraised fist, engulfing the tiny hand in his. "Alright, come on. I'll get you somewhere safe, and you can explain everything on the way." For a moment, Layle reminded him more of Silvana than of Nevina, and he wanted to desperately to pull her into a tight embrace.

"What?" Her voice was thin, unbelieving.

"I said I would help you if you needed it, and you seem to need help pretty badly. I can take you somewhere where you'll be treated kindly, and perhaps you can return the favor."

"I …" Layle's words caught. She opened her mouth to start again, but a horse whinnied close by, and Ajax hushed her.

"Only the King's Guards are allowed to ride horses."

He could hear the crunching of frost under heavy hooves.

Layle's eyes widened, and she turned to run off, heading

for the broken entrance to the cottage nearby. She wouldn't make it before they were seen.

Her hand was still in Ajax's grip, and he pulled her back. "Don't run." Ajax knelt to look into the frightened girl's eyes. "If you run, they will only chase you down."

"Let me go!" Layle pleaded, trying to work her hand free of his grip.

"Stay with me, and I can figure a way out for you."

"I can't go back!"

"Ajax, is that you? Just what the fuck do ya think you're doing with that little girl?"

Ajax sighed in relief, recognizing the voice. "Layle, stop." Layle was beating her fist against his arm, trying to pull free. "Layle, it's alright. He's one of the good ones." Ajax turned to his friend, tugging the still struggling Layle with him. "Dars, I'm glad it's you."

Dars stood across the road from them, leading a large mare by the reins. He looked Ajax over, eyes narrow. "I know you better than to be thinking what I'm thinking, but you didn't answer my question." Dars lifted his chin, indicating Layle. "Who've ya got there?"

Ajax pulled Layle in front of him, though she still fought to break away, cursing him loud enough that he had to raise his voice to be heard over her. "Who does it look like?"

Dars's frown deepened as he looked Layle over. "Looks like the Matriarch, though she's too young." Dars sniffed, lifting one eyebrow. "Her daughter, maybe? One of the girls that went missing with her?"

Ajax nodded, struggling with Layle. She lifted one hand, palm out, and shouted at Dars. "Tell him to let me go, or I'll kill you."

Dars sniffed again, frowning at the threatening hand. "Go ahead, girlie. Put me out of my misery. I've just about had it with this place anyway." He addressed Ajax again, ignoring

Layle's faltering hand. "Did you find the Matriarch, then? Or just the girl?"

"Just the girl. She just appeared …" Ajax raised his free fist, flicking the fingers open. "Right in front of me."

"Just poofed right in front of you, huh?" Dars considered the girl for a moment as she continued to beat her small fist against Ajax's arm. "What're you gonna do with her?"

"I'll take her to Martyn and Nana, see if they'll leave with her. Take her someplace safe." Ajax grunted as a small foot missed his scrotum by half an inch.

Dars wheezed out a small laugh, the first Ajax had heard in months. "Think old Martyn would like a new horse?" He offered the mare's reins out to Ajax. "Might make it easier to get her out of here, if he had another beast of burden."

Layle stopped struggling, looking from Dars to Ajax and back again. "You're not going to take me back to the castle?" Her eyes were wide, the blue irises bright and cold.

Dars shook his head. "Not all of us like the direction things have been moving, girl. And if you are the Matriarch's daughter, I find it best to get you the fuck away from here." He addressed Ajax again. "Now do you want the damned horse or not?"

"Where did you find her?" Ajax took the reins, leaving Layle to stand on the side of the road, sure now that she wouldn't flee.

"She belonged to the family further up the road a bit." Dar's lips thinned. "Don't go in that house, Ajax. It's not pretty. Looks like the da went bad in the head. Butchered his own family." Dars sighed heavily, lifting his face towards the sky and blinking rapidly, and Ajax realized he was struggling to hold back tears. "Only thing he left alive was her." He waved a hand towards the horse. "I was gonna take her back to the castle, throw her in with all the rest, but I think the girl here could use her more."

"Thank you, Dars," Ajax muttered, not sure what else to do.

Dars shook his head, shooing the two of them away. "Just get out of here. I didn't see you. I didn't see the girl. Just make sure you make it back before dark, Ajax."

Ajax once again watched his old friend turn and walk away. He led the horse to Layle, picked her up and set her into the saddle. "Do you know how to ride?"

"N-no."

"Just hold tight right here," Ajax pointed to the saddle's pommel, "and don't kick her."

Ajax led Layle along the king's road. The walk wasn't very far, but Layle was quick to answer many of the questions he had. She confirmed what he had originally thought, that they had been kidnapped from the cottage and led back to the castle. She then tried to describe how they were taken into the castle, although confessing that she wasn't sure how the mysterious Dragon Door worked or even where it was anymore. "I was trying to console the other girls and I didn't see what happened. All I know is that one of the men that took us ended up dead, and we got into the castle."

She went on to describe some of what had gone on during the last several months, including the deaths of her Coven sisters. Ajax could only listen, shocked, as Layle described her imprisonment in a numb monotone.

"Nevina is still alive, although very weak," Layle finished. She stopped, looking at their surroundings. "Where are we?"

They had stopped at an old farmhouse set on a large plot of land, with a horse stabled off to the side. "Don't worry, I know these people. I'm sure they'll help."

Ajax pulled Layle from the saddle, leaving the horse to nibble on frosted grass, and knocked loudly on the door to the farmhouse. There was some shuffling inside, and after a few moments the door opened just a crack, enough for him to see Martyn's black eye and bruised face. Ajax thought he heard a sob deeper in the house, but he couldn't be sure.

"Please, sir, my wife can't do anything more right now. Last time hurt her pretty badly. If you could see it in your heart to wait, we could pay you."

Ajax raised his hand to silence him. "Martyn, it's me. Ajax."

The man looked Ajax over, eyes narrowed skeptically. As Martyn's eyes swept over his face, the old farmer's grim frown faded, and he cried out in relief. "Oh! Thank goodness, it's you!" He threw open the door, ushering him inside. "Please, please, come in. We don't have much to offer, but I'm sure we can find something." He called out to his wife, who came peeping around the corner from the far end of the house. "Nana, look who it is. Commander Ajax has come back."

Nana came out into the room looking pale and sickly. She was thinner and quieter than Ajax remembered, and there were dark circles under her eyes. "Hello, Commander." She smiled, but it was forced. "And who is this with you?" She nodded towards Layle, who had stepped in behind Ajax.

"This is Layle. She is ... *was* the Matriarch's daughter," Ajax answered. "And I'm no longer the commander," he added automatically, but they ignored him.

Martyn tsked sadly. "I'm sorry about your mother, darling." He motioned to his wife. "We don't believe any of that nonsense about her summoning demons to attack the king. Not a word of it. You have nothing to fear from us."

Ajax stepped between Martyn and Layle, pulling the girl behind him. "I need a favor, Martyn, and I'm willing to pay."

"Anything, anything for you," the farmer said earnestly.

"I need you to take care of Layle. She's pregnant, a result of some of the same kind of attacks your wife has been through." Nana made a soft sound, her hands going to her mouth, but Ajax continued. "I need you to feed her, clothe her, then pack your things and leave with her and go somewhere safe." The farmer started to protest, but Ajax once more raised his hand to quiet him. "It is the only way these attacks against you will stop. You two will be much safer. I can give you funds to start a new life elsewhere, as long as you give me your word that you will take Layle with you and treat her as your own." He turned to Layle. "Does that sound fair?"

Layle nodded, although not as enthusiastically as Ajax would have liked.

"That's all well and good, but we haven't the food or resources to make a trip of that kind any time soon. The crops are gone, the well has dried up, and we're already running through our reserves as it is. It would take months to save up supplies for that trip, and we have no means to carry them."

"There's a horse outside for you, if you'll take Layle with you."

Martyn sighed. "That solves one problem, yes, but what about food and water?"

"Show me your well." Layle spoke up suddenly. Her voice was a little timid and uncertain.

"I'm sorry?" Martyn looked around Ajax at Layle, his brows knitting together.

"I think I can help. Show me your well," Layle repeated.

They were led outside. Ajax helped the farmer lift the cover from the well, and they circled around it to peer into the depths. Ajax dropped a small stone over the lip of the well, and they listened for the dull thud as it hit the dry bottom.

"See, no water. It's been like that since last week. We've been traveling down the road to some of the abandoned farms to gather water from their wells, but that takes time, and we can never carry much." Martyn's mouth was a thin line as he glanced between his wife and Ajax.

"I think I can fix it. Just give me a moment." Layle closed her eyes, a stern look of concentration on her face. After a few seconds Ajax heard a low rumbling sound, growing louder with each passing second. After almost no time at all, a great splash of water came up and out, wetting their clothes a little, and the well was once again full.

Martyn and Nana looked at Layle in amazement.

"How did you do that, lovely?" Nana asked in a quiet voice.

Layle shrugged. "Magic. There's water down there. It just needed a bit of help being found."

"I didn't realize magic could be so powerful," Nana said, stepping closer to the well.

Layle was staring at her hands, flexing them slightly. "I didn't either."

For a moment, she seemed very young again, and Ajax could find no words of comfort to share with the girl in front of him.

Martyn dipped his hand into the well, smiling at the clear water that filled his palm. "I've never seen it so full and clean before."

"Go get some seeds," Layle said, eyes bright with excitement.

"Some what?" Martyn asked, brows pinched together.

"Seeds, go get some, quickly." There was a strange sort of determination about her. Color had flushed her cheeks, and her eyes glimmered that bright blue again.

"What … what kind?" Martyn stammered.

Layle smiled. "What would you like to eat for dinner tonight?"

The farmer smiled, rubbing his hands together eagerly. He trotted off, a slight limp in his gait, and returned after a few cold moments with a fistful of hard yellow seeds in one hand, and a few small potatoes in the other. "How about corn and some tubers?"

Layle chuckled, nodding. "Now throw them on the ground."

"But it's not tilled."

"It doesn't matter."

The farmer threw the seeds far out to his left and tossed the potatoes to the ground on his right. Layle closed her eyes, concentrating once more. Within moments, full stalks of corn with beautiful ears stood higher than their shoulders. Plush and twisted vines with tubers twice the size of a clenched fist stretched out across the unbroken earth; the seed potatoes had not even had time to pierce the soil. Nana shouted with joy, rushing to Layle and kissing her cheeks.

"Oh, thank goodness. With a little more of that, we could be out of here by morning. We just need—"

"A wagon?" Layle asked slyly. She took a deep breath, closing her eyes tightly. Ajax watched, fascinated. The horses whinnied loudly, and they ran around to the front of the house to see a large wagon standing just where the stable had been a moment before. Layle followed up behind them, looking tired and weak. "It looks like you've got just about everything you need." Layle wiped her hands across both forearms, smearing trails of blood from her wrists.

"Layle, you're bleeding." Ajax knelt to her, taking her hands in his and searching for the source of the blood.

"It's the cuffs," Layle muttered. "They cut into my wrists when they sense arcane energy. I can get around them, but I always bleed." She looked between Nana and Martyn, who were staring down at her with wide, concerned eyes. "I can keep going, I just need a moment."

Nana tsked. "Nonsense. Let's get you inside. We can get you cleaned up, get you dressed in something a little more suitable for someone as beautiful as you, and get your belly full of some of those wonderful vegetables. We can finish all of this later, darling." She wrapped an arm around Layle's waist, supporting some of the girl's weight, and the two disappeared inside.

Ajax turned to Martyn, who was staring after his wife with a faint smile. "Will you still help her, knowing what she can do?"

Martyn nodded. "With a gift like that, she'll be needing someone to protect her. I can't do much, but I can try. And with a baby coming … It'd be evil of me to turn her out. I'll help her, and we'll get her out of here first thing tomorrow."

"Thank you. I just want her to be safe. I'll give you however much money you think you'll need."

Martyn shook his head. "That isn't necessary. We still have some of the money you gave us before. And once we get to where we're going, we can sell one of the horses." Martyn flexed his hands; his fingers were long and thin. "I think I've still got it in me to work and odd job or two, until we're settled."

"Thank you," Ajax said again, smiling faintly. He turned back towards the farmhouse for a moment. "I should go."

"You don't want to say goodbye?"

"No, no. I'm not sure she'll even miss me." *She hardly knows me.*

Martyn nodded. He offered an arm to Ajax, and the two shook. "Goodbye, Commander."

"Goodbye, Martyn. I hope things are better for you and Nana."

Martyn nodded then turned to follow Nana into the house.

Ajax headed towards the castle, his thoughts already focused on finding Nevina.

42

LAYLE

Layle watched from the open window in the house's single bedroom as Ajax left. Behind her, the farmer's wife prattled on excitedly, but she could hardly hear the woman's words. She could only stand there, watching as Ajax turned back down the dusty road and started the walk back towards the castle. He hadn't even said goodbye.

Had she wanted him to? She hardly knew him, but he was the only person she could remotely trust. And he had just abandoned her.

"What do you think, darling?"

Layle turned, finding the farmer's wife standing behind her, a simple white cotton shift in her extended hands. There was an open trunk on the bed beside them, with clothing folded neatly within.

Ajax had said that she could trust this couple, that they would protect her. She reached out, taking the dress from the old woman. In doing so, she brushed a hand against the older woman's and stole a glance into her eyes.

And there it was.

He had been right.

She would insist on being called Nana, and that was fine enough with her.

She fingered the heavy fabric. "It doesn't have to be white, if that was your concern."

Nana's eyes widened. "Oh? But I thought—"

"I can't go back to the Coven. Not anymore." She draped the white dress carefully onto the bed, turning to look inside the trunk. "Can I wear this one?" She pulled the top article from the neat stack, unfurling it and holding to her frame.

"That one? Are you sure?"

Layle looked down at herself. She could no longer see her feet over her swollen belly, but she could still tell that the dress would fit fairly well. "Yes, I think so." Despite everything, she could still find it within her to smile.

"I've never worn blue before."

NEVINA

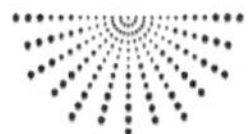

Nevina dreamed of Areanath, as she often did. His arms wrapped around her waist, pulling her closer to him. The warmth of his bed felt so real, so relaxing to her tired and worn body. His lips found her neck, and she let out a contented sigh.

Our last night together. This is what I'm dreaming of.

"Areanath …" she breathed, opening her eyes. "I've missed you." The surroundings were familiar. They were in Areanath's rooms, just as she remembered them. A little colder, perhaps, but still the same.

Areanath said nothing, only continued to kiss the hollow where her neck met her jaw.

She stretched, feeling the warmth of him against her. He was naked; she could feel him hard against her as she pressed close.

"Still not finished with your work?" she asked with a tired yawn. "Do you need my help again?"

Areanath's lips stopped moving, and Nevina tousled her hair with one hand, the weight of the metal cuff heavy on her wrist.

She froze, staring at the circle of metal on her arm. The

warm weight pressing against her suddenly felt hostile and strange.

"You helped my brother with his curse?" Mothlenor asked quietly, mouth against her ear.

Nevina leapt from the bed, pulling the covers after her and wrapping them around her body. "Elir damn you, Mothlenor," she cursed, pressing herself to the adjacent wall. "I've had enough of your games!"

Mothlenor sat in Areanath's bed, one of the pillows Nevina had so often laid her head against draped over his lap. "I only brought you here to see if you had considered my proposal, but you've already said more than I hoped you would." He stood, reaching for a robe on a nearby chair.

Nevina looked away, cursing him again under her breath. "I refuse your offer," she muttered, "and ask that you leave me in my cell to die."

"You refuse?" Mothlenor sounded surprised. His feet were still bare, and he padded softly over to where she stood motionless. "You've lost another girl in the last week." His brows knitted together as he looked her over. "You only have one Coven girl left. And you would let her die and refuse my offer?"

Nevina thought briefly of Layle's attempts to learn the spell she had taught her. "She would do the same, if our roles were reversed."

"Do you truly find me that revolting?"

"Yes." Nevina's voice was flat and quiet.

Mothlenor's eyes darkened and he stepped away from her to sit once more on the bed. He looked her over again, his gaze more calculating than lustful. "You helped my brother with his curse. Tell me how it worked."

"I don't know." Nevina's eyes flitted to the door on the far side of the bedroom and to the study beyond, where a second door led out to the hall. *If I can reach it before he does, perhaps I can flee into the castle.* The idea was ridiculous, there was bound to be a guard just outside the study door, but it was her only chance.

"You just said—"

"I know what I said," Nevina growled, angry with herself. She should have realized that everything felt too real to be a dream.

Mothlenor studied her for a moment, his eyes narrowing. "You didn't lend him your knowledge. You lent him your power." He sneered up at her. "Your Gift."

Nevina said nothing. She couldn't bring herself to look at him. He looked too much like Areanath, in his brother's robe, in his brother's rooms. Nevina felt a lump form in her throat at the thought.

"If you don't know how it worked, perhaps you know exactly what his curse did."

"I don't know."

Mothlenor snarled. "You are trying my—"

Nevina bolted for the open door before he could finish. The door was close, only a few strides away.

She could make it.

A blur moved into her field of vision and the door slammed shut against her.

Mothlenor had one hand on the handle, the other on her upper arm, shaking her. "No!" he growled through gritted teeth. His eyes were alight with anger, and the sight of them frightened her. "You can't leave. You are mine to summon!"

His grip on her arm was painful, and Nevina let out an involuntary whimper. "I don't know anything! Let go, you're hurting me!"

Mothlenor let her go instantly, but his hand swept back and he struck her across the face. Nevina collapsed to the floor in a sprawl, cupping her throbbing cheek.

"Where did my brother hide the amulets?" Mothlenor stood over her, one hand still holding the handle of the door, the other flexing slowly.

Nevina could taste blood in her mouth. She touched a finger to her lip, wincing as she felt the split in it. "I don't know what you're talking about." It was true enough. Areanath had never mentioned any amulets in their time working together.

Mothlenor was breathing deeply, nearly panting, seeming to struggle to control his anger. He locked the door with a quick spell and collapsed onto the foot of the bed, mere feet from Nevina. "He really told you nothing?"

"Nothing," she repeated, sitting upright and pulling the covers around her once more. She spat a wad of bloody saliva at Mothlenor's feet, too fatigued to even stand.

Mothlenor's eyes shifted to her for a moment. "Do that again and I'll kill you."

Nevina only shrugged, closing her eyes and leaning her head against the wall at her back.

"When I killed him, I watched his soul leave his body," Mothlenor said quietly, his breathing still labored. "I knew then that he had done something, but it wasn't until the night before the coronation that I knew what."

Nevina opened one eye to see Mothlenor rubbing a hand through his wiry beard. His expression was neutral again, his gaze distant. *No longer a threat, for the moment.* It worried her how easily she could read him, now.

"My brother, as King of Etritia, was the keeper of one of the four Amulets of Power. The Amulet of Air has been passed down through our family since the close of the Great War."

Nevina sighed. "Earth for the dwarves, in their halls of stone. Air for the men, in their castles tall. Fire and Water for the brothers opposed, so that they might remember their elven kin."

"Not precisely the way we learned it, but the point is the same," Mothlenor muttered. "Together, of course, they—"

"Summon the Great Soul," Nevina finished, lifting her

head. "This isn't a history lesson. You killed your brother so you could get the Amulet of Air. What stopped you?"

"My brother. His curse," Mothlenor growled.

Nevina frowned. She'd never realized that was what Areanath had been planning.

"The Amulet of Air is gone. Vanished. I'm sure the other three are missing as well, though I can't be certain."

She snorted. "There goes your grand plan, Mothlenor. Foiled by a dead man."

"Not if you help me reverse it, Nevina."

Nevina's skin crawled with the way he seemed to almost whisper her name. "You keep calling it a curse. Curses can't be broken or reversed. Only carried out until the energy holding them together ceases."

Mothlenor was silent, his eyes fixed on her.

Perhaps he knows better than I do ... "I will not help you."

Mothlenor's eyes narrowed again. "Do you even know why I want the amulets?"

"Areanath said you wanted to spark genocide. Using the amulets to summon the Great Soul would help you eradicate all non-human life." Nevina closed her eyes again. "Foolish, but effective enough."

"You're just as narrow-minded as Areanath was," Mothlenor grumbled. "You assume that the Great Soul can only be used to destroy. I believe it can also be used to create. It will bend to the will of its master."

Nevina raised her head again, looking Mothlenor over. "And what would you create?"

"A world of peace."

Nevina sneered up at him. "A world without elves and dwarves, you mean? A world where the races you deem unworthy have been wiped out, leaving only humanity to reign?"

"It's the only way to ensure our survival," Mothlenor insisted.

"You are the one who is narrow-minded, Mothlenor."

He stood, bare feet once more padding closer to her. "It's no matter that the amulets are gone." He knelt before her, staring into her eyes. "If I cannot simply create, then I must destroy, and rebuild from the ashes. And I have a creature capable of that, and more." Mothlenor's head tilted slightly. "At least I will, once I force it to hatch."

Nevina wanted to laugh, but the look in his eyes silenced it. "There are no more dragons, Mothlenor. There hasn't been an egg sighting in over a hundred years."

"There is one more dragon, and its egg is mine." He leaned in close, his thumb lightly touching the cut on her lip. "Will you not reconsider my offer? I can be compassionate, Nevina."

His voice was quiet, his eyes sincere. And they caused a shudder to run down her spine. "When it suits you, I suppose you can be." She shook her head gently, pulling away from him. "But I will not reconsider."

"Very well." Mothlenor leaned away, his voice suddenly hard. "Then you will die alone and in the dark."

And with his words, Nevina was once more in her cell, naked and shivering. But she was free from his touch.

MOTHLENOR

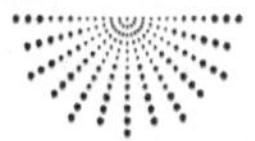

Mothlenor eyed the crumpled mess of bedcovers where Nevina had been seconds ago.

"Perhaps I am too considerate, and to my detriment," he said to the empty room. He dressed in silence, thinking over Nevina's words. She refused him, an honest enough surprise. He had been sure that she would choose to accept, especially with only more Coven daughter remaining in her care. Instead she had chosen death over him.

Perhaps I could have offered her more ... Perhaps I could have persuaded her to stay by my side.

"No matter, what's done is done." Mothlenor frowned, regretting the hasty dismissal he had given Nevina. He took a second to focus, then spoke a quick word under his breath. The walls of his brother's rooms faded away in an instant, replaced with his own familiar study walls.

There was the matter of Nevina's involvement in Areanath's curse to consider as well. She might not know how Areanath's curse worked, but if her Gift had been used to create it, perhaps her Gift could also be used to destroy it.

"Curses can't be broken or reversed. Only carried out until the energy holding them together ceases."

Her words had been only half right. But if Areanath had created the spell, its power should have died with him, not been activated with his death.

Unless that's why his soul left his body. Unless Areanath's soul was providing the energy necessary to keep the curse active.

He shook his head, ashamed he hadn't made the realization sooner. "My brother was far more talented than I ever gave him credit for." *And he actively hid it from me, letting me perform little tricks for his amusement, laughing all the while.*

Mothlenor stepped around to the far side of his desk, fuming silently. He yanked open the bottom drawer, hastily snatching up the Dragon's Eye and peering into it.

If my brother's soul is indeed still out in the world ... But the Eye remained still and unchanging.

"Useless thing." He tossed the Eye lightly onto the desk, watching as it slowly rolled across the top. His eyes narrowed as it rolled closer to the far side of the desk. *So useless ... It would be easier to let the damned thing fall ...*

With a sudden lunge, Mothlenor reached across the desk and plucked the Eye from the far edge, just as it began to topple over and onto the floor. He straightened, staring into the dark depths of the stone. "Perhaps that will teach you," Mothlenor said to the Dragon's Eye, realizing even as he spoke the words how ridiculous they sounded.

It was an expensive find, he thought as he stared at the dark surface of the stone. *And it did help me locate the Coven.*

With a quiet huff, Mothlenor dropped the Eye back into the open drawer.

"At any rate, my brother's curse *can* be broken, Nevina, once I learn how it was made. And in the meantime ..." he turned, spotting the misshapen lump of golden stone through the open doorway of his bedroom, "I have other work I can attend to."

45

SILVANA

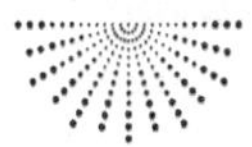

Silvana slowly paced the length of Hasani's study, though her feet ached and her legs felt swollen. She placed a hand on her heavy belly as the baby within stirred. "Shhh, shhh. It's alright. No need for you to get upset too."

But, Great Ones take it, where is he?

Hasani should have returned to their rooms long before now, even if only to grab some small thing or check in with a quick kiss and an excuse about Mothlenor needing him before he darted away again.

And I need to tell him about Ajax ...

Silvana bit her lip and made a graceless turn to continue her pacing for a few moments more. The baby continued to writhe and squirm inside her, and she whispered small comforts to him as she walked and waited.

Eventually, Silvana sighed, giving in to the aches and pains of her body, and sat gingerly in the chair they kept by the fire. Even with the flames crackling, the room had a chill to it that only came during the height of winter. And Silvana had heard a pair of serving girls whispering excitedly about the unexpected snowfall that had come in the night. But Silvana had not seen the heavy white blanket covering the city, because Ajax had made her promise to stay in her rooms until the baby came.

Ajax …

Had her brother gone mad, to claim he saw Layle appear from thin air in front of him? It was one thing to say he believed that the Matriarch was still alive, but another thing entirely to swear that her daughter had come to him and told him where she could be found. And if it was true, if Layle had somehow found Ajax … *Why now? Why wait so long to seek help?*

Areanath had died months ago … why wait so long before trying to escape?

And why pull her brother into it? Because he loved the Matriarch?

Silvana frowned, rubbing her stomach absently. *Dars would know; Ajax said he was there.*

But Dars, like Ajax and Hasani, could not be simply summoned by her thinking of him.

Silvana pounded one fist against the arm of the chair. "Dammit, where is he?"

For a moment, she didn't care who came—Dars, her husband, her brother—she just wanted *someone* to come and keep her from going mad. They always left her, trapped in her rooms like a criminal, her only crime that of being their loving wife, or sister, or—in the case of Dars—their chosen daughter. A delicate woman, in need of protecting, even if it meant locking her away and driving her insane with loneliness.

"Great Ones take it, I can't stay here any longer." She stood with a bit of effort, her feet still sore and her back complaining, and hastily unlocked and opened the door to the hall. *If Hasani will not come to me, I will go to him.*

She glanced quickly down both ends of the hallway and, finding it empty, darted from the room and down the hall towards the heart of the castle, as quickly as her legs could carry her heavy belly.

Her steps were already slowing as she neared the far end of the hall, her energy burning more quickly than she had anticipated. She turned, rounding the corner, and bumped into a man leaning casually against the adjoining wall.

Silvana stepped back, mouth working wordlessly in an attempt to stammer out an apology.

"Ah, Silvana, I wondered when I might see you wandering the halls again." Ferrand's voice was rich and smooth, just as it had sounded from her hiding spot in Nana's bedroom; the sound of it made her heart beat harder in her chest.

Ajax warned me; he told me Ferrand might be looking for me. But he was so close, just waiting for me to leave ...

"Won't you even say hello?" Ferrand asked with a pout, his dark eyes glinting.

Silvana swallowed hard, forcing the sudden jolt of fear back down. "H-hello, Commander Ferrand." Her eyes darted past Ferrand, to the hall beyond. It was empty. "I was just going to go find my husband. I should go, he's expecting me." Silvana tried to hurry around him, but he snaked out a quick hand and snagged her by the elbow.

"You mean Hasani just left you all alone?" His grip on her elbow was strong, painful, and Silvana felt a cool wash of terror flood over her. "I've noticed that you've been spending a lot of time in your rooms. I expect the baby tires you easily. Come, I'll take you back." Ferrand stepped towards the way Silvana had come, leading her. "You should rest, perhaps lie down. I can keep you company until Hasani returns."

Silvana planted her feet, trying to pull her arm from his grip. "No, I need to see my husband. He's waiting for me."

"Hasani is currently in a meeting with the king. He is not expecting you, and he will most likely be detained for quite a bit longer." His teeth flashed in a hungry smirk as he pulled her along behind him.

His fingers dug deeper into her elbow, and Silvana cried out in pain. "Please, don't do this. Whatever my brother did to anger you, your fight is with him."

Ferrand turned suddenly, grabbing a fistful of her hair and pulling her head back to look at him. His eyes were dark and dead looking, and Silvana tried vainly to pry his fingers from her hair. "My fight is with your brother, yes. But I can't ignore the chance to hurt the ones he loves when the opportunity quite literally stumbles upon me."

"Stop it, Ferrand." Her finger caught under one of his, and she twisted it, trying to break his hold on her. "Let me go!"

Instead of loosening, his grip tightened, both on her elbow and on the fistful of hair he held. With a sudden lunge, his mouth was pressed against hers, so hard she could feel his teeth cutting against her lower lip. Silvana tried to kick him, but Ferrand remained unaffected. His gaze remained locked on hers, his eyes grotesque in their closeness.

Silvana could feel his tongue against her sealed lips, seeking a way in. Pinned as she was, Silvana relented, and Ferrand made an eager sound of pleasure as his kiss deepened, and his hold on her hardened.

Until Silvana bit down.

With a yelp, Ferrand stepped back, their lips parting. Silvana could taste blood, and it brought bile to the back of her throat.

"You bit me." Ferrand scowled down at her. "You stupid bitch!" His hand was out of her hair and striking her across the face before she had even blinked.

Silvana turned with the blow, her free hand reaching to touch the stinging cheek.

Ferrand's arm raised again to hit her, but Dars appeared from nowhere, stepping from behind the commander and grabbing Ferrand's arm before it could fall again. "That's enough of that, Ferrand," Dars growled. "Get outta here."

"Dars, Imis bless you …" Silvana whispered breathlessly,

looking from the old knight to Ferrand and back again. She could see strands of auburn curls dangling from Ferrand's upraised hand.

With an exasperated sigh, Ferrand jerked his arm free and released Silvana's elbow, turning his back on her and facing Dars. "You have no weapon, *Peace Guard*. You stand no chance against a true knight."

"I don't need a sword to beat your fucking ass into the ground. I told you that once, and I stand by it," Dars said in a low voice. "Now leave. There isn't a knight around to help you, you tall sack of shit."

Ferrand sneered at Dars, but turned and made his way back down the hall. With a glance back at the pair of them, he growled, "Tell Ajax to stay out of my affairs. I can forgive one trespass, but I can't ignore a second."

Silvana watched him leave, the taste of blood still rich in her mouth and Dars's comforting arm around her shoulders.

"You're not hurt, are ya?" Dars asked.

"No, I'm fine." Silvana rubbed her elbow, which stung with the pain of returning blood flow. Her cheek burned where she had been struck, and her head hurt where hair had been torn from it. But she was better than Nana had been. *Better by far than I might have been ...*

"Come on now, back to safety we go." Dars's voice was still low and angry, but it was reassuring nonetheless.

Dars led her back to her rooms and poured her a large glass of wine while she paced the floor and cursed both Ferrand and Ajax for keeping her locked away. He handed the glass to her silently, watching as she swirled the first swig around her mouth before swallowing and taking a second sip. The taste of blood still lingered, and she finished the glass. Dars took it without a word, refilling it as she paced the cold floor as fast as she could. Finally, exhausted and exasperated, she once more fell into her chair, and Dars handed her the second glass.

"Your brother is telling the truth, you know. About the Matriarch's daughter."

"I know," Silvana muttered glumly, taking the glass from him and staring at it. *Of course I know, as much as I may not want to admit it.* "Will you find Hasani, and tell him?"

Dars nodded. "Sure, sure. I can tell him. I'll tell him about this business with Ferrand, too. Maybe he won't be so quick to leave you alone so much."

"I'm not sure I can stay here much longer. I can't handle being shut in all the time," Silvana grumbled. "I can't even go down to the library for some nice books."

Dars snorted, reaching for a pouch on his belt. "I don't know about nice, but I do have a book you can try reading." He held up a tiny volume, bound in leather.

Silvana read the title stamped on the front aloud. "*The Identification and Properties of Azimarian Fungi?*" She took the book hesitantly from Dars. "Sounds ... engaging."

"I found some stupid bastard curled up behind the barracks last week, covered in his own vomit, stinking of his own shit." Dars wrinkled his nose at the memory, and Silvana's wrinkled at the conjured image. "He said some of the newer knights were going around daring the young recruits to eat some mysterious mushroom that looked like a dried-up bull's sack." Dars's gaze flicked to Silvana apologetically. "His words, not mine." Dars sighed, crossing his arms over his chest. "Stupid kid took the bait, found himself too sick to do more than lie around, shitting himself and trying to aim his stomach contents into the nearby bush." He flicked a hand at the book in Silvana's grasp. "I thought I'd give him that, in case the idea crosses his mind again. But I can't be fucked to give a damn anymore. You can have it. Might come in handy, you never know."

Silvana frowned, tucking the small book into her lap. "Will you come back? Later today, I mean? Books will only keep me together for so long, Dars."

Dars smiled, his eyes lighting up for the first time in Silvana's recent memory. "Anything for you, Silvana." He knelt and kissed her forehead gently. "I'll go and find Hasani, then stop by the library on my way back. I can't imagine anyone will miss me."

They said their goodbyes, and Dars left. Silvana was careful to lock the door behind him before settling back into her chair. The book on fungi was already open in her lap, her thoughts momentarily distracted from her brother and his foolish quest.

NEVINA

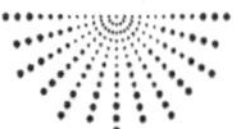

Nevina was once more alone in her dark cell. It had been hours, perhaps even a full day, since Mothlenor had last magicked her to him, and she had sat awake ever since, revisiting what had passed between them. Would it matter, in the end, that Mothlenor knew that Areanath's spell had been created with the help of Nevina's gift? Was he lying about possessing a dragon's egg?

She considered what little she knew of Areanath's spell and what Mothlenor had confessed to her as sleep eluded her.

Thankfully Areanath was able to pass his notes to Hasani ... Hopefully he can make sense of Areanath's spell, and find a way to fulfill Areanath's last wishes.

She began coughing suddenly, a fit that lasted for nearly a minute. She drew a shaky, wheezing breath as the fit subsided, leaning her head against the cool stone.

That had been her idea, she remembered. She had been the one to suggest to Areanath that he leave instructions with someone he trusted, and she was glad when Areanath had chosen his adviser. Hasani would never fail Areanath.

And yet Mothlenor still stood to incite war across the

kingdoms. He claimed to possess a dragon's egg, and had talked of forcing it to hatch so he could use the dragon it held to help him destroy the elves and dwarves. There were so many doubtful possibilities to the whole thing, and yet Nevina still found herself trembling at the thought of a great dragon burning the world to ash. If anyone could find a dragon's egg, it would be Mothlenor.

Part of her was content to lie on the stone floor and forget what she had heard. Layle was surely out of the castle by now, hopefully somewhere safe, and she had nothing left to concern herself with. But another part of her feared the future she knew she would never live to see. What if Mothlenor found the amulets and summoned the Great Soul? What if he did have a dragon's egg, and found a way to make it hatch for him? The beast would no doubt be just as cruel and powerful as Mothlenor himself, and would be tied to his power … There would not only be war, but complete destruction. And what of her Coven? Would Mothlenor find a way to hunt them out? Would they be destroyed as well?

The familiar fumbling sound of keys in the door finally pulled her head up. She watched the door, the heavy weight of the cuffs on her wrists shifting as she wrapped her arms around herself. After a moment the door opened and someone slipped through, platter in hand, a rough-hewn blanket draped over one arm.

"I'm not hungry." The words were already out of her mouth before she realized that the tray was empty. And the figure who strode towards her was far too tall and lithe to be the angry servant woman that usually brought her meals. Nevina pressed her back against the wall, fearing that the man who had tortured her and her girls had returned to molest her again.

Is this Mothlenor's punishment? For refusing him?

She opened her mouth to scream just as the man threw back the hood on his cloak.

Her cry was caught in her throat, and her heart stopped beating.

"Nevina." It was a sigh, and Nevina's fears vanished in an instant.

She finally found her voice long enough to whimper, "Ajax."

He fell on her, wrapping his arms around her waist and pulling her close. He smelled of the outdoors, of sweat and manure and pine. She let his scent waft over her, let his arms embrace her despite the frailty of her body. He pulled away long enough to cup her face in his hands and pull her into a long kiss before wrapping his arms around her again. She held him tight, clinging to the sudden hope his presence brought her. "How did you find me?"

"I found Layle. She just … appeared right in front of me. She told me where you were, and how I could find you."

She smiled, knowing Layle was safe. "Did you get her out of here?"

"She's on her way now."

Nevina held him even tighter, taking in his warmth. "Thank you, Ajax."

"I'm so sorry. I looked for you, even when Mothlenor said you had confessed." He pulled away, searching her eyes. "He lied, didn't he? You didn't kill Areanath, did you?"

She shook her head. "Mothlenor killed Areanath."

She watched as his expression hardened, and he nodded. "I thought so, but I couldn't be sure …"

"How did you know I was still alive?"

"The girl …" Ajax's voice was soft, and his gaze dropped. "The one they took to the gallows in your place. I saw her face." His eyes found hers again, searching them. "It wasn't you."

"It wasn't me," Nevina repeated.

Relief washed over Ajax's face as if he only truly believed it after hearing her say it. "Then it's over. I can get you out of here, we can confront Mothlenor. We can leave. Together." Ajax's eyes were pleading, but Nevina could only look away, ashamed. Suddenly all her fears and worries came rushing back to her.

"I can't leave."

"What do you mean, you can't leave? He killed his own brother, and he'll kill you too."

"Yes." Nevina paused. "He will. And he'll kill you as well, if he discovers that you set me free. I have to stay."

Ajax sighed heavily. "Nevina, please—"

"He's seen my face, Ajax. He can find me, anywhere I go." Her voice was thin but firm. "I can't go with you, or he will find you, too. I can't go back to the Coven, or he will find them. I could hide, but not with these cuffs blocking my magic."

"Then we'll take the cuffs off!" Ajax grabbed for her wrist, but Nevina pulled her hands away from him.

"Only Mothlenor can take them off."

Ajax rubbed a hand against the rough growth of beard on his cheeks, eyes wide in the dim light. "You can still do magic with them. I saw Layle—"

"I am not Layle, Ajax. I cannot do magic around these." Nevina's voice choked around the lump that had formed in her throat. "There is nowhere safe for me to run to." She took his hands in hers, searching his eyes for a hint of understanding. "I have to stay, Ajax."

Ajax groaned in frustration, his gaze going to the ceiling. "Nevina …"

"Stop." She grabbed his chin, pulling him closer to her. She had Seen just a little glimpse … She stared into Ajax's eyes, and he obediently waited, staring back.

A dragon, blue as the sea, soaring overhead. Two elves, both young, stand beside her, laughing as they watch. A boy, nearly a man, runs across the deck of a boat and leans over the railing. A voice behind her calls out to him, and the boy turns around. His hair is dark, and his eyes are the color of midnight.

A small campfire in the middle of the night. A dwarf sits to her right, the boy across from her. The boy looks confused, and a little scared. He pulls a small leather book out of his vest pocket, handing it over to her. He says it belonged to his father, or so his mother told him once.

Nevina blinked her eyes rapidly, her eyes adjusting to the darkness after Seeing so much. Her mind was racing, reeling from the knowledge her short insight had given her. Why had her Gift not worked before? Had Mothlenor somehow blocked it?

There is power in love.

She chuckled a little, shaking her head. "I thought Hasani was the one to carry out Areanath's last task, but he's not."

Ajax pulled away from her, confused. "What are you talking about? What did you see?"

"I saw Hasani's son. Without his parents. But he was with you. And he had Areanath's book."

"You know about the book?" Ajax asked, incredulous.

"Of course I know about the book. I helped Areanath cast his spell, and he needed someone he could trust to finish his work. I was supposed to offer Hasani my aid, but perhaps you will do as well …"

"I don't know what you want—"

She pulled him close again, bringing his lips to hers. *If I can still See, perhaps I can still do this …*

Her lips were warm against his, even though her hands were nearly frozen where they cupped his face. He felt his face flush and his breath caught in his throat as her body melted against his.

Images poured into Ajax's head, flying too fast for him to make any sense of what he saw.

Areanath reclined in a chair, wine in hand. "It's not war he wants. It's genocide."

He was being led through the tunnels under the castle, the Dragon Door behind him, blood still dripping from its fangs.

Mothlenor was kneeling in front of him, so close he could almost feel his breath on his face. "It's no matter that the amulets are gone. If I cannot simply create, then I must destroy, and rebuild from the ashes."

Then it was his own memories he was seeing. Conversations with Mothlenor, it seemed. They shifted quickly, each one lingering for the briefest of moments, only to stop at the conversation in Mothlenor's private quarters as Ajax eyed the items surrounding him.

There.

Nevina's voice was in his head, but he almost didn't

notice it as he realized just what he was seeing. It looked like a misshapen hunk of gold, but it was so much more than that. And Mothlenor just kept it sitting on his desk, so sure no one would realize what it was …

And just as quickly, she pulled away from him. His lips were sore from their mouths being pressed so hard together for so long, and there was a lingering warmth in his extremities that felt foreign to him. But Nevina didn't bother to explain anything.

"You know where the dragon's egg is."

"Yes."

"You have to get it, and you have to get out of the castle. With Hasani and Silvana. You know the way to the Dragon Door?"

Ajax could see the twisting path in his mind. "Yes."

"And you know what must be done once you get there?"

A knot formed in the pit of his stomach. "Yes, I know."

Nevina sighed. "I'm not sure what happens to Hasani and Silvana, but they aren't with the boy in the future I saw. Only you." She touched his arm. "You need to make sure that you're there with him."

Ajax felt the weight of Nevina's task sinking into him. "I … I understand."

"You have to go now, Ajax."

Ajax shook his head. "I want to stay with you a little longer."

Nevina's sad smile pierced him right through the heart. "You shouldn't. You have plans to make."

Ajax shook his head again. "Then I'll get the egg and come back for you. You can still leave this place, Nevina. You can come with me."

She kissed him on the cheek, running her fingers through his hair. "That would be nice. But I don't think it will happen."

Ajax cupped her chin in his hand, his thumb caressing her

cheek. "You are more beautiful than I could ever have imagined, Nevina."

Her face reddened slightly in the dim light. He'd spent
months holding on to the hope that he would be able to find
her, to see her face once more. And when he finally did, she
wanted him to leave.

Ajax ran his hands through her hair, his eyes never
leaving hers. "I love you, you know that? I have always loved
you, since the first time you set foot in the castle when
Nevara was still Matriarch, before all this madness was even
dreamed of."

Nevina smiled. "There's power in love, Ajax. Remember
that. And you would have been a good infatuate. If things
had happened differently …" She sighed. "You have to go
now."

Ajax gave her one last kiss, wanting to feel her warmth
again. Her lips burned against his, the feeling lingering even
when he pulled away. He stood up, pulled the cloak down
over his face, and left her behind.

FERRAND

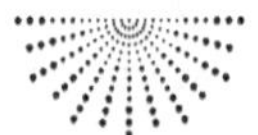

"You promised there would be more time. You said everything would be fine if I did as you asked. If my wife did as you asked." The man before him stank of fear, his voice quavering as he whined and begged. Ferrand was certain he could see small tears forming in the corners of the man's eyes.

His nose wrinkled at the sight, disgusted with this pathetic excuse for a man. *Men do not cry. Men take what they want, and break those weaker than themselves into submission. They do not cry. That is for the women.*

"It seems I underestimated our beloved king's need for increased revenues," Ferrand said, pitching his voice low. It was the same tone he took with women, and it seemed to make the more … effeminate … men more pliable. Easier to bend to his wishes. Weaker. "I'm afraid that nothing you or your lovely wife do can buy you more time at this point. The funds must simply be paid. A Peace Guard should be by within a day or two to collect your debt."

There was a soft noise from the adjoining room, and Ferrand's gaze shot to the closed door, head tilting at the sound. The man froze, eyes darting between the closed door and Ferrand.

Ferrand could only smirk, seeing the panic in the man's eyes. His wife was surely in the next room, hiding from the hungry commander and his insatiable appetite.

Good. Let them cower.

"You must understand," Ferrand continued, turning once more to the man before him. "You are helping your king fund an army. You are helping your country grow." Ferrand paused, his voice hardening as the tension in the man's shoulders eased. "You are helping to avenge the death of our former king."

"I-it's a service, I understand. To help the king."

"Yes," Ferrand answered coolly.

"To make Etritia stronger, and to protect us?"

"Yes."

"Th-then I will gladly pay," the man stammered. He took a half step closer to Ferrand, hands wringing together. "It's just—"

"Yes?" Ferrand was getting annoyed now. It had been the same at each house. Everyone was fine with the increased taxes, *except ...*

"It's just so much more." The man sighed. "I'm a baker, you see. And with the farmers leaving, the mills are nearly empty, and wheat gets more expensive by the day. It's getting harder to provide for the people of the town." His hands continued their nervous twisting. "I'm not the only one. The butchers have no cattle left, and no hunters to bring them deer with the gates closed. And—"

"I understand the concerns you have," Ferrand growled. Why did he have to listen to this ridiculous shit? Was this not the job of the Peace Guards, to take these complaints and bring them to the king? And yet he was subjecting himself to their whines and complaints.

But he needed to show himself. To let them know that he

was still here, in their streets, and they still had cause to cower in their rooms at his presence.

"You are not the only baker," Ferrand said, voice low once more.

"No, no I'm not."

"Then, between all of you, I'm sure you can work together to figure something out." Ferrand turned, stepping through the open shop door and into the filth-littered street beyond. "A Peace Guard will be by within a day or two to collect your debt," he repeated, leaving the man standing wordlessly behind him. The streets were quiet, with only a handful of men standing in open doorways to watch the progress of Ferrand and the two other men with him as they brought news of yet another tax burden to the citizens of Etritia. There were no women or children in sight.

He had walked only a few paces, not quite reaching the door to the next house, when a booming voice rolled down the street behind him.

"Ferrand, I thought we had discussed this. You have no business here."

Ferrand smiled, though his blood was singing with hate. He turned, one hand on his sword. "Ajax. I'm not sure that I know what you're talking about."

Ajax stood perhaps thirty paces away, closing the gap with a glower. "The duty of tax collection falls to the Peace Guards," he said through gritted teeth. "You have no business here."

Ferrand's head tilted, and from the corner of his eyes he could see Clay and Dirk step from the doorway of a house across the street. There was a half-eaten cake speared on the end of Dirk's lucky knife. "I am here only to inform, Ajax. I am not collecting." He caught the eyes of his fellow knights, telling them with a glance to stay back. They did, following his direction without hesitation.

"You are terrorizing them." Ajax halted his advance, scanning the scattered crowd of frightened men. "You should be protecting them. Not threatening them."

Ferrand sneered. "You are mistaken, Ajax." His grip on the pommel of his sword tightened, and for a second he remembered the feel of Silvana's hair twisting through his fingers. "It is my job to protect them from threats outside these walls. To hunt out danger, in whatever form it may take, and destroy it." Ferrand could feel the warmth of anger and lust burning its way from his groin to his stomach. "But while we are all within Etritia, protecting them is your concern."

Ajax only stared, eyes narrowed, and Ferrand felt his hand tighten more, until he could hear Silvana cursing him in his ear, and could smell the faint scent of rose oil as he pressed himself against that damned Coven witch.

"A week's delay to the first man that strikes Ajax." Ferrand was surprised by his own words, as were all those around him.

There was a quiet moment of hesitation, during which those haunting scents and sounds faded.

"Now!" Ferrand shouted. The frightened men around him jumped, but Ajax only blinked.

A single man stepped timidly from the crowd and walked towards Ajax.

"Do your job, Peace Guard. Protect them," Ferrand sneered.

"Don't do this." Ajax's voice wasn't pleading, but the man hesitated anyway.

"Do it," Ferrand growled.

The man straightened, and with a quick motion, hit Ajax squarely across the jaw in an open-handed strike. Ajax made no move to block or dodge the blow.

"Pathetic. But you will get your delay." Ferrand twisted his grip on the pommel of his sword, the decorative edges digging into his palm. The hatred flared again, and Ferrand could once more feel Silvana's thick curls in his hand.

"Two weeks to the one that can bring him to his knees."

The hesitation this time was shorter, and a crowd slowly gathered around Ajax. Fists beat against his back and into his stomach. Ajax said nothing; the only sound he made was the occasional grunt as a strike hit some tender spot. His gaze burned through the assembled group, eyes locked on Ferrand.

Ferrand watched the small group of men as their weak fists pounded against Ajax, and his grip on Silvana's hair tightened again until he could feel her soft curls tearing into the flesh of his palm. The scent of rose oil hung thick in the air, amid the stench of sweat and fear, and Ferrand breathed it in deeply.

Finally, one of the larger men brought down a double fist onto the back of Ajax's head, and the former knight fell to his hands and knees, dazed. Brief and hollow applause went up before the gathered men stepped back, all eyes on Ferrand.

Ajax was on his knees, eyes wide and unfocused.

Silvana was on her knees, eyes wide with fright.

He was telling her to do it properly, or her family would regret it.

The Coven bitch would be next, she was already waiting.

His grip on her hair tightened, deliciously intoxicating.

There would be wine.

Red wine. And white wine.

He had warned Ajax that there would be wine.

"A month to the man that makes him bleed."

The men turned wordlessly, forming a ring around the battered man before them.

Feet kicked his ribs, and Ferrand could hear Ajax gasping for air. Boots stomped down on him, flattening him to the dirty stones of the street.

Ferrand only watched, relishing the feel of his imagined hold on Silvana's hair, breathing in a scent some small part of him knew was not there.

The beating was a short one. After perhaps five seconds, the baker reached down and grabbed Ajax by the hair, and with the help of two other men, lifted him back to his knees. Ajax's eyes were still unfocused, but Ferrand was sure he could see a flash of hatred and pain in them.

With a loud cry, the baker drove his fist into Ajax's face, smashing his nose. Blood spurted from the broken nose, and a cheer rose from the crowd. The baker turned, smiling, blood smeared across the knuckles of his hand.

"Just what the fuck is going on down here?"

The assembled crowd quieted immediately, stepping away from Ajax's crumpled form. Ferrand turned to the newcomer, not surprised to see Dars striding down the street, headed straight for the former commander.

"A lesson in obedience, Dars," Ferrand said, his voice sounding thin to his own ears. "Perhaps you'd care to learn one as well?"

Dars pulled the barely conscious Ajax to his feet, clearly holding most of his weight. He glared up at Ferrand, face twisted in a grimace. "Get fucked, Ferrand," he spat.

Oh, I intend to. Ferrand could still feel Silvana's hair in his grasp, could still smell the Coven bitch's perfumed oils.

Dars turned to the scattered crowd. "The rest of you, go back to your homes. This little game is over." With a faint groan from Ajax, Dars half walked, half carried his friend away.

Ferrand spotted the baker in the dispersing crowd. The man was still smiling, and Ferrand grabbed his upper arm before he could disappear into his home.

"Commander!" The baker's eyes brightened. "Will I really get another delay on the tax debt?"

"I need your wife."

The baker's smile dropped instantly. "But you said—"

"I know what I said." He tugged a leather purse from his

sword belt, snapping the straps that held it in place, and dropped the purse into the baker's hand. "I need your wife."

The baker's eyes were on the purse in his hands. "But—"

"He can have me, husband," came a soft voice from the open doorway.

Ferrand turned, and Silvana stood in the half light of the baker's front room. Ferrand blinked, and Silvana was replaced with a mousy-haired baker's wife, with flour dust on her hands and her eyes rimmed in red.

"He can have me," she repeated, looking over Ferrand's shoulder to her husband. "With that money and the tax delay, we can keep the shop going for a little while longer."

"But—" the baker began again, but Ferrand crossed the threshold and shut the door behind him. It locked with a small wooden latch, and Ferrand turned to see the Coven bitch standing where the baker's wife had been.

"I saw you out there. The fight … it excited you."

"Yes."

"Your hand is bleeding."

Ferrand glanced down at the hand still gripping the pommel of his sword. Bright blood was seeping from between his fingers and under his palm.

"Shut up and undress."

Silvana did as she was instructed, and Ferrand fell on her where she stood, pushing her to the floor. The scent of rose oil clung to her, cloying and sweet and seductive.

When he was finished, Ferrand stood and relaced his pants. He didn't wait for the baker's wife to finish redressing before opening the door to the street. Her husband stood there, purse still in his hands, frozen in place. His eyes shone with unshed tears, and the sight of it disgusted Ferrand.

Not a man at all, just another woman.

"But …" The baker's voice was little more than a whisper. Had he heard his wife's moans? Surely he had, if he'd stood there the whole time.

"Be careful how you spend that money," Ferrand said. He looked over his shoulder, where the mousy-haired wife was hastily tugging her dress back into place. There was a bloody handprint circling her neck.

"The whores of the city will only get cheaper from now on."

"I ain't your damned errand boy," Dars muttered, already knowing it was pointless.

"Please, Dars?" Ajax's eye was puffy and swollen, and blood still leaked from his nose. Silvana had set him on her own bed, and was gently examining the various wounds he'd taken. "You know that if I go to him, one of Ferrand's men will intervene." Ajax winced as Silvana prodded a flowering bruise in his side.

Dars sighed, crossing his arms over his chest. "Alright, fine. I'll give Hasani your message." Dars stepped back to look Ajax over better. "What's wrong with him, Silvana?"

Silvana straightened, hands going to her belly. "I can't be completely sure if there's serious damage to his insides, but it's obvious that he has some cracked ribs. I thought perhaps his nose was broken as well, but it seems to be fine. Lots of bruising to his jaw and cheekbones, but they'll fade."

"I'll be fine," Ajax grumbled, tugging his tunic back over his head with a grimace.

"You will be, in time. I wouldn't try swinging anything heavier than a butter knife around, though." Silvana's mouth turned down into a pouty frown. "It would have been mostly alright if you'd been wearing your armor …"

"If I was still allowed to wear my old armor, we wouldn't be in this mess," Ajax snapped, pulling his tunic down to cover the dark coloring on his ribs.

"What the hell were you thinking, going down there like that?" Dars asked.

Ajax sighed, his glance darting to his sister before he answered. "When you told me what happened to Silvana, I just …" Ajax's voice trailed, and he shrugged, wincing with the motion.

"So you thought it'd be a good idea to go find him, provoke him some more?"

"I did nothing to provoke him."

"Just you being there is enough to provoke him, Ajax!" Dars sighed, closing his eyes and pinching the bridge of his nose. "Ferrand ain't like other men, Ajax. He's a beast, and he's had his eye on you." Dars dropped his arms to his hips, looking from Silvana's worried face to Ajax's angry one. "He'll do anything to break you, you realize that? He started with taking your title, but you resisted. So now he's moving to those you care about." He stabbed a finger in Silvana's direction, spitting his words at Ajax. "Your sister. Your brother, in time. Me, and my family, if they were still here. The Matriarch, if he knew where to find her—"

"He knows where to find her," Ajax growled. "It was Ferrand that took her there."

"You can't know that," Silvana said softly.

"I found her. She showed me everything that happened." Ajax's gaze swiveled between Silvana and Dars, and Dars could sense his mounting anger and anxiety. "It was Ferrand that led her down into the dark, and left her powerless."

Silvana was quiet again, hands moving nervously over her stomach. She couldn't meet her brother's eye, and gave Dars only a passing worried glance.

"Where was she?"

"In the dungeons, as you suggested. There was an … an illusion, Layle called it, blocking the way. I couldn't get through it before."

Dars pressed his questions harder, angry with Ajax for being so stupid and selfish. "And she showed you what, exactly? How?" Dars was nearly shouting now, leaning over Ajax. "Did she tell you that you were going to get your ass handed to you if you went after Ferrand?"

Ajax stood, one hand pressed to his injured ribs. He stood several inches taller than Dars and glared down at him. "Why are you so angry with me, when Ferrand is the one destroying everything we care about?"

"Stop it, both of you." Silvana's voice was thin and watery. Dars turned and caught her eye, realizing in an instant that she was fighting back tears. "We shouldn't be fighting amongst ourselves. We're all that we have left."

Dars took a step back from Ajax, the tension that had been building in his shoulders fading immediately. "I'm sorry, Silvana."

Ajax dropped to the edge of the bed once more, holding his hand out for Silvana to take, giving hers a gentle squeeze. Dars eyed the way Silvana's thin hand clung to her brother's, suddenly missing his family very much.

"I think she gave me her Gift. For a moment, anyway. Though I could only see things that had already happened." Ajax's voice was faint and his gaze distant, as though he were trying to remember. "I saw her being led from their cottage, being pulled down into the dungeons. I saw her speaking with Mothlenor, and he was asking her for help. And she showed me things that I had already seen, but in a way that made everything make sense." Ajax shook his head, looking up at Dars, his expression almost pleading. "I know it sounds crazy, but I found her. And she told me what Mothlenor wanted, and how we can move to stop him."

Dars frowned, arms once more crossing over his chest. "Your father made me promise to watch over your stupid ass, Ajax. And I loved that old bastard, as much as I love the two of you." He sighed, muttering curses under his breath. "Elir damn it all, I'll help you in whatever way I can. Just tell me what you want from me."

Ajax smirked, hand still wrapped around Silvana's. "Be my damned errand boy."

"Ajax …" Dars growled.

"You can get around better than any of us can," Ajax continued. "You're not being watched as closely as I am, or kept as close to Mothlenor as Hasani is. You can help us." Ajax paused, looking up at Dars with a faint smile. "Please?"

Dars considered for a moment, glaring at Ajax. "Fine, but you have to promise me something in return. I don't want you going anywhere near Ferrand until this mess is all over with." He gestured to Silvana, who was sitting close enough to her brother that their knees touched. "If not for my sake, then perhaps for the sake of your sister and her child."

Ajax nodded, looking between them. "I swear it."

HASANI

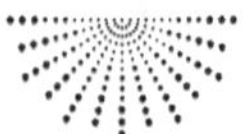

"Hasani, I have heard this drivel countless times. Why continue to pester me with this nonsense?" Mothlenor's gaze was hard, his hawkish eyes focused on Hasani. Across the narrow table, Hasani heard Ferrand let out a small snort, as if he too agreed that their continued council meetings were a waste of time.

"I'm sorry, my lord, but these issues persist, and with no effective way to address them found yet—"

"The issues will continue to persist," Mothlenor said, steepling his hands together and leaning back in his chair. "And that is fine."

Hasani hesitated, for a moment unable to speak. Finally, he managed a numb mutter. "You can't be serious."

"I am."

"But there are hundreds of people out in the city, starving and growing sick." Hasani heard his own voice growing louder and insistent, and he struggled to keep his frustration from coloring his words. "The farmers have all abandoned their fields, choosing to go south or east rather than stay here. There is almost no food to be found, and what little does come through your closed gates is immediately hoarded within the castle walls." Hasani stood, pressing the palms of both hands against the smooth wood of the table. He stared at his splayed fingers, struggling to keep his hands from balling into fists. *Ajax showed his fists, and look where he is now.*

Hasani took a steadying breath. "You refuse to help your own people, my lord, and then demand money from them to finance an army they will die before seeing, in order to fight a war your brother swore was not coming. It is not justified. They are your people. End this madness."

Mothlenor's face was unreadable. Hasani found himself once more annoyed at Mothlenor's ability to simply hide his thoughts and emotions behind a blank mask. Mothlenor's gaze rolled from Hasani to Ferrand, who continued to sit motionless and silent, before settling once more on Hasani. "An impassioned plea. I'm impressed, Hasani. Rarely do you do more than sit and squirm when given unpleasant news." He hesitated, and Hasani hoped for half a heartbeat that Mothlenor might change his mind about keeping the gates closed.

"But you cannot sway me, Hasani." His fingers drummed together, the only movement he made. "The gates will remain closed. We will continue tax collection."

"My lord!" Hasani shouted.

"Have you or your wife gone hungry?" Mothlenor asked, a hint of anger in his voice.

After a moment's hesitation, Hasani answered quietly, "No."

"What about your foolish brother? Is he starving? Is he destitute?"

"No."

"Then calm yourself by knowing that those of us within the castle will not bear the same hardships as those in the city. We will stay strong, Hasani. For the rest of Etritia." Mothlenor's voice grew stern again. "Now sit down."

Hasani did as he was told, falling silently back into his

chair. *Another effort wasted.* He thought briefly of Ajax, and of the task they had spent the last two weeks preparing for. *I hope you are doing better than I am, brother.*

"Now," Mothlenor began again, directing his attention to Ferrand, "you have news on the Coven's whereabouts?"

Hasani straightened in his chair. "The Coven?"

"Yes, my Lord," Ferrand answered, ignoring Hasani. "Thanks to your assistance, my men were able to track the witch Nevara and her maid to an abandoned cabin on the edge of the Felgar woods, to the northeast." Ferrand leaned back in his chair, crossing his arms over his chest. "They watched the house for a few days, but after seeing no sign of the Coven women, they broke into the home." Ferrand's eyes flicked to Hasani's, and Hasani tried his hardest to hide the panic that had gripped him. "There was no sign of Nevara or her maid. They suspected some sort or arcane trickery, and returned for further instructions."

Mothlenor nodded. "An illusion is likeliest, though we can rule nothing out."

"My thoughts exactly," Ferrand said. "They can't be far from that house, and that alone is enough to work out some sort of plan to capture them."

"When did we decide to hunt down out the Coven? I don't recall such a decision," Hasani asked, managing to keep his voice steady.

"Do you disagree with the decision, Hasani?" Mothlenor's voice was quiet, but Hasani could hear the anger simmering just beneath his level tone.

"N-no, of course not, my lord," Hasani stammered. "I only wondered when the decision had been made, and why I was not informed sooner."

Mothlenor sighed, drumming his fingers together again. "The decision was a quick one, Hasani. We did not have time for your whimpering and silly questions. I gave the order for Nevara and the girl with her to be followed, and

Commander Ferrand saw to it that my wishes were carried out."

"And now that the Coven has been found ..." Hasani began, his throat working, "what will become of them?"

Mothlenor nodded to Ferrand, who sneered across the table at Hasani and answered quietly, "The same that happens to all who have wronged the throne." Ferrand's eyes glinted. "They will be brought to the castle and hanged. Or perhaps burned. Or have an axe taken to their necks."

"And you, Hasani," Mothlenor said, drawing Hasani's gaze away from the smirking Ferrand, "will go with the commander to see their capture completed."

"My lord?" Hasani choked out. "Why?"

Because it will be easier to kill me, that's why, Hasani thought. *That can be the only reason to send a troublesome adviser out into the wilderness.*

"Because your king demands it."

51

AJAX

A jax held himself against the curved wall of the tower, listening as Mothlenor's footsteps drew closer. He could hear the low murmur of conversation and Ferrand's heavy footfall, and he pressed himself closer to the bend in the stair where the illusory wall had once stood, clutching a nearly empty bag to himself.

May Imis bless my brother for finally drawing the dragon from his roost.

The pair drew closer, and Ajax held his breath as they neared his hiding spot. But they stopped at the landing that led out to the castle, and at the sound of the wooden door closing behind them, Ajax released the air burning his lungs.

If they had spotted me ... Ajax thought, his heart pounding lightly against his chest. If he had been spotted, Ferrand would have run him through where he stood, and kicked his body down the remaining stairs and into the dungeons.

After a quick peek to ensure the stair was empty, Ajax took the curved ascent to Mothlenor's chambers. Within moments, he found himself at Mothlenor's tower, testing the door. It was locked, but Ajax had expected as much. He slipped a short crowbar out of the bag, sliding it into the groove between the door and the frame. With a quick jerk and the sound of splintering wood, the door was freed. Ajax instinctively winced with the motion, expecting his sore ribs to protest. But they didn't, and Ajax let out a grateful sigh. *I seem to be healing faster than Silvana had anticipated.*

Ajax hesitated, suddenly nervous. This was not the first time he had pried open a locked door. Every once in a while, some young child would inadvertently lock themselves away in a bedroom or privy, and panicked parents with no sense or no finances to keep extra keys around would run to the barracks or a nearby King's Guard for aid.

But this had been the first time he had broken into a place with the sole intention of theft. The idea left Ajax's stomach in knots.

He straightened from his crouch, dropping the metal bar back into his bag. He stepped carefully over the threshold, eyes darting around the room before him. It was empty, looking nearly the same as it had the last time he had been in here. There were papers and books and rolled parchments stacked and piled precariously on every available surface. A small vat of simmering liquid sat on a three-legged stool, tucked against one wall, and the small basin that Ajax had noticed before was now gone, perhaps moved elsewhere.

Ajax moved silently to the desk, shuffling papers and other items around delicately. *The egg had been here, lying on top of some papers.*

But it was gone.

Ajax began opening drawers within the desk, rifling through their contents, searching for the dragon's egg. *I have to find it, for Nevina.*

Ajax desperately tugged open the last drawer, hesitating when he saw the contents. The mysterious stone Mothlenor had shown Ajax sat on a silk pillow, dull and dark. Ajax reached for it, not sure if he wanted to touch it. He could remember Mothlenor's words as he waved the brilliantly colored stone for Ajax to see.

"Do you like it? It can help me see things. Or people."

Could he use this to find the Coven? Or me, if I flee with the egg?

Ajax took a deep breath, not sure what might happen, and grabbed the stone with one shaky hand and pulled it from the drawer.

Nothing.

There was no reaction to his touch, and the stone remained dark and cool in his palm.

Ajax straightened, slipping the stone into a pocket, and began his search of the desk again.

"Return what you have taken, thief."

Ajax jumped at the sound of Mothlenor's voice, looking up to see the king towering in the doorway he had come through. "M-my lord!"

Great Ones take it, I heard him leave! How could he have come back so quickly, and without me noticing?

"Replace what you have stolen, and I will not call the guards," Mothlenor said. His voice sounded oddly hollow, and there was something odd about him that Ajax couldn't immediately place.

"I'm sorry, my lord," Ajax said, watching Mothlenor. He walked around the side of the desk, stepping closer to the king. "I have stolen nothing, but I will leave."

"Return what you have taken, thief," Mothlenor said. His gaze had not followed Ajax as he stepped around the desk, and was instead fixed on a point on the wall opposite him.

"You're not really here, are you?" Ajax asked, inspecting Mothlenor more closely. His hair seemed less grey than Ajax remembered, and his heavy robes hung differently across his shoulders. "You're just another illusion, aren't you? And an old one, it seems."

"Replace what you ha—"

The image of Mothlenor vanished, leaving only a faint scent of something Ajax found vaguely familiar. He sighed, releasing his held breath, and continued his search.

How long can Hasani keep Mothlenor occupied?

"I hope, brother, that your luck has been better than mine," Ajax muttered.

He searched the rest of the study without incident, and without finding the misshapen hunk of gold he needed. Ajax finally turned to the other rooms of the tower, not sure how much longer he might have. It had been nearly ten minutes already, and he still needed to make sure he could get safely away from the tower without running into Ferrand or Mothlenor.

He searched them all, the small library that was just as cluttered as the first room, the privy, just to leave no stone unturned, until he finally worked his way into Mothlenor's bedchamber. The room was unusually empty, with only a large bed and a small writing desk against one wall. He immediately went to the desk and pulled out the single drawer.

And there it was, the misshapen chunk of bright gold that he now recognized as a dragon's egg. He picked it up gingerly, surprised by its light weight. It didn't feel like a normal egg. The surface was rough and cold. He had expected it to be warm, since it held a dragon inside. *But perhaps the creature is dead?*

Ajax carefully slipped the egg into the bag hanging from his shoulder, careful not to bump it against the crowbar. *What would happen if I broke the egg?* Ajax pondered the question for a second, then shook his head and put it out of his mind. He had been in here for too long. He shut the drawer to the writing desk and doubled back. He rechecked everything, making sure it was the same as it had been when he broke in. Finally, he left, shutting the door behind him. The splintered frame he couldn't fix, but the door still shut.

Perhaps Mothlenor wouldn't return immediately, but they should assume that he would. They would have to act immediately. He descended the stairs quickly, cracking open the door to the rest of the castle upon reaching the landing. Once he was sure the path just outside was clear, he slipped through the doorway and made his way to Hasani's chambers. Relief washed over Ajax as he put distance between himself and the tower. *But we still have much more to do.*

Ajax paced the length of Hasani's bedchamber, waiting for his return. His earlier anxiety had only intensified as the long minutes stretched on, and Hasani's absence grew worrisome.

Silvana watched him as he crossed back and forth in front of her, some needlework lying half forgotten in her lap. "Please stop that. It's distressing to watch."

"You do the same thing when you're upset, Silvana."

"I do?" She seemed to think for a moment, and Ajax paused to wait for her. "I guess I do," she said softly. Ajax took it as permission to continue, and resumed his pacing, though he forced himself to walk a little slower.

"Why is it taking him so long?" Ajax growled in frustration, turning to cross the floor once more.

"You asked him to give you as much time as possible, Ajax." Silvana stabbed forcefully at her work, cursing when the fabric tore. She set the whole mess on the floor beside her, eyes fixed on the door. "Isn't a delay now better than one later? It gave us time to pack. And time to plan." Her arms crossed over her belly, one hand rubbing at it absently, and Ajax could see one foot jigging up and down impatiently. *She's just as anxious as I am.*

Ajax glanced at the pile of old saddlebags that he and Silvana had already prepared. *Clothing, money, a few books, plenty of food. Enough to get us to the Free Cities, where we can hopefully start a new life. Just the three of us. Or four, soon enough.*

Ajax sighed, rubbing at the stubble on his chin. "I'm worried we're just losing time now. It's dark, and we should be leaving the castle soon. If we have to wait too much longer—"

The door to the hall opened, and Hasani slipped inside from the dimly lit corridor. Silvana was on her feet in an instant, moving with surprising speed to lock Hasani into an embrace. He held her tightly for a moment, looking Ajax over. "I'm glad you made it back safe. Do you have it?"

Ajax silently pointed to the egg, which sat on the hearth, close to the warmth of the fire. Hasani released Silvana, taking the egg in both hands and gently tracing the rough patches of the shell. "It's not exactly what I expected." He chuckled, turning it over in his hands. "I thought it might be bigger." He carefully handed it back to Ajax, who tucked it into the same bag he'd used to carry it from Mothlenor's tower.

"Hasani, we'll have to leave tonight."

"Of course." Hasani hurried to his desk, shuffling papers and bottles of ink together. "I see we're already packed. Good, that'll save us a lot of time." He took a blank sheet of paper and scribbled furiously on it.

Ajax blinked, stepping to stand over Hasani's shoulder. "I was worried I'd have to argue with you all night about leaving."

Hasani looked up at him with a smirk. "You just broke into the king's quarters and stole one of his most prized possessions. I don't plan on sticking around to see how he reacts when he finds out it's gone missing." Hasani's smirk faded, replaced with a somber expression. "Besides, Mothlenor is going to send me to find the Coven. Or die trying."

Ajax frowned, trying to make sense of the scribbles on

Hasani's paper. "No one knows where the Coven is. You'd have died trying, no doubt about it."

"Mothlenor knows where they are," Hasani said, his voice soft.

"What? How?"

"Nevara came to visit him. It was almost two months ago. She wanted Nevina returned to her. She was sure that the Matriarch was still alive. Mothlenor denied it and had her removed from the city. I was the one who took her to the gate. And from there, Mothlenor had her followed, and she apparently led them right back to the Coven." He dipped his pen into the inkwell again, the motion looking like an angry stab.

"That's impossible."

"Is it?" Hasani asked quietly. "I'm sure Mothlenor was lying about something. Maybe he lied about knowing their exact location. Maybe Nevara wasn't followed at all and Mothlenor used magic to track her down."

Ajax thought briefly of the little stone in his pocket. He had wondered if Mothlenor might be able to use it to find the Coven; maybe he already had …

"But the point is—" Hasani continued. "Mothlenor would have me be the one to lead his army to the Coven, and let them be killed. They are only women and children, sworn allies of mankind. And I want no part in their deaths." He finished his note, dropping the quill on the desk and straightening. "I want to leave tonight."

"How does Mothlenor plan on destroying the Coven?" Silvana asked softly.

Hasani sighed. "We just spent nearly an hour going over what are essentially battle plans. There were maps, and Ferrand and Mothlenor seemed to know a way to subdue the arcane users, though they didn't share it with me …"

"Mothlenor has these strange cuffs," Ajax said. "When they're put on a magic user, it cuts them off from their abilities. Something about the movement of energy within the body." Ajax shook his head, unsure. "Layle explained it to me, but I didn't quite understand it."

"That must be it, then. It sounds right. Though how Ferrand plans on getting all the Coven members bound by those cuffs, I can't guess," Hasani said, arms crossed over his chest.

"Do you have one of the maps to the Coven?" Ajax was almost hopeful. Maybe he could find them, warn them, while Hasani and Silvana fled to the Free Cities on their own.

"I do now," Hasani said with a smirk, holding up the paper he had been writing on. Hasani had scribbled a series of hastily drawn lines and a few written instructions. "I had to draw it from memory, but I'm confident that it's accurate."

Ajax nodded, taking the map from Hasani and tucking in into a pocket. "Good. We need to go, now."

"Wait." Hasani crossed to the bedroom. He pulled something out from under the bed and tossed it to Ajax. "You might want that back."

Ajax fingered the familiar hilt before belting the scabbard around his waist. He was glad to have his old sword back, and grateful that Hasani had kept it for so long. *I might just need it before the next few nights are over.*

Ajax nodded a quick thanks to Hasani, then took up a bag and slung it over one shoulder. "Come on, let's head for the dungeons. Mothlenor has a habit of spending a bit of time in the library after council meetings, right?"

Hasani nodded, taking the remaining bags in one hand and grasping Silvana's with the other. "We'll have to hurry, but we can beat him to the tower, I'm sure of it."

Ajax opened the door out to the hall, checking for passersby. A plainly dressed handmaid turned a corner on the opposite end of the hall and disappeared from sight, and Ajax led the others out. "According to Dars, Ferrand leaves the castle to go drinking and whoring most evenings, so we should be clear of him for a few hours, too."

"Does Dars know where we're going?" Silvana asked from behind him.

"No. He knows we're up to something, but I couldn't tell him everything. For his own sake." Ajax led them down the quiet and dimly lit halls, checking around corners and listening for footsteps. Ajax thought briefly of his old friend, wondering if perhaps they should track him down and bring him along. *Another sword arm would be good, and he could find his family and be with them again ...* But Ajax was sure Dars would only reject the offer, choosing to stay in Etritia and do what little he could to save it from collapse.

The halls were dark and quiet, and Ajax was momentarily grateful that Hasani had held the council meeting for so long. It was late in the evening, late enough that most who lived within the castle walls were sleeping, or otherwise entertained behind the doors of their own chambers. Their path to the Old Tower was nearly deserted, save for the occasional quiet servant that traversed the halls on errands. Ajax was able to avoid these with ease, and they reached the door to the spiral stair unseen.

Once inside, Ajax glanced up the tower steps, towards Mothlenor's rooms. But all was silent. *Still in the library, then. Good.*

Ajax pulled a small lantern from a loop on the outside of his bag and lit the quick with shaking fingers. He grasped Silvana's hand and led her carefully down the steps of the tower. Her hands were also trembling. "The dungeons were closed off decades ago, by Areanath's father, but Mothlenor found a way to uncover them without anyone knowing. Nevina is being held down there." Ajax's voice echoed oddly off the surrounding stone, and he pitched his voice low.

"You said there was a ... a fake wall? Hiding it?" Silvana whispered.

"An illusion. Since you know it's there already, I doubt you'll see it. We should be past it in a moment." Ajax was sure they had already gone beyond the point where Mothlenor's illusory wall had been and were nearing the first floor of the dungeons.

After a few moments of hurried descent, the light from Ajax's lantern fell on a single wooden door, much like the one they had passed through a moment before. Ajax ignored it, continuing their flight down.

"Where does that lead?" Hasani asked.

"There are three levels to the dungeons. That was the door leading to the uppermost floor," Ajax answered.

"And which level is the Matriarch on?" Silvana asked timidly.

"The third." Ajax's voice was hard and his jaw worked in hot anger. "The deepest, darkest level. Furthest from any kind of help. Easier to forget her that way. Easier to let her die, so far away."

Silvana gave his hand a gentle press. "You still found her, Ajax. The deepest, darkest pit, and you still found her."

Ajax couldn't find comfort in his sister's words, and he led them down into the dark without another word.

The air grew damp as they continued, the heavy scent of earth stinging their noses and burning their throats. They passed a second landing, ignoring it as they had the first, only stopping when they reached the bottom of the stairs. The door opened easily, silent on its oiled hinges.

"Someone seems to come down here often enough." Hasani inspected the door in the dim light of the lantern. "The doorknob is smudged with grease, and there are footprints in the dust."

"I imagine that someone comes down here on a semi-regular basis. To bring her food and water," Ajax said quietly, ushering them through the open door and into the darkness beyond. "The key to her cell is kept on a peg outside her door."

Hasani stopped, turning to Ajax. "You could have taken her out of here at any time?"

Ajax glared at Hasani, stepping around him to take the lead. *Does he think I didn't try?* "She refuses to leave," Ajax snapped. He sighed, catching sight of Hasani's wide eyes, and softened his voice. "She believes Mothlenor could find her wherever she went. Better to stay right where she is, and learn what she can, than leave and risk capture again."

Hasani said nothing, and Ajax turned away from him, lifting the lantern once more to cut through the dark.

They continued in silence, Silvana keeping one hand on his shoulder, the other holding fast to Hasani. Their footsteps echoed loudly on the close walls, and Ajax felt his heartbeat quickening with every passing moment.

We're running out of time, he thought, his pace increasing. *Mothlenor will find us.* Ajax's heart pounded in his ears. *We're running out of time.*

Finally, the light fell on a double row of heavy wooden doors.

Ajax's footsteps grew louder as he almost jogged down the remainder of the corridor.

There, just outside the last door on the left side, hung a single key.

HASANI

They walked quickly for several minutes through the maze of tunnels. Hasani was completely lost in no time, but Ajax seemed to know where he was leading them, though he would often pause at splits in the path for a moment. The further they traveled, the stronger the overwhelming sense of a crushing weight all around them became, until Hasani's feet dragged with every step.

Finally, they stopped. They seemed to have reached a short block of prison cells, with a handful of heavy wooden doors lining the hall on both sides. Ajax rushed ahead, stopping at the final door on the left, tugging the key down from the wall and scrambling to unlock the door. He pushed the heavy door open and ushered them inside before carefully closing the door behind them.

The room was just as dark and cold as the hallways outside had been, and with Ajax's torch behind him, he couldn't see more than a few inches in front of his nose. He held Silvana close, and he felt her hands slide down to her stomach protectively.

"Ajax? Is that you?"

Her voice was weak, but Hasani recognized it immediately. Although Ajax had already told them that Nevina was alive, that another was executed in her place, he could still hardly believe his eyes as Ajax rushed to the figure lying prone against the far wall. She was incredibly thin and pale, and hardly seemed to have the strength to sit up. Her face was gaunt, and there was a crust of dried blood under one lip. Her once golden hair was ragged and dirty. But Hasani could glimpse the beauty she'd once had. And the way Ajax held her gingerly and kissed her cheeks despite the filth pained him.

"You shouldn't have come. You should have gone straight for the door," Nevina chastised Ajax.

"I know, I know. But I wanted to see you one last time. And I've brought Hasani and Silvana with me. You can show them what you showed me, help them understand …"

"I can't. I don't have the strength anymore. And you don't have the time to wait around for me. I'm sure Mothlenor will notice what you've done soon, and the first thing he will do is interrogate me. You have to leave."

"We will, don't worry. Just please come with us." Ajax's voice was pleading. Hasani could only stand and listen, unsure of what to do.

"I can't come with you. I am meant to stay here. When Mothlenor realizes that the egg is missing, I can buy you enough time to get safely away from Etritia." She turned to Hasani and Silvana, a weak smile on her face. "Silvana, how is the baby?"

Silvana took a few steps closer, her earlier unease apparently gone. "He's fine. He kicks all day and all night." She knelt beside Nevina, taking her by the hand and pressing it into her belly. "See?"

Nevina laughed, and the laugh turned into a hacking cough that lasted for several seconds. She turned away, wheezing between coughs, then turned back and nodded her head to Silvana in approval. In the dim light surrounding them, Hasani saw droplets of fresh blood staining her lips.

Nevina turned to him. "You still have the book?"

"I do, yes."

"Give it to Silvana."

Hasani looked at his wife, whose eyes had grown large at the command. He did as Nevina instructed, pulling the book from his doublet and passing it to her. She clutched it to her chest, her eyes troubled in the dimness of Nevina's cell.

Nevina clutched Silvana's hand tightly. "You have to get to the Knife. And from there, follow it south until you reach the Free Cities. You will be safe there, for a time, and you must make sure that you always keep that book close. And when the time comes, you will give it to your son. Do you understand?"

Silvana nodded. "I-I understand." She quietly retreated, reaching for Hasani's hand and squeezing it tightly. "Our son, Hasani," she whispered under her breath. "She said our son …"

Hasani had heard, and he dared to hope that it would be true. *A son …*

Nevina was coughing again, head turned and mouth pressed into the inside of her elbow. When the fit stopped, she looked up at Ajax. "You have to go now. You've wasted too much time lingering here."

"I'll go," Ajax started. "It's just …"

"Yes?" Nevina almost sounded impatient.

"I love you. You still won't come with me?"

Nevina smiled thinly, her lip trembling. "I'm not going to be in this world much longer. Surely you realize that. Just remember, Ajax. There's power in love."

Ajax nodded slowly before kissing her on the cheek and standing up to leave. "If things had happened differently …" He sounded hopeful, his voice thick.

"If things had happened differently ..." Nevina's hand tightened around Ajax's briefly, and then she released him.

"Goodbye, Nevina."

"Goodbye, Ajax."

Ajax led them out of the cell, closing the heavy door behind him. Their lantern was beginning to grow low, the oil in it nearly gone. Ajax took Silvana by the hand and she laced her icy fingers with Hasani's. "We have to hurry. Come on." Ajax led them down to the end of the prison block and deeper into the tunnels.

MOTHLENOR

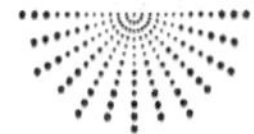

Mothlenor's heartbeat was a rapid staccato against his ribs, and for a moment he forgot how to breathe. *All my work, all my planning. Stolen.*

Why had his theft spell not activated?

He blinked rapidly, forcing himself to exhale and draw in a fresh breath. The spots that were forming in his vision began to fade, and he was able to test his old warding spell.

"The damn thing did activate," he whispered. "And it was dismissed."

Had the thief seen through the illusion? Had it been that hastily constructed?

Mothlenor checked the small table in his bedroom again, knowing that it would still be empty. He considered searching the rest of his tower, just in case he had moved the dragon's egg elsewhere. But he knew it hadn't been moved. And the damage to the door frame was sign enough that someone had broken in.

But who?

He instantly thought of Nevina. Her last Coven girl had managed an escape somehow. Perhaps Nevina had found her way through the dungeon and into Mothlenor's study.

And she knew about the egg.

Mothlenor reached into an inner pocket of his robes and pulled out a long pouch fastened shut with a leather tie. He unraveled the pouch, removing a thin needle; he tossed the empty case onto the nearby bed. The needle was longer than his forefinger, and topped with a large ruby, making the whole instrument heavy. The pointed tip glinted in the light refracting off the gem, making it seem like it was already wet with blood.

With a deliberate prick and a gentle kneading motion, a fat drop of blood formed on the tip of Mothlenor's finger. He stepped to the center of his bedroom, briefly wondering if what he was doing was wise. With a quick flick of the hand, the blood drop fell to the floor, splashing against the stone with a soft smack.

"Nevina," Mothlenor said, his voice deep with the arcane power behind it. "Nevina. You are mine to call."

The blood on the floor began to smoke, first small curls of blue-grey haze, then larger billows of black. Mothlenor stepped back, instinctively inhaling the wafting clouds of burning magic. It smelled faintly of rose oil, and the smell of it stirred some small part of him. The part that still wanted the Coven witch, perhaps? He ignored it, narrowing his eyes to peer through the smoke surrounding him.

As the smoke began to clear, Nevina came into view. Naked, as she had been every other time he had summoned her. But this time she was awake; he hadn't bothered to wait until she had fallen asleep to call her to him. She stood, defiant, waiting for him. Her face was thin and dirty, and her ribs were prominent enough that he could count them. Her hair was ragged, her nails broken and caked with filth.

But she stood before him calmly, as if she had known he would summon her.

"Where is it?" The question was asked before the smoke had finished dissipating.

"I have no idea what you're talking ab—"

His hand flew up to her face, knocking her to the ground. As she struggled to her feet again he bent over her, his anger instantly focused. "The egg," he said coolly. "Someone has stolen it from me while I was otherwise distracted. Was it you?" She had managed to get to her feet again. He grabbed her by the wrist, pulling her close. "Your Coven girl found a way around the cuffs long enough to magic herself out of the dungeons … perhaps you did too?" There was a slight widening of Nevina's eyes, and Mothlenor smirked at her. "Did you think it would go unnoticed? I knew before she had been gone more than a couple of hours. Her whereabouts don't concern me." His grip on her wrist tightened. "Unless she has my egg," he added with a snarl.

"She doesn't," Nevina said quietly. She was staring at him, unafraid.

"Are you certain?" He tightened his hold on her wrist again, feeling the small bones grinding together.

Still, she stared him down. "Yes."

"Then perhaps someone else took it for you?" He could feel his calm decaying under her gaze. He hit her again, sending her staggering back.

But she quickly straightened. "No."

The firmness of her replies ate away at what little composure he still held. "Are you certain?" Mothlenor asked again through gritted teeth.

"I'm certain. Perhaps you just lost it somewhere?" Her voice was coy, baiting him.

He dropped her wrist and hit her in the jaw, sending her sprawling to the ground again.

She remained on the floor, her breathing ragged. Her whole body shuddered as a strong fit of coughing consumed her. Mothlenor watched, curious, as she struggled to control herself. Finally, the fit over, she spat a ball of phlegm onto the ground in front of her. The spittle gleamed red with blood.

"You're dying." The notion was surprisingly serene. "You're dying from a simple sickness, and you can do nothing to stop it from ravaging you."

The witch remained lying on her hip, propping herself up on one elbow, looking up at him in anger.

"How did it start? A small tickle in the back of your throat? Then that feeling of fatigue, perhaps a fever. Then, after a while, it moved down to your chest, making it hard to breathe. And now coughing up blood. You could have healed yourself, made yourself a potion to kill the disease. But in this tower you are helpless." He knelt over her again, dropping his voice lower. "And you will die."

She only glared at him, fresh blood staining her lower lip.

He took several steps away from her, crossing his arms over his chest and looking down on her thin frame. "If you had taken it yourself, you would not have chosen to return to your cell. You would have found your little witch and returned to your Coven to warn them."

She stared coolly up at him, her emotions unreadable behind those terrible eyes.

"You sent someone else after it. You really can't leave the dungeons, can you? Who did you send?"

"No one."

"No one?" He raised an eyebrow critically.

"It was me. I stole the egg. And I did return to my cell, even if it means my death." She looked away from him, wiping the blood from her lips with the back of one hand. "I knew it would be pointless to run away. You would just summon me back."

Mothlenor snorted. "I don't think that I believe you."

"I'm telling the truth!" Nevina slammed her fist into the ground. "I went to the tower, stole the egg, sent it to the Coven, and then returned."

He sighed. "Why do you refuse to help me, Nevina?"

She stared up at him, eyes alight again. "Because you killed someone I love, Mothlenor."

"I loved him too," Mothlenor snarled, surprising himself. After a pause, he added, "I might have murdered him, but he was still my brother."

Nevina turned away from him once more. "Great Ones take you, Mothlenor." She brought herself to her feet, using the nearby bed to pull herself from the floor. "And don't say my name."

"Where did you find the egg?" It was a simple enough question, but Nevina hesitated.

"On … on the desk. In the study." Her voice faltered.

"You're lying."

"I'm not lying! I stole—" Her protests halted as another round of coughing took her.

"You *are* lying. You sent someone else, and I will find out who." A thought occurred to him, and he turned his back on her to leave. Out of the corner of his eye, he saw her rush at him. He turned, easily deflecting a blow to the head. But she continued to fight, kicking and punching his chest, until he was able to grab both of her wrists. "Don't worry." Mothlenor smirked. "You're coming with me. I have a way of finding out who took it, and I would very much like to see the look on your face when I do."

Taking both of her small wrists in one hand, he half dragged her from the bedroom and into the study beyond. She protested, and landed a pathetic kick against one knee, but he ignored her. Once in the study, he shoved her away from him and she stumbled, barely keeping her feet under her. He didn't bother to lock the door to the tower stairs. She had been right; there was no reason for her to run when he could just summon her back to him.

"I made the mistake of telling you about the egg—a mistake I fully intend to rectify, Nevina." He hurried behind the large writing desk, kneeling to open one of the bottom drawers. "But I do have other trinkets besides …" Mothlenor cursed, seeing the empty pillow where the Dragon's Eye should have been. He pulled the drawer clear out of the desk, dumping the contents onto the cluttered top. The pillow was the only thing inside. The Eye was gone.

"Dammit!" he yelled, flinging the empty drawer across the room. It hit the adjacent wall and splintered. Nevina jumped at the noise, her arms covering her bare chest and her wide eyes fixed on him. Mothlenor stalked around the desk again, clenching and unclenching his fists. "Who took it, Nevina?" He raised one accusatory finger to point at the broken mess now lying against the nearby wall.

"I-I don't know—"

His struck her before he was even sure he wanted to. She cried out, a hand going to her cheek. "How did you know about it? Who did you get to take it?" He had never mentioned the Eye to Nevina, had he?

"I don't—"

He fell on her, one hand going around her throat. Her eyes grew wider at his touch, and she clawed at his fingers, trying to pry them loose. "How did you know about it?" he growled.

"Please, Mothlenor," Nevina choked out. "Let me go."

He lifted her to his eye level, her feet barely brushing the floor. Her face began to darken, and her eyes were so wide that they seemed to bulge. "I want to know everything, Nevina."

She squirmed harder, tearing at the hand around her throat. He stared into her eyes until she shut them tightly, tears leaking from the corners. He could feel her throat working as she tried to gasp for air. Or scream, perhaps. Or both. "I want to know what you See when you look at me," Mothlenor said slowly, his voice once again calm. "And I want to know who took my egg."

Nevina seemed to shake her head, her face growing darker more quickly than Mothlenor imagined it might.

He tightened his grip, and her eyes snapped open in surprise.

"I want to See, Nevina."

His vision dimmed, and he could make out the vague outline of a figure leaning over him. The figure came into focus, and Ajax's red hair and concerned eyes swam before him.

"... I'll get the egg and come back for you. You can still leave this place, Nevina."

There was an explosion of pain behind Mothlenor's left ear, and the image of Ajax disappeared as quickly as it had come.

Mothlenor shook his head, trying to shake the spots from his sight. He had fallen back against the desk, and it had barely kept him on his feet. Nevina knelt a few feet away, one hand massaging her throat as she coughed and wheezed for air.

"What did you do?"

"N-not me," Nevina spluttered. She leaned back on her haunches, raising one shaking finger to point at him. "You," she wheezed.

He considered for a moment. The air stank of spent arcane energy, and there were raised blisters on Nevina's neck in the vague shape of his handprint. Had he somehow forced himself into Nevina's memories? He had seen Ajax, and Ajax had mentioned the egg. Could he have used magic to pry himself into her mind?

Mothlenor's head throbbed, and he rubbed it instinctively, wincing as he touched a tender bump. "You hit me," he muttered.

"You were killing me." Nevina's voice was raspy.

"How did you hit me? You can't do magic."

She looked over at him, eyes narrowed. She raised one

arm, shaking her fist in answer. The heavy metal cuff on her wrist seemed to drag her whole arm down.

Mothlenor grunted, straightening with a slight wobble. "It was Ajax, then, wasn't it? He probably broke in during the last council meeting. And he already knew about my Dragon's Eye."

"A Dragon's Eye?" Nevina said. "I'm glad he took it, then."

Mothlenor managed a small chuckle. He offered a hand to Nevina, but she waved it away with a grimace. Instead, he knelt beside her, brushing her dirty hair away from her neck to inspect the welts he had inadvertently given her. "Will you still refuse my offer, Nevina?"

She pulled away from him, unable to make eye contact. "I'd rather die, Mothlenor."

He sighed. "So be it, then."

His arm snaked out, grabbing hold of the hand still massaging Nevina's tender throat and yanking it away. She hadn't anticipated it, but reacted quickly enough. She twisted her body, bringing her free hand up to hit him with the metal cuff again. Mothlenor caught her wrist, holding both between the long fingers of one hand. The other went around her neck once more, and he slammed her to the floor.

Nevina cried out as her head bounced against the stone, and Mothlenor tightened his hand around her neck, once more strangling her. There was no anger in it this time, and Mothlenor was surprised by the sudden stab of guilt that her struggles caused. Her feet kicked out, and she struggled to wriggle an arm free of his grasp. But it was her eyes that made him hesitate the most. Her eyes seemed to plead with him, begging for her life. Bright blue eyes, kept hidden from him for years, now begged for him to stop, to let her go.

"I'm sorry, Nevina." Mothlenor stared into her eyes, leaning over her and slowly putting more of his body weight against his strangling hand. "I can't let you live if you refuse

to help me. I can't let you go if you won't give yourself
to me."

Nevina's mouth opened and closed as if she was trying to
speak. Mothlenor briefly thought of releasing her, of asking
her once more if she would stay by his side. But he was sure
she would still refuse, and it would be harder to try to kill
her a third time. "You would die in the dungeons in a few
days anyway, Nevina." Her kicks were becoming weak, and
her face was dark. "Why not die here, with me?"

He leaned further over her, nearly on top of her, and
watched as she began to lose consciousness. One of her
hands slipped from the slackening grip he held on them, and
the fingers groped blindly for him, finally grasping onto the
billowing sleeve of his robe. When Nevina's kicks stopped
and her eyes rolled back, showing only white, Mothlenor
muttered a spell under his breath. For a moment, nothing
happened, and he maintained his hold on her. Finally, a thin
silver wisp wormed its way through the small opening
between Nevina's lips and drifted slowly upward.

Mothlenor released his grip, catching the floating wisp
between two fingers. His eyes never leaving the silver thing
in his hand, Mothlenor fumbled through the pockets of his
robe, pulling out a small vial and removing the stopper with
his teeth. The silver wisp was tucked into the vial and sealed
once more.

He looked between the vial and Nevina. "I'll find something useful for this, I promise. I won't just make you into a
wraith as I planned to do with my brother." He took one of
her hands and brought it to his lips, kissing the palm. "You
have my word." He leaned over her once more, brushing his
lips against hers. They were soft, and beneath the smell of
filth and death, there was still the faint scent of rose oil and
unspent arcane energy.

"You were very beautiful, Nevina. And very gifted. I wish
you had chosen differently."

Mothlenor stood slowly, tucking the vial containing Nevina's soul back into his robes.

Ajax had his egg. And his Dragon's Eye. But he couldn't have gone too far just yet. There was still time to catch him.

He would need Ferrand. And he would need his wraiths.

But there was still time.

54

AJAX

Ajax pulled them quickly along, the light of his lantern bouncing along the walls as they hurried through the tunnels. He knew the path well, thanks to Nevina. They were nearly there ... *And then the blood sacrifice ...* Ajax's body shuddered at the thought, knowing what was to come.

The light sputtered, the oil nearly burned away. "Shit." Ajax glanced down at the lantern, watching as the light grew dimmer before his eyes. "We'll have to finish the hike out in the dark, I'm afraid."

"Ajax, where are we going? Is there a way out?" Silvana's voice was soft and trembling, and her hand clutched his tightly.

"There's a door. It will let us out in the woods to the north of the castle." The ground beneath their feet began to slope slightly upwards, back to the surface. They were getting closer. "Once out, we head west, towards the Knife. Once at the Knife, we follow it south to the Free Cities." The path steepened until they were almost climbing. *Nearly there.*

"We're going to go through the woods without a light?" Hasani answered Silvana. "Tomorrow's moon will be a full one. There will be plenty of moonlight to see by, don't worry."

They followed the path up and, after a few minutes, the lantern finally went out. Silvana gasped in the sudden darkness, but Hasani comforted her with a few low words. Ajax led them on, stowing the lantern and keeping one hand on the wall for guidance. They continued to climb until they reached a dead end. Ajax groped around in the dark, his free hand feeling first the smooth cold stone of the tunnel wall, then a jagged formation right in front of his nose. He fingered the rough stone, trying to piece together where they might be. Had he made a wrong turn somewhere? Did he get them lost? Ajax's groping hands found a large hole in the structure. His hand slipped in, and he felt his sleeve catch on jagged spikes. He jerked back, his heart pounding. *The Dragon Door.*

"We're here. We've reached the door."

"Well go on then, let's open it."

He felt Hasani move to his side, but Ajax lifted an arm to stop him. "It's not an ordinary door, Hasani." Ajax paused, feeling his pulse quicken. "To open the door, I have to make a blood sacrifice."

The air was still for a moment until Silvana broke the silence. "What do you mean?"

"I mean that the door is magic. It will only open after someone offers up their life to it."

"Then I'll make the sacrifice." Hasani stepped closer to the door.

Ajax reached out again and pulled him back. "I can't let you do that."

"Why the hell not, Ajax? You expect me to let you die to save my wife and son? That's my responsibility, not yours." He shoved Ajax's hand away, again moving towards the door.

"I won't die, Hasani!" he called out. "Nevina Saw that much. The Dragon Door won't kill me." Hasani paused in front of the door. "But if you try to open the door, it might kill you." He put a hand on his friend's shoulder. "Let me do it. And just … protect my sister, if I can't use my sword any longer." He couldn't be sure, but he thought Hasani might have nodded in the dark.

"Imis bless him," Silvana muttered behind them.

Ajax sighed, turning towards the door. He felt his way around the structure until he found the hole again. He positioned himself, ready to plunge his arm into the gaping maw. "Alright, here goes, I guess." *I hope you were right, Nevina.* Ajax took a deep breath and thrust his arm in.

The sound of stone grinding on stone filled the air, followed by excruciating pain as the great stone dragon clamped its jaws down on his arm.

For several seconds, Ajax only knew the agony of the Dragon Door's grip on him. Someone nearby was screaming, a long and terrible sound that seemed to go on for forever.

The initial shock of the dragon's fangs piercing his flesh and boring through his bone faded some, but was quickly replaced with the sickening sensation of his blood being pulled from the wounds in his arm. It left him dizzy in only a few seconds, and he fell to his knees, his initial cry weakening to a whimper as his energy left him. He thought he could hear shouting, someone saying his name, but he could not answer. His eyesight reddened, and he wished he would pass out, even if it meant he would be unable to remove whatever might be left of his arm when the sacrifice was over. His nose filled with the metallic scent of fresh blood, and Ajax was sure that she had been wrong.

Nevina had been wrong.

He would die right here.

And then the great maw of the dragon door opened, and his arm was free. Immediately, his vision cleared, and the pain from his wounds seemed to fade away. *Is this what dying feels like? All the pain, just going away?*

He felt Hasani and Silvana rush to him, pulling him up and supporting his weight between them. He let them carry him out into the moonlight, his legs too weak to support his own weight. They set him gently on the ground, and Hasani cradled his head in his lap. He could hear Silvana, crying somewhere he couldn't see. Ajax could see his mangled arm perfectly in some perverse clarity he was sure only the nearly dead experience. There was still blood bubbling out of the wounds. He saw four deep puncture marks, where it looked like the fangs of some great beast had bitten down on the arm. But the pain was gone. Some part of his mind knew he should be in agony, but he felt nothing more painful than an odd pinching sensation in his arm.

"Silvana, I'm alright," Ajax said, his throat hoarse from screaming. He turned his arm this way and that, examining it. "The bleeding has already stopped."

The bleeding had indeed stopped, and the skin began to carefully seal itself together again. Ajax heard Hasani utter a low curse, but he could only manage a tired snort. Within seconds, the wounds were completely healed, with only four bright pink scars to show where they had been. Ajax turned his arm over, amazed, and saw four identical scars where the fangs had bitten clear through the arm. Ajax peered up at Hasani, who sat open mouthed, with blood smeared on his shirt and jawline.

"Ajax, how did you …"

"There's power in love. One last gift from Nevina, it would seem." Ajax sighed. "Now, come on, help me up. We need to keep moving."

Hasani helped him to his feet. A wave of dizziness nearly knocked Ajax back to the ground, but Hasani caught him, letting him lean against his shoulder for support while Silvana cried and examined the fresh scars.

"Do they hurt?" She traced a finger carefully over one round mark, sniffing quietly.

"They're only a little tender. Nothing to worry about." Ajax gave her shoulder a quick pat with his good hand, which she seemed grateful for, then pointed west. "We're headed that way. I need you to lead the way, until I can keep my feet under me. Hasani will help me, and we'll keep an eye out for danger. You just keep us moving."

Silvana nodded sharply, wiping her eyes with shaking fingers, then turned and started in the direction Ajax had indicated.

"You knew the wounds would heal, didn't you?" Hasani asked quietly, so Silvana wouldn't hear.

"No, actually, I didn't. But I'm not too surprised that they did. Nevina knew I would survive. She knew I would be there to help your son."

"You know much more than you've told us, Ajax."

"Maybe." He shook his head, the movement making him a little nauseous. "I'm not sure. I need time to think everything over, once we get safely away from Etritia."

"Why not cross the river? Hide in the woods on the Vyrisian side?"

Ajax had already considered the idea and ultimately discarded it. "The Knife is still iced over, but spring is coming. I'm not sure it would hold our weight any longer. Better to stay on this side and cross at the King's Bridge."

"We won't get there before light."

"I know."

"Do you have a plan?"

"I think so, but we need to keep moving."

They continued on as quickly as possible. Ajax regained his strength after a few moments, and once again took the lead. They found the Knife soon enough, and Ajax pressed one foot onto the dark ice. There was a soft crack, and Ajax jumped back. The ice held, but just barely. They moved on, keeping the Knife to their left. They left the woods, and kept to the embankments on the side of the roads, headed south.

Ajax could see the bend in the road that would eventually lead them to their first stop. Silvana was at his side, Hasani behind them. The egg bounced gently against his hip with each step as if it was hurrying him on. "We can't make it to the King's Bridge tonight. We'll have to stop, and cont—" Ajax stopped, his hand going to his throat. His lungs were suddenly burning and he fell to the ground, sharp rocks digging into his knees and his bags falling from his shoulders.

"Ajax!" Silvana and Hasani rushed to him, each putting a hand on one of his shoulders.

He reached for Hasani, clinging to his arm, trying desperately to take a breath. His mouth was open, his throat clear, but no breath would come.

"Hasani, he's turning blue! What do we do?"

"I don't know, I'm not sure what's happening." Hasani bent closer, his dark eyes the only thing Ajax could see clearly. "Ajax, are you choking?"

Ajax shook his head. He knew what was happening, he just had to hope it ended before it killed him.

He could hear Silvana's frantic voice, but he couldn't understand her words anymore. His ears were ringing, and his vision had narrowed to little more than red spots through which he could make out Hasani's blurred figure. His heart beat frantically in his chest, and the burning in his lungs seemed to be the only thing keeping him conscious.

Finally, whatever had been holding Ajax disappeared, and he fell to his hands, coughing and breathing in deep mouthfuls of chilly air. Hasani and Silvana both sighed, and Silvana knelt beside him while he crouched in the dirt, sucking in the blissfully cool air.

"What happened, Ajax?" Hasani asked quietly, eyes darting around them, searching for danger.

"It was Nevina," Ajax coughed out. "She's dead."

"H-how do you know?" Silvana asked.

"I'm not sure. I just know it." Ajax stood, letting Hasani help him to his feet. "And that was how she died. In agony, choking to death."

"Ajax ..." Hasani put a hesitant arm around Ajax's shoulders. "I'm sorry."

Ajax shook his head, shrugging Hasani's arm away. Nevina knew it might happen. He could mourn her later. "We have to keep moving. Mothlenor knows the egg is missing. He'll be after us now."

They hurried along, Hasani helping Silvana as Ajax guided them. They followed the bend in the road, coming to the first of the farmhouses. Ajax avoided each one, not sure which were still inhabited. The fields were empty, and Ajax could neither hear nor see any sign of animals, though their scent was still in the air. *Have they all gone, then? Have Mothlenor and Ferrand driven them all away?*

Ajax knelt in the tall weeds that grew along the road and pointed out one of the many dark houses. "There," he whispered. "That one is empty, I'm sure of it. We'll hide out in there until nightfall, if we can, then make our way to the King's Bridge tomorrow night."

Hasani opened his mouth in answer, but an unearthly scream echoed around them, drowning out his words.

The scream was high pitched and hollow, and Ajax felt his skin prick out in gooseflesh. The sound of it seemed to bore into his mind, paralyzing him, and Ajax clamped both hands down over his ears with a groan. Silvana and Hasani did the same, eyes wide and searching. It did nothing to drown out the horrible screech.

As suddenly as it came, the sound was gone. In an instant, the world was silent. Even the crickets ceased their chirping.

"What the hell was that?" Hasani whispered to Ajax. His voice was loud in the stillness.

"Demons. Mothlenor has sent them. They've found our trail." He pulled Silvana behind him and carefully crept his way closer to the road, Hasani just beside him. From the edge of the road, lying flat on their bellies, Ajax and Hasani peered out across the flatlands outside the castle walls.

Four long shadows swept their way down towards them. They were dark things, no amount of moonlight piercing through their shadowy veil. They moved swiftly, racing across the ground without ever seeming to take a step.

"Should we run for it?" Hasani asked quietly.

"We won't make it. And if we did, I don't think walls will stop them."

"What should we do?"

"I don't know." Ajax's mind raced, thinking of a way to get them all safely into the farmhouse without being noticed. There was so much he knew about demons—they were made from the soul of someone who had been murdered, they were incredibly fast and difficult to control, and they—

How do I know all this?

How do you stop a demon? Or four?

There was no way. And the demons were coming their way.

"You said Nevina saw you with my son. Did she see me?" Hasani's voice was quiet in his ear.

Ajax hesitated, afraid to answer.

"She didn't, did she? She knew something would happen to me. That's why she made me give the book to Silvana. For her to give to my son, not me."

"Hasani ..."

The demons pressed closer.

"Perhaps this is where I part from your company, Ajax."

Ajax turned to look as his lifelong friend, whose midnight-blue eyes stared at him with a kind of sad resignation. He nodded, unable to speak around the lump in his throat, then turned back to watch the demons rush across the plains towards them.

Ajax heard rustling in the grass behind him as Hasani

retreated. He heard the unmistakable sound of a kiss, followed by Hasani's low voice. Ajax quietly backtracked to where Hasani was holding Silvana, who was weeping.

"We can run from them … don't do this, Hasani!"

"We wouldn't make it. It's the only way I can protect you."

"Hasani." Ajax kept his voice low. "They're nearly here."

"Right." Hasani nodded, prying Silvana from him. "I'll find you both again, if I'm able."

And with a final quick kiss on Silvana's cheek, Hasani was up and running for the Knife. The movement instantly caught the attention of the demons, who altered course to follow him. Silvana tried to stand to follow him, but Ajax held her down, pinning her against his chest and covering her mouth with one firm hand to quiet her cries. Ajax watched, numb, as his brother ran for the icy waters of the Knife.

Hasani's legs were long, and Ajax remembered with sad relief that he had always been the faster of the two of them. He fled into the dark, the moonlight giving just enough light for Ajax to see him cross the frozen river in half a dozen strides. The ice cracked, the snapping sound echoing in the air around them, but it held long enough for him to reach the other side. The demons crossed only a moment behind him, unhindered by the cracked and broken surface of the Knife. Ajax kept watching, breath held, until Hasani disappeared into the strange Vyrisian woods on the other side.

Silvana's cries grew louder, and Ajax pulled her against him. He wrapped his arms around her shoulders, and let her beat his chest. "You killed him. He's dead because of you!"

"Silvana, I'm sorry." The lump in his throat grew larger and his chest constricted.

She beat him harder. "Those things will kill him. You should have told him to stay. We could have kept moving, we could have outrun them."

"Silvana, look at me." She did, her eyes already red and

swollen, tears streaming down her face. "We would not have been able to outrun them. They would have overtaken us in an instant, and we would all be dead right now. He sacrificed himself so that you and your son will live." Silvana dropped her gaze, turning away from him. His chest constricted further until he thought his heart might stop. "Come on, we have to keep moving. We need to get to the farmhouse. We should be safe there." He stood, taking her by the hand.

Ajax pulled Silvana along behind him, avoiding the houses around them. Lights were beginning to brighten the windows of a few, where the inhabitants were likely watching quietly through half-shuttered windows to track the source of the eerie howl the demons had made. Silvana hardly made a sound, though Ajax occasionally caught glimpses of her as she wiped tears from her eyes. Their route was circuitous, and by the time Ajax cracked open the rear door of the farmhouse and peeked within, the sky was beginning to brighten into grey. He dumped the armful of bags onto the open floor and ushered Silvana inside, shutting the door behind her.

"Nana and Martyn's house," Silvana muttered numbly as they entered. One hand traced the back of a wooden chair with one mended leg as she walked through the living area. "I'm not sure I want to be here."

"It's the only safe place I could think of. There are dozens of farms all around it. If the King's Guard come searching, we'll hear them coming."

Silvana turned to him, eyes dry but still red. "And then what?" She scowled at him. "Hasani has already given himself to save us. Or would you let me sacrifice myself, so you could flee?"

"Silvana …" Ajax reached for her, but she slapped his hand away.

"Hasani is dead, Ajax." Her hands went protectively to her

stomach, and her glare darkened. "My son won't know his father, and you are to blame for it."

Ajax wanted to answer, but he couldn't find the words to argue with her. She was right. He should have thought of something different, something that might have saved them all. But he hadn't, and now Hasani was likely dead.

There was a quiet moment, while Silvana continued to glare at him, and Ajax could only shrink away in regret. Finally, he turned away, setting the bandaged chair against the far wall. "I'll keep watch while you sleep. Try to rest."

Ajax didn't hear her go, but after a moment the heat of her eyes on him had dissipated, and Ajax looked up to see that she was gone.

He settled himself further into the chair, pulling the small stone he had stolen from Mothlenor's desk out of one pocket. *I saw Hasani in it once before ...* Ajax thought of Hasani, hoping he might still be alive in the Vyrisian woods somewhere. But the stone remained dark.

There was a soft sound, and Ajax looked up, body tensing. Through the closed door at the far end of the hall came Silvana's quiet cries. Ajax relaxed some, though it hurt him to hear her.

Silvana is right. Hasani's death is my fault.

Ajax turned back to the small stone in his grip, trying in ignore the sound of Silvana's grief. In the smooth surface of the stone, a small image of his sister glimmered. Ajax stared, wondering how he had conjured it. *It showed me nothing when I thought of Hasani. Is he too far away now?* Ajax swallowed hard, staring at the stone. *Is it because he's dead?*

The image of Silvana showed her lying in a small bed, the covers stripped away to reveal the straw beneath. She was lying on her side, curled around her large belly. One hand caressed her stomach, the other clutched a wadded cloth to her chest. *A shirt, maybe? Hasani's shirt?* Ajax glanced at the bags still sitting on the ground nearby. One of them was slightly open.

Ajax returned his attention to the orb, but it was once more blank. He thought of Hasani, wishing the thing would come alive once more and show him his brother. But the stone was stubbornly dark. After a moment, he dropped the stone back into his pocket and took to listening for hoofbeats.

But all he heard was the sound of Silvana's crying.

55

SILVANA

Silvana hardly slept, and what rest she got was fitful and restless. She wanted Hasani's warmth beside her, his gentle breath on her neck as he slept. She wanted his arms around her, protecting her. And she would never have any of those things again.

It was not entirely Ajax's fault, she could admit that much to herself. Mothlenor apparently dealt with demons, and it was his demons that had killed her husband.

But it was Ajax's quest they were on. It was Ajax that wanted to find the Matriarch, and who had refused to leave well enough alone. It was also Ajax that had insisted on stealing from the king and fleeing the castle.

It was Ajax that had let Hasani run off into the night to be chased by demons.

And for that, Silvana blamed her brother for Hasani's death.

She wasn't sure she could ever forgive him.

And she never wanted to forget Hasani's warmth, or his scent, or the way his eyes lit up when he looked at her.

She clutched one of his shirts to her chest. It was cold, but it still smelled like him. It had been one of his favorites, and she had been sure to pack it before they left.

She held it tight, thinking of him, thinking of their child, who would grow up fatherless, and wept into Hasani's favorite shirt.

She must have fallen asleep at last. A heavy hand was gently shaking her awake, softly calling to her.

"Hasani?" she mumbled sleepily.

"Get up, Silvana." Ajax's voice cut through the fog of sleep.

She had been dreaming of Hasani, but it was already fading.

"Go away, Ajax."

"The King's Guard is outside. They're searching the farms. You need to hide."

Silvana sat up, fear coursing through her and cutting away at the last dregs of sleep. "How long do we have?"

"Not long." Ajax pulled her to her feet. "Come on, you can hide in the larder."

Silvana resisted, pulling her hand from his. "No, I wouldn't fit." She was remembering Nana. She wobbled over to the wardrobe, which had been left behind when Nana and Martyn had left. "In here." She opened the doors, half expecting it to still be full of clothing and finding it empty. "This is where I hid last time."

Ajax helped her inside and shut the door. It was smaller than she remembered, but her belly had probably grown since she had hidden before. She heard Ajax hurry to the far side of the room, then a set of heavy footfalls and a loud voice came from the front of the house.

Silvana found herself reliving her visit to Martyn.

Ferrand is here. He's here for Nana. But Nana is gone. He'll only find me. He'll find me, and then—

The footsteps drew nearer, and Silvana covered her mouth with one trembling hand.

"Ajax?" a familiar voice called softly. "You in here? It's just me. You can come outta your hidey-hole."

"Dars," Silvana breathed, bursting from the wardrobe and rushing towards him.

Dars seemed both surprised and relieved, and caught Silvana's embrace. "Silvana." He brushed his thin lips across the top of her head and pulled her close. "I'm glad you're safe. Where's Ajax?"

"Right here."

Dars turned, Silvana still in his arms, as Ajax stepped out from behind the door to the bedroom, sword in hand. He held it up, pointed at Dars.

Dars scoffed. "Put that thing away. You don't need it just yet."

Ajax's arm dropped a fraction, but he didn't put the sword away.

"Ajax!" Silvana hissed. "What are you doing?"

Dars patted her head gently. "No, he's alright. Just being smart."

"Is there anyone else with you?"

Dars pointed off to the back of the house with his chin. "Just one of Ferrand's newest boys. Don't know his sword from his asshole. I sent him to search the next house and told him I'd check this one. I thought I'd find you here." Dars looked around them as Ajax dropped his sword back into its scabbard. "Where's Hasani? He left with you, didn't he?"

Silvana pulled away from Dars, wrapping her arms around herself. She suddenly felt very cold. "Hasani is dead."

"Dead?" Dars looked between them, open mouthed. "How?"

"The demons. He led them off, so we could get away." Ajax's voice was quiet as if he was ashamed to admit that Hasani was gone.

As he should be.

"Silvana …" Dars reached for her again, but she shook her

head, turning away from him. "I'm sorry," Dars finished softly behind her.

There was a quiet moment, during which Silvana silently retrieved Hasani's shirt and folded it carefully, holding it against her chest. She couldn't look at either man.

"Did you get the egg before you left?"

"Yes, it's just in the other room—"

"Hasani had it," Silvana said. She lifted the shirt to her nose, inhaling softly. The scent of him would eventually fade, but it was still strong enough to soothe her some.

"What?" There was a hint of disbelief in Ajax's words.

Silvana turned, finding both men staring at her. She wanted to laugh, and a small chortle escaped her lips at the sight of Ajax's wide eyes. "You didn't realize? When you fell, choking, your bags fell to the ground. Hasani picked them up. He had the egg when he ran into the Vyrisian woods."

"I-I thought he put it inside my bag, I thought I still had it." Ajax hurried from the room, his footsteps clomping towards the living area.

Dars followed behind him, whispering loudly after him, "Be quiet, you damned fool! That boy out there might be stupid, but he ain't deaf."

There was the sound of rustling, followed by a low curse from Ajax. Silvana drifted through the house to the front room, where Ajax had fallen into the damaged chair, his head cradled in his hands. "I thought I still had it," he groaned.

"Was it for nothing, then?" Silvana asked. Dars and Ajax both looked up at her. "Did Hasani die for nothing?" She stepped closer, stopping herself only a few feet from her brother. She wanted to hit him, but she restrained herself.

Ajax looked her over, one hand running over the stubble on his chin. He didn't answer, and he didn't meet her eyes.

Dars found her eyes, though, and he seemed to plead with her. "Maybe he hid it. Maybe the demons won't find it, and it'll be lost in those woods forever."

"Maybe this was all a mistake," Silvana said quietly. She glanced at her brother, his head hanging low again. "Dars, will you take me back to the castle?"

Silvana watched her brother for a reaction, waited for him to protest. But he said nothing.

"I can't do that, Silvana."

Silvana's gaze shot back to Dars, eyes narrowing. "Why not?"

"Mothlenor has ordered your execution." He spoke slowly, weighing his words. "If any of you are found, Ferrand has ordered for you to be killed on sight, and your body taken back to be displayed in the square."

Silvana laughed, but it was hollow and cold. "Ferrand wouldn't kill me. I'm going to have a baby."

"He's done worse," Ajax said, lifting his head long enough to make his voice heard. "And he would do worse to you, just because you're my sister."

Loud footsteps beat against the dirt outside, followed by a hard knock on the back door. They all jumped at the noise, and Silvana and Ajax drew back. A young voice called from the other side of the door. "Dars, are you still in there?"

Dars lifted a finger to his lips, and Silvana glanced nervously at the shuttered windows. "I'm fine, I just need another minute."

The man outside hesitated for a moment. "I checked the next house. It seems empty."

"Then go check again," Dars growled through gritted teeth. "I'll be just behind you."

The young man huffed, but walked away, muttering to himself. Silvana sighed, and carefully stepped further away from the windows, pressing Hasani's shirt closer to her chest.

"Stay with Ajax, Silvana. He can keep you safe."

"Like he kept Hasani safe?" Silvana snapped. Across the

room, Ajax's shoulders slumped, but he held his head up, staring ahead at nothing.

Dars already had one hand on the door, ready to leave them, but he hardened his voice. "Hasani chose to protect you. It was his decision, and you cannot fault Ajax for that." His tone softened, and he shrugged. "Anyway, those damned demons haven't returned yet, it seems. He might still be out there, keeping them running after him."

Silvana wanted to say more, but she bit the words back, thinking Dars's words over. *Hasani might still be alive …*

"Stay with Ajax," Dars repeated. Turning to Ajax, he offered out a hand. Ajax stood, taking the offered arm and pulling Dars into an embrace. "If you find the old Missus Dars," Dars began, voice thick, "will you tell her why I've stayed?" He released Ajax, holding both of his shoulders, looking him over. "And tell the boy, too. I'm not sure he'll understand yet, but he will in time."

Ajax nodded. "I will. And thank you, Dars."

Dars sniffed once, his hand returning to the door. "Be ready for Ferrand, Ajax. I'm sure he'll be waiting for you at the King's Bridge. I hope you've got enough in you to kill him." He smirked at Ajax, though it was a worn and sad look. "It'd do us all here a good deal of good."

Ajax nodded again. "I'll try."

Dars dipped his head once, sniffing softly, and opened the door just wide enough for him to squeeze through.

And then he was gone.

AJAX

Night fell, and Ajax led Silvana through the remaining farmland to the King's Bridge in the quiet darkness around them. The moon was bright, lighting their path nicely, but still giving them enough shadow to conceal themselves. They never spoke to each other. Ajax knew that Silvana still blamed him for Hasani's death, and he was willing to accept the blame.

They followed the roads, sticking to the ditches to hide themselves. When the road ran out, they followed the river, walking in a stiff crouch through the tall weeds. Silvana seemed to struggle some, carrying the weight of her child, but she said nothing, brushing Ajax's hands away when he offered help. Ajax made no protest, burying the hurt her anger caused.

At last, Ajax spotted a handful of lights in the distance, and the light wind carried the sound and scent of horses to their hiding spot among the reeds.

"It's the King's Bridge," Ajax said. "From here, the Free Cities are another week's ride."

"How long will it take on foot?"

Ajax considered for a moment, watching the motion of

the lights on the bridge. "Judging by the lanterns, there are five, maybe six of them. I'll run up, dispatch a few of them, take one of the horses and lead the others off." He turned to look at Silvana, her face red and puffy in the moonlight. "Then, when we're all gone, you can take another horse and ride for the Free Cities. Larten is directly south of here. Just keep the river on your left, and don't stop for more than a few hours at a time." He pulled her bag from his shoulders, dropping it at her feet. "There should be more than enough food for you to make the trip in there." He caught Silvana's hand in one of his own, surprised by the chill in it. "When I'm done with my part, I'll use Hasani's maps to find the Coven. I'll warn them, help them if I can." Ajax spoke quickly, his words almost tumbling over one another. "When this is all over, I'll find you in the Free Cities, I promise."

"I'd rather you didn't." Silvana's steely eyes and cold words cut him. She wriggled her hand from his grasp, wrapping her arms around herself protectively. "Now go. Save the Coven, if you feel you must." She wiped a tear from her cheek. "Once you ride off, you are dead to me, Ajax."

Ajax opened his mouth to protest, but couldn't find the words. *I should have gone in Hasani's place. You could have found some comfort in him.* He nodded, pulling his outstretched hands away from her. "If you can, find yourself a weapon. The world can be a dangerous place."

Silvana said nothing, offered him no final embrace or a word of comfort. And Ajax was content to let their affection end that way. *I deserve it, after letting Hasani die.*

He doubled back through the reedy growth around the Knife, tightening his bag down against his back as he went. When he felt he had put enough distance between himself and Silvana, he left the riverside, angling his course so that he would come out and back around to the King's Bridge on a curved path. He wanted to see the men waiting for him before they saw him. And he wanted to protect Silvana from being discovered if he were to fall, or if one of the King's Guard left the fight to hunt for her.

The horses sensed him before anyone saw him. He could see them fidget, tossing tails and stamping feet. He had spent many hours in the stables when he had been commander, and most of the horses there knew him well. Ajax's lips stretched into a thin smile. Perhaps they recognized his scent.

He stepped carefully into the glowing light of the nearest lantern, drawing his sword as he approached. The quiet words passing between the knights stopped, and they turned to face him. There were five of them, each with a lantern tied to their saddle, just behind their horse's shoulders. A sixth lantern hung from a pole at the foot of the bridge, and between them, there was light enough to see them all, and for them to see him.

"Ah, Ajax." Ferrand's voice rang out across the distance between them. "I thought you might make your way here. Fleeing into Vyris, perhaps? After your brother?"

Ajax said nothing, watching as the other four knights brought their horses around to circle him. He didn't recognize the other men, but they seemed fairly young. *New recruits, perhaps eager for blood.*

Ferrand smirked down at him, the effect eerie in the lantern light. "Return what you have stolen, and you will be taken to the king alive, for his judgment to be passed down on you. Refuse ..." Ferrand's smile deepened, and he nodded at the men around him, "I'll kill you here, and take the egg from you anyway."

"The egg is gone, Ferrand," Ajax answered. Around him, the men were dismounting their horses, waiting for Ferrand's command. Ferrand himself stayed in the saddle, apparently content to watch. Ajax returned Ferrand's smirk, though his eyes were on the men around him. "I seem to have misplaced it."

"Good." Ferrand's voice had taken on that dangerous silken tone, and the sound of it turned Ajax's stomach. "I had hoped it would come to this." To the younger knights, he added, "Wound him, cut him, just make sure he's alive." Ferrand's teeth were bright in the surrounding light. "I want to be the one to finally kill him."

The men surrounded him, and Ajax turned to keep them in sight. One man slipped just out of his line of sight, then charged in for an attack. The move was foolish. Ajax heard the man's footsteps and turned out of the path of his poor downswing effortlessly. The man was hunched over, apparently struggling with the weight of the sword he held. Ajax stepped in, bringing the point of his sword to the back of the man's bare neck and thrusting the blade through, both hands on the pommel. There was a gargling scream, and hot blood splashed the ground. Ajax pulled his sword free, bracing one foot against the dead man's back. He sidestepped around the blood pooling in the grass and eyed the other three. *A horse for Silvana.*

The others hesitated for only a moment, then all three began their separate charges. On the left, Ajax parried another downstroke, turning the blade away and pulling the man off balance. On his right, a heavy-handed attack aimed for his shoulder, which Ajax caught on his blade. Ajax stepped away, and his attacker followed. The man brought his sword up for another attack, exposing his side. Ajax stepped into it, the point of his sword piercing first the man's leather armor, and eventually his lung. Ajax pulled his sword free of the man's ribs, shoving him aside, to meet another attack from the third fighter. *A horse for me.*

The two remaining men circled around him, eying him carefully. Suddenly, one charged in, and Ajax's blade met his once again. They struggled, until the man he was grappling with looked over Ajax's shoulder, his eyes widening. Ajax instinctively ducked and rolled away, a terrified scream cutting the air behind him. He looked over his shoulder to see the last of the four men pulling his sword out of the other man's neck, knowing the blade had been meant for his own. *A horse for Hasani, should he make it back.*

Ajax took his chance to spring up and dash to the closest horse, leaping into the saddle and urging the beast forward with a shout, leading him away from the King's Bridge. He heard Ferrand calling out, and turned to make sure they were following. Ferrand was already galloping behind him, and the last remaining fighter was climbing into the saddle not too far behind. Ajax turned, cutting back towards the farmland south of the castle, leading them far from Silvana.

He remembered her last words, guilt cutting through the excitement of battle. He urged the horse on faster. *Just be careful, Silvana.*

SILVANA

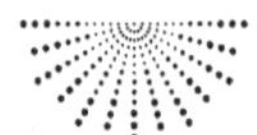

Silvana kept her back to Ajax as he left her in the reeds by the Knife. The night air was frigid, and her fingertips were numb. She wanted to be home, in bed, with Hasani next to her.

Instead, she was stuck out in the cold, unable to return to the warm life in Etritia that she had known for so many years. And she hated Ajax for every moment of it.

She was beginning to wonder if perhaps he had lied to her, if he had decided to flee on his own, when she saw him emerge from the shadows just beyond the circle of light cast by the Knights and their lanterns. He seemed small then, unarmored and frail against the men he stood before. Silvana felt a moment of regret at thinking ill of her brother, but she brushed the feeling aside, steeping herself in the pain of Hasani's death.

Ajax was the reason Hasani wasn't there beside her. And she could never forgive him for that.

Four of the five men left their horses and began circling around Ajax. One lunged at him prematurely, and Ajax cut him down with ease. Silvana's stomach churned at the sight, grateful there was enough distance between her and the fighting that she could not easily see any blood.

It was Hasani's decision, even Dars said as much, part of Silvana reasoned.

"No," Silvana whispered, her breath steaming the air. "It was Ajax that stole the egg. It was Ajax that led us from the castle. We were his responsibility. He is to blame."

Why? Because he loved a woman, and she gave him the knowledge he needed to try to stop Mothlenor from destroying her people?

Silvana considered for a moment. She brought her hands to her mouth, breathing on them to keep the frost from biting at them.

Hasani would have died anyway. Mothlenor said he wanted Hasani to help Ferrand find the Coven, but it was a lie. Ferrand would have cut him down as soon as they were out of sight of the castle walls, her inner voice continued to argue. *Just as Areanath was killed.*

Ajax was being assaulted from all sides now. Silvana could hardly see what was happening, but she could hear the shouts and the clanging of metal on metal. She watched as Ajax sank his sword deep into one man's ribs, then lost sight of him for a moment. She shifted her position, searching for him. He was locked together with one of the men, struggling for the upper hand. Silvana held her breath in apprehension, hoping he could strike the man down. Suddenly, another man rushed at him from behind. She wanted to shout a warning, but her throat caught. She watched as the man charged in, his sword raised; her heart was beating wildly. But Ajax ducked and rolled away, unscathed. She flinched in horror as the man's sword lodged itself deep into the shoulder of his comrade. *At least it wasn't Ajax.*

"Besides, Hasani might still be alive." And Silvana desperately wanted to believe it. She wanted to hope that her husband would still meet her in the Free Cities. Dars had said that Mothlenor's demons had not returned; perhaps that was a good sign.

Ajax was running, heading for one of the horses. He leapt into the saddle and dashed off, riding towards the farmlands. The man still on horseback rode after him, shouting to the surviving fighter to follow. The last man sheathed his sword, jumped back into his horse's saddle, and joined the pursuit.

Silvana waited a moment, making sure no one else was around, before picking up her bag and ambling towards the bridge. She gave the three dead men a wide berth, trying to keep from looking down at their bodies. There were puddles of wet earth, and when one of the horses shifted nervously, the light that crossed over the damp ground showed the grass stained red. She took a few deep breaths, trying to ignore the metallic stink of blood in the air, and continued. The smell reminded her of Ajax's sacrifice in the darkness of the tunnels beneath the castles.

She neared one of the two riderless horses, taking it gently by the reins. "There, there. It'll be alright." The horse only snorted in reply.

She tied her bag to the back of the saddle, something she had seen her brother do a number of times. She tried to mount the horse, but couldn't lift herself up into the saddle. After a few tries, the horse stomped it hooves impatiently.

"Well you try getting a big swollen belly like mine off the ground—it's pretty damn difficult." She had never been any good at mounting a horse before her pregnancy, anyway, and had always needed some kind of ladder. With a snort, the horse folded first his back legs, then each foreleg, until he was sitting on the ground at a perfect height for Silvana to ease herself down into the saddle. "Well, aren't you a smart one, then?" Silvana said, rubbing a hand over the horse's neck. She settled herself as best as she could into the saddle and waited. Slowly, carefully, the horse got back onto all four hooves, and Silvana clung to the reins as she was jostled around.

Once she and her new horse were moving, the ride was easy, almost pleasant. She thought of Hasani, hoping he was still alive somewhere in those woods. *He'll come for me, I know it*, Silvana thought. *And Ajax? Will he come for me, too?*

She rode quietly for several days, each day warmer than the one before it. The landscape around her changed and she continued south. First, the farmland off to her right disappeared, replaced by grassy plains. Then, slowly, the woods to her left faded away, replaced by plains stretching out to a distant mountain range. She thought she could see a large lake in the distance, but she couldn't be sure. After the third day, the air grew hot and dry, and the grass her horse walked through became shorter and sparser. The rich ground turned to hard-packed, dry earth, and then to sand. On the other side of the river, which seemed to be the only source of water for miles, the land looked much as it did on her side. She often stopped her horse for a moment, standing in the saddle and craning her neck to see all around her. To her left, the land of the elves, the sands stretched for a while, but she could see green, and perhaps some trees, then massive mountains far off in the distance. Directly in front of her, sands for miles, but a heat haze obscured her view. Eventually, it would have to end. The Free Cities lay along the southern coast. The land was sure to be fresh and fertile there. But to her right, nothing but sands and stubby cacti.

The Desert. Where the Great War was, all those years ago. So many people had died in those sands—men, elves, dwarves, even dragons. Their dried bones were probably still lying in the sands. Silvana shuddered at the thought. She was just passing through the outskirts, and would be through in no time. Still, she urged her horse on faster, just to get through the hot sands faster.

At night, she camped along the river. She didn't know

how to make a fire, but she didn't need one. It was warm, as winter seemed to be long gone this far south, and a thick bedroll was all she needed at night. At first, she had worried about creatures coming out of the woods, but after the first night spent wide awake, gripping a small knife she had found strapped behind the saddle, her fears subsided. She supped on salted beef, a loaf of bread, and a wheel of cheese. The bread lasted for the first three nights, the cheese was gone by the fourth, but there was more than enough salted beef. The water, thankfully, she could get from the river. She could even bathe, in a way, and was content to ride in her underdress and cool her burning skin in the waters of the Knife.

By the afternoon of the sixth day, green plants had begun to reappear, and she let her horse munch on each one for a moment before urging him on. The horse got water enough, but he hadn't eaten anything more than the occasional apple in two days, and Silvana wasn't sure how much longer he could last. Silvana grimaced in discomfort as the baby kicked inside her. He had been so quiet all morning, she was glad for the reassurance that he was still alright in there. She rubbed her belly, smiling.

She still had to pick a name for him. Hasani had wanted to wait until he was born, and let inspiration find them. But Silvana had secretly been considering some good ones over the last few weeks.

He kicked again, harder, and Silvana winced at the pain.

"Shhh, shh, it's alright. No more fussing in there, now." She rubbed her belly again, hoping the sound of her voice would soothe him. But her smile melted as she felt a sudden gush of fluid from between her thighs. "No, no no no." She slid a hand awkwardly up her skirt, feeling her underclothes. They were soaked through. The horse neighed irritably under her, sensing her distress. "I'm sorry, darling," Silvana said to the beast, rubbing a shaking hand down his warm neck. Silvana's mind was racing. How much further was it to Larten? How long would the baby wait for her?

"We're going to have to run for it." She took the reins firmly in hand and kicked the horse hard in the ribs, sending the beast into a full gallop. She just had to hope that there was a midwife in Larten. She bent low in the saddle, as low as her belly would allow, and put all thoughts of Hasani and Ajax out of her mind, focusing only on making it to the Free Cities before the baby came.

5 8

AJAX

Ajax led Ferrand and his last man to the far eastern edge of the open farmland south of the castle. It did not take long, surprisingly, though the farmlands were fairly large and the ground sloping. The empty fields made the ride faster, as Ajax was able to lead his horse through lands that should otherwise have been full of growing crops or tilled earth. Ajax considered leading them into the Felgar woods, which loomed in front of him, and perhaps losing them or killing them among the trees. But it would be dangerous, and he was just as likely to get thrown from his own horse. *Better to finish this on open ground.*

Ajax turned his stolen horse, leaping from the saddle to the ground. He carefully removed the lantern still hanging just behind the horse's shoulder and set it on the ground beside him. It was still lit, the small flame protected by a glass cage. He removed his bag from his shoulder, dropping it on the ground beside the lantern, and smacked the horse firmly on the rear to send her away. He waited in the dark, the tree line just behind him, as Ferrand and the fourth knight brought their horses to a skidding halt. They jumped from their saddles, drawing short swords as they came within fighting range.

"I'm surprised at you, Ajax," Ferrand said. "Fleeing a fight? I thought you were noble, prepared to stand until you were cut down." Ferrand drew a second sword from his hip, this one short and curved. "I suppose I was wrong about you." He smirked, eyes bright. "But you're here now, and this will be the last time I have to deal with you."

The fourth knight's footsteps quickened until he was within striking distance. Ajax met him, and they struggled. The knight was slower than Ajax, but he was also heavier. And better suited to the sword than the other three knights had been. Ajax deflected a blow, his whole arm vibrating with the force behind it, and sent the tip of his sword into the meat of the knight's stomach. The stab was shallow, but the knight grunted in pain, redoubling his offense. From the corner of his eye, Ajax could see Ferrand watching, annoyed, a sword in each hand.

The knight brought his sword down, and Ajax caught it across the flat of his blade. But the knight was larger and stronger, and he pushed against Ajax's blade until Ajax's leg gave out. He fell to one knee, still holding off the knight, fighting to keep the blade from him. But it inched closer, Ajax's arms burning with the effort.

The knight didn't notice Ferrand stepping closer, his scowl deepening. But Ajax caught glimpses of him over the knight's shoulder as they struggled. *Ferrand will kill me, while this one has me pinned in place. This will be the end.*

Ferrand lifted the curved blade, and Ajax shut his eyes, preparing for the blow. A hot spray hit Ajax's face, and the knight collapsed against him. Ajax struggled, opening his eyes to see the heavy knight clasping both hands against his own throat, trying to stem the blood that flowed from a deep cut beneath his chin. Ajax wanted to scream, but he managed to get one foot between himself and the knight, and he kicked the dying man off him and dragged himself further away, unable to take his eyes off the knight.

"I told you I wanted to be the one to kill Ajax," Ferrand said. He was watching the knight as he flailed, still scowling darkly. "You should always listen to your commander."

Ajax's stomach turned as the knight's struggles grew weak. Ajax had killed men before, of course. But never one of his own, and never when the man could not defend himself.

The knight stopped moving quickly enough, and Ajax could finally look away. Ferrand stood close by, his short sword and the curved blade still unsheathed.

Ferrand smiled, retreating a few steps and motioning for Ajax to stand. "Get up. I can wait."

Ajax found his knees, searching the ground around him for his sword. It was still where he had dropped it when grappling with the knight, and he picked it up, pointing it weakly at Ferrand as he pulled himself to his feet.

Ferrand wasn't even looking at him; he was inspecting the small curved sword he held. "I've never had the chance to use this one in combat, and I have to admit that I'm rather pleased with it." He held it up for Ajax to see, stepping closer as he did. Ajax followed him with the tip of his own blade, his knees and arms still weak. "Do you like it? I found it in a market some time ago." He paused, his teeth glinting. "The same market, incidentally, where I found that Dragon's Eye you took. That was a gift. From me to Mothlenor, before he became king of Etritia." His eyes narrowed, and his smirk turned into a snarl. "And I don't appreciate my gifts being stolen."

"Who the hell are you?"

Ferrand shrugged. "I am the man that will kill you. I think that's enough." Ferrand set his feet, bringing both swords up. "Are you ready, then?"

In answer, Ajax lurched a few steps forward, taking a stance and bringing his own sword up.

Ferrand's teeth glinted once more in a smirk, and then he was moving. He rushed Ajax, attacking first with the curved blade. Ajax blocked the move, but barely turned a stab to the ribs with Ferrand's short sword. The blow glanced off his leather vest, and the bite of it made Ajax grunt. There was no time to counter, as Ferrand was already bringing in another swing of the curved blade. Ajax blocked again, falling back a step.

He's too fast. Faster than I am.

Ajax blocked and countered over and over. Every time he thought he had an opening for an attack, Ferrand pushed his own, forcing Ajax to defend again. Ajax was pushed closer to the tree line at his back, step by step, until he could almost feel the pine needles against his neck.

Ferrand lunged with the short sword, and Ajax side-stepped to avoid it. As he moved, pain lanced through one leg, and he fell to one knee. Blood was seeping through a cut along his right thigh, where Ferrand had somehow caught him with the curved blade. *I'm done. This is the end.*

Above him, Ferrand brought the short sword up, aiming the blow for Ajax's neck. The sword fell, and Ajax brought his own up to catch it. Once again, Ajax found himself struggling against the weight of a larger man, and he wondered how much a sword to the neck would hurt.

Except that Ferrand was not putting much weight behind the short sword. No more than it took to hold Ajax in place, and certainly not enough to subdue him. Ferrand's weight shifted slightly, and Ajax realized his mistake too late.

Pain erupted from his middle as the curved blade found his unprotected stomach and cut through it. Ajax screamed, falling to his back in the grass. His hands went to his stomach, sword forgotten, and pressed against the cut. It was long and deep, and Ajax could feel organs pressing their way through the split flesh.

Above him, Ferrand dropped both of his swords to the

ground and stood over Ajax. Ajax could make out the glint of Ferrand's smirk through his greying vision.

"Look at the great commander now," Ferrand sneered.

Ajax groaned, pressing his hands as tightly as he could against his stomach. Hot blood washed over his hands, and he sucked in a gasping breath through clenched teeth.

"Reduced to nothing more than a sack of meat, bleeding like a stuck pig." Ferrand leaned closer, bracing his hands against his knees. His face swam in Ajax's vision, clearing long enough for him to see the grin stretching his face grotesquely. "Who will follow you now?"

"Fuck … you … Ferrand," Ajax managed through panting breaths. "You're a monster."

Ferrand's smile faded, and he reached one hand out to poke at the bowels visible through Ajax's wound, driving his finger deep into the cut. Ajax screamed, pushing Ferrand's hand away, one long finger red to the last knuckle. "I had hoped that would have killed you a little more quickly, but you're a stubborn one even while dying." Ferrand went to his knees, wrapping both hands around Ajax's neck. "I'll have to settle for killing you with my own hands, and I can live with that."

The pain of his stomach was worse than the choking hands around his neck, but part of Ajax was sure it would be Ferrand's hold on him that would kill him first. He struggled, his hands slick with blood, but was unable to pry Ferrand's hands away. His vision continued to darken, but he could see the glint of teeth as Ferrand smirked down at him.

Ajax groped wildly in the grass around him, his numb fingers searching for anything that might save him. His fingers wrapped around a twig, but it snapped almost as soon as he touched it. His other hand brushed against the soft canvas of his bag, and he tried to drag it closer, but something fell over onto the back of his hand as he tugged. Ajax's vision was only a few pinpricks of light, and he could feel consciousness slipping away. His fingers wrapped around the new object, grasping it as tightly as he could manage, and he brought it up and smashed it against Ferrand's face.

The tiny pinpricks of white light suddenly flared red, and Ferrand screamed. Instantly, Ferrand's hands were gone, and Ajax breathed in deeply, groaning at the agony of his stomach again. He could smell burning blood and flesh, and his right hand hurt. He brought it up to inspect, vision still blurry and grey. The hand was burned, with shards of glass stuck into the flesh. He pulled one out, numbly, and dropped it into the grass. Ferrand was still screaming, and Ajax could vaguely see him nearby. He seemed to be on fire, clutching his face and rolling in the dirt, and the smell of burning flesh grew stronger as he rolled nearer.

The lantern, Ajax thought numbly. His vision was going out again, and he could feel his heartbeat slowing. *I smashed the lantern against his face, and the oil ...*

It won't be enough to kill him, but it was all I could do, Dars.
And the world around him faded.

59

SILVANA

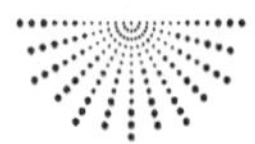

Silvana rode her stolen horse hard, only letting him slow down when she felt her labor pains. The desert sands melted away quickly enough, and to Silvana's relief, she occasionally caught the scent of saltwater on the wind. It started raining a few hours into her mad dash south, and the rain soaked her to the bone. The sky was a deep purple when she was forced to stop altogether every few minutes or so as the labor pain increased, and she continued on foot, worried that riding further would hurt the baby. By the time night had fallen completely, she could see the low walls of one of the Free Cities, and she led her horse towards the gate light as fast as she could, relieved she might make it.

The gate, once she found it, was completely open and unguarded. She led the horse through, looking around her for someone who might be able to help. There were so many buildings, but most had no lights in the windows, and there was no one in the street. But further down the road, Silvana spotted what might have been a small inn, with light still spilling into the dark road from a lantern hanging under the eaves. She hurried down the street, another wave of pain doubling her over. She beat on the heavy door, hoping someone was inside to hear her. "Please, help me, I need a midwife!" She beat on the door again, but stopped when she heard movement and cursing on the other side.

The door opened to a tall, red-faced man with sand-colored hair. "What is it, what do you want? It's a bit late to go askin' about rooms." His accent was thick and southern, like Dars's, but his harsh tone startled Silvana.

"I-I don't need a room. I need a midwife," Silvana cried out, clutching her belly as another wave of pain came. "The baby is coming." She looked up at the man, pleading. "Is there a midwife nearby?"

The man shook his head sadly. "There ain't no midwife here no more. Not another one until you reach the town of Emery, about another twenty miles east o' here."

"I don't have the time to get to Emery. Please, is there anyone that could help me deliver this baby?" Silvana pleaded with him.

The man sighed. He rubbed the side of his face, looking her up and down. "I could help you, I s'pose." A wave of alcoholic stink rolled off him, stinging Silvana's nose.

Silvana's eyes widened. "You? You could do it? But you're drunk!"

He laughed at this. "Aye, I'm drunk. I could still do it."

"Is there not a woman that could help me?"

The man grew defensive. "It was my wife that was the midwife here. I helped her with many of her birthings. You want someone to get that baby, I'm the man to do it." He thrust a thumb into his chest, face set. He suddenly fell quiet, adding, "The other women in this town will butcher you trying to pull that baby out."

Silvana hesitated, but nodded her head as another wave of pain struck her. "Alright. I don't have much choice."

The man stepped back, and Silvana hurried through the door, leaving her horse to stand just outside.

"What the fuck is going on down here?" Another sandy-haired man, younger than the first, came rushing through an open doorway from an adjacent room.

"Tomas, take the lady's horse around back and take care of him. And bring her bags in and put them in one of the rooms on the ground floor. I'll need some towels, first. And a big bowl of warm water. And then see to Jaimes, if you don't mind."

"Are you serious? It's raining like a pair of pissin' dragons out there!"

"Are you sayin' you're scared to get a little wet, you lousy sack of shit? Go do it, and I'll give you a couple of gold pieces."

At the mention of money, the man ran off, and Silvana was led into a small room and taken to the bed. "Take off your underclothes. You can leave the dress on if you want. But be quick about it, you don't have much time before the baby comes."

Silvana quietly did as she was told, peeling off her wet boots, then removing her small clothes. The man ran about the room, collecting the towels from the younger man as he returned with them, and setting a great bowl of water to rest on a nearby chest. He motioned to Tomas, then to the floor next to the bed. "Take her things to the washroom on the way out."

Tomas sighed but did as he was told, shutting the door behind him.

"Alright, let's take a look, shall we? Stand here, feet apart, hold onto the frame if you need to."

Silvana, embarrassed, did as instructed. The man went to both knees, reaching beneath the skirt of her dress. Another wave came on, and she gritted her teeth through it. She waited as the man tsked and muttered to himself for a moment, then tried to break the silence. "Tomas, who is he, your brother?"

"Only by law. He's daft as shit, but good help around the inn."

Another wave came, more painful than the last. They were coming more often, every other moment or so. "And you?" she gasped through the pain. "Who are you?"

He looked up at her, face still red with alcohol. "What, don't want a stranger poking around down here?" He smirked. She wanted to kick him, but only glared at him. "My name is Harlan. I run this inn."

"Silvana."

He nodded to her. "Right, well I have some good news. Your baby is already well on the way. His little head is already startin' to peak through. Just a few minutes of pushing, and he'll pop right out. You ready?"

Another wave of pain came along, but she nodded to Harlan.

"Alright. Then, push!"

She did, gritting her teeth together.

"Come on, keep pushing! Push!"

She pushed harder, straining. She could feel sweat dripping down her brow.

"Almost, almost, keep pushing!"

"I swear, if you say that word one more time, I will strangle you when this is over," Silvana growled through clenched teeth.

Harlan only laughed. "You've got it now, here he comes!"

The labor lasted only a few minutes, and when it was finished, Harlan silently handed her a damp cloth and a rough wool shift and turned his back on her, cleaning and dressing the baby as Silvana cleaned and dressed herself. "I can get a proper bath for you in the morning, but rest is best for now."

Silvana was too tired to protest. "Is the baby alright?"

Harland wrapped the tiny thing in a soft cloth and handed the infant over to her. "It's a boy."

Silvana held the baby in both hands as Harlan went about cleaning up. The baby was so small and fragile looking wrapped in the little blanket. His tiny head was covered in little tufts of dark hair, like Hasani's. Silvana smiled down at him, tears in her eyes.

"Has he got a name?"

Silvana looked up at Harlan, thinking. She'd never had time to pick one, she realized. But inspiration struck her, just as Hasani said it would. "Alastor. His name is Alastor."

***

Silvana slept well for a few hours, Alastor close at hand. She awoke early in the morning to the sound of a baby crying, instantly jumping up to check on her son. But he was fast asleep, his tiny hands curled up into fists. Lifting him out of the little cradle Harlan had lent her, she held him close to her breast and slipped out of the room, searching through the inn. She found Harlan sitting in the kitchen, holding another baby in his arms, rocking it to sleep. This one was a bit larger than Alastor, and lacked the little tufts of hair on his head. "Another baby you've delivered?" she asked.

Harlan jumped a little in his seat, turning to look at her. "No, I didn't deliver this one. This is my son, Jaimes."

Silvana pulled out another chair and sat down gingerly, her body sore and stiff. "You said your wife was the midwife in this city. Where is she now?"

Harlan muttered, "She died, giving birth to him."

Silvana bit her lip, sorry she'd asked. "My apologies."

Harlan nodded. "It's been about a month now. Still hard to think about. She didn't want me to do it, thought I might get distracted, with it being my son and all. She asked a couple of ladies from across the street to help, thought she could talk them through it. But something happened, something went wrong. Before I realized what was going on, she was already gone. Jaimes would have died, too, if I hadn't broken the door down to get in there." Harlan's eyes were tearing up. "I could have saved her, if she'd just let me do it, instead of those evil cunts across the way." Jaimes fidgeted in his arms, crying out. Harlan groaned in exasperation. "He's hungry. It's such a pain in the ass to feed him. I'm not as well equipped as Sarah was." He chuckled, tears running down his face.

"Let me do it, I'm equipped well enough." Silvana reached out, placing an arm on Harlan's elbow, smiling softly at him. "Alastor's already eaten, and I've got enough to feed them both, if need be."

Harlan looked her over, skeptical. "You don't need to. I can look after my own."

Silvana shook her head. "I'm not offering because I think you're incapable. I'm offering in gratitude. Let me do it, and you take a break. It'll be fine."

Harlan hesitated for a moment, Jaimes's cries growing louder. Finally, he nodded, holding him out for her to take. She carefully placed Alastor in the cradle sitting on the table, then took Jaimes in her arms. He was heavier than Alastor, but not by much. She draped a towel over her chest before letting the baby attach himself to her. His cries instantly stopped, and Harlan relaxed a little in his seat.

"You don't have a wet nurse?" Silvana asked.

Harlan shook his head hard. "I don't trust none of them ladies in this town, not after Sarah's passing."

"I'm not from this town. Would you trust me?"

Harlan squinted at her. "Perhaps." He paused, looking her up and down quizzically. "Where are you from, if you don't mind my asking?"

Silvana bit her lip, not sure if she should answer. But she did, after a moment. "Etritia."

Harlan raised an eyebrow in surprise. "The castle? You don't look much like a farmer's wife."

Silvana said nothing, rocking Alastor in the cradle.

"Very well, I won't pry." Harlan leaned back in the chair, crossing his arms over his chest. "And the boy's father? Where is he?"

"He's dead." Silvana choked on the words as they came out. There was the small chance that Hasani was alive, Silvana admitted to herself. But a week had passed, and there had been no sign of him on the Vyrisian side of the Knife during her long ride to Larten. "I have a brother who might come for me. But I'm not sure."

"So you'll be needing a place to stay then, it seems."

Silvana jumped at the opportunity. "I don't have much money. But I can clean, and I can cook." Silvana frowned. "Some."

"You don't look like you've ever done much of either, I'm afraid." Harlan's lips curled into something that could have been a smile or a grimace.

"I can learn. And I can learn how to be a midwife, if you'll teach me. I can help you, should anyone come needing it."

Harlan still looked unconvinced.

"I'll help you take care of Jaimes as if he were my own son. I'll feed him, care for him, and if I'm still here when the time comes, I'll teach him."

Harlan stared her down, thinking. After a moment, he nodded. "Alright."

Silvana smiled, relieved.

"You do all those things you said you'll do, the cooking, cleaning, taking care of the babes, and I'll let you stay. I can't pay you none, but if you'll help me run the inn on top of that, and do some midwifery when needed, I'll make sure you want for nothing. You need clothing, things for the babes, books to study, I'll try to see that you can get them." He shook a thick finger at her. "Mind you, we don't have none of that fancy stuff they've got in Etritia, but we got the bare necessities, and the occasional oddity comes through when the traders come in. That good enough for you?"

Silvana beamed up at him. "That's wonderful. Thank you, Harlan." Harlan grunted, leaving her in the kitchen with Jaimes and Alastor.

Silvana looked down at her son, still asleep in the little crib. "Did you hear that, Alastor? We have a new place to call home."

60

HASANI

Hasani ran as fast as his feet could carry him, vaulting over fallen branches and ducking under low-hanging boughs. His lungs burned, the muscles in his legs ached, and the cuts and scrapes to his face and arms from running through the Vyrisian woods stung with sweat. But he could not stop moving. He couldn't hear his pursuers, but he could sense that they were catching up. He kept running, trying to maintain a path that would lead him deeper into the woods.

He was in elven lands now ... surely Mothlenor's magic would not work here?

Hasani slid to a stop, pausing just long enough to look behind him. Four shadows swept their way across the forest floor, sweeping towards him. He cursed, instantly moving again.

He clutched the little bag containing the stolen egg close to his chest. He should have given the egg back to Ajax before leaving them behind. But he had acted so quickly, without thinking ... *Could these demons take the egg back to Mothlenor?* Hasani briefly thought about ditching the egg somewhere. It could be lost for forever that way, but Mothlenor wouldn't have it. He pushed the thought out of his

382

head, forcing himself to run faster, to put more distance between himself and the demons. It was nearly morning, he realized. How long had he been running like this? How much longer could he keep it up? Hasani focused on his breathing, trying not to trip on his own feet. He vaulted over a large log, his pursuers just behind him—

And landed in a large clearing. Hasani blinked, surprised and very aware of his sudden vulnerability. He saw another figure, half hidden, standing just across the clearing. He ran towards him. "Please, you have to help me." He was vaguely aware that the other man held a bow, aimed right at him. "Help, there are demons—"

Hasani felt a sudden piercing sensation in his chest, knocking the breath out of him. He stumbled forward a few steps before falling to his knees.

Did he just hit me? He looked down. There was no arrow, but there was blood. *Great Ones, so much blood ...*

He felt someone grab him, guide him down to the ground. Looking up, he saw a man with long dark hair and kind eyes. Long ears with sharply pointed tips accented the otherwise normal features. *An elf*, Hasani thought. His head rolled to the side, and he saw the little golden egg roll out of his bag and come to rest just out of his reach. He tried to stretch out his arm, to grab hold of it, but he felt too weak to move, and his eyes grew too heavy to focus on the egg.

Please don't let him get it, Hasani thought. He shut his eyes, too tired to fight any longer.

MOTHLENOR

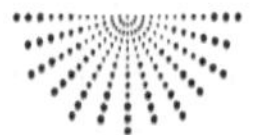

Mothlenor's demons pulled up just shy of the clearing. He could see Hasani, fallen and probably close to death. The man had put up a good fight, evading the demons for several hours. But Mothlenor had known all along that he would fall eventually. The elf had been a surprise though, he had to admit. Through the eyes of his demons, he looked down on the elf as he struggled to stem the flow of blood coming from Hasani's chest.

"Leave him, this does not concern you, elf." He spoke through all four demons at once, their unnatural voices blending into one.

"He asked for help. It is my concern now." The elf ignored the demons, apparently unconcerned with their presence. He tore at the front of Hasani's tunic, placing a hand over the hole in the man's chest.

His lack of fear irked Mothlenor. "Do you know who I am, elf?"

Still, he did not look up. "You are a fool, to delve into necromancy. That much I know."

Mothlenor bristled. "I am the king of men, lord of the Free Cities, and protector of the known world. And you are in my way." He summoned up his energy, sending a fiery barrage down onto the elf from his demons.

But his attacks missed, fizzling out into nothing several feet away from the elf. Mothlenor hissed in frustration.

The elf finally looked up, scrutinizing the demons with disgust. "You are well out of your realm, king." His voice was laced with disdain. "Your powers are not so effective so far away from your castle walls." He frowned, turning back to help Hasani. But something glinting on the ground caught his eye, and he turned towards it. Picking it up from the ground, the elf stared at the golden egg, his fingers tracing the whorls and ridges of the surface. Blood stained the egg where his fingertips touched.

"Give it to me," Mothlenor demanded. He could sense the frustration of his demons growing as his anger mounted.

The elf tilted his head to look at the demons. "It does not belong to you."

"It doesn't belong to you, either, elf. Now give it to me!"

"It does not belong to me," the elf replied. "Yet I sense that it belongs more to me than it does to you." He paused, staring at the egg in his hands, a puzzled expression on his face. He blinked, shook his head forcefully, and tucked the egg back into Hasani's bag, which he then slung over his shoulder. "At any rate, this man had it. And he requested my aid." He stood, lifted Hasani off the ground and slung him over one shoulder effortlessly. "You can find your own way back, I'm sure." He turned, walking out through the clearing and disappearing through the trees on the other side.

Mothlenor growled, furious. He tried to send his demons further into the woods, but they protested, too weak to continue through elven lands without being destroyed. Mothlenor howled in frustration, the unearthly sound emitted from the demons echoing through the woods all around them.

AJAX

Animals were already sniffing at him. Ajax could feel a wet, slimy nose burrowing into the palm of his good hand, while a fuzzy-faced creature nuzzled at his neck. He pushed them both away, muttering. "Go away, I'm not dead yet."

Or was he?

He remembered the fight with Ferrand in broken pieces. Ferrand killing the knight. Ferrand cutting his leg, then slicing his stomach open. Ferrand's head on fire.

Ajax groaned, trying to lift himself from the ground, but he didn't seem to have the strength.

His body didn't hurt. His burned hand didn't hurt. His knee didn't hurt.

His stomach, though …

Ajax groaned again, trying to lift an arm to feel the damage once more. It ached, a terrible, deep pinching and burning sensation. But it was better than the intense pain it had been before.

"That's no way to talk to someone trying to help you," a hard female voice said.

Ajax opened his eyes, catching sight of a round-faced woman with long brown hair peering down at him.

"Am I dead?" he groaned.

The woman gave him a crooked smile. "Do you feel dead?"

Ajax groaned again, then answered, "No, not really."

The woman's face disappeared from his line of sight, but her voice was still nearby. "Then I think you can probably say that you're not dead."

Ajax tried to turn his head to follow the sound of her voice, but a large pink blob blocked his view. Ajax grunted, trying and failing to shove the thing out of the way. It squeaked, but didn't move. "Where's Ferrand?"

"That hot-headed guy you were fighting?" She snorted at her words, an unladylike sound if Ajax had ever heard one. The woman's voice had moved, but Ajax couldn't quite place it. "He put his head out, then got onto one of the horses and fled for the castle. I would assume he thinks you're dead." She paused, then continued. "You certainly *looked* dead. Reminded me a bit of that time my uncle Roland got into a fight with a bear. That bear cut him clean open. Except Uncle Roland died. Piggy, move."

"What?" Ajax muttered, but the squeaking pink thing moved at her command, and as Ajax peered at it, he realized it was a fat little pig. "How am I not dead?" Ajax's mind was still unfocused, his limbs still numb. "I should have died."

"I agree." The woman's face was peering over him again. "But then I saw the wounds on your body healing, so I came closer to check you out." She smiled again, the points of her teeth visible over thin lips, and Ajax felt an odd shiver roll over him. "Are you ready? I'm going to grab your arms and start pulling. It'll hurt, but you're too big to carry."

"You're not human, are you?" Ajax asked.

"Eh, no, I'm not." She grabbed both of his wrists and tugged. Ajax was too weak to either fight her off or help her, so he just let her drag him along. He barely moved, though the woman was pulling his arms hard enough to rip them off.

"Succubus?"

The woman snorted again, dropping his arms. "Do I look like a succubus?"

Ajax craned his head slightly, surprised to find that the woman was completely nude, wearing only his bag strapped over both shoulders. "Well, you're naked."

"Yeah, but besides that." She was staring at him, one hand on her chin. "You're kind of a big one, aren't you?"

Ajax considered for a moment, his neck aching slightly as he tilted his head to stare at her. Her breasts were small, and her arms and thighs hard and lean. There was mud caked on her palms, and a smear of it on one cheek. It was getting hard to keep his eyes open. He shut them, muttering, "I guess you're not attractive enough to be a succubus."

She huffed, and Ajax opened his eyes again to see her glaring down at him. "Piggy, nip him."

The pig obediently nibbled at his leg. Ajax could hardly feel it.

"Don't worry, he'll get better at that." The woman knelt and wrapped her forearms under his armpits. She began tugging again, and Ajax closed his eyes once more.

"What are you going to do with me?"

The woman snorted again, her breath warm on the back of his neck. "I'm going to save your damn life." She sighed. "My brother is going to have my ass over this one."

Ajax half listened as she continued to drag him in small bursts into the woods.

"He'll say, 'Myra, what did you bring back this time?'" she grunted as she yanked painfully on his arm. Ajax wondered briefly if his arms might end up ripped from their sockets. "'Another pig, a skunk? It smells like a skunk. A human?' And it'll just be a mess from there."

"My sword …" Ajax mumbled.

"Piggy, get his sword," the woman panted as she pulled him another few feet. The pig oinked once, then Ajax could hear his little feet hurrying through the underbrush.

"I'm going to need it," Ajax said. *But why?*

"What was that? You're mumbling."

Ajax could feel himself drifting away again, but something nagged at him. There was someone he needed to help. Someone he needed to protect …

"I have to save the Coven," he said, unsure if he said it aloud or not.

"I think we're losing him again, Piggy." The woman's voice was faint, and Ajax hardly bothered to listen to it. "You'll be fine soon, I promise …"

MOTHLENOR

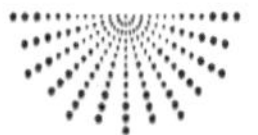

Mothlenor eyed the women and young girls before him. They were battered and bruised. Many looked particularly abused, and he wondered briefly if Ferrand and his men had forced themselves onto more than a few of them during their long trek to the castle. It was the blondes, mostly, that looked the worst. Ferrand had a taste for blondes, it seemed. Their white dresses were tattered and dirty, and every last one of them was missing her precious veil. He could look each one fully in the eyes, and see the terror and anger reflected in them. It had taken quite a bit of effort, and he had lost several members of his King's Guard. But they were here, and he had done it without Hasani, that damned idiot. *No matter,* Mothlenor thought. *He is surely dead, and his family will join him as soon as they can be found.*

"How exactly did you manage to get so many of them to come peacefully?" he asked. His voice echoed oddly around the stone walls of the dungeon.

Ferrand answered, watching the gathered Coven with his one good eye. "We got a bit lucky, and found the nursery." Ferrand's words were oddly slurred, and Mothlenor had to fight to keep the disgust from his face when Ferrand stepped to stand beside him.

"The nursery?" Mothlenor was intrigued.

"Where they kept all the babes and the youngest brats. All snug in their cribs," Ferrand replied, gloating.

Mothlenor watched Navara, her clouded eyes pinched in a furious glare. But she said nothing. "Go on," he prompted.

"We told them that if they didn't stop with fighting us, we'd kill every darling in there," Ferrand crooned. "So they stopped fighting, and let us put those iron cuffs you spelled on them. They worked wonderfully, by the way. We haven't had any trouble from any of them while those cuffs have been on." Mothlenor only nodded, waving a hand for Ferrand to continue. He was sure the cuffs would work, but it was always nice to be commended for his work. "Then we loaded them all up into the wagons, locked them in, and killed the babes anyway." Ferrand sneered at the women before him, but none of them made a sound.

Mothlenor was irked at the idea of children so young being murdered. *But they were Coven children*, he reminded himself. He took a second look around the room and noticed that even the youngest girl in the room was still old enough to be bedded. Barely.

"I've asked the commander here to collect all of you so that you might pay for your crimes against my brother, the late King Areanath. You have been found guilty of—"

"Stop with the lies, Mothlenor," Navara cried. "You've had us brought here so that you can kill us all. We should have expected something like this from you, but then we can't see our own futures, can we?" Navara sneered up at him, the effect strengthened by her eerie dead eyes locking on to his. "I suppose you already knew that, didn't you?" She spat at the ground, missing his foot by inches. She clung to the young woman beside her for balance, teetering slightly as she straightened. "Just say your worst and be done with it, you monster."

Mothlenor felt his temper flare up, but months of dealing with Nevina had given him the chance to grow accustomed to witches, and he kept his anger in check. "Very well. I'm offering you the chance for freedom, but this will be your only opportunity to accept. Either join me, and help me find a way to reverse the curse my brother has cast …" He paused, staring into Navara's eyes. "Or die down here, in the dungeons. Your choice. You have ten seconds."

There was instant uproar, but it seemed to consist only of curses and threats thrown at him. There was no arguing amongst themselves, only outrage at his offer. He waited, counting down the seconds silently. Without a word, he turned, content to leave them all down there in the filth and the dark.

"Wait!"

He turned, searching the crowd for the one who had spoken up. They were all quiet now, stunned into silence.

"I'll go with you." It was the woman supporting Navara. Mothlenor recognized her as the same woman who had come with Navara to his study weeks before. She was young and thin, her brown hair tangled and dirty.

"Anna, no! You can't!" Navara clung frantically to the woman, but she freed herself from the witch's claws.

"I'm sorry, Matriarch. But I'm not ready to die." She stepped away from the rest of the women to stand timidly beside him.

"Anyone else?" He paused, waiting, but the room was silent. "Very well." He turned and left, the woman hurrying behind him.

Once Ferrand and his men had left the room and shut the door, Mothlenor turned to his commander. Ferrand's face was still red and oozing, despite the weeks that had passed. And no amount of time, and no potion or spell could fill the hollow where his left eye had been. The sight of Ferrand angered Mothlenor, not only because one side of his face looked like half-chewed meat, but because he had somehow managed to let a dead man disappear.

Mothlenor snarled at Ferrand, "Bar the door, nail it shut, and don't open it again until the smell reaches the floor above." He didn't wait for Ferrand to reply. Instead he took the woman by the elbow and began leading her through the maze of tunnels to the castle above. "Anna, was it?"

"Y-yes," the woman stammered.

"Yes, my king," Mothlenor corrected.

"Yes, my king," Anna repeated, more forcefully.

"Can you See?"

"No." Anna shook her head, then quickly added. "My king."

Mothlenor frowned. He should have specified that he only wanted Gifted women, but it was too late to toss her back in with the others. "That's too bad."

"I'm Ungifted, but I am skilled in the arcane."

Mothlenor stopped, turning to Anna with an eyebrow raised. "How skilled? Show me."

Anna lifted her cuffed hands for him to see. "I can't ..."

With barely a flick of his wrist, one of the cuffs fell open. "Show me."

Anna snapped the fingers of her free hand, and fire lit upon her fingertips. With a gentle wave of her hand, the fire writhed into the shape of a small bird, which then flitted from her fingertips to soar through the air around them. Mothlenor watched it for a moment, amused. Then with a wave of his own hand, the dark shape of a dragon's head emerged from the shadows the conjured bird cast on the wall, and with a silent snap of its jaws, the bird disappeared. Anna gasped, seeming very young for a moment, but Mothlenor only smiled down at her.

"Very good. You might be useful after all."

Anna gave him a small smile, which quickly disappeared when Mothlenor wrapped his hand around her wrist and snapped the cuff shut again. He took her by the arm once more, pulling her gently along beside him. "How old are you, Anna?"

"F-fifteen, my king."

So young, and so afraid. But there would be time to show her that he could be a generous man.

"What do you know about curses, Anna?"

I hope you enjoyed *The Book of Death.*

If you would like to get a FREE short story that follows Ajax's hunt for the Coven, download it from Book Funnel by using this link:
https://BookHip.com/FZADKM

To get your FREE download of the *The Lost Archives* short story, *The Remains,* you will have to provide a valid email address, which will sign you up for my newsletter. Once you have downloaded your FREE story, you may opt out of my newsletter if you wish. However, I hope you choose to stay!

Jacklyn Hennion

ABOUT THE AUTHOR

Jacklyn Hennion is an avid lover of sweets and wine. She enjoys Netflix and video games, and often spends the evenings winding down with a bit of crochet work. She and her husband currently live in Oklahoma. *The Book of Death* is Jacklyn's first published novel.

Follow her blog at: JacklynHennionAuthor.com

 twitter.com/HennionJacklyn
 instagram.com/JacklynHennion

www.ingramcontent.com/pod-product-compliance
Lightning Source LLC
Chambersburg PA
CBHW031612180726
48284CB00005B/1506